TREASURE REVEALED

SISTER SEEKERS BOOK 2

BY
A.S. ETASKI

Published by Corpus Nexus Press
ISBN: 978-1-949552-03-4

etaski.com
etaski.com/sister-seekers
miurag.etaski.com
www.patreon.com/etaski
www.goodreads.com/etaski
www.bookbub.com/authors/a-s-etaski
www.facebook.com/asetaski
mastodon.online/@etaski

Cover Design by Eris Adderly
Book layout by DocKangey

Dedicated to each of us seeking a place to simply be.

CHAPTER 1

MY SISTER AND I WENT STILL AND HELD OUR BREATHS WHILE A SOLITARY HOUSE Guardsvrin passed by. She sounded bored and distracted as she grumbled something in her throat. I didn't catch it; a pair of battling beetles I'd been watching a moment before had fallen off their fiberstalk perch and clacked together in the dirt to my right.

We waited. No one else appeared.

You hear? I signed to Gaelan.

Teasing slut, she replied.

I frowned. *What *now*?*

My Sister blinked. Her brows arched. *She said, 'Teasing slut.'*

Ah.

My first thought was that the Guardsvrin must be referring to the Bred Consort from the Royal Court currently in residence here. There could be no bigger tease on the whole plantation, I knew from personal experience. Then again, she could have been talking about another bua who had rebuffed her.

My first feeling was relief.

Gaelan isn't inexplicably angry with me again.

The enclosed garden of Tenth House Itlaun was crafted with refined rock formations and mushroom rings of all sizes as their bases. Several were large enough to crouch behind. Fleshing it out more were stands of tough, sculpted fiberstalk, many varieties of lichen crawling over any surface. Attractive bits of moss decorated the cobbled pathways, and soft-glowing root-crawlers illuminated them.

It took considerable effort and expense to have a garden like this, and of those I'd seen, I thought they followed this pattern and only varied in size based on wealth and status. The ones at the Palace were the oldest and largest of them, with more enchanted spiders draping reflective veils of intricate design above the walking stone. This one wasn't that much larger than the one my Mother owned at the Twelfth House.

It wasn't easy to hide in these gardens, either; not if your target was at all wary. Mages and Red Sisters had the advantage for camouflage and determination over the mundane Nobles and servants, no matter their motivation and care. Here, a combination of Gaelan's magic and our unique red cloaks aided in blurring our outline and encouraging other Davrin eyes to slide over us without focusing on us.

Come, Gaelan ordered, and I followed, a tight ball of tension and excitement nestled in my gut.

We had been briefed before coming here. I had studied the layout and routine of the House for some time. The Sisterhood knew where the single, laughably-termed "Matron only" passage lay, and the wards set upon it were no match for the counter-magic within my new bracers or Gaelan's honed experience. We silenced any potential alarm, shifted a stone panel used infrequently, and entered the mansion's secret passage.

My heart beat stronger in my chest as we slid through the black guts of the House, gaining height mostly through dusty, cobwebbed ladders rather than stairs. I imagined the Matron herself squeezing through here and thought it an indication that the Tenth House hadn't been too long in its coveted place. After another generation or two with Consort blood, however, Matron Itlaun might garner enough favor with those above her to remodel these spyways to be more comfortable.

They already have one such Consort-bred heir on the way.

I recalled too vividly for my own comfort how Tulia, the Third Daughter of this House, conceived upon the altar at the last Worship Ball.

The new sire gifted to Tulia's Matron was the same Priestess Son whom I had discovered alone and unprotected during my trials. He was the one I had attacked in my insanity, in that breeding madness clinging to me after surviving the ritual of Braqth's Threshold. The Consort had not been willing. I had tied him down, forcing his staff erect before jamming it up my hungry cunt.

Gaelan pulled me off just in time.

I had almost conceived. With Priestess fertility magic saturating my very essence, I *would* have conceived, if this beautiful bua hadn't been extraordinary in his climax control. Had I become pregnant, I would not have become a Red Sister. I would have belonged instead to the Priestesses until I birthed the child of a poached male to which I had no right.

After that, I would have had no place at Court or at my House. I thanked pure luck for my narrow escape, my fate now backed by the Sisterhood instead of the Priesthood. I did not like to think about what might have become of me after the Spider Queen's handmaidens had claimed my own blood from my womb.

My Sister led us to the hidden exit we sought, and I protested nothing, though I double-checked the route. Gaelan signed to me.

Remember your orders?

A nod, a sign of my own. *You lead. I observe.*

I spotted a subtle smirk touch her lips. *Excited?*

Fuck my crutch.

I will observe, I repeated. *Be aware. His head is not a silk-void.*

No?

No.

Gaelan grinned. *So clear, was it? As if your eyes weren't lust-crossed when I caught you straddling him.*

I managed not to huff so one could hear it. *That was Priestess magic! I wasn't sober!*

Sure. A silent snicker. *I bet his pretty face didn't help.*

Shut up, Sister.

Satisfied, Gaelan turned to study the mechanism and chant a soft spell to "see beyond" the wall before we entered. The Consort had to be alone.

Two cycles after an indulgent party such as the Matron had just thrown, he usually was.

There had been some Nobles in previous missions, other places, both male and female, who never heard us enter. Gaelan had touched one Davrin's shoulder before she knew we were there. It always helped start off an interrogation well for us. I hadn't killed or arrested anyone since my final trial with Kaltra. I mostly shadowed older Sisters, gathering information for Elder D'Shea in what appeared to be a sporadic need. Meanwhile, I learned the tricks and methods of the Sisterhood's many roles.

My Consort knew the moment we entered. His half-naked back was tense, and he stood up with practiced grace from where he had been sitting. Before my eyes were captured by his face, I glanced at what was in front of him while he sat: a modest meal slowly consumed, several colors of thread bundles, and a half-finished, soft decoration likely intended as a gift for his Matron.

Such slender fingers. Talented in more than one way.

I cursed myself for hesitating one step as the Royal Consort turned around and looked at us, soon lowering his gaze to the floor.

Get a grip on your slit, Sirana. He's just a bua.

Yet he was the most alluring one I'd ever seen, to the point I questioned if there had ever been a Davrin with his face before. His lean, delicate features seemed sculpted from someone's dream, surreal and unrevealing of his lineage as if he'd come from no known House or Matron's family. His pure white hair was loose and thick, his nose straight as a blade, his mouth soft, full, and sensitive. His scarlet eyes seemed larger and as reflective as an ornate mirror, inviting like a warm hearth. I knew many Nobles with this same shade of red to their eyes whose needle-sharp gazes offered only a taste of hard metal or poisoned blood.

This Consort was not recognizable as the son of any Priestesses I'd seen, although I'd not had the opportunity to study them all, and I could not imagine such a sire wandering around the Court without comment. This may be one of the older Consorts, and therefore he had been shared frequently by more females — always a downward trend for a male's favor with his protectors — but that face was probably why he still held a coveted place as a breeding sire.

Where are they keeping such births? Entirely unseen, revealed only at Worship Balls?

I wanted to know. My Elder had told me I would find out in time. She knew, but as a first-turn novice, I wasn't worthy of that information yet.

"Look up, Consort," Gaelan whispered. When he did, she signed, ★You remember us?★

His throat flashed as he swallowed, his eyes flicking to me before he refocused on Gaelan and her question. ★For certain, Red Sister. I do.★

★You will not tell your current Matron of this meeting. You will not tell any Davrin, servant, or slave of this House, nor any of the same visiting it.★

He nodded. ★Exactly as you sign, I will not, Sister.★ After a pause, he added, ★You do not mention my Priestess.★

His Priestess. Who is she?

★Tell her what you must,★ Gaelan replied glibly, a perfect dismissal of his powerful owner, as if she already knew. ★I trust you confessed to her your defilement in the kitchen?★

I heard a subtle pulse in the quiet, clean room. Then my eyes widened. *I hear it. I hear your heart.*

★I have not told my Priestess of your visit,★ he told us.

What?

I held still, determined to give nothing away on my face while my Sister displayed her pleasure clearly to him.

★No? Why not?★

★She is ... not merciful,★ he answered as his gaze wavered.

An understatement for any Priestess in the Sanctuary.

★And if she finds out?★ my Sister probed.

My Consort looked at her face, at her eyes. ★The Priestesses do not discover everything. In this event, I leave my fate to the Sisterhood.★

Goddess. I wanted to fuck him. Here and now.

Gaelan turned her ear toward the outside hall; we three were perfectly still. ⋆You have time to talk about Matron Itlaun and her Daughters, Consort?⋆

⋆If you wish, Red Sister. Ask your questions.⋆

It was far easier than I might have guessed, getting him to cooperate. He answered Gaelan's inquiries while I observed. He and I were always aware of each other, although he never glanced at me. My crotch was warm by the time the first noise warned us of an impending visitor. We left with such insights on the Tenth House from an observant and underestimated plaything, I almost felt proud to have found him.

His head is not a void.

I had learned more than a quarter-turn ago that the Priestesses used their Sons as spies. All Matrons anticipated this but accepted these gifts regardless; the trade in status far outweighed a pair of Sanctuary eyes watching those in the home. It wasn't a concern if a Matron believed herself faithful already.

The Priestesses also knew that the Sisterhood tried for the same, testing their Sanctuary Sons and their loyalty to their Mother-Priestesses. Our success in compromising them would vary on many factors, including circumstances, and the intelligence and will of the Consort in question.

We had this mature and experienced male under our thumb, thanks to me. Elder D'Shea would be pleased, but I could already imagine the jab in which she might phrase it.

At least something useful came of your Braqth-inspired idiocy.

I LOOKED FORWARD TO GIVING OUR REPORT WHEN WE PASSED A RUNE POINT outside the Cloister. The mild enchantment responded to a rune fixed on the inside of a Red Sister's uniform — each in a different place. I wouldn't have known where to look for this rune on most Sisters.

When the two matched, a spell sent voiceless notice of our approach to the rooms of our Prime, Elders, and Leads. While it was possible to return unannounced, those specific Sisters had to be in their respective quarters or in the Prime's strategy room at the time, in which case we usually received instructions later.

As if to make a point, the spell responded instantly, deep inside my ear like a buzzing insect delivering the order:

Every Red Sister collect in the Prime Room immediately.

"Shit," Gaelan whispered, glancing at me.

We hustled inside the Cloister and began a smooth run through the dim-lit curves and ramps toward the Prime's room, aware of the moment we passed the next rune point. The double, dead-end door opened without us touching it, and we entered to the altar room to see the Prime, Elders D'Shea and Rausery, and ...

The Priestess Lelinahdara?

A Daughter of Braqth, inside our Cloister. More than that, the one who had wrenched private and bitter memories of my childhood tormentor from me, drawing out the hurt and truth of my barrenness like ancient pus.

At the Prime's order, Lelinahdara had forced me to go through that same ritual again, and where my elder sister had failed, this Priestess had succeeded. My body was healed and strong, fertile, not as Jilrina had left it. Perhaps something to be grateful for.

I still didn't like a conflict of interest being here.

In the plain, black-stone room, a score and more of Red Sisters had gathered. Upon the platform were our Red Sister leaders with the Sanctuary Priestess, the table still covered with maps and scrolls, but also an odd collection of materials and objects.

Half of them looked to me as though they'd be used in ritual. Jaunda and half her teams were here, along with Qivni and those subordinate to her. All of them looked ready to tear down half of the Deepearth.

Elder Rausery glanced up at Gaelan and me, joining the other Sisters under Lead Jaunda, and nodded to us. She spoke to the Prime but looked to D'Shea next. "Twenty-seven, more than half."

My Elder agreed while the Prime smirked like she looked forward to something.

What's happening?

"I shall need a conduit with experience," Lelinahdara said to D'Shea, but we all heard. Her voice was powerful yet lyrical, a sharp contrast to the gruff Prime and grounded Elder Rausery.

"Red Sister Gaelan," Elder D'Shea answered.

This role had been decided before we got here. Now, it was formalized.

The Priestess gestured my age-mate forward onto the platform; only with a definite nod from our Elder Sorceress did Gaelan obey. The Red Sister Prime turned toward the rest of us, her hair streaked with the gilded color of the aged, her eyes and face hard, the lines at the corners of her mouth that much more profound.

"Three Ornilleth have entered our territory. They brought with them powerful thralls numbering over three hundred. The company dispatched a mark ago engaged in the last quarter but is struggling to push them back and starting to dwindle. We believe the Ornilleth are here to capture new bodies, whomever they find, they are not known to be picky. But most certainly they want Davrin, or they wouldn't have come this far."

My brows rose high despite my attempt at a still expression like my Sisters. This would be my first pitched battle.

Against thought-flayers of all things.

The only other intelligent race in the Deepearth of which the Davrin were genuinely leery. If only a portion of the Tragar Dwarves were said to be mind-mages, then the entirety of the Ornilleth were precisely this. At even greater ability.

Enough for only three to control three hundred as extensions of their body.

I felt a subtle urge to piss.

"Twenty-seven of you will tip the balance in our favor," the Prime continued, a rare show of confidence but also a demand. "Elder Rausery will lead in the field. Elder D'Shea is magical support, passing the intelligence between us. You will hear her voice in your head. Act on her orders as if I'm talking straight in your ears. Share information in return, I will need it. Braqth's Priestess will shield you from mental attacks as she can but use your training." The Prime seemed to look right at me. "An attack starts with pressure like water filling your head."

I remembered that feeling, intimately, though no one here knew because I hadn't claimed it.

We signed as one: *Acknowledged, Prime.*

"Good. Priority is to let our army see you destroy as many of the thralls as possible, rebuild morale. When the power shifts, you'll know it. Then I want those tentacled mind-eaters filled with poison from afar. Do not engage in melee or attempt a close kill under any circumstances. The last thing our Queen needs is for the Ornilleth Elder to gain the knowledge you all have. Not even one of you is to be captured alive."

My whole body flushed with a sick fear as I imagined my Lead Jaunda killing me rather than letting me be dragged off. To be subverted, turned into a thrall — a monstrous, entirely different creature — after my mind was stripped and drained of anything useful. Like it or not, a quick death was the preferable outcome. Did that mean I would kill another Sister if necessary?

It must be.

At least Gaelan is staying here.

From atop the platform, Lelinahdara rested both hands on Gaelan's shoulders, perhaps becoming accustomed to her mage aura. That moment, my Sister glanced at me. Like in the candle-lit chamber of my trials, she was the only one who held an expression I could read. Back then, it had been pitying. Now, she was concerned.

I grinned, offering something she could read in return. *Bring it on.*

Her mouth twitched.

"Stockroom," the Prime barked. "Two ticks. Now."

We moved; Elder Rausery was coming with us, and that tangibly boosted the sense of eagerness in the air. We restocked essential weapons and useful tools if we didn't already have them, each of us ready in as much time as it took me to run here from that first call. I removed my cloak, rolled it up and set it in the supply room; no other Sister was wearing one.

"Each of you," Rausery said as she flipped open the lid on a small, locked box bolted to a shelf. "Quaff one."

Lead Jaunda took one first, breaking the seal and drinking without hesitation, and Qivni after her. The rest of us followed by rank. I was last, and Lawret gave me a hint of what it had been.

Extended healing, she signed with a wink. *No pain, no bleed-outs.*

Ah-ha.

I wasn't sure if the calming warmth was all potion or just my anxiety leaking away, but I saw how we'd help the morale of the army.

No pain. We are unstoppable.

My heart still throbbed in my breast as we regathered before the Prime.

"Into the ring," she commanded, and Elder Rausery led us within the subtle onyx inlay in the center rear of the room, which I had missed my first few times in here.

"Don't puke on the Army Commander's boots, Sirana," our Elder said, a playful twinkle in her eye. "We want to impress them."

The other Sisters chuckled, except for Qivni, of course, and I allowed my mood rise with a white grin. "Yes, Elder."

D'Shea and Lelinahdara cast a spell together from where they stood. We blinked out of the Prime's strategy room and into the deep passage-ways. My stomach rose and lurched. The quiet and cleanliness were replaced with the dirt and clamor as I attempted to get to my feet.

My eyesight shifted immediately; all color had faded in darkness but life's movement and the Radiants all around created the shape and depth I needed navigate without light. We stood on a ledge above a more massive cavern, somewhere outside of Sivaraus.

The noise of battle was intense; the edges of my ears prickled from vibration alone. Elder Rausery signed high while facing the fight; simul-taneously, I heard Elder D'Shea inside my head.

Fan out, avoid clustering together. Quick kills, no taunting or torture. We want quantity.

The orders matched Rausery's hand sign commands. As soon as our General gave the signal, tightly bound energy unraveled in every Red Sister, flooded us as one. Novice or not, I felt it, was caught up in it, and

I moved on instinct, my fear oddly muted.

We drew swords and daggers, hand crossbows, and barbed lashes. Our shields must be our speed, for every Sister fought with two weapons and changed them as needed. No one pointed out I was a novice; no one told me to stay behind the experienced ones.

I would fight with them.

Forward, Sisters!

CHAPTER 2

LEAPING DOWN FROM OUR HIGHER VANTAGE POINT, WE COULD BE SEEN CLEARLY as someone lit a light above. Our uniforms blazed, and a wave of voices rose, a cheer to fill the ceiling. I questioned nothing; my boots flew over the rock.

The thralls of the Ornilleth were bigger than us, heavily muscled, and capable of both tearing through or seizing a body to hold it tight. The bulky creatures possessed the empty, blank eyes and a beak without tentacles, only hinting at a thought-flayer lineage. Bodied grey-skinned and streamlined for swimming, with a tough hide that made quick kills more difficult unless one aimed her thin blade just right, either in a sunken, yellowed eye or in a soft spot beneath the jaw.

Stab the brains or the thralls keep moving. They feel no pain and are still controlled by their masters.

As soon as one Red Sister discovered this, we all knew it. D'Shea and Lelinahdara shared that knowledge along with that same sense of elation and power, as though each of us had unveiled this on our own.

I heard Jaunda's roar as she took out two more thralls in quick succession. Kiren and Lawret shrieked like demons, sending a shiver up the spines of at least two fighters as they joined in the attacks with glee.

The potion's magic still thick in my blood, my energy seemed limitless, my budding skills unleashed without restraint or boundaries on our targets. Another first time since I'd joined the Sisterhood; something inside me sang with terrible joy at the vortex of violence, threads of all my Sisters quivering through the bond connecting us on the battlefield.

My own battle-hungry cries were answered many times over.

As the enemy bodies at last began to fall faster than the Davrin around them, I heard a new rumble of bloodlust arise from our army as they redoubled their efforts to fight off the invaders. Unlike them, however, the Sisters did not cluster together, nor did we get completely out of sight of one another. I could always see at least one of my Sisters, blurred, spinning, slashing, and stabbing.

We could always sense the presence of one another; if the mind did not become a void, we knew who still stood.

I absorbed the information of many seasoned fighters at once; I knew things which were happening inside the chaos, even if I did not witness them. We knew we were winning.

Qivni and her team blasted a swath in the middle of the thickest pack of thralls, heat and purple light cracking in the cavern, pain and injury breaking up the mass of bodies and allowing parts of our army to flank them and finish them off.

The regular units who'd begun fighting again were female and male. Their mass of defiant bellows blended in a pleasing pitch of fever and rage. One fighter drew my eye for a few instants within the mass of bodies. She was young, even younger than me, dressed in brown and of low rank but she radiated will and fearlessness.

Quick and vicious, precise but making sure she tore as much flesh as she could in each withdrawal. From the damage and splatter on her clothes, from the fixed scowl on her face and the determination stiffening her spine and pushing back fatigue, she hadn't paused for a long time.

Even when others were falling back, before the Sisterhood had arrived, I could imagine her holding ground. Her snarl shifted to a wild smile when I got close, and without speaking we selected the same pair of thralls to attack. The plunge of her blade took longer to extract because she sawed at the throat. Another thrall noticed.

"Roll left!" I shouted, and she obeyed.

A long-armed swipe of claws narrowly missed us. The cait laughed in challenge and charged as I pitched a fist-sized stone right between its eyes, giving her that opening. My teeth gleamed in the darkness as she leaped onto the abomination, taking it down by herself.

As the dominance of the field shifted inexorably in our favor, the ranged attacks began. I heard a Sister scream, and streaks of red light and fire struck both fighting Davrin and grey mind-slaves alike.

They know they lose, D'Shea said. *Those are the reserves. The masters are visible now.*

Panagan had spotted the three Ornilleth at last after climbing a jut of rock to get both the high view and a chance to use her spell-touched arrows. The flayers were on the far side of the cavern, she told us, opposite of where the Sisterhood had appeared.

In front of them was a line of gaunt, spindly thralls capable of releasing heat and fire from their fingertips. Behind the thought-flayers were not only a few smaller tunnels, but Panagan watched her own arrow strike whatever invisible shield protected them.

The rest of us knew. We couldn't get at them, and they had an easy exit strategy if their forces failed.

Lunent Agalia, Corpora Cilyan, Sister Moria, Sister Sirana. Defend the battle mages nearest you. They must collapse the tunnels and overwhelm the shields. The rest of your Sisters are nearly in position. They will take any opportunity the mages can give them.

Elder Rausery dispatched more Sisters to guide several officers and their units to deal with the ranged attacks, but we four were nearest to the mages holding their line in the back yet were under direct threat. The buas were distracted by incoming fire and rays as the melee thralls on the frontline pressed closer with urgent tenacity.

The single Ornilleth standing a quarter-circle around the cavern had focused on our male mages and our soldiers desperately defending them. Among them, I glimpsed a familiar wizard, read in an instant that all four were losing their nerve as less of the army was close enough to help with simultaneous sources of threat. Their choices splintered as some hesitated or alternated between one method of attack or defense and another.

You can't do everything at once. That's why we are here.

"Ranged offense, Callitro!" I shouted with force over the din. "I've got the fools in front of you, they won't get through!"

The battle mage I'd met at the last Worship Ball blinked when he recognized me, and he grinned realizing I'd be guarding him personally. I shot one thrall through the eye with my crossbow, and it stumbled, crashing into another and opening a breather for the army. I'd lost track of the young female fighter for a bit, but heard when she cried in a cheer and joined back in, connecting with another unit to fight the same line threatening the mages.

Laughing at the sight, I placed my body between Callitro and the nearest harm. His focus tightened to a pinpoint in his next spell, and the distance was impressive.

The concussive blast centered right in the middle of the fire-thralls opposite of him. It echoed, reverberated, sending more than a handful of the backline to their misshapen knees, clutching their earholes.

"Well done!" Lunent Agalia called, taking up the lead and preparing her own magic stone from a pouch. "Mages! Prepare this spell with your brother! I'll shield you until you're ready — !"

Retaliation was swift, and a red line of scorching heat missed me by two finger's breadth as I withdrew my crossbow bolt from a thrall's eye. Another seared Moria's thigh before clipping the Lunent's ear; another mage jerked and lost his focus, falling to his knees. Obeying nonetheless, the three standing buas became entirely vulnerable, their eyes closing to speak the next words.

"Shit!" Agalia groaned, and that moment my head began to get that pressure inside like it was filling with water. More than one Sister around me shook her head, their eyesight becoming fuzzy as mine.

I stumbled back a few steps, unintentionally opening the way to Callitro. More red streaks incoming. The young cait in the brown uniform hid behind a lurching thrall as it was struck in the back. The flesh smoked a little, and she gripped it like an unwieldy shield until fate decided which way it would fall.

"Hey!" she shouted at the top of her voice. "Sisters, wizards, watch out! You're dangling in an open web!"

Not only that, but something colorless plucked at those threads, trying to wrap them tighter and tighter around our ankles and hands so we couldn't move.

~*Kill the Self-abductors. Silence the Song. Claim the bodies.*~

What ... ?

I locked eyes with Agalia. I heard a voice her and yet not *wholly* hers, accusing me: **Novice. Weakest link ... affecting us all.**

No.

Terror and truth flared at once at the back of my head.

It's not true.

Far from it.

Focus! D'Shea said to us all, as if she, too, struggled to keep us connected.

I closed my eyes in the center of a battle.

~*Noch berte. Itsche craug.*~

As fast as it happened, the pressure lifted, the mental manacles came off, and my vision became sharp. My ears were filled to the very tip with the rumble of the rampaging battle. The Lunent shook her head, confused but quickly hiding it in front of those waiting for direction.

"Battlemages!" she ordered, pointing at each Tower wizard in turn as Moria poured a potion down one male's throat. "One, two, three, four ... two flicks apart and equal points above the Ornilleths' heads!"

The injured wizard wiped his mouth and nodded, rebuilding his spell as quickly as he could; he would be the last to release. Meanwhile, four Sisters and more defended the wizards as the viciousness escalated in our tight space. It would have been easier if the mages could have gotten to higher ground, but that only made them a better target for the rays.

At last, we gained enough time and ground for the magic users to attack the stone above the Ornilleth. If we had had even one less blast or if it hadn't been timed right, it wouldn't have worked as well as it did.

Callitro and his brothers all used the same spell, centered side-by-side on the far wall, and each delayed those successive heartbeats, filling my chest and my ears with a threatening earthquake.

Boom. Boom! *Boom!*

BOOM.

Noise and vibration sent general confusion abounding but, more importantly, masses of stone began to fall, collapsing in a deliberate wave. The crushing weight of rock struck the shields around and above the thought-flayers, weakening it with constant assault while creating an obstruction behind them over which they must climb and hope to squeeze through without being trapped or smashed.

I saw in my mind what I could only describe as "mental sparks" arching around an otherwise invisible dome every time rock struck the surface. I believed I understood how they did it. I almost knew why it was failing.

"*Sivaraus Archers!*" Rausery bellowed. Her voice sounded far from me but uplifting all the same."Aim and release at that shield! Do not stop until you run out of arrows!"

Our army's archers sent arrow after arrow to the dome, the intent not to penetrate but to add to every pebble and boulder wearing down the Ornilleth defense. There seemed a rise in anticipation, as if a dam was about to break. Over and over it happened, and I heard D'Shea's voice.

Prepare.

I held my breath.

NOW!

Fifteen Sisters had since gotten in range to shoot poisoned arrows and darts at the Ornilleth. Three seemed overwhelmed, their minds blinking out and they were not able to send a second dart, but the other twelve shot again, and again. I listened and knew each thought-flayer received more than ten doses of our most potent poison.

Meanwhile, I attacked with my thinnest blades, now so slick with life fluids it was harder to grip them. My nearest foe slowed suddenly, then stopped moving entirely. It stood with blank eyes blinking in confusion. The creature possessed not command nor guidance.

Next, it was without breath or heartbeat as well.

"Move in and slit the throats," Rausery commanded three of our best. "Search them and bind them for transport."

"Yes, Elder," Jaunda said, taking a step forward.

~*NO! Contact after death is dangerous!*~

"Hold a moment, Jaunda," my Elder ordered next, rethinking her approach.

Who said that? D'Shea demanded as the odd, underlying bass faded away.

I waited as if someone else would claim the breach of command, but no one answered. The cavern gradually became quieter as each Davrin unit realized their enemy was not fighting back. About half of them finished off the grey-horror or fire-flinger in front of them while the rest stepped back and regrouped, looking for their officer to instruct them.

Meanwhile, Elder Rausery herself backed by Lead Jaunda and Corpora Kiren finished the Ornilleth by setting them aflame with an incendiary dart each. As the bodies began to burn, I could breathe again, and a cheer began to swell; I couldn't help but join in.

"We won!!"

Chapter 3

Rarely were there moments of unity such as this, where all Davrin stood on the same side.

I laughed as loud as my lungs could manage, pointed to the ceiling, my next affirmative cry half-shout and half-growl as I turned to see Callitro's handsome face, his bright eyes watching me. Sweating and disheveled as I was, he was a pure delight to snap into my arms.

He tried to speak.

I claimed his mouth, thrusting my tongue in and grabbing his buttocks through the robes. I pressed our groins together and felt him respond instantly, his staff growing longer and very firm between our bellies as I drank deeply of my stolen kiss. My hand slid toward the front, stroking that gorgeous erection, although I didn't know what I expected to happen next.

Corpora Cilyan hissed an order at me. "Let him go, Sister."

I felt the reaffirming command from Elder D'Shea. *No, Sirana. Not where commoners can watch you act common.*

Damn it.

I released Callitro with an internal grumble and stepped back. The battle mage was charmed and dizzy, his robes visibly tented; he was gasping, regretful as well that I'd stopped, but glad to take the attention.

He glanced over at his mage companions, his smile filled with bragging rights before he noticed the guts and slime that I'd transferred to his robes.

Then I heard D'Shea's voice again.

Kill every thrall. Leave none breathing. Find the field menders. Any with available restorative potions are to tend the wounded.

Oh, yes. The clean-up.

The order passed through Elder Rausery and the Sisters to each officer. I was surprised to hear one dissenter; she was gesturing to a cluster of the thin, lanky fire-shooters and addressing our Elder as she made her way back to the center.

"We shouldn't destroy them, Elder Sister, they were once our own mages! Think of their use against our enemies if we can get them back! And if we can't, surely the Priestesses or sorceresses can find a way to control them —"

The Davrin eyes went wide as we all only just realized that Rausery had moved. Our Elder scowled into the eyes of the dying officer as she slowly sank down to the ground. Rausery held a glistening blade in her right hand. She looked around at those watching, and her voice projected without having to shout.

"Kill. Every. Thrall. No exceptions."

There were no more dissenters.

Rausery called the Red Sisters closer to her, and I noticed some of us were missing. The spell linking our thoughts had receded, however, and I could no longer be sure if they were alive or not. Lead Qivni hadn't been one mind to "wink out," but she also wasn't here, along with two others. There were six in total not standing with us.

Three fallen, and three still standing to carry them back.

Not the Prime nor the Elders would want a Red Sister's body and equipment loitering where ally and enemy alike could see it, or worse, loot it.

Rausery next selected us in twos and threes for various tasks. I was instructed along with five others to oversee the healing so those able to march back to Sivaraus would do so on their own two feet.

"Set more lights and watch them," the Elder grumbled before moving on to her next duty. "Make sure they're actually *healing*, not selectively bumping off their wounded rivals." She paused, focusing on me and answering my unspoken question, the same way the Prime had. "Watch the faces of the wounded. You'll know."

I had to admit this was an excellent opportunity to make sure a rival died. If Jilrina and I somehow had been in this battle together, it would have been my high priority. Searching with my Sisters for the army's brewers and menders, I looked for the patch formed like a small bottle on their back. They were not all together at first, but we located them and called them to our side.

"Very good, Sisters, I'm ready," one younger brewer said after listening to our instructions. She pointed to a group of collected wounded three clusters away. "I'll start there."

"No, you won't," Corpora Kiren said, stepping to stand chest-to-chest with her. She took a whiff of the cait with a familiar, leering grin. "You start with the group closest, Number Nineteen. Protect that trade agreement with the Fifteenth House. Careful that I don't step on your heels."

The youth swallowed. "Y-yes, Red Sister."

Kiren pinched her ass on the way over, inciting a yelp, and the rest of us laughed. We followed the Corpora's lead in the attitude, acting as their escorts and superior officer as I grasped for knowledge D'Shea had required I study.

Identifying to which House each mender or brewer belonged was essential, as none could choose their own patients. Plenty attempted to try but all were stopped, and I was astonished at the frequency of the mismatches.

Elder Rausery was right about watching the wounded.

If they were conscious, a quick glance at them when they laid eyes on the mender told me whether it was a neutral pairing or a deadly one. The healer herself never gave it away.

"Hey, Sister!" one of ours called. "Send me your healer, you can have mine!"

It would become a frequent call among those in the red uniform.

My own damaged armor indicated that I had received a few injuries as well, though it took me this long to realize it. I hadn't felt them although might have recalled receiving them, and the wounds themselves were already healed.

This was the case for every Red Sister present. We appeared perfectly fit, and we needed none of the resources from the Queen's Army whatsoever.

I found among the wounded the same feisty cait who'd fought beside me. By chance, I stood in front of her with a mender. I watched her face and the others; they didn't like this first choice. Some of them looked briefly afraid, vulnerable, but the youth scowled defiantly and spoke for the group.

"Toss off a cliff, Fifth House," she snarled, holding a bleeding gash on her thigh.

I couldn't help grinning, looking to the highest-ranked mender in the army — who had yet to heal anyone. "You heard her. Toss off. Send me the Fourteenth House brewer. She's more competent."

Pure pleasure it was to watch this much older female try so hard not to sneer at me. Instead, she sniffed at the rejection, muttering, "Gutter fringe," as she was traded for a third time.

The wounded before me all relaxed as soon as she was gone, some glancing in apparent gratitude at my scrapper, who maintained that winsome scowl.

"Quite a reputation the Fifth must have," I said.

"Trudin only heals commanding Davrin, Sister," one soldier volunteered. "The rest get a salve of her choosing, and you're lucky if it doesn't burn a hole to cripple you before it heals. Everyone knows it."

"Commanders find this amusing, I take it?"

"They don't have much pull to punish her properly, Red Sister. Fifth House."

"Right." I looked at my fighter-cait directly. "You're Noble, aren't you?"

She glanced around, realized the others would remain silent, and shrugged with a nonchalance reminiscent of when I first arrived at Court.

"Barely."

'Barely' Noble. From the Bottom Three, then.

I studied her leg as we waited, and the replacement mender approached. The injury wasn't life-threatening yet, but the youth wouldn't be able to walk back to the city with her unit and it would only get worse from here. Her armor was covered with blood and black goo, and the design was common level but reasonably made.

Strands of white hair stuck to her forehead and temples and her hair had been tied in a tight bun before the fighting but was mostly undone now spreading over her shoulders. In the light, she had fierce, red eyes shaped a little like D'Shea's, but wherein my Elder there was all calm and grace, this one was aggressive challenge and stubbornness.

I made room for the tending female from the Fourteenth House and saw that they approved of her with unanimous, placid expressions. At last, I asked the wounded cait, "What is your name?"

I watched her face heat up when the mender and a few soldiers chuckled, very softly. Then she cleared her throat.

"I am Jael Aurenthietti, Red Sister."

She was a Noble, yes, but a Fourth Daughter and of House Aurenthin, the bottom rung of the Noble Houses at Twenty-Fourth.

"Jael." It felt nice on my tongue; a soft, sensual buzz through my teeth and lips before ending on a sigh as my tongue lightly touched the roof my of mouth. *Jzahhl.*

"Not one to give up easily, are you?"

She withheld whatever opinion she held of my small talk and answered. "No, Red Sister. Only the dead give up the battle, and I'm not ready to hang up my skin."

It was an odd twist on a common saying, but I liked it.

Activity in the cavern was rising again, and these low-born Nobles were one of the last groups who must get to their feet. I saw they would make do with whatever leftover potions and half-used salves remained. Before too long we'd be pulling out, but I took the time to observe as much as I could of the aftermath of my first real battle.

Logic suggested this cavern and its surrounding area would smell for spans. We had burned the three thrall masters to be safe but could not burn every dead body, or we would pollute and use up our air with results worse than the smell. I knew from simple talk that we depended on the scavengers of the Deepearth to clean up afterward, but it took time.

Before we left it to that fate, scores of able bodies combed the battle-field for interesting objects; they investigated the bodies and checked the area for stragglers.

With thralls such as these, there wasn't much to loot, and we could only leave the enemy where they fell. We sometimes took our own dead back along with any slaves, but it depended more on if there was a Davrin present who cared enough to do it. They were usually related to the dead but not always.

"Ow," Jael said, darting a narrow look at the mender even though she cooperated.

"Ah, yes, my favorite of the six signs of life," the Fourteenth smirked as she tugged a little firmer on the wrap, making the youth grimace.

"What's that?"

"Complaining."

Jael muttered something about her Mother — either the mender's or her own — but I didn't catch it as I spotted Lunent Agalia signing high to me to reconvene.

Leave them.

I did without announcement, consciously resisting the urge to look back. It helped that the "Battle Buas," as I'd overheard a few say already, were collected with their female captain, waiting behind the reforming Red Sisters.

Callitro perked up, smiling a little but managing not to show his teeth this time. Another wizard leaned over and murmured something to him, and he shrugged as though he hadn't a care in the world.

I must make time to visit him at the Wizard's Tower.

Rausery gestured that we were to leave. I assumed all was under control, and it was clear we wouldn't be walking back with the army. We followed our Elder to the rendezvous point where we had appeared and then past it, heading deeper into the highest tunnel.

Twenty-one of us, healed by the magic in our bloodstream, moved without any appreciable sound, weaving a confusing crawl through another two passages before we came upon a stone wall and a feeling familiar to me.

A Ward. And an opening behind an illusion.

I proved to be correct on both counts as Rausery suspended the Ward with what appeared willpower alone, striding straight through the stone without stopping. The rest of us followed her, vigilant and in formation. After all the torches and glow-stones lit for the healers to do their work, it took time to adjust to a close, still, black space again.

"Any change?" the Elder's low voice asked, though at first, I knew not to whom.

"Their bodies are healed and whole, Elder," Lead Qivni answered, sounding tired and a little uncertain. "Deep in Reverie, perhaps."

"Not natural Reverie."

"No, Elder."

"Coma, or temporary mind-sludge?"

"I don't know, Elder, but there's no reflex response."

Several bodies blocked my view, and I moved to glimpse even a little of what I sensed. The three Sisters we knew had fallen were laid out within another onyx-inlay circle, Qivni and two of the other Red Sisters who had some mage ability, Dieri and Nyllel. All three looked baffled and wary, not a good sign.

"Alright, Sisters," Rausery said, "back to the Cloister. Maybe Varessa and Tarra can put their heads together."

Who?

I did not have much time to guess as we were ordered to stay still inside the circle and wait for the Elder Sorceress to bring us back. In her time, she did. It was only when we all stood back in the Prime's strategy room did I recall my Elder's given name, as I hadn't heard it since my trials.

Varessa. Does that mean 'Tarra' is the — ?

"Congratulations, Red Sisters," Prime said gruffly, looking just a little proud. "Your skills and your obedience to your Elders, to me, and the supreme communication of the Sisterhood defeated this invasion. This is why we are the best there is at what we do. There are no demons but us."

"No demons but us," murmured more than a few Sisters in reverent answer, causing the Priestess to raise a white eyebrow.

"We have three casualties, Prime," Elder Rausery said, respectful but delaying celebration just yet. "Permission to move them to the cots as soon as possible. We need D'Shea and Lelinahdara."

"Casualties are inevitable in battle, Elder."

"I know this lesson well, Prime. They were psionic attacks. We must bring every Red Sister back from a battle, that is our law, but there may be a holdover threat undetermined."

The Prime's face lost any trace of pride and became the one of which I had learned to be afraid. "Just kill them, Rausery. Destroy their bodies. Their willpower was too weak to withstand the Ornilleth. We can always recruit more."

"I agree with Elder Rausery, Prime," Elder D'Shea spoke then, her voice rich, standing with poise and one palm resting on Gaelan's shoulder. My closest Sister seemed dizzy and unfocused, kneeling with her legs under her between the Sorceress and the Priestess.

"What's that, Varessa?" the Prime growled.

"I heard a voice not one of ours within the Priestess' Weave. It was close to the time these three fell. I must try to determine who spoke to us. Perhaps it spoke to them first."

"What did she say?"

"She, or 'he.' The voice may have been male."

The Prime bristled. "And?"

"And it warned us not to touch the thought-flayer bodies after we'd poisoned them."

Other Sisters murmured, some nodding, all confirming their Elder's claim. I nodded with them; I had heard it, too.

"Davrin male?" the eldest Red Sister said with great suspicion.

No ...

"That is to be determined."

As D'Shea seemed intent on speaking what the Prime didn't want to hear, Elder Rausery chose then to break back into the discussion.

"We've never tried to wake up those dropped by Ornilleth before," our battle leader said, taking a step forward to stand before our Prime with a respectful bow. "This fight felt different. We were unified, more than we've ever been. I've never known so much of what was going on with the battlefield, with my subordinates."

Rausery motioned toward the mages as she continued. "I think Varessa's and Tarra's methods are reaching a pinnacle we shouldn't shy away from now. I want them to look at our fallen Sisters, see if we can recover them. Even three is a harsh loss to us, Prime. Recruitment and training take time."

My Sisters around me nodded in agreement. The Prime wanted obedience, and she would get that, but she didn't miss the fact that nobody seemed to want to celebrate our victory just now as questions hung in the air.

What about our three Sisters? Which of us fell? Can we get them back?

"Move them to the cots," the Prime commanded Rausery, then looked at the rest of us. "Restock your supplies and see to your equipment. Clean up, go to the Mess. Relax while you can, you'll know when you're next summoned. Get out of here."

We moved in roughly familiar units, although I rolled myself closer to the wall to linger for as long as I could until I determined that Gaelan wasn't standing up to come with us. I saw when the Prime looked between Rausery and D'Shea and jerked her chin downward, dismissing them and herself officially while offering Lelinahdara a more reverent gesture on behalf of Braqth.

"Report as soon as you have a theory, D'Shea," our leader said, already walking toward a much smaller doorway at the back. "Or if any of those three ever wake up again."

"Come on, Sirana!"

Cilyan snagged my arm again, and I caught Jaunda glancing my way curiously, gauging whether she was needed to enforce the Prime's orders. Rather than disobey in front of her and so many others, I left with my

Sisters to restock, repair, and replace, then finally visited the sluicers to clean up—

And spread against the wall for a few who badly needed a release.

"Take it," she whispered, thrusting her Feldeu in hard. "That's it, novice, squirm on my pole."

"Ngh!" I grunted, my cheek pressed to damp stone. I felt tits pushed to my back and the thick phallus sinking into my slit as Thena kicked my ankles wider apart.

I wasn't the only one penetrated under the cold water; there was a lot of grunting and fucking surrounding me, and this aroused me despite my distaste for Thena in particular. Although, I *was* the only cunt presumed to be available without verbally volunteering.

Because I'm the youngest. Bottom rung.

I could have tried to refuse her, to fight her off as Rausery and Jaunda had each taught me, but all of us beneath that cleansing water had been in the battle, and no one else had started a fight. No one had rejected another Sister after the serious threat we'd just faced.

Thena wouldn't be the only one, anyway. The endurance potions had worn off, and I hadn't the strength to fight off four of them. Nor did Thena have strength left for much beyond driving fast between my legs.

She just wants to cum.

Jaunda watched on my other side, her own cock dripping water and being joyfully serviced by Lawret on her knees, but I caught a silent exchange between the Lead and Corpora Thena. Both our tugging exhaustion and my Lead's hard eye were the likely reasons the Corpora and her favorites — Sisters Suna, Panagan, and Moria — merely took their turns in my cunt, relatively quick and not rough enough to injure.

I managed to cum, crying out nice and loud to let them *know* that I had.

"Yes! *Ahhh, yes!*"

I thought Suna might have just finished up, or Panagan had just entered me. I knew it wasn't with Thena; I heard her chuff in annoyance as I twitched, standing on the balls of my feet, my pelvic muscles milking another Sister's cock, not hers.

Jaunda purred in approval and murmured to Lawret to suck harder. I was released with a well-ridden twat and a few hard slaps to my wet ass. After that group had left and Jaunda had pulled out of a swollen set of lips, she approached and leaned near my ear to speak.

"Good work getting them all off, Sister. Keep being smart, choose your battles. Things'll change."

I smiled a little, only sorry that both of us were too tired to go for a second round or, in my case, a fifth.

After all that, after leaving clean and dressed and taking myself to the Mess Hall, I still wasn't hungry. While sitting and attempting to eat, more of the battle returned to me in flashes, things that happened too quickly to absorb at the time.

I relived the water-weight in my head, the mental attack on me and Agalia and the others. That feeling like *I* was the one dragging them down, the belief that I was the rotten part in an otherwise robust body.

Then I had heard the Tragar language, a gruff voice such as D'Shea told the Prime had been there. *She and I may not have been the only ones.*

Instead of that revolting weight landing even heavier upon my back to defeat me, however, that deep, male voice had instead broken the chains, freeing us to think clearly once again. To fight back. To reinforce the weave of connection between the Red Sisters.

What happened when we were all linked through that spell?

Was the need to understand it enough to confess what had occurred between Kain and me deep in the wilderness tunnels?

Move in and slit their throats, Rausery had said.

~No! Don't!~

I curled my fingers tighter around my fork, poking uneaten food on my plate.

Contact with dying psions is dangerous.

Chapter 4

Given enough downtime, I might have hovered near Gaelan's quarters, waiting for her to return. My thought was that she might need a Sister's help if Elder D'Shea didn't have time, and I could volunteer as the tender because maybe no one else would.

Gaelan and I were the youngest Red Sisters and far from having earned the benefits of the Leads and Lunents, or even the Corporas. All of them would have — *did* have — Sisters falling over themselves to offer aftermath care, if for no other reason than status and having valuable ears to oneself for a moment.

I didn't have the time to volunteer, however. Barely a few marks and a magically mended uniform later, I was running errands for Corpora Cilyan and creeping around Sivaraus as if an Ornilleth invasion had never occurred, even as the Davrin on the streets talked about nothing else.

Bold, noisy spots of celebration had spread at the Palace Court and various Houses, as well as the marketplace, but nothing cohesive. It was too early for the Valsharess to make an appearance and the Priestesses had yet to spin their own pronouncement of their essential role in preventing our populace from being dragged into the thought-flayer's dungeons.

*Wherever that is. The Sisterhood barely needed the help of **one** Priestess, useful only to our Elder Sorceress.*

Yet those two and the Prime had taken my Sister Gaelan away, and I still waited for news from someone, anyone, about this crisis; how it started, what we planned to do next. The Sisterhood had responded as directed, as we'd been trained, and it had felt like I had understood what was happening around me. Within the crisis, within that "mindlink" spell, I had known what was going on as it had been staring me in the face.

Now, a heavier, lonelier thought had settled in, likely enough that I wondered at my own naivety.

Nothing will be explained now, but well done. Continue on, Sisters.

I watched. I reported. Once, I asked my Corpora if the battle mages — the male ones — had returned safely to their Wizard's Tower.

"Of course," Cilyan replied, making a face. "If you have time to think about that bua you kissed, you have time to work on a few other things. Follow me."

I'd expected that. I was given "grunt" tasks: helping to gather food and equipment and cleaning the Cloister. There were no outside servants to do it; we had to be self-sustaining. It was better than acting on my impulses, which might lead to House Itlaun and the Consort again, or perhaps to House Thalluen, to see if my former Matron had given birth yet.

After all that danger and excitement, my mind strained against the feeling that my world was shrinking again, not even a full turn after all I'd suffered in body and mind to enter the Sisterhood. After I had thought the cage of my Nobility had been blown wide open by my trials.

Patience. Opportunity will be there. Just look at Jaunda and D'Shea.

This assumed I wasn't trapped by another with a grudge against me. It also assumed I wasn't killed in action. Or punished for insulting a Priestess. Or got on the Prime's permanent bad side. The truth was that I didn't know how many Red Sisters died young compared to how many earned rank like my Lead and Elder. We didn't talk about the dead, and I had not been around long enough to witness it.

But I decided, with Elder Rausery staring at me. Asking me outright. I decided.

It was better to die young as a Red Sister acting under our own agency than live longer by sucking up to Matrons and Priestesses as a Noble. It was better to do my own scrub work than wait for servants; better to serve my Sisters as I had in the sluicers, for pure pleasure and release than to fumble around negotiating for suitable studs, my only important duty being to breed more Nobles.

I reminded myself the only one with true authority over the Sisterhood was the Valsharess. I had risen very high, very young, even doing lower work than I ever had before, even yielding my body to be used in the basest ways by older females. The contrast was an awakening for me, and I would only figure out more of the system the longer I lived.

It must be enough. There's no going back.

Eventually my mind returned to the three Sisters who had been struck down by Ornilleth.

Sister Feini. Sister Berayne. Corpora Reishel.

Primarily under Lead Qivni's command. Middling rank, solid fighters as I understood it. Their bodies whole but comatose, their minds injured. According to Elder Rausery, we'd never attempted to retrieve such casualties before. Why now? Do such things heal with time? Did the extraordinary willpower we all possessed reassert itself? Was there anything we could do to help beyond caring for their bodies?

And how long might we perform such a draining duty before the Prime orders their throats cut? Not long. Elder D'Shea must discover something for Rausery quickly.

"There you are."

I jumped but kept hold of my bristle brush, getting to my feet swiftly and standing at attention. "Lead."

Jaunda wasn't smiling as wide as she could when she had distinctly lewd plans for me; she held Gaelan upright by her arm. "Here, got something else you can clean up."

I scanned her and frowned. "What did they do to her?"

Our youngest mage was awake but exhausted, barely paying attention to her surroundings or the voices talking about her. Gaelan's disheveled, white hair stuck to her forehead and cheeks from sweat already having dried. I wasn't sure, but thought I glimpsed a pleading look in her dull, red eyes.

"No point in asking right now," my Lead said, passing Gaelan over to me, and I dropped my brush to reach out and hold her up with both hands. "Just get her clean and fed, if she'll eat. And guard her, will ya?" She pulled out a message pellet and came close enough to tuck it in a pouch on my belt. "Call me if there's trouble."

"What kind of trouble?"

"Do as I say, novice."

"I apologize, Lead."

Jaunda left for her next task, whatever it was, and I stumbled with Gaelan to her familiar quarters, laying her down on her pallet. She closed her eyes and didn't speak while I gathered the water, basins, and cloth I needed to cleanse and dry someone unable to clutch the tools herself. The door could be warded with a finger pressed to a gem embedded in the frame and a word spoken. I tried that, discovering that Gaelan hadn't changed it since I had slept here more often before claiming my own room in the barracks.

Most of her weapons and armor had already been removed; Gaelan wore just the red leather and boots, easy enough to strip off. I knew what stale sex smelled like, and furious physical effort; the whiff I caught coming off her skin wasn't either of those. The closest thing I could compare was the unctuous, alchemical odor upon my body after being released from a ritual or being forced to drink a potion not in my best interests.

The 'real' ones by the Priestesses, not any my pretentious sister attempted in the back plantation shed. I leaned closer, opening my nostrils to draw in the strange mix of scents as I wrung out the clean cloth. *D'Shea's scent, too.*

Our Elder hadn't left her alone with Lelinahdara but had remained close and presumably called Jaunda afterward. This kept my protective resentment in check while I tended Gaelan. At one point, Gaelan's eyes fluttered, her head turning on the edge of consciousness as she moaned and reached out with her hand.

"N-Na —" she stuttered before her throat closed and she gripped my forearm like she feared to drown.

I watched her, letting her squeeze my arm as she swallowed desperately, gagging before taking a deep breath to fill her chest.

"*Ungh,*" she choked again, her eyes rolling up inside her skull. "Tr … *ey-guh* — !"

What are you trying to say? Why do you strain like this?

I felt tiny bumps rise from my neck all the way down my back and arms beneath my uniform as a thought occurred to me. How well I knew this feeling, of not being able to speak when thoughts and cries rang loud and clear inside my mind. I hoped it was only the shadow of a childhood fear in a helpless Sister who was not well.

What did they do to you?

In time, Gaelan was clean, warm, and resting peacefully, if only because she had used any remaining strength in an imaginary struggle. I stayed to guard but grew bored enough to explore her room, to see what she'd changed since I'd left. It was not much. There wasn't a lot of furniture to change around anyway, and although her chest of drawers could be locked, they weren't right now.

I found her Feldeu wrapped in a shiny, black pouch within the second drawer. I paused with my fingers on it, feeling it through the silk. This one was the first Sisterhood phallus I'd felt, first, in my mouth and then parting my slit. Gaelan had been attached to the other end, and I'd made her cum while kneeling on all fours.

I'd since received and serviced many others. Some Sisters swapped places, taking turns wearing it. I knew Gaelan wasn't opposed to trying this with me, but D'Shea had forbidden it until I passed some unknown test and earned the right.

Thus, I didn't know the command word to make this one transform from a cold, floppy, unwieldy thing to a warm, rigid, sensitive extension of a Red Sister's whole cunt.

Sighing, I removed it from its drawer anyway and pulled the bag off, cradling the dark tool in my bare hands. I was already familiar with one end but less so with the bulb at the base, which always disappeared inside the Sister about to fuck me. I imagined it was broad enough to make clamping down on it with one's belly muscles an effective way to keep it in place even if the command word hadn't been spoken.

Hm. I could still try it on, see how it looked. *Wash and dry it off later.*

With my boots already off, I tugged at the leather ties at my hips, loosening the blood red leather enough to push it down my thighs. The act alone made me receptive, and it took only painting a few other lovely cocks in my mind — real ones — that I either had long ago or still coveted and strumming my nub to make me wet enough to work the firm, smooth bulb around in my cleft like a dessert in its sauce.

Oh, yes.

Soon enough, I pushed. My body gave but I was fully aware of every measure of the unusual girth.

Thick as a Dwarf ...

The bulb slipped in, abrupt and startling, as my body clutched down harder than necessary. My face grimaced in disgust and I tossed the flicker of Kain from my head. A stupid comparison to make, as if I wanted to reimagine how *that* particular cock felt.

Feldeu in place as well as it would get, I settled back on Gaelan's pallet near her feet while she lay curled up on her side. I explored both my sex and its burrowed lodger with my fingers, briefly caressing and tracing the shape of the unfeeling rod itself. It was turgid enough, and I could press it to my stomach like an erection, but it was far too cool to help my impulsive fancy. I knew it could become even firmer with the arousal of its wearer. Hard and hot.

The faces Jaunda, Gaelan, and the others make when they use it on me ...

I could only imagine the sensual pleasure alongside with the taboo of turning the usual power dynamic on its head. Whatever enjoyment a female could glean from using the pole to scratch her itch, it was secondary to the Red Sister's magical rush.

Magic I wasn't feeling this moment.

I sighed again, the initial excitement in donning the Feldeu waning as I reflected that I'd never done this at Court *because* it would have made me the lesser. The submissive female, the play-acting bua attempting to touch those refined spots inside a "superior" female without ever reaching her own peak. Not unless the unfeeling, awkward phallus was pulled out and more knowledgeable fingers or lips and tongue replaced it.

Jaunda makes it look easy.

My Lead wielded her cock with such confidence and power that sometimes I forgot her tastes were backward from every Matron, Noble, and commoner following them. It only seemed natural to submit and spread my legs to her, for her to mount me and let her ride the pleasure her way.

Elder Rausery, too.

What she told me once in my earliest training still confused me.

"I've already seen how you take a cock, Sirana. You'll do fine if you're ever on the Surface. Now show me how you fuck one."

If I ever go. And what did she mean, I'd do "fine"? At what?

At taking a cock. That seems obvious.

It still left so many questions.

Meanwhile, Elder D'Shea hadn't yet coaxed me into her bed after inviting me to sleep there a few times early on, which was assuredly another test of my impulse control at the time. I'd never seen the Sorceress wear the Feldeu at all. Nor Lead Qivni. And other Sisters switched all the time. At least my curiosities and the malleable status of such a tool might stave off stagnation for a while.

I tugged on the black toy with my fist, stroking the length of it. I felt nothing except my body resist giving up the bulb inside. I tapped a bored tattoo on it, just for the subtle vibrations, as I turned my head, letting my eyes wander. My eyes fell on Gaelan's shapely ass, on the pretty, purplish netherlips peeking out from between her dark thighs. I smirked at my thought.

She's not well. Probably can't enjoy it, and neither would I. Numb pole.

Unless she told me the command word.

Gaelan twitched in her sleep, muttered something unintelligible again, and I watched as she stroked her clean slit with one hand, her fingers trapped between her legs as she relaxed again. I perked up.

"Truh … Treh …"

She breathed out, her lips forming the same syllable even if her voice was gone. Her hips moved in a clear, sensual invitation, one hand reaching to cup one buttock, spreading herself a moment for a better view. Then she relaxed again, and my smirk had crept higher to a grin.

Do you still dream of buas, too, Sister?

I hadn't asked her whether she had taken real semen inside her since joining the Sisterhood. She had been off and on again agitated with Elder D'Shea or cold to me ever since my mission to execute the Second Daughter of my former House. That had been a task I was only too glad to fulfill, and yet ...

Somewhere, I'd disappointed my Elder. I should have asked the Matron more questions. I should have taken a sample of that drugged wine. Gathered more intelligence on the male guardsvrin and the orphaned cait.

But I'd been afraid of seeming weak and beholden to a family which was mine no longer. I did not want to appear distracted or, worse, obsessed. There was self-discipline to impress a superior — something the Prime and Rausery wished to see — and there was inquisitive discovery, which D'Shea made clear she wanted more. She wanted me not to feel fear but pleasure in revealing that which was hidden in plain sight, just by gathering and interpreting the right details.

Did that mean not as many Sisters showed that tendency? It was one of the few compliments D'Shea had paid me, and she had framed it as an expectation. A demand.

"Ohhh ... mmm."

Gaelan was feeling better. Her spine curved elegantly from shoulders to hips, one thigh shifted up, her sex just a bit damp now after I'd cleaned it.

I scooted on my butt closer along the wall, within reach to brush my fingertips along her sex, and she sucked in more air. Left herself open, inviting. My cunt ached as it swelled around the base of the Feldeu, and I rolled forward onto belly and elbows, attaching my mouth to her lips while grinding my mound against the cool pole trapped between my thighs and the pallet.

Oh, that's not bad.

I might climax this way, given enough time. My hips undulated, my mouth chewed and sucked on my Sister. The two together was a heady combination.

"Ah!" Gaelan cried, reaching back and catching the back of my head with her palm, pressing my nose deeper between her ass cleft. I chuckled, slurping her pucker.

"Truh — ! Ungh!"

She hadn't formed one clear word this entire time I had been watching over her. It was like a collar was around her neck, unseen yet someone kept tugging it each time she tried to speak. She only grunted as she scrambled up to her knees then, spreading them while curling her arms against her breasts, shoulders planted to her bed.

Braced. Demanding to be fucked. Serviced.

Her tasty slit now well above my reach, unless I sacrificed my own pleasure for hers.

Damn it.

I nearly reached out her ankles, tempted to pull her back down and continue my grinding upon the Feldeu while eating her. I paused, however, watching her quiver. A thought came to my mind, muddled by her personal perfume, and I pushed myself up using both arms.

"You want it, huh, Gaelan?" I murmured how Jaunda often did to me. Crawling behind her, taking hold of one hip while rubbing the fake phallus along her ass, her inner thighs. I couldn't feel a Braqth-damned thing.

I asked, "You want this inside?"

I nestled the tip between her petals, and she lunged backward, surprising me. She'd taken it halfway before I could yank it back out. She moaned a complaint.

"What's the command word?" I murmured softly, then repeated myself. "The Feldeu. What's the word, Gaelan?"

"H-huh?" she asked, her toes curling, which made me smile, although now she might be straining to listen.

Or to wake up.

"What's the command word?" I tried again, keeping the same, calm tone. Confident. Not too eager or impatient; not like when I'd botched the bluff with the Tragar. I teased her opening, slipped the tip inside then dragged it out and down across her clit. She jerked and shivered, her toes curling again. She moaned, but no word came out with it.

My own slit drooled like hers, I could feel it. I was tempted to thrust in, to see her response, and yet … I didn't. I only wanted it if I could feel something, too. Like when I mated my buas. I enjoyed watching their genuine reactions, their faces, their straining and climaxing bodies. I could delight in Gaelan's responses to *taking* a phallus instead of using it, but …

I pushed in, bottomed out.

She gasped. "Oh, yes!"

Her first clear words.

My beginner's thrusts were awkward, every bit as much as the first bua I'd ever mounted yet different. I humped, experimenting. Unfocused. I tried grinding my clit again, realizing it didn't suit the angle for filling her in any way she liked. Not if her weaving, uncooperative gyrations were any indication.

Fuck.

I pulled out, held onto her hips to keep us apart when she groaned again.

"Command word, Gaelan. Tell me."

"Ss … suh —"

"Yes?"

Her dazed, maroon eyes flew open. "Sirana! N-no, *wait!* Oh, Braqth, what did I say?!"

In a moment of pure frustration, I plunged in and folded over her back, pinning her in place for that instant of fear I saw in her eye. My mouth wasn't far above her shoulder and one sharp, upturned ear.

"Nothing interesting," I replied with a wry sneer. "Just a lot of moaning."

She shook her head in denial, but I imagined she might have squeezed the phallus inside her then, testing to see if I reacted. If I felt it.

"Get off me, Sirana."

It seemed I couldn't fake it.

"Alright. You'll have to tell me about that dream, though. It was a good one, I could tell."

She didn't reply, and I pulled out and released her without further posturing, except to stand up and turn around. I pulled out the large bulb before she suggested that, too, hiding my grimace from her.

Goddess, my slit throbbed. So unsatisfied.

I went to the cleanest basin I'd been using to bathe her and gave myself a cursory wipe before cleaning her Feldeu thoroughly and properly, the same as I had been taught to maintain any piece of equipment. Gaelan was quiet as I patted it dry and slipped it back into its silk pouch. I placed it atop the chest rather than put it back where I found it.

Pulling up my leathers only then, I glanced over. "Well? Say something."

She shook her head, to refuse, I thought at first. But she had had enough time to back her questions up to the beginning. I was more impressed than I'd admit.

"How did I get there?"

I shrugged, sitting back down on her pallet. "Lead found me. She was leading you around by the arm, like you were in a trance. Told me to clean you up, watch you until something changed."

She glanced to the top of her chest. "Did she also say to find my Feldeu and fuck me with it?"

"No." I started to grin, mimicking Jaunda to hide my unease. "You suggested that."

She pursed her lips, narrowing her eyes skeptically, but something kept her from blurting out whatever she was thinking. For a moment, she looked afraid again.

"We won?" she asked quietly. "Against the thralls. And flayers. You weren't hurt?"

I nodded proudly. "We won. And I made it in one piece. It was almost a cycle ago, Gaelan. How long have you been in our Elders' clutches?"

"Too accurate," she grumbled, looking down at her naked body, lightly touching the damp folds I'd been clumsily prodding between without completion for either of us.

"You *were* moaning in Reverie," I muttered, trying not to sound defensive. "And touching yourself. You liked me eating you. Then you got up on your knees and pointed your snatch at me. I ... I thought I'd give it a try since the Feldeu was where you left it."

Checking over the rest of her body, her face was very warm, Gaelan found herself cleaner than she might have recalled. She found herself unhurt, as I knew she would. Next, she studied the used basins and damp towels and sighed to herself. Perhaps she decided to take me at my word.

"Maybe soon," she said. "But I *know* it'll be better for you as well as me if I'm goddess-damned *aware* that we're fucking, Sirana."

I sucked the inside of one cheek, shrugging again with my arms folded. "Sometimes it can be. Other times your mind just goes elsewhere. Where in the Abyss was *your* mind, anyway?"

She stared determinedly at her bare feet. "Remembering someone I'm better off forgetting. Happens sometimes when D'Shea and Lelinahdara's magic rides me for long enough. I relive my life, like walking in deep shadows. A deeper Reverie than most."

"Huh," I said, thinking over how sexy she'd been acting. "A bua, then? From when you were a commoner?"

Gaelan stiffened but gave me a nod.

"Is he still alive?"

The shake of her head was so slight as she stared into the void that I almost missed it.

"Oh. Well. At least you won't run into him on a mission."

Her throat flexed in a hard swallow, and she curled her lip like there was a bad taste in her mouth. She took a slow breath and let it out. "Do you feel lucky to be out of where you were?"

Odd change of subject.

"Yes," I answered. "But I also wanted it enough. There've already been many chances to fail and die."

"Yes," she agreed soberly. "For all of us here. But some of us might have had more to lose than you did, taking those same chances."

I watched her eyes, recalling how hers were the only ones to show any concern for me in my trials. Gaelan expressed more emotion than most Red Sisters — unwisely, perhaps — but then again, maybe it had something to do with her being a mage, or why Elder D'Shea would choose her to help when there were other mages with seniority.

I felt a pinch of unease at what I'd just done while she still recovered from whatever the Sorceress and Priestess had needed from her in their "weave."

*But if a recruit was in a **better** place before facing the challenges of the Red Sisters, and taken away from it ...*

I didn't see how it was possible that one might survive the loss of that old life unless she thought she could return to it.

She made it here only five turns before me. Maybe she does want to go back but keeps it secret.

"You seem to wear the Feldeu a lot when you'd rather not," I said. "What's keeping you from telling me the command word and getting what you want?"

"Elder D'Shea," she said, arching an eyebrow. She'd told me that already.

"And what is *she* waiting for? What do I need to do? Can you give me a hint?"

Gaelan shook her head. I didn't know whether that meant she knew or not, but either way, she couldn't say a thing about it. My sigh sounded like a pouting growl even to me, just before my Sister's stomach echoed the sentiment.

"Food here or at the Mess?" I asked, knowing it depended if she could face anyone outside this room after whatever she'd been through.

Gaelan watched me a few moments and seemed to read me. "The Mess."

She stood up to dress, and I smirked, satisfied, and once again impressed without saying.

Chapter 5

A couple cycles passed without word about the battle's aftermath. Elder D'Shea was regularly in meetings with Lelinahdara and Elder Rausery, and only glimpses of the latter's face told me of the Prime's impatience. That we were running out of time for something other than execution for our fallen Sisters.

Perhaps the Prime had already chosen. The Guardsvrin at the infirmary had been heavy at first, but soon better uses were found for an experienced Sister's time.

"Report to the infirmary, novice," Elder Rausery said, the first direct words she'd spoken to me since I'd slept in her room just before the Worship Ball. "Keep the place clean until I come back around. Shouldn't be long."

"Yes, Elder."

I sighed inwardly though I made my sign of respect and reported for duty. I took over for Moria, who was clearly glad for the relief. She shoved me toward the cleaning supplies, giving me a summary of how to use the storage and drainage closets.

She directed me to the water source, large wash basins, the shelves of clean cloths and bedding, the bins holding those soiled, and the lines to which were clipped those washed and hanging to dry.

"Get started now, Sirana," she said, "because at the very least, they're going to piss their clouts again. Then you have to make sure they drink without choking so they can do it again. Like being a wet nurse for the wrong hole."

She chuckled, and I wished — far from the first time — that I had learned even a few cantrips our House servants had used to keep up with the volume of dirty fabrics, dishes, and vessels generated by a mansion.

"Consider yourself lucky their bowels are as empty as their stomachs," she growled on her way out.

I smiled. *If you insist.*

Moria had taken all she'd brought with her, and I removed and placed my own equipment on the hooks she'd just cleared. I worked on the soiled laundry, got a few clean lengths hung up to dry, and wandered back to the room containing the three cots. Their hair had been unwashed for several cycles but at least they were wiped down and not starting to shrivel from lack of water.

I went over to check their clouts for changing, briefly distracted by the tits of each in doing so. I hadn't seen many bare Davrin breasts in a situation where they held still with nothing else going on so I could simply look at them. Curiosity had me comparing the lighter and darker shades of nipples, fuller and more pointed mounds, even the placement of each on their chest varied a bit.

Sister Feini. Sister Berayne. Corpora Reishel.

I watched them, and on impulse decided to check their eye shade in the better light. I'd never been able to do something so daring as peel back an eyelid on another sleeping female. As I studied the faces and eyes of the comatose caits, it returned to me that I'd just molested Gaelan in her sleep, too, with little hesitation, with no guilt until she woke and discovered me.

I could have done so with a Court male or two back then, but …

I didn't. More appealing just watching the bua sleep, somehow.

It was an odd difference, perhaps, but I could compare it to my Sisters doing what they liked while I was under the Priestess' influence as a new recruit.

Do as was done to me.

Reishel's pupils reacted to the candlelight in what seemed to me a normal way, contracting smooth and timely, but Feini's and Berayne's didn't. Theirs were sluggish and remained open far too long in light that should have stung. The eyelids on all three stayed open when I lifted them; they only closed if I brushed them back down, which I did for each.

Their bodies were whole, no visible injuries, nothing seemed wrong, yet they weren't aware. They breathed but otherwise made no noise, no moans or grunts. Some similarity to a corpse perhaps, but too warm, and clearly the body functions still worked.

I stayed closer to the Corpora, taking a seat on a squat stool next to her simply because I was better able to picture the exact shade of her eyes and their normal response to the light. The silence was heavy excepting the muffled activity of other Sisters outside, deeper in the Cloister, and there was only so much work or cleaning I could do.

I kept guard, trying to put myself back in that calm mindset I'd learned being on stake-out for multiple cycles watching House Itlaun. It wasn't easy. I was tense and distracted, and I didn't understand why.

It's only been a few marks. I could be here for a span easily. Nothing to do except think about buas.

I thought about them — a lot. *Micraen, Reaf, Tohni, Yeri ... that ass-raping, cowardly wizard and that stunning, Braqth-damned Consort.*

Eventually, I would weigh pleasuring myself to pass some time with not knowing the next time the Prime or the Elders might step in and catch me with wet fingers and pants down. I might get off lighter with the Elders, depending on the mood they were in, but the Prime ...

She just waits for an excuse.

A rush suddenly swept my body, and I sucked in air, leaving my pants in place.

Only once I'd "fought" the Prime in a grossly imbalanced match, and Elder Rausery had needed to drag me out to wash and heal. It had taken so little to earn the eldest's sneer, her brutal hand and burning Feldeu; the Prime's boredom and displeasure meant only my pain. There was no subtlety, no game to play. Just dominance and submission; all I could do was stop fighting and hope I survived.

That terror and defenselessness was only half a turn old, but it seized on another invasion not many spans earlier.

The Tragar. Kain.

Our bodies linked by Elven magic, our minds bound in Dwarven hatred, both of us pushed to simultaneous peaks of terrified ecstasy, our free wills lost, sanity threatened. The raw holes and thick semen coating my insides had been the least of my worries. I couldn't submit and hope to survive that time; one of us had to die to break that endless loop.

It wasn't me. I won that fight.

I wondered if it took something like that to persuade the Prime that a Red Sister wasn't soft just because she was new, or a Noble?

I'm still alive, am I not?

I hadn't told anyone about Kain. I feared what they'd do to me. What I'd be blamed for.

Corpora Reishel moaned, and I looked over at her. Her mouth was closed, and she hadn't moved that I could tell, yet for a moment it seemed she had. That sound had come from an open mouth.

*Help ... *

I frowned at the voice. It was not an Elder or a Lead using a magic pellet to summon me. I looked around the empty room even as my heart sped up. I knew it was pointless. Much as I feared to accept it, I knew the voice had come from the bed next to me.

Slowly, I turned in my stool toward her. *Corpora?*

Another moan. Her mouth was still closed. Her voice box didn't flinch. My heart began to race as if I fled through the wilderness tunnels once again.

Stupid. She could be passing air.

I smelled no gut gas even as I sniffed. Again, I reached to peel up her eyelid, standing to lean over and look at her pupil. At how it responded to the light, if it was the same as before.

"Corpora Reishel?"

Pure terror punched through an unseen barrier, rushing straight down my spine; abruptly Reishel's red-violet eye focused on me.

She saw me.

I threw myself back from the cot as she bolted straight up, starting to scream. I stumbled backward onto the floor, staring at her as she shrieked wordless sounds. Bumps arose on my arms and legs; my weapons were still hanging on the wall.

"What in Braqth's web?" someone shouted in the hall.

"Sirana?" Sister Delia called. "Sirana!"

"She's awake!" I cried. "One of them woke up!"

BOTH ELDERS RAUSERY AND D'SHEA ASKED ME FOR THE DETAILS LEADING TO Reishel coming aware. The Corpora had been removed from the infirmary down to the holding cells where her cries went unheard by the rest of the Cloister. If she couldn't calm down or speak intelligibly, if she didn't know who she was or remember her training, then she wasn't worth keeping alive any more than the two who lay unmoving and pissing their cots.

"We can give our Sister some time to get her head together, but not a lot," Rausery said.

I was in a closed room with them just down the hall, and Rausery looked over her shoulder as if expecting the Prime to enter any moment. A lot more Sisters were guarding the infirmary and holding cell all of a sudden, and one should expect whispers to spread.

"If you can give us something to work with, novice — ?"

"Even the smaller details might offer insight," the Sorceress said.

"I was finished cleaning," I said, knowing what I had wouldn't help. "I ... checked their eyes."

"Why?"

"Um. I was bored. I wanted to watch their pupils in the light."

"What would that have told you?" D'Shea asked me with apparent curiosity.

I shrugged. "I don't know. I noticed only Reishel's eyes were normal. The other two were ... sluggish."

"Did you do anything else to them? Hit or shake them?"

"No, Elder. I just looked at them."

She stared at me, waiting to see if I'd squirm in a lie. I didn't, because it wasn't a lie.

"You were sitting next to Reishel," Rausery said, having noted the overturned stool when she had come in; I nodded. "Any warning she was about to wake up? Movement? Complaining?"

"I heard some moaning," I said.

D'Shea hadn't blinked. "You were to report any response."

"It happened too quickly, Elder."

"Moaning to screaming and thrashing?"

"Yes, Elder."

I recited the moments as they ordered, and the Elders listened to the details, which I knew wouldn't help them or Reishel. There was nothing to see, nothing to describe except that chilling feeling when I looked into my Sisters eyes. And neither of us were mages.

I spent the next three cycles tending the other two. I avoided peeling back their eyelids again. The mood outside the infirmary varied, but I caught a few words once, standing next to the door.

"She's coming back," Corpora Cilyan said, sounding glad about it. "She recognized me and the last three Sisters to tend her, and I even heard her humming a tune she likes."

"But is she a Red Sister ... ?"

The voices had faded down the hall past my hearing, but I considered it good news. The other two weren't so well, but one was strengthening. That made the Sisterhood better off than we were immediately after the battle, even just by one.

The Prime arrived, scowling at me, at the cots and the sheets hanging to dry. I was already on my feet at attention.

"Nothing?" she asked.

I weighed lying to delay her until Rausery could come by but was too afraid. "No change, Prime."

With a nod, she drew a long dagger and approached the cots. I wanted to back away but remained where I was. She spun the naked blade on her palm, letting it rest to offer me the hilt.

No …

I glanced from blade to her hardened face. She was smiling a little.

"Permission to touch your weapon, Prime," I said, hoping it was just a test of obedience and not an execution order.

"Heh. Permission granted, novice."

Fuck. Fuck …

I took firm hold of the thick handle, lifting the heavy dagger into my hand. I was cold but desperate to hide any uncertainty from her.

"Orders, Prime?" I asked.

She tilted her head just a bit. "Kill them, novice."

The subtle shaking began despite my efforts. I'd only killed two with a blade before the battle with the sightless thralls. Both of them had been staring me in the eyes.

My sister. And Kain.

These Red Sisters wouldn't be staring at me. Did that make them more like the thralls? It didn't feel like it; we'd met eyes before, and like Kaltra and the Tragar, Feini and Berayne had cum on me, too.

The Prime narrowed her eyes dangerously and drew breath to repeat her order.

I acted before she could. I made it quick.

CHAPTER 6

ELDER D'SHEA GESTURED FOR ME TO FOLLOW HER ONE EVE, ABOUT A SPAN AFTER Reishel could speak again from the holding cell. I obeyed without speaking. Her gait was leisurely and swaying as if she were in her silken robes instead of her reds.

I'd just returned from the outskirts of Sivaraus, and from the smell of her, the Sorceress had been somewhere in the center. She didn't speak at all until we reached her quarters; I followed her lead in that as well.

The door slid shut behind us, she called light to her heatless candles, and I looked around the spacious room more familiar by now, even unusual as it was in the Cloister. The high bed, the bath, the bookshelves, the enormous desk, the tidy counter with a mirror, used either to dress or to store and prepare a small snack or a drink of wine, and a bench set at waist-level, with two chairs nearby.

If D'Shea had a collection of vials and magical components and small burners at her disposal in her quarters, they could only be in the locked closet built into the stone.

Rausery's quarters had been a touch smaller, with a low pallet, basic square table and two chairs, a standing chest used for hygiene but not storing food. Hers had no bookshelf although she had a desk just as large, and there had been a tall pile of pressed parchment that looked like maps, plus a few way-finding tools.

It was plain that the Elder Sorceress spent quality time here, where in contrast, I hadn't seen much evidence that Rausery stayed in her quarters a moment longer than she had to.

"Bathe, Sirana," D'Shea said with a little wrinkle to her nose as she began the water flowing in her tub. "Set all equipment on my bench."

I did as she said. My skin was cool and sticky in places where I'd sweated through, and some grit had even gotten into the few breaches in the armor, but there was no blood or damage. I had no conflict or execution to report on this time. I untied my braid, letting it fall, and began to comb it out with my fingers. D'Shea nodded in satisfaction and indicated that I should sit in the tub even while it was still filling.

As I cleaned myself using her soaps, silently enjoying the warm swirl around my legs climbing up my torso, D'Shea inspected my uniform, weapons, and other equipment, muttering a few magical words. Seeming to find nothing of interest, she undressed as well, trading out her armor and uniform for a soft and comfortable, pale purple robe. It didn't resemble the wizards' robes in appearance, but its elegance suited her, and she seemed to prefer it.

By the time my Elder sat with a glass of wine with her desk's chair turned toward me, I'd finished scrubbing my skin and hair, had dunked myself to rinse. I sat a moment longer before she said to empty the tub and dry off. A towel was within my reach, folded on a low caddy next to it.

I observed her as I ran the absorbent cloth over my dripping body. She didn't speak to me, and she seemed low on energy. It was hard to decide the difference now, as normally she stood or sat calmly, rarely paced, never fidgeting. She was like that now; she did not slump, sag, yawn, or do anything that made me think she was worn out.

Yet she still seemed that way.

My Elder turned her head to look at me with that face clearly from Nobility and smiled. "Good. Now, come sit. Have some wine."

I blinked as I realized she had moved one of the bench chairs to sit at a right angle from hers. As she lifted her glass to her mouth, I saw the second, empty glass on the edge of her desk beside the open bottle. That was a first.

"Come sit, Sirana," she repeated.

She hadn't instructed me to dress, and I knew enough by now that it wasn't an oversight. A creeping feeling crawled up the back of my neck as I wondered if she intended to fuck me this eve, this many quad-spans after my initiation, long after I had my own uniform and was fully of the Red Sisters. Perhaps the set up suggested it, but her languid motions and drifting eyes didn't.

I accepted the chair but hesitated at pouring any wine for myself. The open bottle missed roughly the same amount as was in D'Shea's own glass, but it meant nothing as I hadn't watched her open the bottle and pour to drink it straight.

D'Shea watched me and softly chuckled. "No other way to test, Sirana?"

She lifted her glass toward her mouth. I smiled. "No, Elder."

She shook her head, tilting it and letting the transparent, brown-tinged liquid slide down her throat as she swallowed twice. Then she reached to pour another half-glass from the same bottle and emptied that as well in three large gulps. I stared at her, and her smile was impish as she set down her glass and leaned back in her chair, one leg crossed over another.

"How long will you wait now?"

My fingers closed on the seat beneath my bare ass. "Until my report is over, Elder?"

Her mouth twisted with silent laughter. "Sufficient. Tell me about your trip to House Itlaun."

That was easy as I told her everything I had observed, which was very little.

"Very well. Now let's talk a little about House Aurenthin," she said. "You wandered out that way recently, did you not?"

Damn. Had someone reported on me?

"Yes, Elder. Just now, after my last check-in."

"Why?"

"You were still in the city, Elder, and no one gave me a specific task."

"A little evasion helped, I'm sure."

The Sorceress leaned forward to take the wine bottle again as she made that remark. She filled the empty glass nearest to me then upended it to fill hers near to the brim. I watched the last couple of tan drops land in her cup before she set the bottle down. She leaned back in her chair again, leaving both glasses full between us, and my eyes chose to study her breasts beneath the robe instead. I could see her nipples standing up, and the dark arrowhead of skin coming to a point. I knew she wore nothing underneath; a shrug of the shoulders and a loosening of a knot, and she'd be nude like me.

I figured she sensed my confusion, or at least my tension.

"You are off task, Sirana," she said, "yet I never see you drink any spirits. You've even refused when Jaunda offered."

I shrugged. "Too many burning tonics forced down my throat as a child, Elder, and more than one tampered with at Court. I don't understand compromising my wits with intention and leaving myself vulnerable."

My Elder nodded thoughtfully, resettling to look comfortable, and her gaze was far away for a few moments. She blinked and focused on me. "I've heard this before. We're agreed. Anymore, I partake of a substance *too* restful only while sitting here. Locked in and secure."

I frowned a bit. *Where else did you 'partake' that you don't anymore?*

This was what I wished to ask but it was too specific about her past. I knew nothing of where any of my elders had come from, not even Jaunda, and Qivni had kicked me in the head when I probed her about a link to the Sanctuary. The most I knew of any Sister was that Gaelan had been a commoner with a bua she still thought about — but she refused to tell me anything about him.

Instead, I asked, "Why imbibe at all, Elder?"

D'Shea smiled, relaxed yet sly. "A necessary part of any mage perfecting their craft, Sirana, whether or not they brew potions. Testing and confronting magical effects of any kind is not unlike swallowing a liquor or eating a mushroom which changes your senses, placing us in an altered state. It *can* compromise the body, and a mage best not forget this, but if we are to learn magic, if we are not to stagnate, we cannot afford to fear those altered states of mind and body, or losing control of them on occasion."

There was a clear warrior's parallel there, I didn't miss it. This was no doubt why Jaunda sometimes indulged in recreational "alteration." And D'Shea was correct, my Lead *had* offered the same to me, and I *might* have been safe to try, but ...

I was afraid.

I didn't trust even my Sisters to pick me up out of the hallway if I collapsed, as I had once chosen to do for the young Noble, Micraen. Upon waking, he had rewarded me with my first ride upon a young pole; he had given me the pleasure of the body I had protected, but that hadn't been my purpose at the time. I'd only been afraid of what others would do to one who couldn't defend themselves.

Afraid and angry.

As I'd been for so much of my youth.

My Elder reached for her glass and changed the subject, still watching me as she took a sip. "Do you remember the young fighter from the Ornilleth skirmish? She broke rank and assisted you with defending the mages."

I saw where she was going with this from a cavern away.

I nodded. "Yes, Elder. We spoke again briefly after the battle. I saw to her healing, among others."

"Of what did you speak?"

"I asked her name. Complimented her fierceness." I thought back. "That was all."

D'Shea's dark red eyes did not blink. "What *is* her name?"

You already know, don't you?

"Jael Aurenthietti," I said, pausing. "Is that the first you've heard her name?"

D'Shea half-smiled. "No."

"She is someone of interest to us?"

"Perhaps. She is to you, yes?"

"Not her alone, more what made her. I'm curious about the bottom House."

"That's why you took your own task after House Itlaun, waiting for me?"

Just spill the 'report,' Sirana.

"Yes, Elder. The Valsharess' Army drills on the Matron's lands and she cannot refuse. The Fourth Daughter of the Twenty-Fourth spoke to a *Fifth* House healer like she was nothing. More of them seem outspoken, probably due to their severance from the Court. They are vulnerable to retaliation, petty or devastating, yet seem active on poorer lands."

The Elder nodded, slow and thoughtful. "Active. How is that?"

I tried to put what I'd seen into words. "They live in a slum, like the Lowgate on the other side of the Great Cavern, but not so cramped. I didn't observe the same … slinking lethargy. They didn't so much hide in holes as stay alert on an open expanse doing things. Sneaking scouts seem a regular thing."

D'Shea was smirking. "You deduced all that from a single observance?"

"I admit it took more, Elder." I smiled back. "Three times."

She huffed. "Without explicit instruction."

"You don't want me to cling to explicit instruction, Elder. I did not interact."

"Heh. Nothing so blatant as kissing Callitro on the battlefield?"

My face flushed. "No, Elder. They didn't see me. I never spoke."

She stared at me, wine glass in hand. The silence stretched.

"Are you displeased, Elder?"

She inhaled, the shape of her breasts apparent beneath her robe. "Yes, but not entirely. Perhaps I should consider this a genuine mark in her favor."

"Her favor?"

"Aurenthietti. The Fourth Daughter."

A sudden possibility settled in my mind. "Recruitment?"

"Perhaps." D'Shea's expression was hard to read yet her words struck hard. "You are aware we are two Sisters down."

I looked at the floor, folding my hands. "How is Reishel, Elder? I haven't seen her."

"Retraining. We'll get her back."

"Is she the first one, as Elder Rausery said?"

The Sorceress nodded, her mouth solemn. "True clashes with a mind flayer are rare, but all our Sisters struck down before were killed either where they fell or soon after being pulled out."

Rare? A mind flayer is rare?

"Why did *three* of them attack us, Elder, with an entire mob of thralls?"

"Unknown." D'Shea took a drink and gestured with her glass, swirling the liquid. "Have the wine I'm offering before I take offense, Sirana."

A Noble at Court would have already.

"Yes, Elder."

I lifted the generous helping, held it beneath my nose. I could smell nothing unusual until I tasted it. The mushroom wine had a tart bite to it that I wondered how it had been done. Bitter was the most common undertone, and sweet because of the need to add consumables other than fungus to the process. It was sour enough to cause the inside of my mouth to pucker and salivate; that was an accomplishment.

"What do you think?" she asked.

"Different," I responded, smacking my mouth once, holding up the glass to note the coloration.

She laughed quietly and sipped; she was on her third glass, and I could see the relaxation in her shoulders and her eyes. She felt the effects and kept watching me sip from the glass. She was silent for quite a while, and her copper eyes drifted over my breasts and belly, my legs and back up. I hadn't done more than finger-comb my hair from being in the tub; it was unkempt but not in total disarray as it dried, but she studied that, too. Over that quiet time, I could feel the wine warm my insides.

"Do you still prefer males over females, Sirana?"

I swallowed the wine on my tongue and wondered whether there was a right answer to this one. "I've had only females since joining the Sisterhood, Elder."

"I'm aware, Sirana. And you failed to answer the question."

I gathered my wits even as they'd grown fuzzy around the edges. "I prefer living erections to numb appendages, Elder."

"Living erections?"

"Real, or magical. The sex doesn't matter."

"You don't care for the synthetic rods." Her tone was wry, and she rolled her eyes upward. "Few females do, given their position in being forced to wear them. What about wearing a Feldeu yourself?"

My mouth was open, but I paused. My Elder rested her cheek on two elegant fingers.

"Have you thought about it?" she added.

"Of course, l — "

" — especially when you made a *vulnerable* and altered mage take the one she should be using on you?" D'Shea lifted an eyebrow. "That was the 'numb appendage' that came to mind, I take it?"

Gaelan. Flustered, I swallowed my answer mid-thought. "Yes, I've tried it. Only once. I won't do it again."

"Do what? Pump a Sister's cunt for her without feeling anything yourself, or take her while she's 'altered,' as you dislike yourself?"

Fuck.

"Take her while she's altered, Elder," I answered with sincerity. "I haven't ever ... i-it's happened to *me* a lot, but she didn't like it after, and it wasn't the best idea I've had — "

"You realize saying that won't stop another from taking you while altered again, and I *guarantee* you won't be able to keep that boundary yourself as a Red Sister, Sirana, so don't attempt to think so."

"I mean Gaelan only," I pressed. "Just between us, as Sisters. I never equated mage spells with potions and liquor, Elder. I won't do it to her again."

"Hm." D'Shea smirked. "And if she asks you to use her Feldeu on her and work her to climax while awake? Serving her needs with a numb appendage? Never your preference at Court, we know."

"We'll find something that works between us, Elder. I can't say what it is."

The Sorceress considered me as though I had suddenly said something intelligent and it surprised her. Briefly, she shook her head as if to refuse a request I hadn't heard spoken.

"Touch yourself, Sirana."

It was an order that sent tiny bumps of surprise spreading over my shoulders. My heart beat harder as I opened my legs a little and touched between them, my fingers slipping between my netherlips. She watched for a bit but then gauged my glass beside me on the corner of her desk.

"Finish your wine."

I knew better than to take my hand from my crotch. I reached out with my other and gulped it in four large swallows before setting it down again. The brown liquid coated my stomach, which heaved a little. My mouth puckered, D'Shea sighed in mild disappointment but otherwise didn't comment.

As she watched, and to help my responsiveness, I imagined Jaunda and Delia, recalled their recent "surprise" quickie, jumping and wrestling me to the ground in the Mess Hall. I'd used some of what Elder Rausery had taught me, what I'd been practicing, and I almost got away. Almost. Other Sisters had heard my Lead compliment me as she jerked down my leathers and I stayed in position with legs open.

"Goddess-damn. Making us really earn it now, eh?"

I had taken them both at once, deep and willing. I'd sucked Delia with such enthusiasm, flicking my bean with one hand while Jaunda determinedly reamed my backend. I'd cum so hard for them as others watched, as several bent over a table to join. My Sisters were so different from seducing and climbing on top of coy, Noble buas.

As soon as my Elder heard my touch as well as saw it, she spoke.

"Show me your fingers."

A hot flush swept over me, and my mind had fallen in a heavy haze just in that short time. I held onto the seat with one hand, to make sure I did not tilt too far off center; I drew my first two fingers out of my hole and showed them to her. My Elder straightened up and smoothly leaned forward, her mouth capturing my fingers, tasting my juices. I felt her soft tongue swirl around them, hot lips press and suck the fragrant fluid off my skin. Her robe was looser in the front and I could see the curves of her breasts, naked nipples teasing me, not quite in full view.

There was no doubt in my mind now, when I least expected it, that D'Shea had decided it was her turn to sample me.

"E-Elder?" I whispered.

She offered a pleasant hum as she sucked my fingers, her inebriated eyes low-lidded and glazed. She stood up slowly, untying the sash at her waist as she stepped to the side and walked to her closet.

"On my bed, Sirana. Upright. Sit on the edge with your legs parted."

There had been a little shake in her voice. *Anticipation?*

My gut was tight for not knowing what she planned, what she liked, how she intended to enjoy herself. It was hot as well, my slit swelling, engorged to an ache to think that the only Red Sister who hadn't fucked me yet genuinely desired me now.

I sat on her bed. She had blankets softer than others, and the mattress beneath gave comfortably. I had lain here before, my very first eve inside the Cloister and a few times after. It hadn't felt different then — just the bedding I was used to myself as a Noble.

Now it felt *very* different, even though it was the same bed.

I watched D'Shea open her robe while facing away from me, revealing her shoulders and her back, the fine in-curve of her waist and the swell of her hips. Her bare arms lifted with hypnotic grace as she hung the robe back in its place on the wall by the tub. I glimpsed the scar again which crossed her spine high on her back before she turned around, and I saw the two on her front as well. One just beneath her left breast and the other near her womb on the right side. I still didn't know why she was scarred at all, but at least understood that, according to Rausery, the scars might be recent and D'Shea had never attempted to erase them.

Unfathomable for a powerful Sorceress.

Or they might be …

Perhaps from Priestess ritual. And will never heal.

I shivered to imagine.

D'Shea murmured a word and opened the storage space set into the wall. From my angle, I couldn't see inside; I only knew it was large but didn't reach the floor. There was a thick stone foundation below with runes on it. My Elder pulled out a box barely large enough to contain the pouched Feldeu she lifted from it. I felt a familiar clutch in my nether regions when I recognized it.

Here I was again, but why had it taken this long?

D'Shea unveiled the magical phallus, releasing it from its confines, and it swayed with weight. My eyes followed it rather than my Elder's face when she came nearer.

"Tha'z …" I slurred.

"Hm?"

She stood directly in front of me, bare feet braced inside mine. I stared at her purple-tipped breasts, felt her warm hand run up my thigh as she leaned down and close.

"It's what, Sirana?" she said near my ear.

"Broad, Elder."

Both ends.

"It is. I like it that way. Ass to the edge."

I shifted forward, and she drew in her breath through her nose near my skin, scenting me, before moving her face just enough to plant a soft, nibbling kiss on my mouth. My eyes closed, the fog in my mind thickening; I spread my thighs wider at a nudge from her knees. It was an awkward position for her, but she had chosen to fuck face-to-face.

Unusual.

I felt the thick Feldeu nudge at my sex and relaxed by reflex, allowing it to enter me. It stretched. A lot.

"Ungh," I groaned, and D'Shea withdrew briefly.

Using her fingers to spread more of my moisture around it, she aimed, pushed again. It was much thicker in girth than Gaelan's or Jaunda's — on par with Kerse or the Tragar. My mouth opened with the stretch, and I prepared to have her push me onto my back, to feel more of her thrusts—

Then the bulb passed in, and my eyes flew open, my body clamping down, holding it fast as the weight tugged from the front. Just as when I'd tried on Gaelan's Feldeu.

"Elder — !"

"Calm." She focused on the cock between my thighs, cradling it although I felt nothing. "Palms on the sheets, Sirana."

I obeyed; she spoke an arcane word with a matching gesture, and suddenly I felt pressure on my wrists. I tried to lift my hands; I couldn't. She'd put invisible cuffs in place.

A fucking Game?

When was it anything else in Sivaraus? Gaelan had said in her initiation, she'd been forced to wear the Feldeu to be treated as the Sisterhood treated a male: weaker, sensitive, his netherhole stretched while his cock was sucked, ridden, or simply slapped and tormented, and Gaelan had felt all of it.

This was worse. A female demoted to the male role without even the benefit of feeling anything. Submissive even to a male, if the commanding female desired.

I spoke through my teeth, my back rigid as metal, the chilly, dense material lodged stubbornly inside me and only slowly warmed by my body. "P-punishment, Elder?"

She caressed the unfeeling pole with one hand, my thigh with the other. "Why assume that, Sirana?"

"You asked my preference and do the opposite?"

D'Shea shook her head in disappointment, reached to grab my hair and yank my head back so I stared at the ceiling.

"Too predictable," she said, pulling and shoving the bulb of the Feldeu one more time, probably lowering her eyes to watch it as she purred against my chest and said, "*Yemennija.*"

Wait, no —

I felt something grab firm hold of me from the inside as if it had created a vacuum, and it unnerved me so that I strained against releasing my bladder. The next instant, I felt the bulb inside my birth canal burst with heat, washing my guts in magical flare where it became one with me, and I could no longer feel it. Instantly I was aware of the severe urge in my groin to couple, taken in by the hyper-sensitive flesh jutting up. The fat tip brushed against D'Shea's thigh first as she kneeled, then she cradled and caressed its full length.

I choked on my scream, at first thinking to move it away to protect the thing, then suddenly trying to aim it, to sink it somewhere hot and wet and tight—

"No ... No, s-stop," I breathed, grimacing as I writhed against the cuffs on my wrists.

The Sorceress squeezed it firmly and lowered her head. At first, I could not grasp the reality that my cock had passed between her lips. I felt her tongue on the crown.

Her warm mouth.

~Suck me.~

So familiar, that voice. The sensation, so strong it was pure agony. A bellowing roar filled my ears, my head.

My head ...

She took all of me, slurping, sucking. I trembled, and she chuckled before she did it again.

"F-fuck!" I squealed, shoving my hips up with a jerk, slamming the back of her throat, gagging her. I tried to grab her ears; I couldn't, my hands were bound.

She coughed and growled in annoyance, "Novice."

"Release me!" I roared, jerking my wrists.

My Elder looked confused, and she did not release me. She sprang up instead, pushed me onto my back on her bed and held me down, climbing on top. I yelled and struggled, yanking against the magical restraints.

"Why are you fighting?" she asked fiercely as she straddled me.

Suddenly, my erection was pressed lengthwise against her sex. The haughty slut was *rubbing* herself over it, her hips swaying side to side and around, I *saw* how she teased me!

Cunt's wet. Cunt wants it!

"Fuck!" I cried, trying to stab up into her if she wanted it that bad. "Fuck it! Fuck me!"

~Fuck it, or kill it. Maybe both.~

I tossed my head, drowning in the voice. My eyes saw only black, picked up only vague Radiants. I was in the wilderness, the aftereffects of ritual stealing my ability to think, chaining my will to the emptiness between my legs, leaving me helpless to run or fight. This time, however, I wasn't empty; I did not ache to be filled. I needed to fill, needed to *feel* that yielding void, the steaming softness wrapped snugly around me like a — a ...

"Sirana ... Sirana, stop! Calm down, you're only making it worse —"

~*Fucking trickster! Who are you? You brought me here to torment me?!*~

I attacked, striking my forehead against the face of the warm, curving body on top of me. I saw stars in front of my eyes, felt the pain as she collapsed, warm breasts pressed to me. I jerked one wrist so hard, the invisible force she'd used to strap me down came free.

~*I'll teach you to hold me, dirty howler!*~

I clutched her to me with my free arm, wrenching my shoulder as I freed my other. My arms held her around her ribs as if I were drowning and I rolled easily upon the decadent sleep space. My weight alone should be enough to hold the slender Elf down. Her legs fell open. I moved my hips to feel the head of the phallus drag across her sex in teasing torture, but within moments I figured out the angle. I pushed. She gasped, coming aware after being dazed.

I was inside that exotic cunt, and she knew it.

"Sira — *ugh!*"

I thrust deep down inside her, groaning against her shoulder, biting the big muscle there. My fat cock opened her wide and I held on for my life as pleasure exploded behind my eyes. I invaded that tight slit again and again, making her grunt every time the length slid in as far as it could go. There was no doubt my eyes rolled back in my head.

~*You like it! Tell me you like it!*~

I-I like it! Don't stop!

She was slick, her breathing ragged, and then there was that rippling grip as her sheath spasmed and fluttered around me! Caressing, worshipping. Only the Davrin were twisted enough to climax on my spear.

I'd never felt the like among *any* of my own kind.

"Sirana!" she cried, panting, and my chest swelled that she knew my name!

~Tugren! Yes!~

I planted my hands upon the too-soft mattress, raised myself up on my arms, strong muscles unified in working my member into her snatch. My eyes squeezed tight, wordless moans sounded in my ears, probably mine, but I felt her body clutch itself around me multiple times. She enjoyed getting fucked, enjoying the fucking.

~Oh Braqth, feels so good, please, let me c-cu — !~

I'd die if I didn't cum.

"Sirana. Sirana ... r-relax. Let go ... Breathe."

I pumped her sloshy cunt. I pounded it harder. I couldn't! I couldn't relax, I couldn't breathe! Every new stroke just curled my toes and pulled me taut as a bow, made me arch my back, stone-hard nipples pointed out. If she didn't stop this forsaken rut, I'd die!

She had to stop fucking me.

Oh! Oh! Oh, no ... please, don't stop — !

I'm going to die!

Why are you doing this, Davrin?

Abyssal sickness ... Goddess magic stronger than me ...

Her arms went around me, pulled me down. Her hands scalded my naked, sweating back. Her body hummed an unfamiliar pitch.

"Relax, breathe with me," she murmured. She was so calm. "*Relnega'shes.* Breathe. Breathe. Listen to me breathe ... Yes, again. Deeper."

I *knew* I was breathing. I felt the pain only as I realized it was fading away. Sensation flooded my groin, the sword piercing her becoming harder, pulsing a few times. My vision was coming back in spots, and so were the colors.

"Yes ... *Yeee — AAAHH!*" I screamed.

Incredible pressure began to unravel inside me as a torrent of pleasure rolled through my cock and back again, exploding at the back of my head. I thrust in and tried to push it in as far as it could go; my muscles locked, and I groaned again through bared, clenched teeth. I trembled and shuddered, gasping with the ebb and flow as it dwindled like sudden destruction had passed, leaving me a crumbled and sodden mess.

She pushed me off her, and I was useless enough to let her. I couldn't even sit up, and staring at her face as she rose above me, I eventually focused on the Davrin mage. She had a bleeding bitemark on her shoulder and a bruise swelling up on one side of her forehead; I could taste blood in my mouth and my head ached right in the center of my brow. Her nipples looked like they had been twisted and stretched, and although I had evidence on me for having caused the first two injuries, I didn't know about that one.

Eventually it came back. I knew who she was.

"Elder D'Shea," I admitted, though I was lost in every other way.

She glared at me, and impossibly, I nearly fell asleep right then. The feeling dragged at me like lead; I just wanted to close my eyes for a few moments, and we'd talk when I woke up—

If I woke up.

"I-I ... apologize, Elder," I gasped, fighting back the urge to yawn and negate my contrition.

She huffed an exasperated, ill-tempered laugh and reached between my legs to take hold of my erection, preparing to pull it. I yelped in fright, my voice masking hers as she spoke the release word. The Feldeu immediately separated from my inner walls and outer folds; once again, it was just a broad thing plugging up my twat. She pulled it out none too gently and I blurted another sound of discomfort as my cunt throbbed.

"Silence!"

I pressed my lips tight, awaiting her judgment. She stared at me, studying me in a definite foul mood. Her voice was clipped when she spoke again.

"I have *never* seen a reaction like that to the Feldeu, Sirana."

"It ... was my first time, Elder."

"Not even a first time!"

I flinched but unwisely spoke again. "I'd have welcomed some warning, Elder."

She grabbed my hair and forced me to sit up, putting her face in mine as she made my scalp burn. "I have the privilege to fuck you any way I want, and no Red Sister needs a warning."

I swallowed, opened my eyes again despite my grimace and met hers.

"I don't drink much. I can still feel it. I f-feel strange. You insisted."

She sneered. "Not your fault, then? Not in your right mind, it was the drink?"

"The Priestesses do it to the young ones at Court," I snarled. "I never knew how many buas I rutted at that Sathoet conception ritual! Do you *always* get a novice drunk her first time wearing a magical weapon?"

I received another slap for that. I had expected it.

Worth it.

"You acted like someone else entirely!" she hissed, still gripping my hair. "Nothing I know of you explains it! You devolved to a point I had to *insist* you keep working your lungs! I waited for any hint of that flexible will to reassert itself, but it never did! I expected more of you, Sirana."

I felt deep resentment at her words. "Then ask me a question, Elder. You've done it every time before closing a report and passing judgment of my actions. Aren't you going to ask?"

"Too bold in your afterglow, are you?" she hissed, leaning back and releasing my hair. "Fine. What in the Abyss did you think as you raped your Elder with her own Feldeu, novice? Explain it to me."

I froze at the truth of the accusation, and D'Shea saw the terror in my eyes. Another time, another place, if anyone else had heard, or witnessed what just happened ... How could I explain it and expect to escape the same torment I'd seen the Red Sisters do at executions? I needed my Elder's tolerance; I needed to beg for it, and I *would* beg.

But how could I *explain* it to her?

A drop of her blood from the shoulder bite had dripped to her breast, and I blinked as a vision of myself in the mirror returned — disheveled, muddy, and injured, dragging a Consort behind me. The Tragar bite had been on my left shoulder, the same as hers.

Someone else entirely.

The thoughts as we fucked had seemed as if I'd thought them before. Not my thoughts, though, not exactly. But male. Genuinely male. As if I had been mind-locked with the Tragar again, when I'd heard his thoughts, felt his sensations as he fucked my body.

Yes. D'Shea had been me. I had been Kain …

I felt nauseated.

"You know what it was," my Elder stated. "I see it. Tell me, now."

Tell her or suffer in ways unknown but far-reaching. She didn't have to add that; I already knew. I would exist with the Sisterhood or nowhere worth being.

I trembled as I swallowed down illness. "It was … as it felt in the Deepearth, Elder. After my trials, after the ritual, when the Sisterhood deposited me out in the wilderness. I told you … I told you then the power of the Goddess, the aftermath of Braqth's Threshold, was 'distracting' for me."

D'Shea nodded slowly, burning eyes watching every tick in my face. I felt anger and fear mix in my middle, and my breasts rose and fell faster as I breathed.

I said, "I underplayed that. It was utterly *crippling*, Elder. I couldn't satisfy myself, I tried. I couldn't catch anything to eat, I barely remembered to drink, I wanted to scream from the isolation! I could have died from the want, all I had to do was give up and let something find me, and I wouldn't have cared if a beast had decided I was in heat! That was the *worst* thing the Sisterhood could have done to me in that state."

She tilted her head at my bold description. "But you made it back."

"Only because I found something to fuck," I grumbled.

"Yes. You found the Consort."

Yes, that's what happened.

"No."

"Oh?"

Despairing, I admitted it. "I found a Tragar first. Psionic. I fucked him to death."

Elder D'Shea was genuinely shocked, putting out a hand to remain sitting on her bed. She stared at me before her gaze trailed over my body and down to where she'd set the uncleaned Feldeu she'd pulled out of me. She was in deep thought, as I'd seen many times before. I waited for her to speak.

"Just the essentials first, Sirana," she began, looking at me. "What happened?"

She was more intrigued than disgusted. That surprised me in return, but now I felt calmer after the confession. There was no other way for me to explain myself without my Elder knowing everything, and I knew she could — and would — use spells if she decided she couldn't trust anything I said.

So be it.

"I encountered a Tragar scouting for gems," I told her. "I needed food and water. He had some. I tried to bluff him to give it up, but it didn't work. He tried ... he went invisible, so I attacked. And we started fighting."

"Invisible?"

I nodded. "Tried. He hurled stones with his mind, but he missed. I knocked him out and went through his pack to get something to eat, but ... it ..." I breathed in, out. "The need overwhelmed me then, and he woke up."

"Ah. Did he decide to rape you first," my Elder asked, "and you took advantage and turned it on him?"

"No, *he* didn't decide." I blinked. *Dammit, absolutely not. No tears.* "I did."

She waited, never blinking. "Go on."

"His eyes were pure white, like an Ornilleth. A long enough stare, and we were in each other's minds. He ... it ... my need overwhelmed him, too. We fucked, Elder, but neither of us was ... willing. I heard *all* his thoughts, felt what it was like for him, being and spurting inside me. I screamed his anger, hatred ... He screamed mine, plundered by his own cock. One coupling wasn't enough to sate Braqth, though, we kept ... repeating."

"Until he died. How, exactly?"

I shook my head and shrugged. "Until he gave up his will, and I had a sliver of my own mind back to seek the nearest stone and strike his temple. I broke the link, retrieved my dagger, slit his throat. After that, I could make it to Sivaraus. Braqth's Threshold only took control of me again when I saw the Consort."

"This was the second time you tried to sate it," my Elder said, "not the first."

"Yes, Elder. That's everything."

Again, D'Shea pondered like she read a scroll with great concentration. I swallowed, feeling my wine-sticky tongue and desperately wanting some water.

"Intriguing," she whispered now. "And you still returned to the Sisterhood after that."

I nodded warily. "I never intended to admit it, Elder."

She smiled. "But you did. And why? Because your first time donning the Feldeu brought up this ... impression a psionic Dwarf left upon your mind." She rubbed her chin with two fingers. "Yes, that makes sense of what I saw. And heard."

At her next look, I scooted a little back from her to sit cross-legged, folding my arms to hold myself. I couldn't grasp what she wanted now.

"It is luck when one meets a powerful psionic Tragar, Sirana," she said. "Most of them are either not gifted or are weakly so. But this one could push deep into your mind, and I believe he trapped himself in our divine magic when he did. He was trapped!"

She sounded almost excited, and I was sorry to learn why as she glanced at her Feldeu.

"There's no telling what intelligence he left inside your mind."

Oh shit. Fucking shit. No.

I vehemently shook my head. "Elder D'Shea, no —"

She reached out to grip my forearm, peeling it away from my middle. "Listen to me carefully, Sirana. It shall be hard enough for Reishel to survive long enough to be trusted again after awakening from a psionic strike, and now I learn that you kept such an important secret after entering the Sisterhood. These are firsts, novice, which are always the hardest to pass muster. If a whisper of this comes known before I discover a way to placate the Prime and those more ignorant Sisters, our eldest just might do away with the both of you than deal with the unknown and I cannot stop her."

My entire middle froze, and my skin raised to a thousand tiny pebbles across my shoulders and arms as my eyes widened.

"There must be tangible value in keeping you both," she told me, her eyes fierce and confident, and she started to smile. "And I shall find it. Leave this to me, tell no one else, and for the praise of our Queen, do *not* allow another Sister to make you wear her Feldeu."

I grimaced to think of Gaelan wanting to share but nodded. The Sorceress picked up the thick phallus and got off the bed as if the cycle was just beginning. She cleaned it herself, visiting the closet again to secure it and tend to the bitemark on her shoulder from a potion kit she had in there. I sat awkwardly without orders.

"Elder? What about … ?"

"Hm?" She turned around to look at me.

"Using the Feldeu on you?"

The disrespect, I didn't add. *The violation.*

"Oh." My Elder nodded. "We shall try it again soon."

I jerked in surprise on her bed. "What?"

"For certain. I take back my words about the strength of your will, Sirana. What you've told me proves I was right from the beginning. To survive a ritual controlled by a Priestess is impressive for most Davrin, but what you've just described goes far beyond that. We have only to discover your boundaries and learn what you already know."

D'Shea paused, smiled slowly to see my face. "Next time will be good for me, too, you insubordinate, secret-keeping, Dwarf-fucker."

CHAPTER 7

D'Shea began alternating my time between House Itlaun and House Aurenthin.

"Get closer," she'd instructed. "Listen for voices."

At last.

It was far easier to spy on those at Court, I knew; the tunnel system saw to it, and all novices began there. Less easy was it to spy on a House proper, to get close enough to hear or see anything useful while avoiding detection. The situation quickly could become sticky; any slips or witnesses must be dealt with, yet it could not always mean the death of the detector.

So, better to not be detected in the first place.

Regularly I crept close enough to begin recognizing faces, to listen to whispers or potentially read their hand sign. I didn't catch everything, and most of my observation was still regular living not different from watching the carts going to and from a place from afar.

Nonetheless, I enjoyed watching individuals, learning more about them.

I enjoyed watching Jael Aurenthietti, in particular, and the evidence of an iron will behind a gleeful level of furious energy maintained beyond the battlefield where we'd met.

I did not know anything of her past — D'Shea didn't want me to know as it would color my reports — but it was arousing to watch her practice a soldier's skills and push the patience of those larger than her. Jael never showed if she was afraid, wouldn't be intimidated as she readily snarled back, and she wanted more.

She just doesn't know what might count as more, or what she can reach, as I didn't.

The Fourth Daughter wasn't right for the part of a Matron. She was reactive by habit and impulsive by nature. That role was already taken by her oldest sister anyway; three females would have to die before she would get a chance.

Unlike me, she didn't seem to want it. She was solitary in her family, like I had been, but left the grounds with surprising frequency. She volunteered for patrols, and her Matron and sisters seemed content to let her go.

Mine had blocked me off, kept me in place. They controlled me. I couldn't leave. Couldn't become better at fighting back.

Jael fought back all the time, but not against her sisters. Her violent sparring on the grounds of the worn plantation was against others with whom she had no close connection beyond similar training.

Not often did I observe her coupling, but what I saw was just enough. Jael was fierce even then. I witnessed her take a few of both sexes, but slightly more female. I didn't know if that was significant or not, but I was pleased.

Interested.

She usually overbore the other; she was the dominant by using threats and physical means, but it almost seemed she was disappointed when they submitted, even after a healthy struggle. Myself, I liked when they submitted by choice; the buas especially.

It made me wonder whether some part of her wished someone was strong enough to defeat her; other females, perhaps, who might wipe that sneer of contempt from her face.

I know plenty of Red Sisters who could do that for you, Fourth.

I thought she was right for us, and not just for the fact that then she could be the youngest Red Sister to take my place. She was right for Rausery, more so than D'Shea, and we needed candidates to replace those we'd lost. I wanted us to Collect her.

Don't push too hard. Include the flaws in your reports.

Impulsive. Strong temper. Bitter toward Priestesses and Houses above hers — which included everyone — and unwise in some of the things she said even to her allies. Her Matron must be tolerant of that tongue because Jael did nothing with it. She remained on the outside, because she may not survive long if she was required to live inside. She was aimless.

But give her some direction on that outside?

Something to do beyond the norms of a low life, retrain her perception to minimize the lop-sided importance of her House's number. She would go for it, I felt.

Rausery would want her.

By contrast, I quickly grew bored watching Curgia and Tulia with their Mother and Aunt. Middling-to-low status, I only witnessed in the House modest implications of medium-term plotting. Much business and merchant speak, utter fear and compliance with any suggestions, directives, or hints which came from the Priestesses. They over-analyzed every detail, tying their own web tighter and smaller around themselves in their anxiety.

The only interesting part was that, after half a turn, I could spot the same subtle signs of pregnancy in both sisters. One was gloriously proud of it and the other tried desperately to hide it.

D'Shea had smirked to hear this. *"Hm. I wonder which sire matches which belly?"*

Most of my spying was slow-paced; Jael was the pleasant exception. Even watching the Consort mate with one of the House Nobles was boring. They never tapped his potential, never saw him as more than a prize, a status symbol, and they treated him like fine crystal which could be chipped or cracked during a bit of play.

As mechanical as Tulia was on the altar.

As for the Royal Consort himself, he was compliant and placid; he orgasmed oh-so-prettily for them, performing as expected.

Deceiver. You can handle much more than that, bua.

I wondered how his interest in sex did not flag after these many decades of greedy caits and their Mothers shuffling over him as he lay on his back.

Impressive, when I think about it.

Eventually, I would take the opportunity to speak with the Consort alone.

"Where is the Other?" the Consort asked after setting the sound-dampener Ward on his quarters.

"Only myself this eve."

A pause. I smiled. He swallowed. I tried not to laugh.

The next moment, resolve came to his stance.

"What do you want, Red Sister?" he asked, flexing his left hand.

"An update since my last visit, *aus*."

He tilted his head at the compliment, as I implied his potential value in a pet name used for jewelry boxes. He nodded, offering what he knew, or claimed to know, in his steady and pretty voice. What he said amounted to two Daughters of Itlaun were pregnant, and he was "too late" to be the sire of one of them.

"Curgia still carries, but is hiding it," he said. "I do not know who has leverage over her."

Only the same Priestess who owns you, darling.

I wasn't sure I believed him. What if Curgia had confided in him, or what if Wilsira herself made a taunting remark in his hearing before he landed on the Worship Ball's altar? Unlike the reports to his Priestess, he could be lying to the Sisterhood; foolish as I saw that, we must take what he said with a grain of salt. I did have an open objective related to that. D'Shea would want the leverage if I could get it.

"I see. Is that all?"

He nodded.

"Do you lie, either in fact or by omission?"

"No, Red Sister."

He didn't look away at first while I stared at fine, scarlet eyes, but he soon blinked, gazing to the side and shifting his weight on his decorated, sandaled feet. He wore a similar outfit to the last time I'd seen him, but this time the pale blue cloth around his waist and draped artfully over one shoulder was finer quality. He likely wore nothing else beneath.

A gift for the given, wrapped up and ready.

I smiled salaciously, trailing a hot gaze up his legs, lingering on his crotch, waist, chest and shoulders. I admired that his hair was down, free-flowing, contrasted with mine when on a mission: tight-plaited and bound against the back of my neck. He also wore a different circlet around his throat; still of the round belly symbol but integrating House Itlaun's crest. It looked brand-new.

I ended my appraisal with an appreciative hum as I nodded as if having decided. "I have some spare time, then."

His eyes widened a fraction, and he took a step back. "Red Sister, no, please, I have told you before, if my Mistress —"

I closed the distance between us even as he backed up. My voice was coarse. "Where do you think *telling* me anything from your lying mouth is going to have the result you want?"

"I am not lying!" he exclaimed, bumping into the wardrobe with his back and giving it a startled glance before looking back at me. "Forgive my slip, Sister. I beg of you."

I ignored that and stepped chest-to-chest. "It conflicts with another report about Curgia's condition, Beautiful. One of you is lying."

I took hold of the bottom of his wrap, my soft, leather glove brushing along his thigh as I tried to raise it up. He possessed the spirit to grab another part of the cloth — not my wrist, the Consort *did* use intelligence — and hold it down. His resistance made my crotch warm. The fabric was taut enough between us that one sharp tug on my part would tear it.

I wanted to. The sound would be satisfying and stroke my hunger.

But then he'd have to explain it to his Mistresses.

"I am not the liar, the other is," he said. "I cannot be the sire of the child Curgia carries. She would not hide it if I were."

I huffed. "So prideful of your seed, Consort?"

"I am sold and traded all over Sivaraus for the purpose of spreading it, Sister."

I hesitated at the resentful edge of his mouth as he looked down and away from me. I tossed that direction aside although I did not let go of his wrap.

"Under which circumstances would you guess she would hide it?"

He shrugged helplessly. "Anything unplanned and unapproved, Sister."

"Vague theory, nothing more. Any thoughts on Curgia specifically?"

The Consort's jaw tightened. "I do not know what happened to her."

I did.

"Guess, *aus*." I took his chin to steer his eyes into mine. "I *ask* for your opinion."

He breathed out and swallowed, caged against his wardrobe. "My guess, Sister ... is she was forced to conceive."

I quirked one brow. "Sounds unlikely. Could be a dalliance with a low-born servant."

He shook his head. "Obtaining a purging potion is possible for a Noble. I also know how she and her Mother wanted a Consort. Curgia is not impulsive. And ... I am familiar with the signs of force, Red Sister. I have observed it my whole existence."

"Experienced it once, too," I quipped. "Seems no one escapes it in Sivaraus, hm?"

His face flushed warmly, reminding me how he'd looked with the root jammed in his mouth and his wrists tied. The responding thrill in my belly was difficult for me to hide. I kept talking.

"Why would those 'signs' be the same in a cait as a bua? I assume you've been watching limp staffs brought low. It's not common for grown females."

The Consort looked delightfully angry at my bald lie, his life energy churning and spinning beneath his skin from his chest up to his face before he got himself under control. "Females are forced as males are. The signs are the same."

"Oh?" I wanted to hear this.

He stared at me in disbelief. "Consorts all know why even the highest *female* Nobles fear you, Red Sister. You are the worst and most cruel in your power, and none below the Priesthood are excused. I am not even certain children are spared."

He hadn't gone the direction I wanted at all, and a hot flash of anger and insult swept through me instead. I was sure he saw it beneath my skin. However, I smirked and chose not to enlighten him. Yes, the Red Sisters killed children sometimes when necessary, but no children were to know the Feldeu. Elders' orders. As for my own view, there wasn't another rule guiding the Sisterhood that I wouldn't report on faster, should I witness it.

I let go of the cloth of his wrap and slid my hand toward his inner thigh, reaching beneath to cup his testicles. He jumped, and I smiled.

As I thought. Naked underneath.

Our breath quickened, mixed, and he pushed at my wrist in a silent plea. I let my hand return to his smooth thigh and leaned to sniff his neck. I remembered.

"Goddess, you smell so good, bua."

He gasped. "Please, do not —"

"Who would know?" I growled. "No one, unless *you* told them. I know you wouldn't."

"Sister, please, I beg —"

"Aw, poor, pampered slut. Don't you *want* me?"

It was a ridiculous question. I teased him, shoved his reluctance against his words to make them dance for me. I caressed his privates again, this time over the surface of the cloth. I paused to discover him partially erect and swiftly becoming thicker.

Then his secret tremored near my ear. "Yes."

I blinked, my lips hovering above his collarbone.

Yes?

My intentions muddled severely by that one word, I inhaled the sweet scent again, touched my lips to his shoulder, tasting him. I massaged his cock firmly; only a few pumps, and it became fully erect in my hand. Harder than when I'd forced stiffness from him during our first encounter. I heard him suppress most of a moan — a genuine one — which he tried and failed to cover.

I clenched my jaw with how much I wanted him right then. I hadn't had a real bua *since* throwing him upon a table, and I'd been too insane at the time to enjoy it. We hadn't even finished.

Then, before the Consort, was Kain.

Elder D'Shea knows.

I sucked in air and straightened up to look at the Consort's eyes, shoving some of my ardor to the side with difficulty as my higher thoughts focused on his words as he spoke.

"Do not force me again," he pleaded, quivering. "Red Sister, I would lie beneath you if I held the choice, but I do not. That choice is held by my Priestess. Use me as an informant, know I shall never mislead you by fact or omission, you or any Red Sister. But if I join with you, *she* will know, and my life could be forfeit if she so chooses. It will not matter that I had no choice but to submit to you."

D'Shea's objective just dropped into my lap, and I nearly missed it in my distraction, as those words aroused me to an aching fit.

"You speak of Priestess Wilsira," I forced out, removing my hand, my fingers digging into the furniture behind him. *Kerse's Mother.* "You belong to her, but you'll share private words with the Sisterhood?"

He exhaled; his heart pounded in his chest. I heard the regret while seeing it on his face. "Y-yes, Red Sister, I will. Words exchanged are easier to hide than the aftermath of coupling."

He could see my regret as well, I bet, as I recollected my renewed fertility. It struck me how I would never be able to support a favored male or invite a stuffed belly with him, yet the potential remained for the explicit benefit of the Sanctuary. What was the likelihood that, if I was stupid and indulgent enough to become pregnant by Wilsira's Consort, that I would also be *controlled* by her while gestating the baby in the Sanctuary?

Hiding the aftermath from a Priestess. This damned bua couldn't be more fucking right.

I was silent for long moments before I spoke again.

"Why would you lie under me?" I asked him, only because I wanted to know.

He slowed his breath, swallowing before speaking. "You see me. You like what you see."

I narrowed my eyes. "I also hurt you. And enjoyed it."

"You tested me. And did not find me lacking."

How well I understood this in my short time among my Sisters. I watched as he swallowed again, another flash of that lovely throat.

"No one had dared before," he said. "I have wondered how I would respond. Now I know. And you know. You are the only one who does."

The stiff rod still in my hand pulsed once. He decided he had enjoyed the challenge. I almost couldn't believe it.

Teasing slut ...

I said, "Used to being treated like the thinnest crystal, hm?"

He lowered his lashes. "Yes. You frightened ... and thrilled me, Red Sister."

I frightened and thrilled myself.

My obvious uncertainty had made him bolder because he pushed at my wrist with his hand, and, reluctantly, I released his cock. Then, he questioned me in turn.

"When you found me," he began, "the only direction you could have come from was the wilderness. You were naked and injured, someone had bitten you. All you carried was a blade. Were you attacked? Did they rob you?"

I smirked and granted him an answer. "Attacked? Yes. Robbed? No. I was as you saw me when they attacked. I kept my blade and killed them."

Fortunate for me, I'd already confessed about the Dwarf to D'Shea, or this one might have something to use against me. Let him think it had been more than one who overwhelmed me. It was better for the Sisterhood's reputation than what had happened.

The Consort nodded, his eyes wide with interest. His shakes had stopped. "Wh-where had you come from, Red Sister?

I quirked my brow at him. "You received all the information you're getting about *that*, Consort."

He had expected that reply. "Yes, Red Sister."

Give a thread, take a tapestry, as the saying goes.

In petty retaliation, I ran my gloved hand greedily from his neck to shoulder and arm. I couldn't feel the texture, but I felt the warmth; this drew his attention back to its proper place. He realized I hadn't yet accepted his offer. Tiny bumps broke out over his visible skin.

"Wait —" he breathed.

I tilted my head and covered his mouth with mine in a deep kiss, trapping him by bracing both forearms on either side of him against the wardrobe. He tensed, rigid and fearful, but now I knew with desire as well. I persisted, and eventually, he yielded, opened his mouth for me. It was hot and slick and tasted of fine wine and spice.

My hands left the wardrobe and cupped his jaw, holding him steady as I drank deeper. Sliding gloved fingers into his loose hair, I was aware of the location of his hands as well. He kept them flat and open, pressed to the wardrobe as I had my fill of his mouth. My fingers did not slide below his neck, but my hips moved of their own accord; my mound encountered his member, and, damn him to Braqth, he responded in kind.

His body trembled when I drew back. As did mine, if I was honest. *This is dangerous.* I teased and tormented *myself* at this point.

"Agreed," I said, my voice husky. "I will not risk your safety with your Priestess, so long as your intelligence to any Red Sister is complete truth as you know it."

My Consort nodded, his voice a rush of breath. "Yes. Agreed. Thank you."

I released his face and dropped my hands to my sides, knowing I would regret for the rest of my life that there wasn't a win-win way to fuck him. I stepped back.

Time to leave.

Before I did, however, I asked him a question on impulse. "Do Consorts have names?"

My eyes detected another flare in the dim, though his expression hadn't changed much. "Yes, but ... they are different in each House we are given to. The Matron chooses how to call him."

"I imagine your Priestess knows each of these Noble names of yours."

He nodded. "Yes, Red Sister. As I am given them."

I waited, and he read my expectation. He confessed a little more.

"My Priestess holds my first name," he said. "From the Sanctuary. Where I was born."

"Is she your Mother by birth?" I asked curiously.

"No," he answered with clear wariness. "Perhaps ... do not ask more now, young Sister? Please."

"Well ..."

The Royal Consort had not misled me by fact or omission upon this first test and spoke plainly when he was threatened. He had gently reminded me of his age, calling me 'young.'

He's a century older than me, at least, and still alive after every cycle dealing with Priestesses and Nobles.

Recalling my own challenges as a youth and my Elders' many warnings, I would be foolish to ignore his guidance due to my own feminine pride. To play the game properly, I must weigh his position and vulnerability against my aimless curiosities, lest I waste my new and valuable resource. Tasty as it was to know this beautiful sire wasn't Wilsira's blood the way Kerse was, it led only to more questions as to what lay deeper inside the Sanctuary. I also wanted to understand what prompted me to ask. I was afraid I could guess.

I shook my head, more to myself. *No more questions. I can wait.*

A thought struck me which I enjoyed, however, as it smothered the regret of denial in my belly for a moment. I smiled at him, at last answering his plea.

"So be it. But I will call you *Auslan* from now on if that is just as well."

I had stunned him, I could see, as he grasped the context: not just a cute jewelry box, but a secret cache of great wealth, newly discovered and claimed by the finder.

He nodded acceptance. "As you will it, Red Sister. I am Auslan."

My Consort did not ask a name for me in return, and his tone was so careful that I wondered what emotion he'd just experienced. Mine had been the only satisfied pleasure I could expect from him.

Auslan. My treasure revealed.

No other Noble drew genuine desire from him as I just had; they could not see the intelligence and will in this pretty Consort.

And *my* name for him would be the only one that Wilsira Tachnathon *didn't* have in her collection.

Chapter 8

Although I took time and care leaving House Itlaun so as not to be seen, with the distance grew my frustration and the ache between my legs. What Auslan had confessed had a grip on my mind, but I realized something important alone out here in the dark.

This new secret could feed my pride, yet my cunt would remain empty. Like trying to fill my stomach on praise.

He didn't have to admit he wants me. He could have kept that gorgeous mouth shut.

It had been so long. I wanted a bua. A real one, and badly. I didn't want another Sister, and I didn't want to complain and tempt D'Shea to move up the moment where she made me wear the Feldeu a second time to prod me about the damned Dwarf.

I didn't want to *be* the male, I wanted to *touch* one.

I wished to smell another Davrin, to listen to the different timbre of voice, to sense his subtle reactions and hear his gasp from what I did to him. I wanted to suck on a hot, stiff pole, fondle his smooth, tender sack until he spurted fresh seed over my tongue, and I swallowed his offering. Too vividly, I imagined his compliment to me, the proof of his pleasure, leaking out of my hole — my netherhole if I couldn't risk taking him in my slit.

I'd had no time or opportunity to claim a bua until the moment I'd had that Consort pressed against his wardrobe.

And I still … can't … have him!

Sneaking away unfulfilled now, I knew I didn't want my first bua after becoming a Red Sister to be one of the "punishments" selected by my superiors just before the poor fuck's execution. My stomach was queasy to think that could happen. If I waited long enough, the idea would come to the Prime, I knew, like her idea of me slitting the throats of helpless Sisters. D'Shea had suggested as we drank wine together that I'd have to find pleasure in a weaker Davrin's sexual torture. Sooner or later.

To toughen me up.

But not yet.

With a touch of desperation, I changed my direction to head toward the Wizard's Tower. It was time to visit Callitro in his own den. Out of sight of anyone, as my Elder had ordered.

My choice. Take it while I have it.

I had done a little more research about the place since the Worship Ball half a turn ago, where I had first met Callitro. The young battlemage had offered me an invitation to the Tower, claiming he could make me something useful. Only then had I at last *noticed* that true wizards had been a rarity at Court; otherwise, I might have approached one to make me something special decades ago.

I once had read a number: one-hundred twenty-three known wizards in Sivaraus and all of them held permanent quarters at the Wizard's Tower.

In contrast, the females who developed a strong talent for magic studied at Court or sometimes with a private tutor at their own House. At last count, there were two-hundred forty-six sorceresses considered "powerful" in Sivaraus.

This wasn't a high ratio considering our overall population filling the Great Cavern, and nearly every mage, whether wizard or sorceress, was employed in creating magic-touched items for others to use, even the Matrons and Nobles, depending on the status of the recipient.

All the Wards upon our doors and windows were based in magic constructed into the location. All potions, salves, or enchanted gems fixed within jewelry or weapons were created by the mage class. Small mending, cleaning, and warning cantrips didn't count; many merchants and servants could perform those. Perhaps even I could learn if I applied myself.

No, the true conjurers like my Elder D'Shea or Priestess Lelinahdara were the rarest sort, at least in the public eye. They were brought out mostly for battle or rituals in the glory of the Valsharess and Spider Queen. She intimidated simply by stepping onto a platform and raising her hands, lifting her mouth to speak.

I had studied this buas-only space as preparation to find that invisible wizard from my trials, as my Elder had granted me leave to do in my own time. I hadn't forgotten the contemptuous cock which had edged me so long, ruining my hard-earned climax before plowing my netherhole so hard I couldn't even enjoy it.

He must have taken lessons from the Prime.

This place, a school and dormitory for wizards, was called a "tower" because it loomed above all except the Palace and Sanctuary. It *could* be considered free-standing, I supposed. It had been built into and around a gigantic, natural column, where a stalagmite and stalactite had met in the middle of the cavern's floor and ceiling.

There were many levels in a circular floor plan, though the largest few floors both at the base and the crown of the structure contained only twenty or so individual quarters and three to four larger functional rooms, such as a kitchen or washroom. The center levels were smaller than that, made for libraries and archives in addition to the labs.

The wizards were a solitary group, eating, sleeping, and studying away from Sivaraus as a whole, almost all their supplies brought to them by assigned merchants. It didn't mean that they didn't receive "customers" or gossip amongst each other in different parts of the Tower. I was warned they had some of the largest sets of pointed ears, catching all murmured or whispered by whoever came to them, or wherever they were sent should they leave the Tower. Hoarding knowledge was their basis for living, after all.

Red Sister.

A calm, pleasant male voice sounded in my ears as I approached the first gate, although I saw no one; it had no physical guardsvrin.

Your name and purpose here?

It was the Headmaster. We'd never spoken, and I had never seen him, but I knew who managed the place on behalf of the Valsharess. I must have struck a Ward. I focused as it began to get difficult to step forward over the mushroom field leading to the second gate, thinking my answer.

Sirana. To visit Callitro in private.

I heard an amused grunt. *Have you taken an infertility draught, Sister?*

I blinked. Those exist? I didn't even know where to get one.

Um? No.

Then I shall have one ready for you. Proceed. The constructs shall let you pass.

The second gate was guarded by two Dread Spiders. Their mottled and bloated appearance was convincing enough that, if the Headmaster had not told me they were "constructs," I might have turned around.

The forced hybrids stood upon eight, giant spider legs and gripped a primitive spear in both gnarled hands as their arachnid body blended into an Elven one at the torso. Their hair was grey with mud, tangled, and hiding most of a fanged face in which I would have expected to see far more than one set of eyes. Their presence would terrify the curious and the unwelcome. I looked for signs of illusion but couldn't see them; the detail was unnerving.

Constructs. Not real.

I was glad I didn't have to speak to these creatures, but I tensed, ready to move fast if they did. As the elderly wizard had said, however, the Driders remained still and let me pass without looking at me.

These things were not two of the true condemned, not former Dark Elves twisted into a horrifying monstrosity during a ritual, held by Au-ranka, the Keeper in the Pit. Jaunda had suggested that only the Keeper could control them, and the Valsharess controlled the Keeper.

"Not even the Priestesses pull these creatures out of their cage to play," she had said.

That was a relief. I surely didn't want any Braqth-biter wielding her first sacrificial blade having access to these things. D'Shea might have complimented me about surviving the ritual intact, but I doubted *any* Davrin withstood this transformation once chained upon the altar.

The stone double-doors of the Tower entrance parted as I approached; they didn't open wide, but only enough for me to slip through. The Headmaster stood on the other side in an otherwise empty, sparsely decorated entryway, and I was brought up short to look at him.

The mature bua was taller than me, wearing a dark gray robe, threaded with purple and gold elegance, with a slimming cut. When he smiled, there were creases and fine lines that I was not accustomed to seeing in *any* male. The elder wizard had solid blond hair like the Valsharess, and I thought this implied that he was as old as She but then met his eyes.

They were a rich, dark red with gold flecks; his gaze was clear and alert, not faded like Hers. Still, I had to assume that his life and the magic he practiced had taken a toll; the lines around his eyes and at the corners of his mouth were deeper than the Queen's, even as he somehow appeared younger.

The elder offered a small vial to me, his long fingers lightly touching the bottom. "Welcome, young Sister. I am Phaelous, Headmaster of the Wizard's Tower. If you would, please drink this."

"What is it?" I asked, wary despite myself; I did not reach for it.

He was patient, his face oddly warm and soothing. "A bittersweet tonic which will discourage conception for the duration of your visit."

I rested my hands on my hips, lifted my chin, and I smirked. "What if I came for something other than sex, Headmaster?"

He didn't blink, and his arm didn't move; he still held it out. "I am aware of the rules governing the Sisterhood's children and the punishment to the sire if the Prime so chooses. If such rules do not intimidate *you*, young Sister, then consider this the simplest way to protect my own learners. They are rare enough as it is."

Punishment of the sire if I catch? No one mentioned that.

I had no retort, and my hands slid off my red leathers. Arguing with him further would have been irrational hubris, so I took the vial, broke the seal, and quaffed the small mouthful of liquid. He was right; first, it was bitter, then it was sweet.

Phaelous bowed his head to me with astonishing grace. "My gratitude, Red Sister. Give it a quarter mark to fully take effect then have no worry if you find Callitro to your liking."

That easy? Why hadn't either Rausery or D'Shea told me about this? Fuck, I could have had something to take with the Consort just now!

I was staring, I knew it, and the old male smiled again as he reached for the empty vial. I let him take it.

"You have a question for me, young Sister?"

What the web.

"You have anything that lasts longer than a visit?" I asked. "And what do you trade?"

He laughed gently, and it sounded pleasant and polite though he shook his head in the negative. "I have nothing I am allowed to give you, Red Sister."

I felt a flare of anger. *What? Why not?*

"As you are not here with an executive order," he continued, somewhat changing the subject, "then the rules of preservation apply on these grounds."

What are you — ? Oh, right.

I smirked at his formality. "Yes, I know. No maiming, disfigurement, poisoning, or any action that would debilitate a wizard lastingly in applying his trade. Especially his mouth and hands."

I know what he can do with them instead.

Phaelous bowed his head again. "Thank you for your clarity, Sister Sirana. Callitro's domicile is on the seventeenth level. I shall escort you."

This old wizard had long ago lost whatever mystique he ever held for the Red Sisters, I could tell. I felt like a child speaking to him although there was nothing wrong with his manners. Wordlessly, I followed him into the next room, noting artwork and a bit more color before he gestured to a large, garnet inlay forming a circle upon the floor.

"There are no stairs," he answered before I could ask. "We move between levels by jump circle."

I frowned. "And one needs to be a mage to use a jump circle?"

"Correct, Red Sister."

Maybe, maybe not, but it didn't change my current state of needing his aid, and my next thought sank in quick. *Fucking Eights, I can't sneak in here later, can I?*

If I wanted to fuck Callitro, I had to get Phaelous' permission and cooperation each time. No secrecy and he would probably report each one to my Elder, if not the Prime. And what if I wanted to look around for my invisible wizard? How could I get between levels? Especially if the one battlemage I sought was on the *seventeenth*.

No wonder D'Shea was smirking when she granted me permission to look for him.

We went from the base level to another in a heartbeat and a slight surge of stomach upset. Instantly I smelled spice and eclectic components, old fiberstalk parchment and burned powders. My eyes adjusted to the mellow, magical glow emanating from a very small stone pressed into the wall about every ten feet.

We stood in a small alcove spilling into a hall which bent on both sides, curving out of sight with a central column obscuring what lay beyond. Because of the light, I could see carvings above multiple, arched door-slabs; they were numbered. I was aware of at least one door sliding open slightly as we walked past it.

Without looking, Phaelous said, "Return to your study."

The door closed again, but I bet an ear would be pressed to it for some time. Suppressing a smile, I followed the Headmaster to stop in front of the door marked one-seven-five, observing as he placed his bare hand upon a smooth piece of polished stone on the right side of the door. There was no sound I could detect until someone spoke within the room.

" … Master?"

I could hear Callitro's muffled voice coming back through the polished stone. He sounded almost amazed.

This doesn't happen often.

Phaelous said nothing aloud, he simply kept touching the smooth piece, a look of concentration on his face. I pursed my lips. *What are you telling him?*

Callitro opened the door quickly; it was clear that he expected another

Davrin besides his Headmaster. When the bua laid eyes on me, his body surged hot enough for me to detect his excitement, even in the soft lighting. He smiled but said nothing, not even a greeting, as if he'd been instructed to silence while his visitors stood out in the hallway. I followed their lead.

I looked at Phaelous for a hint. Turning to me, the old wizard bowed his head and gestured for me to go inside. Turning again, he left without so much as a word. No warning or instruction what to do, or what not to do, while I was here. I wasn't sure how to summon him when I needed to get back to ground level.

Callitro will tell me.

I said nothing, covering my uncertainty in front of my eager battlemage. I smiled back and signed, *Let me in?*

Callitro stepped back, beckoning, and closed the door as soon as I slipped past him. I glimpsed the tent in his robe as he set the Ward, and all the tension from my secret meeting with Auslan boiled up again in an instant. I wouldn't waste this chance I'd taken.

"Red Sister, welcome."

His attempt at formality mimicked Phaelous.

"It's a pleasure to —"

I didn't have time for this. "Take off your robe."

He blinked. "I ... um — huh?"

I closed the space between us, tugging at his wizard's belt. I whispered to him, "Strip, Callitro. Naked. Now."

His mouth sagged, his burnt-orange eyes wide. He looked down at my gloved hands just as I released the brown cinch on his waist.

"H-here, let me —" he stuttered.

I allowed him to remove his own belt lined with pouches — they could contain anything — and he placed it very gently atop a low array of parchment on his workbench. Next, he removed his rings from his fingers and an amulet from around his neck and secured them quickly in a box marked with runes.

Hmm.

His dark blue study robe was different from his formal one in that it lacked the gold and purple stitching and opened in front, folding over itself to show dark skin of his chest in a thin "V," not unlike that of my Elder Sorceress. I reached for it once he'd removed his belt and magic items, taking hold and pushing it open like a set of drapes. Some lithe flesh was revealed, but there was another knot securing the robe at his waist on the inside, and I plucked impatiently to tug it loose.

Callitro smothered a snicker in his throat.

"I heard that," I growled.

"My apologies, Red Sister. Do you want me to — ?"

I slapped his hand away. "I've got it."

I unthreaded the knot and found myself staring at him nude from the front; an attractive, unblemished package. Eye fixed to his crotch, my hands moved strictly by feel to his shoulders and pushed the fabric off him. His robe fell to his sandaled feet in a heap. His cock jumped once, his testicles contracting slightly exposed to cooler air but recovering as his erection started to grow. My mouth watered.

"You're staring, Sister."

He sounded neither prideful, casual, nor teasing — I could hear the nerves, and he was correct; I was staring. My gaze moved beyond his white-crowned cock to smooth hips and thighs, nice legs and ankles, back up to a flat belly and balanced chest and arms, fit though softer than a fighter. He had a cute face; he wasn't as graceful or as beautiful as Auslan, but I had no complaint. My cunt certainly wouldn't, I knew.

Callitro. You'll do nicely.

Removing my own belt and weapons, I looked around a relatively small, cluttered room. Aside from the workbench, there was a writing desk, bookshelf, bed, cabinet, and a couple of chests.

I didn't know the purpose of half the possessions in plain view, and there would be much more hidden out of sight like his jewelry. Maybe I could ask some questions later, but for now, I selected the least-covered flat surface to move shit.

I grabbed the bowl, pitcher, cloths, and odd grooming items from a simple washing station set as far as one could get from his parchment. I put them all on the floor and turned back to my wizard, standing naked but for his sandals.

"Sira*na?!*" he began, my name ending in a yelp when I pulled him closer and crouched to lift him by his ass, holding him firm against me. He gasped in disbelief, "S-Sister, Goddess ... !"

The young wizard writhed, clutching my shoulders and my cloak for balance as his naked erection touched my blood red leather armor. If I'd been nude as well, his cock would have been nestled between my tits; chuckling, I squeezed his ass.

His body shivered against me as I set him upon that space I'd cleared, and I hummed as I ran my gloved hands along his thighs, stepping in between them. Every measure of my confidence with buas from before the Sisterhood returned to me in a flood, and I could not welcome it more.

He's shaking.

And that pole in front of me was still as hard as I'd ever seen on any Noble bua in my bed.

I tilted my head to press my lips to his naked belly, and he sucked in air. Taking hold of his wrists, I pinned them to the fiberstalk chest, enjoying his little noises as I trailed more kisses down his flank and abdomen. Nudging his stiff prick out of the way with my chin, I buried my nose in his fur and inhaled his male scent, filled my lungs with it.

Fuck Braqth's Tits, yes.

I lifted my head just enough to gulp down his cock, and he pulled much harder against my restraint, uttering a delightfully shocked, "*Guh ... !*"

You've not been taken by many caits, have you? That or my technique had changed after so many Sisters thrust her Feldeu between my lips.

I don't care.

My mouth slid over him, tongue lapping; I tasted his delicate, delicious skin sucking with firm, tight lips. His pleasure climbed, the unguarded, panicked sound breaking from his throat bringing an aggressive rumble from mine, and I moved faster. Stroked him harder using only my mouth.

"Goddess ... !" Callitro shrieked, his hips jerking, egg sack tightening up. "I-I c-can't, S-Siss — oh! *Oh!*"

His cream erupted, coating my tongue and the back of my mouth. I coaxed every drop through that first climax, and the wizard could only submit; he shuddered and shook, his voice pulled down into a stunned silence.

Fuck, he tasted good. Depravity and guilelessness in one gulp.

Our breathing filled the room afterward, the voiceless rush of air contrasting the intense rush such a short time before. I purred in satisfaction, reaching to take his waist in both gloved hands, helping him off the stand although I had to hold him lest he stumbled. He was a little shorter than me, and when he leaned back a little to look up at me in muzzy-headed awe, I grinned and couldn't resist kissing him on the mouth again. It struck me, when he stiffened and tried to lean away, that he could taste his own seed on my tongue.

That's nothing compared to what I've lapped in my time, sweetmeat.

I gripped the back of his neck, my other had his ass cheek, and I held him in place to enjoy my kiss thoroughly while we weren't on a battlefield in front of my Sisters and the Valsharess' army. Upon lifting my mouth, I murmured, chiding, "If I can guzzle it, bua, surely you can sip it."

Callitro nodded, unwilling to argue as my hands drifted over him. "Your pardon, Sister. I was surprised, that's all."

Nodding, I started tugging off my gloves, to feel him skin-to-skin at last. I tossed them onto a stool, dropped my cloak there as well, and kissed him again, my fingertips knowing his texture as my lips already did. I liked that he shivered yet again. I leaned closer, kept my voice as low as could be above a whisper.

"I want to fuck you on your bed," I said with a lascivious grin. "My cunt gripping you hard, taking you deep. Sucking you in, all the way to your hair."

The young wizard stared in a mix of eager, fearful astonishment. "I-I am ... willing, Red Sister, but I just ... um —"

"On the bed," I ordered, pushing him that way while I sat on my gloves and cloak to remove my boots. Callitro nearly tripped over one of his smaller boxes on his floor, trying to step that way while watching me. I laughed, enjoying the reveal of my strengthened, powerful body underneath a powerful uniform. I stripped out of my leathers, keeping certain pieces easy to reach.

"Goddess, Sister, you're —" he began, smiling in his admiration.

"When was your last bath?" I asked, standing up naked. Cluttered space or not, after sucking his cock, I figured he had done basic grooming recently.

His blink was cute. "Um? I wiped down this last waking."

"Good enough for me. On all fours, Callitro. Face away from me."

He didn't speak what he likely thought, but his expression was darling as he reluctantly complied, his freshly milked cock hanging flaccid with his balls. I strode forward, kneeling on the bed behind him, caressing his buttocks. I watched the tension rise in the muscles of his back. As tempted as I was to exploit, I didn't have a lot of time before missing my check-in with Cilyan.

Perhaps a warning might be worth a trade.

"Has anyone rimmed your netherhole with their tongue before, Callitro?"

He looked back at me, eyes widened. " ... No, Sister."

"Stroked your nut gland to make you ready?"

He swallowed. "No, Sister."

"What about ordering another bua to stretch your ass with his pole for her amusement?"

He flinched and sounded grateful when he answered, "No, Sister."

I smirked, parting him with my thumb, admiring a tight and seemingly untouched pucker. "You're not *completely* virgin, are you? Was my mouth the first hole your cock has spurted into?"

"No ... ! Uh, no, Red Sister. Two Nobles shared me at the last Worship Ball. Another before them, some turns prior." Callitro shivered as I passed the flat of my thumb lightly over his back hole. "I-I don't leave the Tower often. Or see many females."

Lucky me. And there's a whole Tower of fresh buas available here.

Sliding one hand between my legs, my fingers glided without drag across my dripping netherlips. Spreading his cheek with my other hand,

I leaned down behind the young wizard and caressed his crinkle with my tongue. No hesitation.

He blurted a cry; the pucker clenched tight.

"So sweet, bua," I chuckled.

I pressed back in to *really* dine upon his virgin asshole, swirling in circles, nudging and tickling, coaxing relaxation of that rubbery flesh ... penetrating it with a hot, stiffened probe. The young wizard gripped his bedsheets with both hands, overwhelmed as he remained in place with his knees wide, submitting to this experience I offered. I couldn't wait too long before I incorporated my cunt-slimed fingers into the play. He learned what it felt like to have a knowledgeable cait stroke his nut gland for him.

First one finger, then two, hot and snug around me. *Goddess, he's tight.*

"Shhiii ..." Callitro hissed in wide-eyed astonishment. "Ungh ... !"

Oh, yes. You like that.

My battlemage's staff plumped up again; soon it was full and hanging hard beneath his belly. It hadn't taken him long to rebound, making me glad to have sucked him to pleasure first. Not only had I claimed my coveted taste of bua cock, but I'd learned the hard way at Court that a cait couldn't play with an inexperienced male before his first orgasm *without* his cock spraying uncontrollably all over the bedding. I hadn't forgotten that Auslan, experienced as he was, had taken my fingers the same way and had become hard without spurting. In fact, his control had been so strong, he hadn't jetted even when I *commanded* him to.

No male should have that much control during sex or be so distracting.

"Sirana," Callitro moaned as I reached around to the front to stroke his rod as well.

"Never had a cait do this for you, huh?" I murmured, the swell of pride adding to my aching crotch.

"Never," he agreed, moving his hips, rolling them like an instinctive slut as I claimed him on both sides.

Fuuuck ...

"Good," I said, panting. "Now, over. On your back. I'm going to fuck you so hard ..."

Callitro obeyed, and I straddled him. No words; I claimed him quickly, putting him straight into my snatch. We grunted simultaneously as our body heat mixed.

I can't catch. He can fill me when I tell him to.

"Don't you dare cum again before I do," I hissed, moving atop him, and his burnt-orange eyes widened as he nodded.

"M-May I … touch you, Red Sister?" he breathed.

His gaze landed on my jiggling tits as he said it. My smirk appeared as a snarl, teeth gleaming. "Go on."

His touch was lighter, gentler than any of my Sisters; he didn't restrain me in any way, only caressed and squeezed where he could while I fucked him. I felt the young wizard's hands on my ribs, waist, and hips, leading back up again, but I focused on climaxing, on the anticipation. Then I felt only the release.

Yes! Oh, fuck, yes, at last …

By the time his hands drifted downward, Callitro was close again, clutching my thighs as he strained beneath me to hold himself back. His grimacing face was adorable, and I growled as I felt my body rise once again toward orgasm. I ground and rolled my hips, gripped his shoulder and the pillow, braced myself, increased force and pace together—

"Goddess!" he cried. "I c-can't —"

He needed practice. He let loose inside me. I watched his face.

His face —

"Shit. Shit, *fuck!*" I barked, my peak taking me by surprise as my cunt clutched and rippled along his pulsing length. My mouth hung open as I shuddered, held in the same ecstatic instant with my first bua claimed as a Red Sister.

It was good.

Really good.

I heard a sound I didn't recognize. A dull chime.

From the door.

Lethargic, I looked over my shoulder. Callitro spoke, his voice thick. His prick still deep inside.

"H-Headmaster?"

"Time for your visitor to leave, Callitro. Red Sister, you've been summoned by your Elder."

Uh-oh.

I stilled my face lest the bua read an expression of concern, even as a further string of expletives sounded in my head. *What in the fucking Pit? Now? Did Phaelous time it this way?*

Disallowed to enjoy any afterglow whatsoever, I got off my playmate and said, "A moment, Headmaster."

I signed an inquiry, and Callitro pointed at a cloth I could use to wipe my crotch. Immediately I dressed and equipped myself with the same thoughtless efficiency learned from the many times I'd practiced before. The young wizard watched me with fascination, lying naked and out of my way upon his bed. Once finished, I secured my cloak and took a step toward the door before spinning around.

"Oh!" I exclaimed. "You offered to make me something."

Callitro blinked. "Uhm?"

A hiss of impatience. "You craft magic items, right?"

"Yes, Red Sister."

"So, make me something useful." I took a step toward the door. "I shall return to check on your progress."

His white brows lifted. *Now* he understood. "What is your desire I create, Sister?"

I don't know.

"I don't care. Something small I can use in a fight."

The wizard sat up straight, pulling a blanket to cover himself as I reached the door. He nodded. "I'll make you a ring. I'll have to think what —"

"Do that. I must report to my Elder."

Stepping out into the hall, I was face-to-face with the old wizard. He smiled without showing his teeth, standing with utter calm, his arms gently folded as he looked me over. Signing for me to follow him back to the jump circle, he did not speak.

A few more doors opened slightly as we passed, the scholars inside better prepared to peek out, and their Headmaster said nothing.

Again, I followed his lead, cooperative as I endured the stomach-lurching jump back down to the bottom floor. He escorted me to the front exit with no opportunity for me to linger, waving his hand in a gesture. It opened only wide enough for me to get out. Once I stood on his front stoop, he spoke.

"The potion you took will last another twelve marks. Have care in accepting further seed in your womb, young Sister, as our essence can remain viable for some time after emission. Give my regards to your Elder."

The dark Tower door closed, and I headed back to the Cloister with male cream gradually staining the crotch of my leathers.

I received the message by pellet that I'd missed my check-in.

Elder D'Shea was annoyed with me.

CHAPTER 9

"By the metal web, Sirana, what have you done?"

I drew a blank card on how to answer that question.

The Elder Sorceress held me in her quarters after instructing I speak to no one in the Cloister and not stop until I reached her. She had commanded me to stand still in the center of her floor after lining up all my equipment on her workbench. I had, wearing only my shirt, leathers, and boots. She had walked around me three times as if she wasn't clear in what she saw.

Whatever it was, I couldn't see it.

"You've been fucking a mage," she answered her own question as a growl. "Pull down your leathers, novice. Now."

I reached for the ties at my hips, noting with a dry smile that my crotch tingled at the demand. "You can tell just by looking, Elder?"

"I can. A powerful enough sorceress or Priestess can, Sirana, if she knows how to spot it."

Good to know.

She scowled deeply, dark red eyes snapping with her words as I pushed my leathers down to mid-thigh.

"Bend over."

I obeyed but tried to speak. "Elder, I drank a —"

"Silence."

Her finger slipped between my netherlips with ease; she pressed in, and her touch was examination only. She murmured something, but I felt no magical effect. She tested the stretched gusset of my pants. She said, "Did I not instruct you to find release only among Sisters, Sirana?"

"Yes, Elder."

"Did you imagine the order had simply expired? Or that I had forgotten to lift the restriction?"

I had probably convinced myself of one or both of those things, yes. "No, Elder."

She probed my ass with a dry finger and I flinched; she didn't bother to murmur an arcane word that time. She sounded incredulous.

"Semen in your cunt, Sirana? Is this deliberate insubordination?"

"No, Elder," I said with force, thinking I should believe it myself before anyone else could. "Not to you."

The Sorceress gave me a narrowed, dangerous look. "Pull up your leathers and explain, novice. Report."

Relieved to hear this, I reseated them without delay. She was ready to listen, and my bare ass and sensitive parts wouldn't be exposed the entire time. Yet another difference between her and the Prime, who *was* at the center of my fear and my decision, if I were truthful.

"I spoke with the Consort again," I began. "I confirmed his cooperation for the time being, confirmed he is willing to keep secrets from Priestess Wilsira as he does not have strong loyalty to her. He's agreed to answer any question truthfully for any Red Sister, as far as he knows it."

"Oh?" she said blandly. "Why? In exchange for what, and what proof do you have?"

"Nothing tangible on either account," I said tightly. "He said ... he desired me but is afraid Wilsira could detect his dalliance —" I blinked as a thought struck me. "The Consort told me that Wilsira would be able to tell if he fucked females outside House Itlaun. Why he wouldn't risk it with me. He begged me not to force him."

D'Shea's nose wrinkled. "So, he has meat between his ears as well as his legs. Yes, that one is a stronger mage, and mature enough to show it."

"How?" I asked. "How does that work? What are you seeing that I can't?"

My Elder shook her head. "Finish your report, Sirana. I recall giving you this objective, but why do you believe him now? Why should I? Consorts survive by telling a Matron what she wishes to hear. They perfect the craft. I see no reason to trust his word here."

"If it were *just* words, I wouldn't, either, Elder, but it was much more. His whole body. His scent, his tone, his heartbeat. You understand reading beneath Court veneer, Elder."

"Did you touch him?"

"Yes. And kissed him." I paused. "He liked it. Even if he put on a show for me, he still liked it enough to offer me the exchange if only I wouldn't *keep* doing it or push him farther."

D'Shea paused. "Did you 'like' it?"

I hesitated then grinned. *Fuck it.* "If I were offered both his pretty mouth and your wine, Elder, I'd get drunk on him first."

A roll of my Elder's eyes. "Charming aside. And you obliged him by walking away. I assume you went to find another bua then, since you can't have your Consort."

"Yes, Elder. Callitro at the Wizard's Tower."

The Sorceress watched me steadily. "Is that whose semen you have inside you?"

"Yes, Elder. Only his." A pause. "I haven't found the invisible wizard yet, but I will."

So many thoughts passed behind her eyes that I kept talking.

"Headmaster Phaelous gave me an infertility draught as soon as I arrived," I said. "I was not allowed to enter without drinking it. He said that was how he protected his students, and it only lasts half a cycle."

D'Shea's jaw firmed up and she shook her head in disappointment once again. "Do not believe everything the Headmaster tells you, Sirana. He is known for lulling females into a false sense of safety. His loyalty is only to the Valsharess. Drink *no more* potions of his making."

"Callitro will be crafting me a ring," I blurted. "I'd like to claim it. I want to go back. I'll just use my mouth and ass, no cunt."

"Phaelous will not allow you in without magical protection, Sirana. Too much risk."

"You can order him to let me in, can't you, Elder?"

Again, the Sorceress shook her head, and with how harshly her face tightened, I believed she would uniformly deny any and all goals I had toward that Tower. I felt my resistance rise, already listening for ways around her coming edict.

D'Shea seemed to notice my expression and frowned in more thought than disapproval; she reconsidered what she'd been about to say. She moved her hands from her hips to the small of her back, drawing in a long breath to release quietly. My own shoulders lowered some, and I waited.

"Rausery warned me you'd seek release outside the Cloister sooner than some recruits," she said, lifting her chin. "So be it. If you intend to receive a new magic item from Callitro, you shall need to return to the Tower. You will coordinate those visits with me from now on, and *I* shall give you a prevention potion to drink in front of Phaelous, so you may decline his."

My heartbeat had quickened to hear this, and I tried to pick a question. *You knew? You have them? Or can make them?*

I asked, "Will he be able to tell what it is, Elder?"

"With a glance, yes. It shall be what I tell you it is. Nothing more, nothing less." She paused to let me absorb that. "What is Callitro making for you?"

My face flushed. "I ... don't know. Something to help in a fight. He suggested a ring."

D'Shea began to smirk. "You had nothing in mind when you asked?"

"I wanted his cock, Elder. I reported to you that he had made the offer half a turn ago at the Worship Ball."

"At least you're being truthful."

My Elder scanned me head to toe, appraising ... something.

"Should I continue my report, Elder?" I asked.

"I don't need a blow-by-blow of your rutting, child. Was there anything of particular interest that either Callitro or Phaelous said or did that I should know?"

I thought back. Callitro, nothing; I'd pounced and pushed him past the point of any coherent gossip. Neither of us had cared for anything but coupling. Phaelous had barely spoken after negotiating the infertility draught and being assured I wasn't there to cripple or kill any of them.

"Mm. The Headmaster asked me to send his regards to my Elder."

Her jaw tightened again, and she exhaled through her nose. Clearly, she didn't think well of him, and I wondered if I'd just delivered a subtle taunt? I could even see the two being rivals, in a way, but dared not ask about it.

"Is that all?" she asked with an edge.

I didn't feel like explaining the motives that sped me toward the Tower after visiting Auslan: the possibility of the Prime ordering my first rape of a bua after the one to kill my Sisters; the confusion of losing myself while wearing the Feldeu and expecting to repeat it multiple times while under study.

I hadn't even mentioned that I had named my Consort, and that he had accepted.

Insubordinate, secret-keeping, Dwarf-fucker …

"Very well," the Elder Sorceress announced, moving to don her red cloak and begin making a pack of items from her mage's closet. "Gear up, Sister. You will escort me through the spyways until we reach the Sanctuary."

I paused mid-reach for my bracer. "Sanctuary?"

"Yes." She observed me in silence until I attached my bracer. "It is time for you to speak with Lelinahdara again. You have several demons distracting you now after Jilrina was exorcized. We shall observe where your mind is at presently."

Damn. That was fast.

D'SHEA LED ME AS CLOSE AS POSSIBLE TO THE PRIESTESS' QUARTERS BEFORE WE climbed out of the spyways into a storage room and then slipped out into the hall on the sixth floor of the Sanctuary. Lelinahdara had been expecting us; there was no delay sliding inside despite the masking spell of my Elder.

I smelled incense lingering everywhere, many different scents shared over time, and it reminded me of Qivni. The Priestess before me wore her purple robes with the silver thread, but not all the jewelry and heirlooms as when she'd been performing before the Sisterhood — both my trial and the Ornilleth battle.

She was tidying up a mirrored vanity when we entered, the door sliding shut behind us. My eyes couldn't help drifting over it, displaying a mix of beautifying items and others I guessed were spell components. Otherwise, they made no sense being there.

The rest of the room resembled D'Shea's quarters in the Cloister more than I cared to think about, but with many more shelves for scrolls and shuffled notes. Lelinahdara turned to my Elder and smiled, bowing her head.

"Varessa. A pleasure as always."

"Tarra."

Those strange, green eyes flicked my way. "And, Sirana. Again."

"As I informed you," D'Shea answered with stiff patience.

Tarra grinned. "Yes, but I'm still not certain what you described, or what I am to do for her."

"It was your magic which snared the Dwarf's mind. We require your insight."

Nope.

I'd have been content with leaving right then, the moment the Priestess shrugged her shoulders and claimed she didn't grasp our point in being here. A few more exchanges like this, and I spotted a Court-like ritual between them, and a familiar one; oddly indirect, coaxing, flattering. I'd always been bored by these exchanges before, but after my initiation and training in the Sisterhood, that feeling fruited tenfold in my chest.

Goddess damn it …

I stood at attention and waited for it to end. Eventually, Lelinahdara stepped closer to peer at me. I looked back, meeting emerald eyes.

"My spell snared him," she repeated softly, fascinated. "Braqth's Blessing protected you when otherwise you would have been another simple mind-death like Feini and Berayne."

Hardly simple. My stomach quivered from the memory of the Prime's blade.

I stared at the Priestess directly, not caring if I challenged my betters. She knew what had formed my youth. Lelinahdara had stripped me of all mental protection upon her altar, had left me that quivering mass in heat out in the tunnels.

Only to be reformed into ... something else. Now D'Shea wanted her to strip me down again, to learn how *that* twitched as well.

~Never again ... ~

"Let us sit her down, Varessa," Tarra said. "I shall examine her. Did you bring the catalyst?"

"I did. Sirana, leathers down to your boots as you sit."

"Elder," I protested a last-instant appeal.

The Sorceress acknowledged my expression only by stepping up close and mouthing words which weren't even a whisper, yet I understood. *"We **must** learn more. Or no shield from the Prime."*

Lelinahdara would not have been able to read lips from this angle. This was between us. Rather than making my Elder appear weak in front of the Priestess, I obeyed her, drawing down my red bottoms and tucking them just beneath my knees as I sat in the padded, armless chair offered.

From her satchel D'Shea removed the large Feldeu — the very same one I'd worn to know my first cunt — and nudged my pants farther down, tapping my knees wider. I scooted my ass to the edge of the chair without being told.

D'Shea caressed my slit gently, testing the moisture. Callitro's presence could still be felt, and she used that to her advantage. Within moments I grunted, the hard bulb again lodged inside me, and Tarra chuckled as she observed us.

"Such strange creatures the Sisterhood makes," she remarked as my Elder tested the fit and angle of my cock.

"Where is your Sathoet, great Priestess?" I muttered.

D'Shea's mouth twitched at one corner, and she stroked my netherlips wrapped snugly around the phallus. It felt very pleasant, encouraging. Had I just amused her?

"Where he always is," Tarra said, blithe and aloof.

"Oh?" I leaned. "Hidden behind purple robes?"

D'Shea cleared her throat before we could bicker. "Ready, Tarra?"

Those green eyes narrowed at me. "Shouldn't we bind her, Varessa?"

"No. That only makes it worse."

"If you say ..."

"I do say."

She could.

D'Shea focused on me, the large toy resting in her hand. "*Yemennija.*"

Scalding magic flooded my guts, and I gasped as the Feldeu retook its hold on me. Without pause, D'Shea stroked it for me, and I whimpered in pleasure.

"Ready," the Sorceress said.

"Very well," Lelinahdara replied, as she thumbed a simple, silver ring on her right hand and stepped closer. "Now, show me this Tragar seared into your mind, Sirana. Let me in as you did before upon my altar. Don't fight."

~*Ha.*~

She laid her right palm across my forehead. Green eyes stared directly into mine. A memory of Kain's blank, white eyes narrowed back at us.

~*Challenge, ulkhein? Understood.*~

I heard the thought rise as I struggled to keep myself afloat. It still sounded like me.

"*Shunvil ssigris dosst,*" the Priestess intoned.

The ring on her finger struck like a dart stabbing into my skull. I flinched as magical claws ripped at the air between us, lunging forward. I blinked, aware I still gripped the padding of the chair, my erection trembling in the open air. I was surprised how soon the sensation stopped. From the look on the Priestess's face, so was she.

The Tragar chuckled deep in the dark.

Tarra neither took her eyes from me nor let her guard down after she lost the spell, proving herself a competent mage, at least. She removed her hand from my head, folding them together in front of her. "I asked you not to resist, Sirana."

"Can't do it," I said. "You want it, Priestess, you earn it."

"Old habits won't help you now." Tarra tilted her head. "I am the Sanctuary liaison with the Sisterhood, your Elder's ally. I am not your enemy. Varessa would rather I not harm you by forcing this."

"Try," I growled, my body shivering. I stared; I pictured how much less intimidating she'd be without those robes. Just another naked, dark-skinned Elf.

All can be stripped naked. Some way, any time.

The Priestess frowned at my rebellious expression. "You want to learn more about what my ritual did to you, do you not?"

"Not really."

"Regardless, you must yield to avoid injury."

"You could suck my cock instead."

A pause. Quiet enough for me to wonder what was wrong with me.

"Varessa?" the Priestess asked nonspecifically as she checked that I kept my own hands in place. Maybe we shared the thought that I'd want to strangle her.

D'Shea smirked a little. "This isn't the Dwarf. I believe Sirana speaks without barrier."

Tarra shook her head. "If that is so, you must temper her behavior. Any other Priestess will be eager to break such defiance. You know it."

"She's not stupid, Tarra, but I believe the Feldeu makes the old harm worse."

"Should we remove it to continue?"

"That's one way. She suggested another."

After a pregnant pause in which I grinned, my Elder shrugged. "Red Sisters get dirty making their discoveries."

The Priestess sounded chilly in her reply. "As do the Daughters of Braqth, Elder."

"It's your magic," D'Shea repeated. "Explore its aftereffects while it's at the surface. There is no formal ritual to follow here, but surely, you've not forgotten the arcane already. I can't tell you what to do."

"Yeah, Tarra," I rumbled, lifting my hips to present my pole. "*Explore* it while you can."

Lelinahdara's green eyes crackled with insult. "You *act* possessed because you believe you can avoid the consequence. You're not clever, Sirana, I have seen it many times."

"I don't care."

As I scowled, my shaking grew visible even to me; I couldn't stop. My Elder reached down to gently stroke my huge phallus, and the soft leather of her grip claimed my focus. I sucked in with astonishment and then sighed. Goddess, how much that helped the tension!

I'd developed a headache without realizing it.

My Elder leaned and kissed me lightly on the mouth, and I returned it on impulse. I liked that she smiled.

"See?" D'Shea said, keeping her soft voice. "Bend a little with her, and she will yield. *Force* her to bend, and she whips back to strike your face. The only other response is to cut down her will, and I'll not allow you to make her useless to me. You want to know as much as I do. I need never have told you about her trial after your involvement."

Although reassured that I had my Elder's protection here, I wondered exactly how much she had told this "liaison," and whether it might harm an agreement I'd just made. I eschewed thinking of specifics in case the Priestess tried to catch me unaware, meditating on the sensitive tip of my new appendage.

I waited. No one brought up any part of my trials before Tarra exhaled, squaring her shoulders as she considered my prick, attempting nonchalance.

She lazily pointed at it with her palm up, finger extended. "You wish me to share *that* with you as an 'informal' method?"

My Elder smiled, taking to one knee beside my chair, cradling the Feldeu; she was quite beautiful as she handled me. "Upon reflection, I agree with Sirana. We want to know, we should earn by *knowing*. Have a taste."

My eyes widened a little.

Tarra crossed her arms. "You first."

Manipulating. Still teasing. She's not really going to —

D'Shea dipped down and put my cock in her mouth, as far as it would go. She stroked it as she sucked, and I reacted just like Callitro, shuddering, eyes rolling up, blurting a cry.

"Elder!"

I reached for that elegant arrangement of white hair without thinking. She anticipated it and snatched my wrist, pressed it down to my thigh, firm but not harsh.

Her mouth caressed me, and I almost choked on my own spit. A low rumble in my head remained, a sound like a Dwarven male might make receiving such service, but the anger didn't burst through weakened barriers; I did not drown in fear of being chained.

D'Shea stopped, looked up at my dazed expression. "Sirana."

She studied me, made sure it *was* me.

"Y-yes, Elder," I gasped.

"Sobriety makes a difference, I see."

"I hate potions, Elder, 'm'sorry," I slurred, shivering. "Goddess, please don't stop."

"Tarra?"

Ignoring my plea, she offered the Priestess a turn. Admittedly, I was desperate for any warm and wet hole, so I cooperated even as I didn't want to swap mouths.

I mean, how good can she be sucking cock, compared to a six-century Red Sister?

The Priestess's hesitation suggested she hadn't the skill she'd witnessed just now.

What? Too important to suck a rod?

I succumbed to the impulse to prick her aloud. "You led with ease before, Lelinahdara. Do you need a larger audience to act your role? Is that how you get off?"

Again, my Elder let the remark stand unchallenged, her slow, subtle hand helping me keep calm. If she was to "temper" my behavior with the Priestesses, she wasn't starting now. Tarra disapproved but showed only annoyance.

"Varessa, it's clear she's resistant to me, but she wants you. I suggest *you* ride her and wear her down, while I try my spell again —"

"I'm not your puppet, Priestess," D'Shea said with resentment. "You can do some of the work."

"Yes, we work *together*, doing what we each do best —"

My Elder's grip on the Feldeu tightened; she was out of patience. "Take a risk like in the other-cycles, Tarra, or don't. But decide. I have work to do and don't know when I can drag my novice back here."

The Priestess ignored the demand. "Yes, why did you 'drag' her here now? Didn't we discuss a different time and place?"

"She's just visited the Wizard's Tower and drank something Phaelous made."

Tarra paused. "Hm."

What? Why is that important?

Anxiously, I waited for more insight than I got. After that teasing grunt, the Priestess lowered herself to a level with the Sorceress and wrapped her bare hand right beneath the red glove.

Her skin was cool and her hold less assertive as my Elder pointed the black, magical toy in Tarra's direction. Wrinkling her nose, she deigned to lean over and wrap her lips around the tip. She offered a lingering suck that seemed the bare minimum she could do to satisfy my Elder, because such a weak effort wouldn't satisfy me.

Given the orgies they orchestrated, given their need for young Davrin to mount each other using every hole, I'd not taken the Priestesses for being *bad* at sex. Yet, while directing it all and seeming involved, Lelinah-dara had let four Red Sisters do all the "work" leading up to the dagger slipping between my legs.

I still didn't know what they had done to Gaelan after the Ornilleth battle, but my Sister hadn't been satisfied.

~Too high to remember how to suck. Arrogant cunt, I'll make you remember.~

A mental image seized me: my hands grabbing the Priestess by the back of her head, my hips jerking up, ramming the pole down her throat to make her gag. To choke her.

My heart throbbed in my chest; it scared me to remember that it had been me. My throat, and Kain's thick prick.

"Shhh," my Elder shushed, stroking me with more skill than the Priestess. She reached to caress my bare hip and buttock with her free hand, touching without restraining me. "Relax, Sirana. Trust me."

Quivering, still frightened, I blinked. *Trust you?*

How many could even ask me that, and I might consider? Only a few new Sisters; Jaunda, Gaelan, Rausery, Cilyan. If them, then why not the Sorceress who wanted me for the Sisterhood in the first place? Why not the one who let me escape unpunished thus far after I'd so brutally forced myself between her thighs. After I'd struck and bit her, used her for one-sided pleasure.

She could have let me give up afterward and stop breathing, as Kain did.

She hadn't. My Elder had encouraged me to breathe.

D'Shea watched me now; I stared back. I sensed a subtle manipulation happening, as if she stroked something intangible alongside the staff attached between my legs. Lelinahdara only shared in it because she had her mouth on me; she let the Elder take the lead this time. It fascinated me to realize it.

No formal ritual this time, she'd said. *I can't tell you what to do. Take a risk.*

Perhaps a sorceress was better than a Priestess at informal spells.

But what are you doing to me?

The Priestess stopped sucking too soon. "Her resistance does not soften."

"Neither do you," I gibed, annoyed.

D'Shea sighed and gave up. She stood and left my cock in Tarra's wan hand, taking a seat at the vanity to drop her cloak and unlace her boots and leathers. I stared at her, felt only wanting; I held a silent wish, but I dared not ask.

"Perhaps I should light some incense," the Priestess suggested.

"No," D'Shea replied. "We stay sober this first time."

Tarra shook her head. "The powerful magic doesn't work that way. You said take a risk."

"Without a crutch. We need a control. A baseline."

"A waste of time."

"If you think so, you *have* forgotten a lot, Tarra."

Though I grasped there was history between my Elder and Lelinahdara which didn't involve the Priesthood, the Feldeu kept my attention on the female flesh being revealed. There was little room for thought as D'Shea stripped down, removing boots, stockings, and leathers, displaying herself naked from the waist down.

Goddess. And I'd had her, my first time. I squirmed, wanting her again.

Her slit was aroused, the color of her netherlips a deep, reddish-purple beneath stark white puff of short and straight fur adorning her mound. Her hips were lush, her thighs strong, legs long with feet made for seductive sandals.

Returning to us, D'Shea stepped in front of me as Tarra moved back. The Sorceress presented her backside to me with a slight sway, and I caught a familiar whiff, untouched by wine. My damp cock ached.

"Will you make atonement for your behavior earlier, Sirana?" she asked me from over her shoulder.

Which time? The drunken rut or the Wizard's Tower?

"Yes, Elder," I responded, staring at her ass.

Answering my prayer, she bent over, legs splayed, and I sucked in a breath at the sight. My heart skipped as I spied her fingers caressing herself. Her other hand reached back and spread a buttock, showing me every fold and crease in the dim light.

"Eat," she commanded.

"Yes, Elder."

I dove in, starting with her slit, my nose pressed to her star. She hummed in encouragement, angled her hips better, and I sucked and slurped, reaching to stroke the Feldeu at the same time. My nose and tongue overtaken with my Elder's essence, my lips and cheeks enfolded by the warmth of her skin, I didn't care how much like a bua I was acting.

I listened to her breathing shudder and change; I heard sounds that she was pleased. Extending my tongue down as far as I could reach, I licked the juices from damp fingers dancing over her clit, and she chuckled. I sucked and tenderly chewed on her netherlips then raised my chin to swirl my tongue around and around her asshole. It relaxed swiftly, much quicker than Callitro, and she cooed.

"Good cait," she breathed. "The Sisters taught you well."

That they had. I served with enthusiasm; I stroked myself harder, drifting in contentment for a while before catching myself in a whine as she pulled my dish away.

"Sit back," she ordered.

I centered myself, and my Elder backed up to settle on my lap, her naked backside pressed to my gut, her red armor protecting her back. I felt her hand take the Feldeu between her thighs, held my breath as she raised up and aimed it for a place which I knew was hot and slick. I saw none of this; I felt her take my cock inside as she squatted down, her body wrapping around me, swallowing me up. I moaned loudly, clutching her hips.

"Sirana?" she breathed. "A-answer me."

"Y-yes, Elder," I forced out.

The memory of Kain was not rising, I knew, although I continued to experience flashes of impulse or profound thoughts which seemed alien. Outwardly, nothing changed as D'Shea fucked me, riding the broad Feldeu, although my glimpses of the act, my perception flipped from serving to being served and back again. Perhaps only the tone of my growl might be an indication which view I had at any given moment.

I can't focus. I can't choose.

Then something fluttered against my shaft, and I opened my eyes to see another pair of Davrin hands holding D'Shea by the thighs. Tarra kneeled in front of her, moving with us, her mouth's focus tight on my Elder's flesh right above where I speared her; the lick I'd felt had been an accident. The Priestess pleased the Sorceress to such an extent, I felt the clutches and ripples around me, I heard the Sorceress' delight as her climax approached.

Tarra *did* have some talent. It just wasn't with a phallus.

"Yeah!" D'Shea grunted like she'd just reached the top of the Great Cavern itself. Swept along with her, I rammed my cock inside, good and hard.

"*Yes!* Oh! Again!"

She likes cock.

Bracing my heels, I thrust up, held her tight to me as I fucked her, my head seeming about to explode as the Sorceress howled her release. Her body milked the phallus that connected us, fiery magic arching from her to me. I couldn't stop it. I came so strongly my body and mind locked up.

I heard a whisper like scattered grit blown over naked stone, and then I blacked out.

When I could breathe, when I could see again, I still sat in the padded chair, now wretchedly stained. My legs were splayed; pants were trapped around my boots; my fur was matted down, and my cunt was sore, empty, buzzing. I felt satisfied, so relaxed I could barely move. Elder D'Shea had had time to put her leathers and stockings back on, though she was still in the process of putting on her boots. Tarra stood with her back straight, arms crossed, her robes barely wrinkled.

They noticed me waking at the same time.

"You stopped breathing again, Sirana," my Elder said, jerking at her boot, stomping her foot into place. "But it returned to normal after you lost consciousness."

"Inconvenient," the Priestess remarked, smirking at me. "But not invariably lethal. How do you feel?"

Tarra seemed much more confident now. I wasn't, and I knew I sounded groggy.

"Like after the trials."

"Be specific," my Elder ordered.

"The altar," I lied. "The Threshold."

Tarra tilted her head in surprise. "Oh? This is not what I feel, Sirana."

"Maybe not," I grumbled, "but it's the only other time I passed out after cumming."

"Hm. Well, the Dwarf we sought never surfaced, so that is a failure."

"I have my baseline, Tarra," my Elder objected as she stood up, her uniform complete.

"I'm not sure what we have, Varessa. I am only certain it's not *my* magic lingering." The Priestess glanced at me, appraising. "It's someone else. Or some*thing* else. Perhaps we'll need a psion to make any progress."

My Elder snorted, offering me one of her cloths from her belt. "Finding one of those as an ally would be like finding a live spider encrusted with diamonds."

"There are one or two weak ones in the dungeons." The Priestess snickered. "Psions, not diamond spiders."

My Elder made a face, answering seriously. "No. We'll test all the arcane and divine paths, first. Something is sure to break loose." D'Shea noticed me holding her cloth and staring. "Wipe down, Sirana. Get dressed."

I obeyed, but Tarra filled the silence while I did.

"Varessa and I have purged the Headmaster's potion from your body, Sirana. No ill effect we could sense, just the suppressed fertility as he claimed. It's been neutralized now. You're back to a normal state."

I glanced at my Elder to test that truth and saw confirmation. *Fuck.* "Why heighten my chances sooner than necessary?"

"Discipline," the Sorceress said, browsing an item atop the vanity. She didn't look at me. "The Sisterhood must control their demons, Sirana."

Tarra laughed in delight. "Almost on level with the Priesthood, no?"

"Almost," D'Shea replied.

If the intent of the Priestess had been to barb the Red Sisters, my Elder sounded bored. Or distracted. The moment I was ready, she spoke formally to our liaison.

"Thank you for your assistance, Priestess. We'll discuss the next step after I've refined the method."

Lelinahdara shrugged. "As you wish. Keep me informed, and we shall keep this between us for as long as we can."

"As agreed."

Although I was the subject, I was not part of this deal.

Wordlessly, I followed my Elder out and back into the spyways with more leather-cleaning on my chore list. I was dazed, still unsure what to think or how to feel.

I knew I was being used and would be used yet again, but I was also protected. I didn't know enough to take action alone or fight too hard against either Elder or Priestess.

Lelinahdara was right. I only 'acted' possessed because I could say those things without being lashed. This time.

It seemed stupid of me in retrospect, though. Tarra wasn't a wannabe like Jilrina.

In the tunnel leading toward the Cloister, D'Shea gestured in front of my face, demanding my attention. ★Thoughts, Sirana?★

She still asked that question. I was lucky. That whole tangled scene played through again. I lifted my hand. ★Proud to serve you, Elder. I am fortunate to have your tolerance.★

She expressed her surprise with a raised eyebrow, but she nodded. ★Will you cooperate if I must alter your mind next time?★

★You?★ I asked clarification. ★Or her?★

★Me, with her assistance.★

★Then, yes. Although forgive the question, why need her at all? She said the magic wasn't hers.★

★Because she knows enough detail, and this is the deal between us. She is not useless to us, I only needed to remind her of her roots and the workings of my Feldeu.★

★Meaning the Priesthood didn't create them,★ I claimed on gut instinct.

My Elder paused, her expression turning a little cold. ★No, they did not. I doubt any female mage could create one so realistic to satisfy the Prime.★

I guessed the obvious. ★The Headmaster?★

Elder D'Shea held her eyes on me so long, my skin itched. ★His grandsire. And the acting Headmaster retains the grimoire.★

Grand ... sire?

Unable to fathom the time between an already ancient Phaelous and his *grandsire*, I fell silent. Knowing how long a Feldeu lasted and whether it was passed down among Sisters might tell me whether Phaelous had made my Elder's tool or not, but D'Shea didn't have to spell out that I'd reached my quota of answers.

I'd received my reward for making the connection so quickly, but she was finished with the subject.

Nonetheless, the Headmaster's warm, soothing voice returned to me on the way back to the Cloister.

Give my regards to your Elder.

CHAPTER 10

OVER THE NEXT SPAN, D'SHEA KEPT ME OUT OF MISSIONS WHICH REQUIRED two or more Sisters; in fact, very little of it needed me to go far from the Cloister.

Auslan received a reprieve from my spying, and Houses Itlaun and Aurenthin would have gone about their doings without me there to watch. Although I was certain Gaelan noticed — given we were both avoiding the other's quarters, probably by instruction — she never had an opportunity to remark on it in my presence.

Jaunda did, once, as she received a mission to retrieve a familiar healer-Noble from the Fifth House for "questioning." She gestured at where I measured shelf-stable rations, though our Elder Sorceress didn't even look my way.

"Want me to break her in?"

"Not this time, thank you, Lead."

"Yes, Elder."

I read from the dry smirk on my Lead's face that she knew I was in trouble. Other Sisters even seemed to avoid me, leading from one span to two.

"It's Reishel," Corpora Cilyan had offered as a hint after the first span, when I was hungry for any morsel. "The Prime is testing her. Elder

D'Shea aids the process."

I nodded, my stomach flipping to recall the other two, dead in their cots almost a quad-span ago. I remembered the sound of Reishel's scream as she woke up a couple of cycles earlier.

Aids the process? More that my Elder keeps Reishel alive.

That was enough motivation for me to want to stay out of trouble and not draw D'Shea's focus at a bad time. I was stable; another Sister was on the edge.

I slept in no one's quarters but my own during this time, and I was left to my own discipline to carry out my tasks. My Lead or a Lunent checked on me frequently enough to see progress — the collecting and inventory, the modest repairs, the distribution of supplies — and to prove my Elder had neither forgotten me nor had her orders expired.

Whatever the Sorceress had wanted to do next about the Tragar in my skull had to wait, especially as none of my behavior suggested any impression of Kain at all. I felt entirely right in my own head.

I waited through the second span and avoided trouble for as long as I could. Through sixteen cycles of menial work and solitary martial exercises, without any attention from my Lead or Sisters, I managed well enough though grew bored and antsy in the closed space.

I wasn't the only one.

Thena and Suna decided to take offense at my avoidance. They had not brought Panagan and Moria this time; it was two versus one, and I had a choice to make.

"Not fighting?" Thena sneered, her mouth too close as I was pushed to the wall, a set of knuckles digging hard into a pressure point in my back. I gritted my teeth, flinched at the way her breath fouled my ear. "Again? How disappointing."

Wait, slit.

"Panni and Moria coming?"

"Soon, Corpora."

"Good. Get her pants."

Elder Rausery's methods didn't need my rage; in fact, it worked against me. I kept my temper as they bared my ass without letting up on the pain in my back; I took the first fuck from Thena without a fight, hoping the other two didn't arrive while waiting for the contempt to rise, knowing the controlling pain would lift at the same time.

As soon as both knuckles and cock left me, the Corpora received an elbow between the eyes. She dropped like a stone.

"Cunt!" Suna cried, Feldeu already poking out, ducking low as I feinted a follow-up punch.

My Sister charged me as I relaxed into my next stance, slipping to the side to trip her as she flew past. Suna hit the wall cock first, and I chortled. Both Sisters were down but coming around, so I ran, righting my leathers as I went.

One detail they didn't know that I did: Lead Qivni was in a nearby equipment room. I barged in, panting a respectful, "Lead Qivni."

She read my disheveled state in a moment; her shoulders slumped, and her eyes rolled upward. "I don't have time for this."

"Lead, I request an assignment outside the Cloister. Anything you need done, I shall do." I dropped to one knee, the fingertips of my left hand upon the stone, head lowered. "Keep me out of trouble here, so as not to distract my Elder and the Prime from Sister Reishel. I know it's her last chance."

Qivni paused, reconsidering in the face of my humility. We both heard the shuffling and grumbling down the hall, and she exhaled. "Come with me."

We soon approached Thena and Suna standing at attention in the barely-lit hallway. The Lead paused.

"Exercise each mount in the stable, Corpora, Sister," Qivni told them. "Clean up anything they pass outside our Cloister."

I controlled the grin on my face as Thena's jaw flexed and she narrowed her eyes at me. "Yes, Lead."

I followed Qivni up a ramp and around two more bends, recognizing the way to the Prime Strategy Room. Elder Rausery waited inside with Lunent Agalia; it was clear each of them had expected the Lead, but not me.

"Well, well," Rausery remarked, palms holding open a map spread on the table. "Having fun, Sirana?"

"Immeasurable, Elder," I answered with a relieved smile, bowing my head.

Without replying, Rausery looked at her Lead.

"Thena and Suna have noticed she's not leaving the Cloister, Elder," the Right Hand explained, folding her arms. "They can't resist."

"Indeed, they can't." The Elder shared a look with the Lunent that I couldn't read, then asked Qivni, "Recommendation?"

"No objection. Tradition suggests presenting a spread, Elder."

I had no idea what that meant but it sounded like what I'd just endured.

"It was oddly timed," Qivni added with suspicion, most likely against my Elder.

Agalia smirked. "Well, she is an odd cait."

Rausery nodded, although not to agree, I didn't think. She pondered something related to why she was here. "Right, then. Sirana, any orders from your Elder which might conflict with you coming with me?"

"None, Elder," I answered with confidence. *Just get me out of here!*

"Grab your cloak and gear up. You have five ticks."

That risk paid out like pure sex. I wanted to kiss her.

Equipped and ready in four ticks, I left the Cloister under the best protection I could wish for. Nobody told me where we were going, but I didn't care. I received no dirty looks for excess noise, so I kept up well enough to the first jump circle. Like those in Phaelous' Tower, I still needed an elder Red Sister to use these to shorten any distance.

I learned our destination only after we'd arrived, after leaving a second circle and coming out of a tunnel to see a familiar field where the Valsharess' army conducted their drills.

I stared. *House Aurenthin?*

Elder Rausery crouched down, and we followed her lead. She observed the plantation in poor repair for a while then nodded to her Right Hand.

"Go do your thing, Collector. We'll wait for you here."

OUR WAIT WAS QUIET FOR A LITTLE WHILE, MOSTLY STILL, ALTHOUGH IT STRUCK me that we'd come in what would be the business part of the cycle for most plantations, when the most eyes would be watching.

Not Aurenthin, more of them are resting now.

I knew from my stakeouts that they were more active when the others weren't, trading with more cautious Davrin from the slum or races other Houses wouldn't — or couldn't — bargain with.

Being on the Fringe has that facility.

The Valsharess would have all the justification She wished to destroy the entire House at any time because of this. Most saw them as a "weak spot" where other races could walk into our territory by crossing a stream, barely getting wet, and any outside merchant group who got too large for the tastes of Elves were always blamed on House Aurenthin letting them in.

For the time being, however, the Queen let them stand in their place, and had for some time. How long, I didn't know, but even I could tell it had been some time since the last upheaval.

My Elder had shrugged during one of my earlier reports when I asked. "Remove House Aurenthin from their place, and another must act as the border hub, probably farther in from the Fringe. We'd lose ground. We watch the Twenty-Fourth House as well as we watch the others, Sirana, and you already know the army is sent to their grounds for training regularly."

She had paused to sip her wine. "And the Valsharess adds Her own intimidation from time to time."

"Intimidation? Like what?"

D'Shea had smiled. "Watch long enough, you'll see it."

I hadn't seen it by the time I crouched with Elder Rausery and Lunent Agalia, waiting for Lead Qivni to enter the bottom House. I hadn't been told for whom we'd come.

But I rather hoped.

Elder Rausery focused on me with a shrewd smile. She signed,

How's it been, novice?

I had only received brief orders and tasks from the Elder General since she had taken me under her arm to train me both in defense of my body and in acting the elite guard for the Worship Ball earlier that turn. My recollection of pleasuring her the one eve alone in her quarters still warmed my middle, and she'd given such practical advice proven to be useful time and again.

Now she asks me how it's been. Easy as that.

Challenging, I signed with a smile.

As the recruit wanted when I asked?

Yes, Elder.

Good.

Lunent Agalia relaxed, seeming content with my clear appreciation for the Elder General. I wished I could say more, but I had to wait until our Sorceress figured out what to do about the Tragar shard in my head. Before that could happen, I had to give the Sorceress space to deal with the Prime and claim Reishel once again for the Sisterhood.

I wondered what Elder Rausery might know about that. The timing of this other "Collection" seemed either entirely oblivious or full-on intentional. If asked, I'd assume Rausery knew plenty about what was going on in the Cloister, even if I'd learned she spent the least amount of time there, which explained the sparseness and lack of personal touch in her quarters.

But does that mean the Prime isn't aware? How could that be so?

Something drew the Elder's attention — a message pellet from Qivni, I guessed — and Rausery looked to the plantation. Rausery reached into a pouch with one hand, signing with the other.

Follow, she signed to Agalia and me without checking if we obeyed.

As if I'd refuse.

The three of us quickly slipped a quarter-way around the rough perimeter before Rausery led us inward. We hid behind stone, in crevices, and under boughs of fruiting mushrooms, our cloaks masking us from the Dark Sight of other Davrin. Only the flash of true red in visible light would reveal us, and first rule was always to use that to one's advantage to surprise one's quarry and make them piss themselves.

Suddenly, two sets of desperate feet scrambled straight toward us, making my skin prickle.

I watched the Elder rub the base of her ring finger with her thumb while holding the small stone she'd pulled from her pouch. Simultaneously, she whispered a word of power before clenching her hand to make a fist. I assumed she had quickened some magical enhancement.

With her free hand, she signed, ★Neutralize the Davrin. Do not kill. Do *not* let her escape.★

Agalia and I both answered. ★Confirmed, Elder.★

Rausery chose her moment well, standing to step out and block our targets. She revealed her own light source in the palm of her red glove, her uniform blazing bright, shocking our targets and tripping them up.

With a shriek both angry and terrified, Jael Aurenthietti skidded and skirted the Elder's side by grabbing a jutting rock, pulling to launch herself in a new direction sprinting away from us.

Rausery let her go, her focus tight on the naked Sathoet right behind the youth. She was braced for attack, and it was perfectly timed.

Our Elder closed her fist, dousing the light, and drew her arm back. *She's not — ?*

Rausery punched the Priestess' Son right in the face, so effective that it threw him backward off his clawed feet, his exposed erection bobbing and flopping with his balls.

I gaped. Rausery was taller and stronger than me, true, but there was no way she was *that* strong.

Guess I know what that ring is for.

Agalia was already running after Jael. In my distraction, I got a late start. This wasn't a test of endurance to close the gap, however, as the Lunent only waited until she was close enough to pitch her own pellet at Jael's back. It struck center mass and split with a small crack, then an explosion of webbing ensnared her, dropped her like a weighted net had landed on her.

Jael stuck to the stone where she fell and screamed so loudly it echoed off the stone above us.

"NO! Noooo! Let me go! Let me GO!!"

Agalia had caught up to her by then and kneeled to force a gag on her, shoving something in Jael's mouth to muffle her, although the young fighter still bellowed her fury as she struggled against the sticky webbing.

Caught in between the Elder and the Lunent doing what they planned before I had begged to come along, I glanced behind me, spotting Lead Qivni catching up to us.

As she had sent Kerse away when he'd attacked me at the Palace, now the mage raised her hand in command, snarling a ruthless pattern of sounds that caused the demonblood agony just speaking them.

The Sathoet howled once, growled as he contorted, doubling up to crouch on his knees upon the ground. Her body as hot as his to my Dark Sight from the magical effort, Qivni jerked her fingers in the general direction of the Palace.

"Cryczefiina!" the Lead commanded with the confidence of any Priestess.

Snorting air, drooling, and with a whine, the Sathoet left at a flat run. I watched while I could, until he had cloaked himself; his outline vanished from my view whether there was a light source or not.

Rausery stayed ready for a possible reversal until Qivni gave her some positive sign he was gone. Then she noticed where I stood. She grinned, and my face flushed to the point I knew she could see it.

Well. I was utterly pointless to this task.

The Elder signaled Qivni and me to come with her, and we joined Agalia and her captive. As Rausery set a sound-dampening Ward in our vicinity and signed for me to keep a look-out, Qivni pulled one of the bottles at her belt and approached Jael. I had nothing to do but stand beside Rausery and watch.

Dampening a cloth with the liquid inside the bottle, Qivni kneeled and ran it over the white threads covering Jael's hands, dissolving the webbing as the Lunent grabbed and pulled them behind her back.

They bound Jael's wrists together then attached a black length to her throat designed for that purpose — the more the Aurenthin struggled to free her hands, the stronger she choked herself. Fortunately for her, Jael figured that out before she fell unconscious.

I wouldn't say she was docile, but she stopped moving so that Qivni could break down more of the webbing to free her. The Lead and Lunent then picked her up, one holding each arm, leaving her legs free as they expected her to stand or walk on her own.

The Sisters turned her around to face us.

Jael's hair was long and straight, and earlier it had been pulled up into a simple band at the top of her head to flow down her spine. Now, however, it was a mess, with strands escaped and loops and tangles frizzing the back of her head, the main body of it spilling over both her shoulders. I also noticed how torn and rumpled her clothing was, far beyond what would have been caused by the webbing.

What happened just now?

Jael didn't focus on Rausery first. Her fierce eyes landed on me, and she made it clear she remembered me. Her eyes narrowed, and she bared her teeth, chewing aggressively on the wad stuffed in her mouth. Words tried to rise from her throat, but they were unintelligible.

"Remove the gag," Rausery said, standing with hands on her hips as she looked the youth over.

Agalia obeyed, and Jael coughed and spat, seeming in no sweeter mood for having the dry packing removed from between her lips.

"What did you say?" the Elder asked.

"I-I said," Jael gasped, looking at me, then the Elder, "I knew it."

"Knew what?"

The cait quivered with rushing emotion, swallowing against the choker attached to her wrists, her eyes moist as she glanced back toward her House and back. "I knew ... the moment *she* talked to me, after the battle ... you would come to grab me."

"Clever cait."

Jael took a deeper breath, needing the air to speak all at once as she stared Rausery in the face. "I didn't *do* anything! None of us have! Why won't you leave us the fuck alone?! If you think I'm grateful you stopped them, you're wrong! *You* sent them, you red cunt!"

Stopped them? Stopped who?

Qivni scowled at the blatant accusation and insult, and Agalia's mouth was tight, but Rausery maintained a calm smile. Only now that I stood close and still long enough that I could smell Jael's sweat, soured from an extended period.

She hadn't been fresh when she sprinted out of the House and over the grounds. I smelled musk and dirt and spit all muddled together, plus a familiar tang like curdled milk. There were not only a lot of torn places on the youth's clothing, but also damp spots caused from things other than sweating.

Now I realized her bottoms were set askew, as if they'd been yanked up only as she started running.

"How many Sathoet were there, Lead?" the Elder asked.

"Four," Qivni answered, both hands tight on the youth's right arm. "In the barn. One of them escaped me and gave her chase."

"Snared three on your first word, eh? Impressive."

The mage nodded once, acknowledging this but probably not in agreement. Jael listened but wrinkled her nose in dismissal at what this might have told her. I could read it on her face.

Lying, don't believe you.

"Seems the trials started a little early," Rausery said. "Red Sister?"

It took a moment to realize she meant me. "Yes, Elder?"

"Clean her."

That was a familiar order.

Without the same hesitation Qivni had once known, I stepped forward and around behind the two Sisters holding the young Noble. I took hold of her rough-cloth pants, and Jael tensed and tentatively shook her head. She wanted to fight but was having trouble breathing.

"N-no, don't," she said hoarsely.

Sorry, cait. Knew this was coming for me, too.

It could be worse.

I went to a knee as I pulled the torn clothing down to her knees, and she quivered again. The scent of multi-male sex filled my nose — I would know — and I could tell without touching that her skin was tacky with drying slobber and semen.

I decided to take off my gloves to keep them clean, tucked them in my belt, and reached to part her cheeks with both hands. I recognized the look of two freshly fucked holes even in the dark.

Qivni interrupted a gang-rut?

Unlike the young Aurenthin, I didn't think Rausery had sent them. More likely she had caught some report of Sanctuary activity out this way and decided to act on it.

I leaned forward, and Jael flinched as my tongue touched one sticky thigh first. No worse than licking Kerse's cum off the black glass floor during my own trials, in fact, a bit better being warmed by the skin of a female I had been curious about anyway.

I cut a wide swath across her legs with my tongue, twisting awkwardly to get as close to her snatch as I could. Jael breathed very quickly, I pushed my face in, and Rausery stepped closer; I saw her boots appear right in front of the cait, taking hold of her choker, giving it some slack.

The Elder spoke quietly.

"Bend over. Keep the feet apart."

Jael would have fallen over had the Sisters not been holding her.

Given such access, I closed my mouth over her sex, sucking and cleaning the male seed from her flesh. She squirmed and squealed even before I moved up to her loose, tacky netherhole. Jael gasped and grunted at the first penetration of my tongue, but it was not pain, I knew. Confused, she remained off-balance as I serviced her as Gaelan had done for me.

Rausery picked her moment to force Jael back upright, lifting her chin and tightening the choke a bit more. I held her cheeks wide open and kept eating her ass because I hadn't been told to stop. The Elder chuckled in approval.

"Is my Sister doing a good job?"

Jael jumped again, but not from something I'd done. Rausery had reached down and cupped her mound, still wearing her gloves. She stroked the sore flesh, gentle and slow.

"Ungh!" Jael gurgled as I swirled my tongue around in circles, rimming her swollen ring with full focus as the Elder's fingertips stroked back and forth.

"Is that a 'yes,' recruit?"

Rausery's voice was low, hinting aggression; Jael's was tight from a constricted windpipe.

"Y-yes, Elder …"

"Good. How many times did a Sathoet spill seed into your quim?"

"I-I don't know," she wheezed.

"That many?"

Jael shook her head. "M-Maybe none? *Oh!*"

Rausery had flicked her bean; I felt her pucker tighten around my probing tongue. I could agree with the cait; all the thickest gunk seemed stuck on her skin or was oozing from her ass. Maybe she had swallowed more of it, or maybe that was why her hair was a mess.

"I … I," she panted, sounding baffled in her pleasure, "I mean … they fucked it. Always pulled out. Sprayed it somewhere else."

"Not trying to fill your belly, hm? That's interesting. This happen often, Aurenthin?"

Jael's slit was wet with fresh moisture, and I liked the way it smelled now that the half-bloods' spunk was gone. She trembled constantly now, close to cumming.

"Elder?" the young fighter tried, sounding more confused.

"Answer me, recruit. Have those same Sathoet rutted in your holes before?"

"N-no!"

"What about other demonbloods?"

"No …"

"But?"

"B-but … Ah … Ah!"

Jael pulled at her wrists; she couldn't help it. We stroked her harder, my Elder and me, from front and back. She couldn't escape the constant sensation; it grew worse when our Elder slipped a hand beneath her shirt and took hold of a tit as well, doing something which made the cait squeak.

"What's wrong, recruit?" Rausery snickered. "Losing your chain of thought?"

"*Ah … A-AH!!*" Jael cried as the Elder jammed two fingers up her twat and ground the heel of her hand against her furry mound.

The cait's anus squeezed tight around my tongue, fluttered, then began a rhythmic flex that matched the gasps the youth struggled to complete with the choker around her neck. If not for Qivni and Agalia, Jael would have crumbled as she peaked and then came down. Her slickness and scent smeared all over my chin and throat, and this made me smile as I leaned back.

Rausery noticed and chuckled. "Taste good, Sister?"

I smacked my lips and giggled by accident. I cleared my throat when Qivni frowned. "She does, Elder. Delicious."

Rausery snorted. "Guess we'll bring her in, then. See if the other slits agree."

I stood up, the crotch of my leathers damp as Agalia and Qivni worked together to cut and strip every scrap of clothing from the young Noble's body. Jael had no choice but to remain still and allow it to happen or pass out.

When she was barefoot, I obeyed my order to collect her boots and the shreds of her clothing to take with us; I already knew they were to be destroyed. She'd never get them back.

At last, my Elder pulled a familiar, black bag out. She put it over Jael's head, and a light stream of urine trailed down the cait's left leg.

Suddenly, I realized that the feisty Aurenthin might not survive the span.

This might have been my first and last time I'll know her taste.

The memory of when I'd made it into the Sisterhood returned. Jaunda had squeezed my backside as a gesture of welcome, saying how she'd enjoy having it around. She'd grinned like she was proud of me, though at least just plain randy for a new slit. A new Sister.

As I am already.

I wondered how many times Jaunda had been disappointed wanting that.

CHAPTER 11

JAEL VANISHED FROM ALL VIEW. ONLY ELDER RAUSERY KNEW WHERE SHE WAS.

The recruit hadn't been tossed in the holding cells below, I'd checked. A good thing as far as I was concerned, as a "lowbie" locked up there would be easy meat for Corpora Thena and her followers.

I'd only learned, through the effort of being a pain in Agalia's ass, that the disappearance would last until the Prime and D'Shea reappeared from wherever they had gone.

It had already been three cycles.

"It should be obvious, Sirana," the Lunent said. "Elder Rausery can't start testing a recruit until she's spoken with her own elder about it."

"But four Sathoet attacking her," I pushed. "That wasn't chance, us arriving just then to take her."

The Lunent sighed, frowning at me. "No. You weren't intended to arrive there at all. *That* was chance."

I nodded. "Then why? House Aurenthin has some serious enemies among the Priestesses?"

The older female chewed the inside of her cheek, looking at the floor as she considered; she lifted her white lashes. "I don't know, Sirana. I've heard sending Sathoet to harass the Nobles is something the Valsharess decides every so often, not the Priestesses, but I don't know."

"I've never heard of that happening to *any* House," I protested, "and I was one of those Nobles at Court."

"Only for a decade and a half," she countered. "You're young, and for what it's worth, this is the first time I've seen it happen. It's been a half-century easy since the last time I was told that it did."

"*Any* other House?" I persisted. "The last time? The time before? What?"

Agalia shrugged. "No. It was House Aurenthin then, too."

What in the Weirding Web has the Valsharess got against them if She wants them where they are?

The Elder Sorceress would know more, I knew, but she was in no mood to discuss it when I next saw her. Or rather, heard her, as her voice struck me while I was working.

★Sirana, to my quarters. Immediately.★

Yes, Elder.

I dropped the shelling Qivni gave me to keep me busy and loped my way through the dim, curving halls and rampways to land outside her door. Intentionally, I braced myself and tripped her Ward, the pain only flaring once before I backed off. A moment later, I could feel the magic was suspended, and I opened the door.

"Close it now."

I did so quickly, and the Ward was in place an instant after I'd managed to lift my hands off the stone. I turned around, saw my Elder sitting on the edge of her bed and Reishel collapsed on her knees upon the floor, her head resting in the Sorceress's lap.

They were both naked, exhausted, and I was struck by the number of bruises and abrasions on both of them. The damage was clear on their skin because the dirty, blooded water was still draining from the Elder's tub.

What did the Prime do to them?

"Elder?"

"We shall be fine," the Sorceress said in her normal voice. It clashed badly with the painting of vulnerability in front of me, especially as she stroked the younger Elf's damp hair, who moaned softly. "The Prime has decreed Reishel will remain part of the Sisterhood."

I didn't reply at first, then pointed out, "You haven't made a declaration."

"No, and I shall not like this," she agreed.

"Does Elder Rausery know you're back?"

"She will." D'Shea watched me steadily with dark, dark red eyes. "I … need you to do something for me, Sirana. A secret, and no resistance on your part. Just do your best."

"Do what, Elder?" I asked warily.

"Normally I would call Gaelan for something like this, but I already know how this affects her." She lowered her chin pointedly, staring. "As do you."

I shifted my weight. "Is this anything to do with how fucked up she was after the Ornilleth battle?"

"Yes." D'Shea took a breath. "I need a conduit."

My chin jerked once to the side in my doubt. "I'm not a mage."

"Correct. You've been touched by a psion, as has Reishel. And I felt … great clarity after the last time with Lelinahdara. My aura revived. I believe you can help us best, and quickest, with your cooperation. You can help us heal."

"You can't just … drink a healing potion?" I suggested uncomfortably.

"We have already used what the Prime allowed," she said sternly, frowning at me. "We don't have time, Sirana. I am not a hands-on healer, but I believe I can strengthen a spell I do know with your help."

"No secret stash?"

"Sirana."

"Nothing? Truly, Elder? For urgency like this? You're much more intelligent than that."

The Sorceress emitted a growl at me. "Yes, I have a cache. But the Prime is familiar with the results. It is better to present Reishel back to the Sisterhood in a better state she's in now but without the 'cheats' the Prime already forbid me to use."

It finally sank in. I blinked at her. "So, you want to use a 'cheat' she *doesn't* know how to recognize?"

Her smirk was downright crooked. "Exactly, novice. Well done. And you have motive to say nothing of it, am I right?"

I swallowed.

"Will you cooperate, or not?"

She was asking, not commanding. "You ... want me to wear the Feldeu again, Elder, and ... cooperate?"

"That's a start. You said you would do this for me next time."

True.

"Well ..." I looked around. "Where is it?"

"Over here on the bed already, behind me. If you've decided, Sirana, strip down, and help me with your Sister."

If I've decided. I supposed I had, wary though I was. I got naked and joined them, sitting on the edge of the bed opposite of Reishel. D'Shea and I both looked at the large, magic cock behind her, and I took it up to put it into place without further nudging. I waited for the command word.

"*Yemennija.*"

KAIN SAID NOTHING; WE SAT HIGHER UP ON THE WALL, LISTENED TO THE DAVRIN language as Reishel had heard it, at once mysteriously insidious and finely nuanced.

"What is your final word, Prime?" the Sorceress asked, never once leaving the younger Sister alone with their superior and owning the cuts and bruising for that as well.

The three of them were all naked for this challenge, this final trial. The spans spent in the underground wilderness showed on their bodies. Reishel swallowed a whimper, biting her lip to the bleeding point, waiting upon her back for the Prime to get off her and take it out for good.

I could hear her terror.

No ... help ... inside ... something's truly hurt inside.

Finished at last, the aged Elf stood up, scowling down at her subordinate as the younger cait closed her legs. "Same as always. Make it back to the Cloister, no potions, you're back in."

"I shall, Prime," Reishel whispered. "Thank you."

The Prime finally lost interest in her, and Reishel murmured a mind-prayer that it would remain so for some time. The powerful female turned to face Elder D'Shea, squaring off, and the six-century mage met her eyes without flinching. The Prime reached for her naked tit and D'Shea snapped and brought up a hand glowing a royal-purple warning like a lighthead pincerworm. Neither blinked, but the Prime grinned in a rare show of pleasure.

"Remember that trick," she growled full in her throat. "The last one you pulled as the final member of your House. Before I destroyed it."

There was delight in her tone, and D'Shea smiled back, more a baring of teeth. "The 'trick' has grown for the strength of the Sisterhood, elder. Care to sample its current potency?"

"It'd be fun."

The Prime stepped closer, noses barely touching, the purple glow just hovering over her heart. Her whisper was harsh as granite slabs grinding hard seeds to meal.

"If I did, though, I'd have to kill you after, like I almost did then. But I don't think she's done with you, yet, D'Shea."

The Sorceress said nothing, waited on raw, bare feet; her hand maintained its light, and she looked powerful even without mage's robes or armor. How the Prime still had the energy to strut looking for a fight after all this time out, Reishel did not know. She only watched the blooded Feldeu attached to their leader from under her lashes, wary that it had not been removed even one time.

The Prime had just spent the entire time with a constant erection. Reishel thought that would have driven any Red Sister rut-rabid.

"Are we not finished, Prime?" D'Shea asked.

"Yeah, we're done," the Prime said. "Meet you back home, Court slut."

She walked off, her strong back flexing as if she missed something as her raw-knuckled hands clenched into fists more than once. Kain and I watched as my Elder waited to make certain the Prime did not return, then kneeled to help Reishel to her ragged feet.

The younger Elf clutched her belly, murmuring that she was hurt.

"No potions," Reishel croaked. "I'm dying … Elder. I won't make it."

"Don't give up yet, Sister," Varessa D'Shea said. "There are always other ways to follow orders."

"Sh-she expects that … looks f'n'excuse …"

"She must understand what I do first, child. I assure you, she never has. Not from the first cycle we met."

~Always another way to follow orders.~

I held her.

I held on to her and kept myself inside, as our Elder had her arms around the both of us. Braced on my elbows, I tried not to crush my fragile Sister.

Reishel had whimpered for mercy when I first penetrated her, before I'd gone under, drifting in her last clear memory before she'd come here, and I had pressed in slow as our Elder chanted and spun her own magic, her body hot and strong beside mine.

Mercy.

I knew Jaunda would have given it to a fellow Sister, especially if no one else was watching. No one else knew about this. We would never say.

I shuddered, blinking as I came aware of where I was. I barely moved my hips but was surprised at the pleasure now rippling through me in gentle waves. Perhaps it was because Reishel had voluntarily kissed my shoulder. Then my neck. She sighed. She sounded healthier than before I'd lost focus. Her sex clenched down around my cock, milking it.

Deliberate.

I gave a harder thrust, and she moaned.

"That's enough, Sirana." My Elder panted with exhaustion. "Stop. And withdraw."

~No.~

"E-Elder?" Reishel asked.

Her arms were around me, hands flat. No fingers hooked like claws.

"The wounds have just mended, child, and your reserves are low."

~But she wants it — ~

D'Shea took a breath and firm hold of my shoulder, warning me not to start humping. "Better treatment than Reishel received beneath the Prime will still reopen her injuries, Sirana. Obey me, for her sake if not because I just invested the most risk that I *ever* have in two young Sisters this close together."

"F-fuck the Pit," I growled aloud, frustrated, planting my hands on the soft mattress to push myself up and back.

Just *feeling* that incredible, slow drag of Reishel's wet hole slurping my staff along its entire length nearly had me collapse upon her again. Then our eyes met as I hunched above her; my Sister's naked gaze was warm, grateful to feel pleasure.

She wouldn't have resisted.

D'Shea would have none of it. Both hands upon my shoulders, she pulled me back and away, steering me off the bed to drop onto the floor. There, smooth as silk, she kneeled beside me, grabbed firmly the base of my prick, and spoke the command word to detach the Feldeu. I grunted then whimpered myself as she pulled it out.

Goddess, I ached. A couple spots of cunt-drool landed beneath me.

With an exhale that sounded like relief, D'Shea nodded. "My gratitude, Sirana, for your cooperation. My efforts paid for themselves."

I inhaled and nodded as I let it out. I had an easy and necessary way to distract us as the last few cycles returned. "You may wish to make your declaration with Reishel soon, Elder, so you can take whatever potions you need to recover."

"Oh? Why is that, novice?"

"Elder Rausery snatched Jael Aurenthietti from her House three cycles ago. She's holding her, waiting for you and the Prime."

"What?!" D'Shea exclaimed. "Wh ... why would she do this *now?*"

"Four Sathoet attacked Jael in the barn," I reported. "Elder Rausery sent Lead Qivni in to get her. They hadn't even finished, her holes were still wet."

My Elder eyed me suspiciously. "And you know this because?"

Because I licked them clean.

"Rausery brought me with her."

"Why would she come seek *you?*"

"I sought *them*. I needed to get out of the Cloister, avoid some other Sisters. The Elder indulged me, but she didn't tell me where we were going. I figured it out when we got there."

I heard D'Shea swallow. "I take it Qivni banished the Sathoet back to the Sanctuary."

"Yes." I smiled. "But not before I witnessed Rausery brick-fist one right off his feet."

Reishel laughed softly, still lying upon the bed, and the Sorceress stared at me, no doubt quickly sorting her plans and priorities. She pushed herself to her feet and swiftly sought her uniform, secured in here this whole time.

"A question, Sirana," she began as she dressed.

"Yes, Elder?"

"Why did you *avoid* your Sisters instead of fighting them? Isn't that how Rausery taught you to handle it?"

"I still can't fight off *four* of them when they get the jump on me, Elder, any better than the Aurenthin could that many Sathoet. I need distraction and tricks instead when I'm alone like I was while you were gone."

"You couldn't go to Jaunda or Gaelan?"

"I couldn't find them."

"And how in the Deepearth did you convince Lead Qivni of this desirable idea?" she said with irony. "She'd have protested strongly, I think, and I know Rausery always weighs her opinion."

I paused, glancing at Reishel, who listened with unblinking eyes. She did seem better, mentally alert, less distracted by the weakened state of her body. Her white hair held a soft wave now that it was dry, cut just below her shoulders, and watching her now, I wouldn't have been surprised if she might have been a distant cousin to the Sorceress.

"I told the Lead what she wanted to hear," I said.

My Elder's eyebrow arched. "Explain."

"Qivni thinks I'm selfish, and only that. That I'll never be fully loyal to the Sisterhood. I told her I needed to avoid a fight with Sisters so as not to draw the Prime's attention and cause trouble for you and Reishel at a bad time."

My Elder rejected that. "Chances are greater you'd have simply been fucked to exhaustion and left alone. Hardly needing the Prime's or my attention."

"No, Elder," I snarled, "not again. I mean it. Next time those cunts pile up on me, it *will* need someone's attention. I told Qivni the truth, I *knew* it was a bad time to pick that fight. I wanted to delay it any way I could." I nodded to my Sister. "For her sake. Qivni believed me."

"Did she tell Rausery that?"

"Only that I was being picked at. Not what I said to her."

"And her Elder replied with?"

"Very little. Asked for a recommendation from her Lead, checked against your orders for me, and made her decision. She took me along without saying why. But we captured Jael Aurenthietti, and Rausery used me to 'clean' her just as you had Qivni and Gaelan do when you captured me. She wants to test the fighter from the last battle for the Sisterhood."

My tone wasn't resentful of that, I made certain of it. Neither my Elder nor Sister spoke for a few moments, and D'Shea continued to prepare herself. She became stronger before my eyes with each layer and leather tie, more determined.

"A good read of the situation, novice," she granted. "And a clever solution. Leading to valuable foreknowledge for me."

"Yes, Elder. You needed to know."

D'Shea gestured for me to dress and waited while I did so. Reishel would remain naked until after she was presented back to the Sisterhood.

Before we left her quarters, the Sorceress said, "Think about a reward you'd like for your initiative and success, Sirana. I will try to grant it."

CHAPTER 12

I WONDERED IF THE FOURTH DAUGHTER OF HOUSE AURENTHIN WOULD BE dragged to the Palace for her trials, sent to the same candle-lit chamber where I'd first seen the Sisterhood standing together. Jael was technically a Noble, although she'd never been to Court and acted more like a commoner. Particularly in her crude and frequent cursing in the hallways of the Cloister.

"Let me go or just kill me and be done with it, you curd-dripping, spinneret-suckers!"

Somehow, her Matron had let her get away with this behavior, while my sister Jilrina had never let me step out of line where she could see it; even my words had been taken away. Jael also lacked any patience to read the powerful females around her, which might work against her, or ...

I glanced at our eldest. *Or the Prime might get a charge out of her.*

This was Rausery's pick, not D'Shea's.

We didn't go back to the Palace when the cait was revealed before our top superior. Instead, the Red Sisters were crowded into the same room where I'd first been presented, where Jaunda had been the first to pick me up and drag me to her quarters to give up my holes to her pleasure.

We took our places with backs to the same wall, red uniforms lining the entire room, and Jael was in the middle, surrounded, terrified, but using her fear to make herself seem downright dangerous for one about twenty turns younger than me. Small, quick, and poisonous.

She was comfortably old enough to breed and fight in the army but hardly more than a novice if she'd been training with the Palace Guardsvrin at Court as I had been at her age. It quickly became clear she had had different tutors from the unfamiliar stance she took.

"One more twitch, and I'll rip your egg sacs out through your cunts!"

I sighed inside, trying but failing to catch her eye. The taste of her slit was still fresh in my memory, but wherever she had been with Rausery, waiting for us, Jael wasn't thinking about that moment as I was.

The Prime wasn't the only one grinning at a fiery, puffed-up insect ready to blast us in the face with a caustic fart if we got any closer. Corpora Thena clearly liked what she saw, swapping whispers with Panagan and Suna while Moria leaned in.

I stood near Cilyan and Gaelan, and Reishel had joined us now re-dressed in her full uniform. Lead Jaunda stood beside Qivni, appraising the naked recruit with the rest of us; I couldn't read either of them very well, but I could tell Elder D'Shea wasn't too impressed. Elder Rausery gauged the Prime more than she did the youth, having already watched her for a while before now.

Suddenly, the Prime took three long strides into the middle of the room; she was huge in her approach, like a boulder set to crush. The nude cait experienced a whole-body jerk, releasing the tension built up in one bad flinch, but I'd been watching her feet braced wide and her knees bent. Her heels hadn't moved backward one finger-width. The Eldest Sister noticed, too.

"Either too stupid or too stubborn to know you're in slime gut-deep, Aurenthietti," the Prime said. "Which is it?"

"Trick question." Jael's voice shook badly but she continued to snarl at the cruelest Sister. "I *know* I'm chin-deep in loose stool. Everyone at my House knows who *you* are, Red Sister Prime. Doesn't mean I shrivel like a mushroom spent of its spores now you've finally shown yourself."

"Why not?"

"Because you already picked my fate by now. Begging and whimpering won't change that, it never has. So just move the fuck on with it, I'm getting bored."

The Prime struck her so fast I didn't see exactly where it landed, only that it threw Jael to the floor in one strike. The old female kneeled and took hold of her throat, jerking to get her attention. Jael gave it to her, baring her teeth even as she struggled for breath. The Prime was smiling in a way she hadn't at my trial; she had seemed so bored then.

"I hear you don't like Sathoet," the eldest rumbled.

"N-none of us do," the youngest wheezed.

"Sorry I missed that show. First violation can never be repeated. Still, I relish the look on their faces. How about a repeat performance, just for me, recruit?"

That needle pierced right through the youth's armor; her bright copper eyes widened, and she jerked her head in refusal, denial. The Prime exhaled, her grin wholly malevolent.

"Beautiful. D'Shea? Go suck your Priestess, or whatever you need to do to make sure I have a room in the Sanctuary in under a mark. Call Tachnathon as well."

"Yes, Prime."

"Rausery, pick five to go with us. The rest to wait and see how this ends."

"And then?" the Elder prodded her, calmly curious as she signed to Qivni and Jaunda then scanned the rest of us, looking for specific Sisters.

"Then she gets the *real* test of wits. We'll see if she has any."

A few Sisters were disappointed when they weren't chosen, I noticed, although most didn't show an opinion. I wasn't selected, either, and felt frustrated — *more* waiting — coupled with that same trickle of dread now mirrored in Jael's face. I wasn't certain whether she had seized on the fact that the Prime had called her a recruit or not; I wasn't certain if she realized the same thing I had by this point.

That she would return a Red Sister or not at all.

Survive, little scrapper. It's all you can do.

The young Aurenthin blurted a frightened roar when the five chosen — Leads Qivni and Jaunda, Lunent Agalia, the healer-Lunent Nyllel, and

Jaunda's Corpora Kiren — picked her up and bound her.

The chosen Red Sisters then left with the Prime and Elders without delay, Jael's vociferous struggles fading from our hearing. The rest of us were left with orders to follow-up on our current assignments and continue the endless list of tasks and maintenance chores.

I slipped away to avoid those chores. I'd been doing mostly that for nearly quad-span now and was careful not to catch Corpora Cilyan's eyes as I left Gaelan and Reishel to their own. Heading back to my tiny quarters for a few supplies, I knew I would leave the Cloister and go ... somewhere.

I considered returning to the Wizard's Tower to visit Callitro again, but my Elder was abruptly and deeply engaged in delicate politics once again, and I didn't have a Sister-made infertility tonic to satisfy Phaelous, so I opted to avoid earning that displeasure on all sides.

I'm not that stupid or stubborn.

Yet it was a waste to just sit. D'Shea had approved of my initiative with Auslan and in slipping into the Collection of Jael. She was pleased in a way she *hadn't* been when I'd failed to explore anything outside my given objective at my former House Thalluen.

My Elder had offered me a boon just now, in exchange for allowing her to manipulate the psionic wounds between Reishel and me to somehow speed her healing with the arcane. I still didn't understand how that was possible, even for a Sorceress, but couldn't deny the results.

I also didn't know if Reishel knew I'd been eavesdropping on her own harsh test with the Prime. I didn't know if D'Shea knew. I hadn't asked because I hadn't wanted to.

I had become aware in such a strange way, floating barely tethered, feeling as if I had just traveled time itself, only to find I had been sleep-fucking my critically wounded Sister for who knew how long?

Maybe what I saw wasn't even what happened. Perhaps it was just a dream in Reverie.

I left the Cloister and returned to House Itlaun. In no hurry, I drifted carefully around the plantation for some time. It was my Elder's most vague mission still outstanding, watching this Matron, this set of Daughters, and this Consort. I had learned patterns, become familiar with schedules and faces. The only thing I hadn't done was what I'd been told to avoid.

Letting them see me.

I had been a Red Sister for almost a full turn now. Not long relative to others, but I'd just aided to bring a vulnerable Sister back into the fold and had witnessed the selection and initial testing of another. I was no longer dangling free and without foothold at the bottom of the line.

D'Shea showed me secrets. Already, I learned to circumvent the Prime's precise orders with something that worked better for D'Shea. I had survived to become a Red Sister, and I was deep into the muck of it now. I'd never get out, no matter if I ever wanted to.

I wished to know how Sivaraus saw me. If I was in fact still pretending, or if it showed to Noble and commoner alike. I wanted my own test, and if it displeased my Elder, I could make it my reward to avoid punishment. Then I'd know better.

If not?

I'll ask for something else.

House Itlaun had a garden with secret places deeper within clustered growth which I had to think were included deliberately. It was not easy to find a spot that few household servants visited at least once in a cycle. Nearly all these places visited unveiled either trades or trysts but few actual plots; all were short-term, materialistic, and the immediate satisfaction of some flash of want.

I had decided that the servants here were content here, as they were at my Mother's House, and this was how they played, whether they believed they were unobserved or not. There was a certain wisdom to the Matron allowing "secret" bargaining in a controlled area. Even pets needed to scratch their itches and groom their nests to keep them healthy and clean.

Auslan, Callitro, and other males here and there crossed my mind as I waited through the cycle before my target came into the garden alone. The Consort was just inside the plantation's residence, and I'd even glimpsed him once through a partly-covered window. He was the reason I hadn't gone inside to reveal myself to her.

Because going inside is exactly what I want to do.

I couldn't dream too much about the males, though; my body responded to pure sound, and I held still when I saw Curgia enter at last.

Without pause she sought one of the back clusters to duck down. My ears detected the working of a small mechanism, and I didn't think it was the lock of a secret door or a hatch. I was already moving, concerned I'd somehow lose track of her, when I heard her gasp in pain just before she dropped something on the soft ground.

I slipped into position so that I could see her form in the dark, swirls of her life's heat helping her stand out from the ever-present Radiants.

She was hunched over, her knees spread wide beneath a plainer gown bunched around her mid-thighs. The skirt was too generous for me to be able to see any tell-tale bump in her abdomen. Something cylindrical was lying in the dirt.

She cursed Braqth and one Priestess in particular, a blasphemy very close to one I'd used in the wilderness with insatiable rut-hunger eating at me. I heard the despair in her voice, saw her punch at her own gut — more in frustration, as it was not nearly hard enough to cause damage.

She is not handling her condition well, then.

This seemed a good time.

I tested how close I could get to her, slipping from the foliage to crouch near to her, my fingers threaded together and my stance one of a predator considering whether to pounce or not. My cloak and cowl broke up my outline, hid much of my own energy, and only someone looking directly at me would make out my face.

I kept my expression placid, observing, and neutral.

When Curgia sniffed and picked up the tool again, trying without success to flick the dirt and grit from it, she sat down on one hip. I could see half of her miserable face when she shifted just enough to catch me in her periphery. She reacted quickly, turning her head, and wrenching herself around to see who or what was beside her.

Wide eyes. The searing flash of the flight response choked in its progress. She was paralyzed as if a Drider had bitten her. I smelled the sour pulse of fear and wondered whether she would lose her bladder as well.

So, this was how a Noble saw me.

"Y-you heard me, didn't you?" she whispered, her hand partially obscuring her mouth.

"Perhaps." I gestured to the tool in her hand. "What ill-begotten Ketro made that? And do you mean to jam it up your slit? Not for pleasure, I'd think, unless you enjoy uncontrolled bleeding in solitude."

Curgia's face paled, turned greyer. "I-I …"

"You're too far along, I think," I said. "You need a brewer's help, at the least."

She glanced at the cylinder as if having to recall why she'd brought it, then she swallowed. I could see her body quivering. "A-are you here to kill me?"

I tilted my head at her tone. "Do you want me to?"

She gripped the womb-scraper tighter in her hand and tendons stood out on her neck. She shook her head uncertainly before she hesitated again.

"Is that a yes or no?"

She opened her mouth, but no sound came out; it was possible she didn't really know. For certain she couldn't think well enough to answer me.

"Have you thought whether the Priestess wants the demonblood in your belly?" I asked.

In revealing that I knew her secret, I had to give her time to get over her shock. This was the first time she had ever spoken to me, but I had already watched her for a very long time, starting when she kneeled prostrate before a Priestess and was mounted by her half-blood son.

I cut her off with a gesture when she started, "How did you — ?"

She obeyed and bit off the question I wasn't going to answer.

"Well?" I asked again.

Curgia blinked and took too long to answer for anyone I'd consider reliably useful, but at least she did answer simply. "No, Red Sister. I hadn't thought that. She ... just wanted to clog up my womb with this ... thing. So I could not be blessed by the Consort before my sister."

"That's all she wants, hm? Well then, what next? Sooner or later, you'll have to drop 'the thing.'"

Curgia shook her head; she had no idea. Astonishingly, she hadn't thought that far ahead.

"Here's a question," I said with a smirk. "Have you noticed any Nobles raising mixed bloods sired by Sathoet?"

The Noble stared at me. "I ... I haven't been to other Houses much ... only a few times at Court."

"That should be enough."

"They're ... not common?"

Close enough.

"She also told you something important," I prompted, handing her the figurative spider's egg sac. "Her opinion about her demon's son compared to the Royal Consorts."

Curgia stared at me with muddled horror. "You were watching."

I just smiled.

She shuddered after a moment and shook her head. "I don't know what you mean, Red Sister."

I rolled my eyes and shrugged. "I mean, either the Priestess will take the Sathoet child — her grandchild — once it's born, or she will end the pregnancy herself. Those are her choices, Curgia, and not yours. She won't leave it with you regardless, she's just letting you suffer in silence so you'll be malleable when you see her again."

This had clearly never occurred to the pregnant Davrin, and it was difficult for me to understand why not. However, I could see her mind working as every Davrin's did eventually.

"A gift from the Abyss, half divine, through her, she said," Curgia whispered, and I nodded when she looked up at me. "It's magical, this ... baby is."

I smiled wryly. Perhaps she wasn't entirely stupid. "Very. It's power to her, in some form or another."

The rate of the Noble's mind finally reached a normal level, and her eyes brightened considerably. "She won't let me keep it, I can see her taking it. But I wanted ... her help to end it. She's refused."

"For now. She has time."

At last, it hit the Noble on the head. "Wilsira will give me what she planned to do anyway, but for a price."

I couldn't help chuckling. "Good. Pull your head out of your twat much sooner next time, before trying to dig your guts out with dirty metal."

Curgia swallowed and made no action, no expression, no comment; she clearly did not know how to take an insult from a Red Sister except in silence. I wasn't finished anyway.

"Now think," I prodded harder. "What might the Priestess do if you do not ask her for help at all? If you carry as if you want it and have every plan to birth it?"

Curgia was still from a merchant family, deep down. "She'll make me an offer first."

"And if you respectfully decline the first offer?"

The despair which had been framing the young female's eyes ever since the Worship Ball seemed at last to begin melting away. She nodded her understanding; she had more power and her unwelcome unborn had more value than she had been willing to consider.

"Easy to overextend your reach," I warned her. "Were I you, I would give the Priestess exactly what she wants in the end. Just get something for it. If you defy her, you'll wind up dead or worse. This will be over in another turn at most. You'll have the Royal Consort much longer than that, so you'll have another chance. If you don't kill or make yourself infertile first."

She nodded, her brief glance at the tool telling me that she hadn't considered wrecking her womb. Meanwhile, it had been the *first* thing to cross my mind watching her. I knew well how it could be done.

If it occurred to her to be suspicious of my generous advice, it might be later; she was too busy grasping on to new hope. I had held her hand already far too long; the only thing I'd held back was that the Sisterhood would be interested to see if Wilsira tried to take and hide a newborn Sathoet child somewhere.

Unlike Curgia, I already knew they weren't allowed, by order of the Valsharess.

"Do you ... want something from me, Red Sister?" she asked hesitantly.

I hadn't considered that yet. I had acted on the desire to see the game change from the direction it had been going. I wanted to add an extra loop in the Priestess' plans just because I could.

I still disliked Wilsira Tachnathon for many reasons, even never having met her face-to-face. I disliked her for being Kerse's Mother, for owning Auslan and making him too afraid to fuck me. For being the one the Prime called upon to further torment Jael Aurenthietti.

For being the type of Priestess my late sister had emulated and aspired to be.

"When it's time to repay me, you'll know," I said to the Noble.

Curgia nodded, accepting the debt as an easier thing to swallow than what the Priestess had done. "Whatever you wish, Red Sister. If I can grant it, I will."

I enjoyed hearing that.

I waited until she looked away, distracted by her thoughts and the noises of the gardens and household, before stealing backward and away from her. I hadn't managed complete silences because she knew I was there; I just wouldn't turn my back on her while she watched.

Well-practiced as I was in getting out of the area unseen, I slipped out in good time. Treading the pathways away from House Itlaun, I felt strange despite my view being so familiar.

I'd done something definite with my own time just now. I had changed something significant, counseled, made an open-ended bargain, and swapped information instead of just observing and reporting.

Would D'Shea be at all pleased with me about that? Would she be annoyed at my lack of planning or outright furious with the interaction, given her own engagement right now?

She will make it clear, I expect. My Elder always has before.

I considered whether I found such a conniving Sorceress that easy to read in private without distractions, or if she just showed me what she wanted me to see.

CHAPTER 13

"SIRANA! *Hsst!*"

I slowed, turned around on my heel. She had gotten close, damn her. I smiled. "Gaelan."

She frowned, and I caught her scent. "You've been avoiding me."

"Huh." I looked to the side. "Thought you were avoiding me."

"Piss crystals. Go to my quarters, novice."

My resistance and my interest in her tone arose like twin pricks. "Mmm, no. I'm busy."

I turned to leave, and Gaelan slipped an arm right between my cloak and arm, hooked my pit and snapped me into a decent hold against her body. I grinned at first.

"I know D'Shea initiated you," Gaelan murmured by my ear, and my smile dropped. "You've worn it now. The Feldeu. Why didn't you tell me? I've been waiting."

"The Elder forbid it," I said without thinking.

"Why would she do that?"

Oh, that's a spider's nest.

I twisted to get out of the hold; she was prepared to block my first attempt but not my second. Wrenching the other way harder and dropping, I slipped free and launched myself up and forward, ready to challenge her to a chase. I discovered Gaelan had brought an ally when my forehead connected with a knee, an abrupt thump in my ears.

I fell over with a light flashing behind my eyes.

"Ow."

"Oo, sorry, Sirana. You moved too soon."

I blinked up in the dim hall. *Reishel?*

Now I knew how Gaelan had found out. Each Sister took an arm and hefted me back up. The twin eagerness in their eyes surprised me; it was playful. Reishel's smile was warm and Gaelan's more aggressive, watching for sudden movements from me to try again to escape.

"Come with us," Reishel whispered, eyes flicking each way like we may be discovered at any moment. "Please."

Worm shit.

My resistance drained out looking at her hopeful face, and I was quietly led away. We did not stop until we were inside Gaelan's quarters, the door secured and her mage's Ward set. By then, watching one Sister efficiently strip down, my mind had seized upon all the reasoning I needed to take this risk with both hands.

Sobriety makes a difference. I've been in control and have been myself the last two times. I can do it again without D'Shea. When the Sorceress had the time available to "alter" me while wearing the thing, *then* I would worry about who was around me at the time I lost control.

Reishel was the first nude, her body unblemished now and better fed and watered, though still weakened from what the Prime and the Sorceress had put her through. I was still dressed when she came into my arms, and I let her.

She pressed her mouth on mine with a sensual linger that recalled Callitro and Auslan, and how I'd kissed them. The similar softness genuinely shocked me, and the impulse to rip my lips away from her, to deny her was strong. I *knew* my older Sisters wanted me to wear the cock for them, but I was *not* just a pretty bua to be taken and fucked!

I won't be seen that way!

My arms tightened around my Sister, reminded her that my body was the stronger one, healthier. I explored her, my gloved hands caressed her naked back and waist, squeezing her buttocks, and she moaned. I speared my tongue inside, tasted her mouth, and she dared not bite, although she twisted her neck to break the kiss and draw in air.

She said, "Want you on top again. This time, don't stop until you've cum."

I relaxed a little. This was what I wanted to hear. Her murmuring voice even quivered a little as she offered me a low-lidded, suggestive gaze. Her eyes a bright ruby red. Submissive. Beautiful.

I looked at the first Red Sister who had bent me over and rutted me to her own pleasure first. "And what about Gaelan?"

Watching us, the mage had been touching herself through her leathers. She met my eyes, removed her hand, and did not answer before leaving to retrieve her Feldeu from the secure compartment in her desk. She placed it atop the flat surface, then reached up to take down her hair. My eyes trailed over familiar curves just hidden by custom armor, though not for long.

"Whatever way we get there," Gaelan said as she finished and walked away from the magic tool, stripping down closer to us, "I want my slit sore and satisfied at the end of it."

I nodded. Other Sisters rarely plowed Gaelan in the way she preferred. Almost all the time, her Feldeu was attached, which meant Jaunda and others reamed her asshole to their own satisfaction. Maybe they reached around to stroke her cock, and maybe not.

Or, as with D'Shea, they instructed Gaelan how to use her magic tool to pleasure their own slits. She was often allowed to climax with the focus being the attachment, but I knew the mage didn't have high standing yet to demand what she *really* wanted.

She had been waiting for me. A Red Sister lower in seniority, wearing the cock. Despite that, I was looking forward to it, although I still had one question for Reishel when next I could wet my mouth and speak.

I looked her in the eyes. "Mended?"

She nodded. "I just drank a stronger draught. I can take it, Sirana."

That must mean Reishel was out from under the Prime's eye. I exhaled in relief, although I still had a distracting thought. *Now Aurenthietti is in her place to take the abuse. She isn't even a Red Sister yet.*

Naked Gaelan leaned close as I still held Reishel; the mage kissed the edge of my ear in the spot I liked, nibbled on my neck. My desire flared in my chest and between my legs, and Reishel smiled to see my expression. She kissed me as well, her body language pliant and welcoming, and Gaelan's hand slid down my front and between my thighs to stroke me through my leathers.

I wasn't accustomed to receiving this softness. I sometimes showed it to males, but only in a way where I still felt *female*. The Red Sisters each held my unwavering attention now, even as I felt some trepidation how this was going to work.

They worked together to strip me, squeezing my breasts, caressing my haunches, and I let them. My nipples were hard, drawing tight and proud with my skin bared. Their hands were on me, their scent wafting up from their white thatches, dark purple folds eager for a Sister's cock to penetrate. I wanted that, too. I wanted the release and was willing to wear the cock between them.

I can sample every hole before we're done.

The two of them grinned when Gaelan's fingers made a squishing noise between my netherlips, my flesh so engorged she needed to press in harder to make any depth.

"You're ready," she whispered, touching her sensitive mouth to the corner of my mine. "Go get it, I'll teach you the command word. You asked before when you were behind me, filling my slit. When it was *your* idea."

My heart pounded to hear her low, smoky voice. To hear her words. She was right, and now I didn't need to trick her into saying it. *She will teach me.* I would be able to don the first Feldeu I'd known with no one's help, control, or instruction.

Gaelan stepped back to her pallet then, getting down on all fours. She spread her knees apart for our view, arching her back, smiling back at me over her right shoulder.

I stared at her dark maroon eyes, at her sexy smile; a slick, pink tongue snaked out from between dark, full lips. Then, when she waved her hips to draw my attention, I studied her plump, glistening netherlips and the purple crinkle right above it. My lungs struggled to draw in enough air as I felt a shiver pass through me.

"Go get it," Reishel nudged me, almost a plea. "Put it on."

"I want to see it on you," Gaelan added. "I've waited for this, like when I first saw you in your reds."

I smiled, and Gaelan reached back to run the pads of her fingers over her sex, through her white thatch, showing me some of the pink between her folds. She oozed clear, sticky desire, rubbed herself a little faster, and I breathed harder and in sync. Between shifting hips, my netherlips brushed my inner thighs, and I had to wet my drying mouth again.

I wasn't even wearing the cock yet, but I wanted her.

When I left for Gaelan's desk and her Feldeu lying on top, Reishel knelt beside our Sister in heat. Soon, Gaelan moaned as the Sisterhood's newest survivor gently caressed her hanging breasts. Listening to them both, my hand shook a little as I reached for the familiar toy. It was smaller than D'Shea's, but that was preferred. I could fuck them both hard, and I wouldn't hurt them like the Prime did us.

Although I'd be certain to make them scream.

Because they want it.

I took the wobbling tool and moved to the pallet, choosing to stand near Gaelan's head where she could easily see me. I rubbed the bulb of the attachment against my sex, quickly slickening up the surface. I felt a tingle which might have been magical, and my channel pulsed hungrily, knowing what to expect.

Gaelan's large, dark eyes looked up expectantly, desire clear on her face. She did not look away as I pressed more of the bulb inside, my body stretching so willingly around it and clutching tight, relieving my hands of their duty.

"Say 'rah-vel-ish-tah,' " my mage Sister instructed in a flat tone. "With the accents on the second and third parts."

I repeated how that sounded in my head a few times before speaking it myself.

"Ra'*vel*ish-ta."

I felt a strong tingle, but not securement. Gaelan's fingers played between her folds, and Reishel's eyes grew wide in anticipation; her mouth was still closed.

"Second just less than the third," the mage corrected. "Step up, then down low. Try again."

I did. Another light sizzle, and another tweak in a tone that Gaelan couldn't say herself or she'd just do it for me.

Reishel sat back to wait, spreading her legs to caress her cunt as well, and I had to work even harder to concentrate on the preciseness of the command word. I glanced at her snatch without meaning to as I spoke, and Reishel laughed softly when I failed again.

Slut. Wait until you're flat on your back.

"Ra'*velish*'tah," I growled, eager and urgent.

That completed the connection.

My knees weakened as the Feldeu seated itself and bonded with me, and I sank down on the pallet, shuddering and gasping. Awareness of my skin heightened so that the subtle heat of Gaelan's body caressed my face, and I inhaled as I gripped my pole to anchor the fierce hunger radiating from my gut.

A smooth, indulgent stroke eased the ache and offered me patience.

"*Ohhh*, Sirana," Reishel cooed, enraptured by whatever she saw on my face. She crawled forward to put her face in my lap, and I felt her tongue flick out to caress me.

"D-don't —" I gasped, my hands shaking badly as I tried to grab her hair, to pull her off of me.

I missed and next felt her mouth engulf my turgid rod. The embarrassing sounds which escaped me as she worked her mouth up and down the phallus—

Goddess!

Gaelan laughed out loud, waved her hips; I could still see her slit. Fumbling, I grasped Reishel's shoulders, bracing myself, digging my fingers into her flesh.

For a while, I was helpless, staring unseeing at the ceiling as I fucked that hot and wet mouth, and my Sister accepted the thrusts I made with my hips, pushing the tip deeper into her throat where it grew tighter. She would swallow against it, squeezing, or lurch, or gag.

Nowhere else I'd plunged so far felt quite like this.

"Don't stop," I whispered, a roar rising in my head as I imagined cumming this way.

Reishel disobeyed me. After pushing the blunt end a little farther down her throat, she withdrew. A sharp bleat of frustration escaped me as I shuddered. I felt the need to grab her ears and put her face back in my lap, but my Sister took my arm and pulled, her voice as delighted as mine had been bitter.

"Take her!" Reishel encouraged, tugging me toward Gaelan. "She *needs* it. Pay her back for times she's done you."

Our mage still waited on all fours, knees spread. She glanced back, nodding, wanting it. My eyes traced up smooth legs and buttocks, the pink slit a beacon in the dark. She was lean, long, muscular. I shuffled up, put my hands on her hips. Held tight. Reishel reached between us, helping me aim, because I wasn't nearly as precise as Jaunda in my first crude thrusts.

"Oh, goddess!" Gaelan cried as I at last lunged in, burying the magical toy in her searing, live cunt. "Oh, *yes!* Fuck me! Please!"

The Feldeu now in place for us both was incredible, yet the right side of my head began to ache. I ground my teeth, pulling my cock out and thrusting in again, and her ass pressed back against me in response.

She enveloped me, and I ached in the two most extreme ways, good and bad. My groin felt her wet ecstasy while obsidian slivers inserted themselves at shallow angles in my mind. I moaned aloud, agony covered with joy.

~So different from Tugren. Why do I want her so? She's tricking me, controlling me.~

I lowered my throbbing head, stayed mounted on her and humped that tight, willing hole. I kept my eyes closed and inhaled, drawing in the scent of Gaelan's skin and her sex as she climbed toward her peak.

~Disgusting! Depraved, Abyssal caster!~

This mage had been far better to me than many Davrin I could name.

No. Not disgusting. She needs it.

~Of course, she needs it. Trickster Elf in heat. All of you!~

Mistrust. Distaste. Hate.

"No," I gasped.

Not hate. I don't hate her.

Warm. Generous. Beautiful.

"Sirana," Reishel whispered from somewhere close. A hand trailed down my spine, a welcoming caress. "Oh, Gaelan ..."

"Gaelan," I repeated.

I fucked the first Red Sister who had tongued my gooey nether-hole during my trials, and she grunted in pure welcome every angle of penetration I sampled. Her fingernails scraped the pallet.

"Harder ... Sirana. Harder! Oh, Goddess, yes, it's been so long!"

Her cunt clenched tight once around me then rippled as the rest of her shivered. Reishel reached between the mage's legs; Gaelan's cunt tightened on me as she yelped. The mage grew even more vocal as I plowed her and our Sister held pressure with her fingertips, circling and rubbing. Her hair draped down, covering her face.

"Oh, I-I'm ... gonna ... !" Gaelan cried.

~Yes! Take this pole. Feel me!~

"Ungh!"

"Gaelan!" Reishel cried.

As my Sister hit her peak hard and soon to tumble quickly down, I was afraid.

For an instant, this act *terrified* me. This truth flashed across my face.

~I'm trapped. Your Goddess is stronger than me!~

I shook my head, closed my eyes, the splinters still stabbing at my mind. *No! Not afraid, won't submit! No!*

I refused to go under!

And nobody was there to make me.

"Fuck, no," I growled, pounding, wallowing in the scalding Elf slit kneeling before me.

She gasped in surprise and my renewed vigor but fell into our rhythm again, clutching her pallet, grunting, tensing, working to rise again as I rubbed her hole raw for her.

My cock sizzled with her magic, and her whole body seemed to meld with mine, much beyond the toy which connected us. I found something sustainable in the beating of our hearts, and I drifted there for a time.

Yes. Yes ... Yes!

*~She is Tugren. Yet **not** Tugren ... ~*

My pace settled, grew steady. Gaelan climaxed again.

Tugren. What is that? What?

I knew no answer. There was no equivalent in the Davrin language, only a possessive feeling of *want*, spoken in my own voice, just slightly changed. I experienced a flash of memory then, of using a pickaxe to dig out raw gems from the tunnels.

Are my eyes open or not? Am I awake or asleep?

It didn't seem to matter.

The Dwarf wasn't solely looking for gems but testing rock and soil for threads of an element the Tragar people used for psionic weapons.

~Very rare. Only used by those gifted ones. Only found by those with that gift, though others may help to mine it.~

Is that why you were there?

~Yes. Often it lies where Davrin magic permeates the rock. We don't know why, but there must be a reason. We must get closer to the Valsharess' mad city to find what we seek. We must leave our Tugren for many cycles, but we always came back to reclaim her.~

Why come this far? Why risk it?

~Too important to the forges, to our survival. This last-found spot had been promising ... rich in the element, the closest to Sivaraus yet. Dangerous, but we must leave signs for others to follow. No area is abandoned by all, even if one of us never comes back — ~

"Sirana?"

I turned my head.

A second Tugren found my lips, covered them with hers. Sucked gently and let go.

Goddess, yes ...

Like a full drink of water when I needed only a few drops to continue living.

My eyes closed as tension drained like poison from a lanced wound; I took a breath and a slower stroke of my cock inside the female before me. The fingers of the second female slipped down and behind me, between the cheeks of my bottom. They had been lubricated with her own juices.

My eye opened, and I saw a Davrin as she touched my netherhole. *A Davrin?*

I must have stared like I didn't recognize her.

"Sirana," Reishel breathed, "it's me."

Fingers circling my tight star, preparing to penetrate, and I liked it too much to remain confused. My relaxing pucker wasn't hairy; I was smooth enough for any Elven tongue.

Memories of so many Sisters tonguing my netherhole flooded back.

It was *me*. My own memories.

Sirana.

No demons but us. There is no conflict here.

This is not the wilderness of the Deepearth.

We are safe. We are willing.

My asshole yielded to a slender finger, not a stout Dwarven club. Then my Sister gave me two fingers, a twist of her wrist, and I sucked in my breath.

So familiar, the sensation helped clear my throbbing head.

"Reishel," I groaned, my Feldeu still buried deep in another Sister. I spoke her name as well. "Gaelan."

"Sirana," the mage sighed, sounding exhausted; her head hung down. "I'm sore now. A-are you done?"

"I-I haven't cum yet," I said.

But I remember why Kain had been where I found him.

I wanted to laugh. Had I just done what my Elder wanted of me from the moment after I'd taken her, by surprise and by force?

It seemed so.

But the consequences of that would be later, when the Elder herself had time for me. Right now, as Gaelan's cunt wrapped hot and tight around me, I knew what *I* wanted.

I was myself; these impulses, these strange, worried thoughts were not *me*.

After a few more deep breaths and more pleasure from both ends by my Sisters, the pain in my head began to subside.

At last.

"You were going at it for some time," Reishel cooed, squeezing her fingers in and out of my back hole.

"Mmm," I said, trying to form a coherent thought inside the Sisterhood's Cloister, not outside it.

Now that I'd stopped fucking and held myself inside, Gaelan lifted her head and pushed herself up slowly, coming vertical on her knees and leaning back against me. The Feldeu was still inside her, and Reishel's fingers were still inside me. My arms went around Gaelan, and I stretched to kiss the corner of her mouth when she turned her head toward me.

"Worth it," she murmured, like she expected to get in trouble for this.

She's probably right.

"My turn," Reishel urged, making me gasp as she shoved her knuckles in deep. "Come, Gael, she hasn't cum yet."

A languid sigh. "Oh, alright."

Gaelan pushed her hips against me to fall forward, and Reishel's fingers slipped lamentably from my back hole at the same time the mage crawled forward, pulling herself off my phallus so we could come apart.

The dark pole still ached, even if my head no longer did, and I looked at the unfucked Sister beside me with narrowed eyes and a growing smile.

"Your 'turn,' huh?" I said.

A quick nod. "Been waiting."

Me, too.

"On your back, then," I growled, my lust coming through with a bit of threat. "Like you promised, horny slit."

With a deviant smile, Reishel obeyed, scooting into place to display herself on the pallet, her breasts flattening a little against her chest. Her hands lay even with her shoulders, palms turned up, and remained there as I kneeled upright between her open legs. Gaelan made room, setting herself up to watch.

Before Reishel could reach down to help me, I took the Feldeu in three fingers of my left hand and guided it to my second, eager slit, pressing inside with obvious greed. Her mouth opened in a gasp, and I groaned as I felt the incredible warmth which surrounded me again.

Feels different. The way her body held me.

I settled down on my elbows, covering my surviving playmate for the second time in as many cycles. I was atop her; she wrapped legs around me, her hands still where I could see them. I reached for her wrists, braced myself. I started to fuck her in earnest, holding her down, biting her neck. She squeaked.

This time, she said, don't stop until you've cum.

I sought to go deeper; I wanted more of those sounds, so I returned to my knees and pulled her legs up vertical so that her calves rested on my shoulders. Her bottom rose slightly off the pallet and her body folded as I leaned in, bracing my fists near her waist. I moved instinctively, thrusting in and out.

Reishel's eyes rolled, and she smiled, groaning. "Oh! Yes …"

"Damn, Sirana," Gaelan chuckled. "Getting the feel of it already?"

As sure as the web, I was.

Void take me … Goddess, so good!

This moment lasted for me; Reishel seemed in no hurry for me to finish as she offered her tight cunt, and Gaelan alternated between touching herself and caressing me, sometimes slipping her hand down where my Sister and me connected.

She whispered words I didn't always catch; they might have been encouragement, or they could have been mage phrases which caused my magical toy to tingle even more.

Or it could have been my imagination.

After I'd gulped down this great helping of my own pleasure, I focused on Reishel's face. I could believe she just needed to be fucked, and she didn't care about anything else. She didn't want to fight or to resist. She laid back, opened wide, and let me take her as I wanted, for as long as I wanted.

She likes what I'm doing. She won't fight me. Won't try to kill me after …

Small ripples passed through her a couple times; Reishel might have peaked but was subtle about it, biting her lip as if she didn't want to distract me or Gaelan. Regardless, I saw it as I kept my gaze on her pretty face.

Reishel never said my name, and she murmured encouragement only as wordless sounds. Her hands made the occasional affirmative gesture, silent and probably more reflex than conscious thought. She'd grown much slicker, and when I realized my thrusts had become repetitive, that was when I decided I wanted her other hole.

I pulled out. "Turn over. Face down, ass up."

Reishel not only obliged but did so with a spring and a suppressed peep of delight.

I slapped her haunch as I reclaimed my feet, standing above her. "I heard that."

She arched her back, opening her ass into the slap. "Sorry, Sister!"

Gaelan chuckled as Reishel presented to us, waving her dark bottom, and I quirked my brow at my smug elder Sister.

"You're next, Gael," I tossed casually before looking to Reishel's crack, already wetted from our coupling thus far.

"Only if Reish's mouth cleans you well enough," she challenged with a smirk. "Because I'm not taking it in the ass from *you*. You'll have to rub my cunt raw again, little Sister."

I grinned. "Oh, you'll be waddling afterward, Gaelan. Guaranteed."

Both Sisters snickered, their fingers pressed to their clits as I prepared Reishel's netherhole. She didn't ask for any special lubricant; she remained compliant to my whim and will. I used my saliva and more of her own wetness to prepare both her ring and my phallus.

I did not use my fingers on her as she had on me. We had both been well-trained by the Sisterhood, and I knew her purple pucker yielded readily to such familiar pressure — no prior stretching required.

"Open up, Reish," I cooed as I crouched above her, legs wide and my weight braced as I nudged the head of the Feldeu into her crevice. I squatted to grip her shoulder with one hand, her hip with another, and pressed my hips forward, opening her up with steady force.

Before I could expect it, the tip popped inside. And held.

"*Yyyes!*" Reishel squealed, shivering, waiting.

By the Eights, her body was *hot!* The tightness purely divine. I paused, teasing her for a startling moment before I pushed deeper. Her ruby eyes flew wide, and she moaned the loudest yet, her mouth slack and salivating a little.

"Sirana … !"

I wanted to get every bit inside, all the way, and to hold it there before I began reaming her. I wanted her to feel how fully she was taken. She obliged me, holding still, waiting for me to start pleasuring us both. The self-throttling of my other Sister grew audible to my left; Gaelan panted as she watched us.

I heard the boot steps only as they stopped outside our door.

"*Fuck,*" Gaelan breathed.

We froze in place, Reishel's ring clenching once around my invading shaft. I glanced at Gaelan, making no noise as she crept up beside me.

Who's there? Should we ask?

Then Lead Jaunda's voice rumbled through the door, and my heart leaped.

"Finish up and put on your pants, you two. I got work for you to do."

She's back!

I felt my cock throb, and Reishel's hole seemed to quiver a little in response. Gaelan and I exchanged glances, perhaps wondering the same thing: *Is the Aurenthin still alive?*

Jaunda gave no hint as she struck the door, and Gaelan's Ward wavered. "Gaelan!"

"Yes, Lead!" she blurted. "We hear you. We'll be out!"

Reishel had put her fist in her mouth to prevent making noise as I pulled halfway out and sank back inside her to soothe the ache of my arousal.

"Two ticks," our Lead warned, "then I come in and drag you out."

She sounded rather hopeful about that outcome.

I still needed the release so badly, however, I couldn't stop now. I thrust a few times with more determination, and Reishel tried to swallow her moans as she pulled her fist from her mouth.

"Do it harder," she whispered, gripping the nearest blanket, "please, Sirana, shred me ... you've got two ticks."

And we couldn't even talk about what might happen if Jaunda told D'Shea about what the three of us were doing.

I started my final wallow, enjoying this tight, receptive hole. Reishel stuffed the blanket into her mouth, biting down, and one of her hands disappeared between her legs. Her fingers brushed my inner thigh once before settling and rubbing at her own snatch.

Candle's burning. Come on, fuck the Abyss out of her.

My tempo increased until the only sounds were the slapping of our flesh and the muffled grunts and groans from a filled mouth. As vocal as I'd been before, my mouth sagged open but was silent in anticipation and in dread of a returning pain.

Fuck ... fuck ... !

One sharp stab lanced my head when I climaxed. My vision swam and went black, and I released one, long moan, low and gruff. Reishel's netherhole still clutched tightly, coaxing a few more shudders from me as I came down.

Jaunda hadn't burst through the door.

Made it.

"We have to get ready," Gaelan said, moving forward to hasten the disconnect by planting a palm on my chest and pushing back.

I didn't resist because I enjoyed how the Feldeu was squeezed out of Reishel's shitter as we parted. The sensation forced a loud, twin gasp between us. I couldn't help but want a glimpse of my partner's swollen anus while I had the chance, after I'd used it in such a way.

I felt a strange glee in seeing — even briefly — the way it gaped open and winked while closing back up. I also noticed just how much fluid coated Reishel's inner thighs; clear and glossy from her own cunt, stringy where a thread hung from her dripping netherlips to her leg.

She enjoyed taking it hard.

Such satisfaction and pride.

Then the mage leaned in, taking firm hold of her property. She was already dressed.

"*Ularantha*," Gaelan chanted.

I gasped in shock as the Feldeu disconnect inside me; she waved her hand in front of my face before tugging with one hand.

"Sirana, relax, let me take it out. We can't have thirty flicks before Jaunda will be in here."

I nodded, memorizing how she'd said that word as we eased the bulb out of my sex, finally detaching the phallus completely. Reishel and I had to move quickly, staggering over to the wash basin; we felt the urgency deep now. The washing was barely more than a wiping down, and we scrambled to get back into our uniforms.

We were half-dressed when Jaunda returned, breaking that Ward with ease and opening the door. The three of us stopped like statues as our Lead stepped inside, Gaelan at attention, me bootless and cloakless, and Reishel just securing those. The big grin on the Lead's face covered any surprise.

"Well!" Jaunda said, looking us up and down, and I glimpsed Lawret and Berayla peeking in as well. "Was looking for you, Reishel. Nice to catch you here. Let me guess, you gotta start over at the bottom?"

"Lead," Reishel bowed, catching the other two in the respectful gesture as her movement never faltered. She finished dressing before me, securing her belt and stepping closer to the door. "For the time being, yes. Prime's decision."

"Fun," Lawret remarked, her and Sister Berayla now standing in the door frame. She looked over Reishel with new eyes. "A novice with experience?"

"I've seen worse fates," Jaunda said, then focused on me as the only one not ready. "Come on, sweetlips, time to go."

"Yes, Lead." I hopped on one leg, just got my foot in my boot and stamped it down to settle in place. I started on the leather lace. "What of Aurenthietti? Did she pass?"

Is she alive?

Jaunda tilted her head at an odd angle where her tapered ear seemed even longer, surrounded by short hair. The other Sisters watched for her response; even Lawret and Berayla appeared not to know the answer to that question. I was the first to ask her outright.

"Care whether she did or not, huh?" my Lead said.

I glanced at Reishel and back, finished one boot and started on the other. "We need more Sisters, don't we, Lead?"

Jaunda followed my thought. "If they're right for us, yeah. Still gotta pass trials."

I pressed her as I stomped my other foot. "Did Elder Rausery's choice survive the Prime, after what we saw in the training room? Does she breathe?"

"I wouldn't think so," Berayla remarked. "Too recalcitrant."

"Snarls like a beast at any authority," Lawret agreed with a snicker. "Like all Aurenthin I've met. The Prime might like to play with them, but she doesn't take them on."

"There are more of them here than you'd think, Sister," Reishel said, her voice a bit quiet. "Sisterhood before House, always. They learn not to draw focus."

To survive, she might have added.

Jaunda listened to us but was still watching me as I finished lacing. "Can't wait to get off the bottom?"

"Maybe." I grinned, reaching for my belt and weapons. "I know *I'd* enjoy having that ass around."

The Lead heard her own words spoken back and snorted.

"If you're not allowed to say, Lead, I withdraw the question," I added, cinching my belt. "If I've overstepped, I'll undo all of this and spread my ass for you, Lead, right now. Just give the order."

Jaunda's intelligent, rust-red eyes narrowed as her mouth warped a wry angle. "Some other time, novice. If you're so excited to know, she's alive. Sent outside Sivaraus now, like you were. Might make it back in a couple cycles or a span."

I nodded, perhaps with too much eagerness as I reached for my cloak. "Different direction?"

"No, the same, I think. Prime was worn out from watching the tests." She winked. "She let the Elders pick, and I think they want to give the wrung-out 'cruit half a chance. Come on."

"Yes, Lead," Gaelan said, cutting me off as I drew breath, warning me to stop talking before she and Reishel joined the others.

I held still for a moment, watching them file out the door. I didn't like the sinking sense of foreboding in my middle.

Same direction as my trial?

If the Elders wanted to give Jael a chance, they had made a mistake, but the newest novice convincing either of them might be like reversing a cave-in.

I might need a little magical help.

My eyes drifted to the desk and the unsecured, hastily cleaned Feldeu, and I took it, secured the weapon at the small of my back as I rushed to catch up.

CHAPTER 14

JAUNDA HAD GIVEN ME ALL THE LENIENCY I COULD NIBBLE OUT OF HER FOR THE moment. I was separated from Gaelan and Reishel and sent to do some physical work on a newly transported arrival of supplies sitting in the lizard stables. I would be restocking, resupplying, and reorganizing throughout the Cloister's various stockrooms for the immediate future.

At first, I was anxious, trying to think of a way out of it, but I was surrounded by a few too many less-friendly Sisters upon whom I had to keep an eye out. It gave me time to think, I supposed, at least up until the moment I could run into a Sister looking for entertainment. Then, as always, I would decide if I would fight or accept. This time, I knew, I would fight fang and claw.

As I worked on various tasks, I noticed I was becoming preoccupied, easier to take by surprise, and I worked harder, quicker, trying to focus and get things done as soon as possible. I was so deep in thought that I bumped into Berayla once, my hand accidentally brushing her backside. I was lucky; she chuckled and leaned to kiss me as she moved on to her own project.

"Wake up, sweetlips," she said, her hips swaying in red leather, "unless you mean it."

I'd smiled a bit but got back to work.

Wake up, indeed.

What condition would Jael be in if she woke up in the same water chamber that I had? Not filled with divine lust, I'd wager; perhaps more like Reishel had been — weakened, bludgeoned inside, barely well enough to move. Would she search around the same cavern I had? Would she find a blade from her former House? She would have to take the same path out as well, there had been no other way. She would be heading in the same direction, following the deep pulse of the city.

If I hadn't been hallucinating as I'd been fucking Gaelan's slit raw, the idea that there could be *more* Tragar between Jael and Sivaraus than there had been for me bothered me deeply.

She wouldn't have a splinter of a chance unless she ran and didn't stop. Seeing her fight on multiple occasions, knowing how she bristled at forceful obstacles, I knew she wouldn't retreat at the first hostile sighted. It wasn't her way.

I hadn't, either. I'd been too hungry to leave. There's no telling how much strength the Prime took out of her before they abandoned her out there.

I had been measuring travel rations from one crate into smaller pouches easily carried on belts or in packs when I looked up to see Panagan standing in the doorway to one of the pantries.

The archer had not gone out of her way to harass me ever since our supervised fight under the Prime and Rausery, where I'd won by forcing a Feldeu covered in burning ointment into her throat. Sure, she had jumped on me in the sluicers after Thena and others had me softened up and submissive, but there'd been no initiative of her own.

Panagan usually watched me with a cold, unreadable expression if I passed by, while Moria might scowl but made it clear she would also not act unless someone else did first. There was more reason for this beyond that one fight, I knew.

Whatever had occurred between the Prime and them after our sparring might be one, if the eldest recalled their disappointing performance at any point. There was also the fact I'd begun building reputation using my new tricks from Rausery judiciously and unpredictably. Sometimes I took the fuck, and sometimes I didn't. To some, I was still considered

Jaunda's newest playmate, which held some weight as well.

Panagan now stood watching me with intent. None of her usual group stood behind her and I heard none coming. Even if they had been, I'd show no fear.

"Are you going to supervise or help?" I asked dryly.

She didn't pause long before stepping forward to take a spare measuring cup from the wall and a few pouches. She straddled the bench on which I sat, facing me and within reach to scoop into the large bag of journey mix. We prepared a few pouches in silence as I wondered whether to wait her out or think of something to say.

My older Sister watched me with some intensity as we finished half the bag in silence, the soft rattle of dried meat, fish, mushrooms, mosses, lichens, and hard salt cheese. Very nutritious for us and with a long shelf-life, if a little bland compared to the specialty foods of the Houses.

"Elder Rausery wants this one," Panagan said quietly.

I raised one brow. I already knew that. Still I sighed, "She wants one what?"

"Aurenthietti," she said. "I saw you watching her. Talking with her low-born House Guardsvrin on the battlefield."

I stopped scooping and rested an elbow on my thigh, offering an amused look. "So?"

Panagan had an excellent stare when she cared to use it; her red eyes tried to stick any exposed nerves her opponent might have with needles. I took note.

"Agalia mentioned you were there at her Collection," she said. "It wasn't planned, you convinced Qivni somehow."

But you don't know how. Jealous of your Lead?

I smirked. It seemed I wasn't the only one nudging superiors for tidbits about Jael.

"Are you poking around on behalf of the Sorceress?" Panagan continued. "Does she want to sabotage Elder Rausery's pick?"

I allowed a slight frown of confusion to show on my face, guessing Panagan hadn't directed an interrogation on her own before. Compared to Jaunda or D'Shea alone, never mind with them both in the same room, this was as subtle as breaking off a stalactite and bellowing for answers as she swung it overhead.

I shrugged, answered her question without needing that threat. "No."

Panagan pursed her lips. "Which one?"

"Either. Or both." I couldn't help smiling at her sour expression, waggling my brows. "Why would this matter to you?"

"I'm being sent out to watch for her, as Gaelan was for you," she told me. "And, I'm guessing, so are you, since D'Shea sent the recruit into an area you so recently explored."

"So forthright, Pani," I commented, filling another pouch and tying it off.

Now my thoughts rapidly shifted. Panagan was going out.

That made two Davrin who wouldn't know about the Tragar, if they were there. Panagan also thought the Elders were competing, that D'Shea would tilt the scale to see Aurenthietti fail and die.

Would she do that?

Would Rausery have done something similar if she felt more dislike for me? If it was true, was it a mistake to confront them both about … ?

About what I remember. What Kain knew.

D'Shea had already been caught off guard once in Rausery's timing. I knew how she hated it.

I lifted my head and grinned at my Sister. "How about suggesting it first? Recommend to Elder Rausery that I go with you for that exact reason: I've explored the area recently. You can keep an eye on me and make sure I don't sabotage her chances."

I noticed Panagan's hand squeezed the handle of her scoop before she consciously relaxed it. She narrowed her eyes at me, suspicious that I was being as direct as her. She shook her head once in refusal. "You are a trickster like D'Shea. I'll wait on our superiors."

I groaned inside. *No, don't **wait**! I was being truthful!*

"Well, I've been given no order to sabotage anything," I said, my frustration apparent as I tried to explain. "Whatever you're thinking is speculation, and you're wrong assuming I have instructions to watch for Aurenthietti even by the Sivaraus borders, much less *that* far out beyond them."

"Spider shit," she stated, standing up to leave.

"Panagan!" I growled in protest, but she swept out, red cloak billowing.

While I heard her boots stride away, I thought about what had happened with Gaelan, how that rise in consciousness occurred. That seamless immersion where Kain's most primal impulses had formed some sort of intuitive reason. And a voice. It had been *my* voice, and yet there was no way I had been talking as I was thinking. I hadn't known any of that before.

One of the Tragar had not returned to their stronghold. He would be presumed dead, but he'd left sign for them to follow. More would return to the area to mine it, and Jael had been dropped in the same place, naked, bleeding, and vulnerable. Her intended Elders had no idea.

Would Rausery choose a different place if she knew this, to give the cait a more realistic chance to succeed? She might. What about D'Shea? Well, all I had to do was look at how hard she'd worked to keep Reishel.

They both want ... need ... new Red Sisters. They wouldn't have chosen this if they'd known.

I scooped the last of the journey mix into their pouches and hurried to leave, to find someone with enough pull whom I could persuade. Jaunda was the first I saw, and I practically jumped in front of my Lead to gain her attention.

"I have an important report for Elder D'Shea," I blurted. "Or Elder Rausery. It doesn't matter, but I *must* see them."

Jaunda tilted her head. "Regarding the initiate or a mission?"

"Both," I answered in truth, straining to keep my shoulders square.

My Lead looked me over. "Don't normally see you vibrating like this. Must be something exciting."

"You could say that," I said. "Get me their ears, and you'll be the first I tell after the Elders hear it. Agreed?"

The strong warrior shrugged one shoulder, and she appraised me a bit differently than before. "I always hear what I need to. How about a spar instead? Time and place is my choosing."

I thought that offer was a step-down. "What do you mean, your choosing?"

"Training you need anyway. Cross-terrain. You try to reach a given point before I catch you. *When* I catch you, you play with me until you're as raw as the first time we fucked."

She is truly not curious what information I have?

"And if I reach the given point first?" I asked cautiously.

"I don't touch you." A familiar, smoldering look. "For that cycle, anyway."

I stared at her. "You want a chase?"

Jaunda's face broke into a grin. "You got it, sweetmeat. Call it envy, since you get to go first. It's been decades for me."

I did a doubletake. "I go first?"

"Yep." Wicked, red eyes glimmered with silent laughter. "I can pull you in early to see the Elders. Get you their ears." She paused. "Yes or no, novice?"

You grease-spitting twat.

I may as well have been calling myself names, as I knew very well that it had been my obvious desire and single-mindedness that led to this in the first place. If I'd been more subtle, I'd have figured why she wasn't curious what I had to report without the sex trade.

Yet Panagan had been so blatant and ill-informed ...

I sighed. It could be so much worse.

"Yes," I answered. "Take me early to the Elders and pick a time later to chase me. I'll give my all."

Jaunda nodded. "You'd better. Follow me."

She took me to the strategy room where the Sisterhood often gathered, a place I might have expected to go except that it was warded and locked. Jaunda was able to undo both in just a short pause, then strut in as if taking a stroll in her favorite sex room.

Elder Rausery was there talking with Qivni. Unlike times before, there were no maps or objects spread around the table upon the platform, though I did notice a chalk drawing traced in a deliberate and complicated design on the floor a few paces from them.

They both fell silent as we entered, and when Qivni noticed me, and her expression edged toward full-frown annoyance. I was too late to see anything of interest in Rausery's face; she seemed to be only waiting.

"Yes, Jaunda?" Rausery said calmly; like always, she seemed to have a lot on her mind.

"Sirana has information you need about Aurenthietti," Jaunda said simply and stepped slightly to the side so I wasn't directly behind her. The Elder could see me head-to-toe.

"We were going to call her," Qivni said.

"I know. Let me call my Elder instead. Save some time."

Jaunda stood at ease but lifted a message pellet where we all could see it, pausing a moment before snapping it between her gloved fingers. Her eyes entered a thousand-pace stare as she sent a message, and perhaps received an answer.

Rausery showed some actual surprise. She and scowling Qivni stared at me with such arrow point-focus that I resisted an outright squirm, wishing Jaunda would tone down the dramatics.

"Is she coming?" Qivni asked when Jaunda was back with us.

"Yep. Soon."

I grimaced. *D'Shea will be thrilled being last in again. Joy.*

Rausery caught my expression. "Worried you're wasting that time, novice?"

"No, Elder!" I replied immediately, folding my hands behind my back, underneath my cloak. I was doubly sure when I found the Feldeu.

Gaelan's. The one I stole. Have to explain that, too. Shit.

Elder D'Shea arrived like a rockslide, her face set like stone as she stopped at my elbow. "Qivni, Jaunda, both of you wait outside the door. We'll call you back in."

Qivni hesitated, but Rausery nodded once, and then she complied.

When I was alone with both Elders in the spacious room, D'Shea took my elbow as I'd been expecting, but instead of a dressing-down, she silently steered me onto the platform closer to Rausery. The Elder General watched us expectantly, betrayed no impatience, just an unspoken order to get on with it.

The Sorceress was equally determined to understand.

"Why did Jaunda call me early?" she asked us both.

"She said Sirana has information we need on Aurenthietti," Rausery filled in. "That's all I know. I'm guessing you're the one starting ahead this time, Varessa."

I'd noticed they dropped the formalities around each other; I didn't know if that applied to me, but I picked the most grounded way I could think to open the discussion when they turned to me in unison.

"I presume Jael wasn't taken to the wilderness by cart, but by jump circle?"

They nodded.

"And I heard it was the same place you took me."

"Yes," D'Shea said shortly.

I exhaled. "Then there's probably Tragar entrenched between her and Sivaraus. Many more than the one I ran into."

Rausery stared at me. "You met a Tragar alone?"

"A psion," D'Shea supplied, confirming her prior knowledge.

"And she survived?" the General remarked.

"I'm alive," I pointed out.

"Not without paying a price." The Sorceress had a cunning smile. "What have you discovered, Sirana? Have you been *exploring?*"

I nodded my confession. "Gaelan ..."

"Yes?"

"I wore her Feldeu. Used it on her. As she asked. And ... memories came back."

Like you wanted with Lelinahdara, but it didn't work.

My Elder's eyes glinted with suggestion. "Whose memories?"

Heart pounding, I glanced at Rausery and back. "Kain's. He left signs for others to follow. He was a mining scout. They'd follow the sign whether he returned or not. It hasn't even been a full turn yet, but he found something. So, if they found it in turn ... they could still *be* there, digging for it."

"What did he find, Sirana?"

I shook my head. "I-I don't know. A type of gem or ore they value.

It resonates with the mind mages. They use it in weapons. I don't know what it looks like."

"You'll recognize it, perhaps," D'Shea said, her mind crackling behind her gaze while Rausery rubbed at her eyes as if she was already tired.

"Short version, novice." She looked at me. "What happened? And why weren't we told?"

Abruptly, the helplessness under a Priestess's influence returned; I felt the urge to weep in frustration trying again to describe it. I swallowed, blinked, and made no sound; I would not allow any tear form large enough to fall.

"The Priestess' breeding urge was too strong," D'Shea spoke for me. "Sirana was snared into a life or death struggle with a Dwarf to satiate that urge."

"Ew," Rausery remarked, though she showed surprise again.

D'Shea briefly looked at the ceiling. "It was not just the spell of the Threshold she fought, but the Tragar's mindlink. It's caused some kind of … hmm, wound. An impression of the Dwarf in her mind."

"She said, 'Kain'?"

"Yes. You weren't told because she buried it. Even I didn't hear it in her interrogation. I recently uncovered it after Reishel became aware again."

Rausery narrowed her eyes. "That happened while Sirana was tending her, wasn't it? In the infirmary."

"I didn't do anything to her!" I blurted.

"Quiet," the General said, and she looked at the tabletop like she was thinking this new game over. "Hm. You knew this, Varessa, but still suggested Jael be tested from the same place?"

The Sorceress nodded without apology. "I was going to send Sirana farther out to watch her, as I knew you would send Panagan. I wanted to test if any memories surfaced in her from returning to that area. However, it happened far earlier, with Gaelan as the conduit and a magic cock as the focus."

Rausery stared a beat, huffed, shook her head once. "You *really* know how to pick'em, don't you?"

"I have my sources." D'Shea folded her arms beneath her breasts. "As do you, or this Aurenthin scrapper would be in the dungeon now, having her skin pulled off in strips for insulting a healer so far above her own meager House."

"Hey, she's gone from their sight," the General growled. "That's all House Five has to know."

"She's gone," I dared interrupted from urgency, as much as I ached to hear more. "But was she unconscious when you left her? Or awake and already moving?"

Rausery's umber-red eyes didn't blink as they shifted to me. "Unconscious, like you were. She was injured enough in her trials that she'd have bled out in a few marks. It was only that she finished to the Prime's satisfaction before that happened that we could give a draught to stop the bleeding. But she was weak. I thought the same place we left you would give her some time to rest."

I shook my head. "It's not safe there, Elder. I know it. I'll go out and get her, we can restart the trial somewhere she has a better chance."

"No," she ordered. "We can't know everything in a chosen area, that's part of the test. And *no* recruit is to be retrieved before reaching edge of the Great Cavern on her own, do you understand? Some have died trying, Sirana, that's the way it is, but we cheat and the Prime just kills them anyway. We only want the most resourceful ones in the Sisterhood."

Or the luckiest. "But you wouldn't have put her somewhere she'd have to bypass a Tragar mining operation, Elder. Not in that state."

Rausery glanced at D'Shea. "I might still have. Send a Sister or two to watch, that's all."

I blinked my astonishment. *So easily dropped?*

The two Elders must be accustomed to keeping secrets from the other.

D'Shea watched my anxious face for a few moments. "What would you suggest, novice?"

Well-timed relief. I felt gratitude just to be asked. I had an offer.

"If she can't be retrieved and replaced in another location, Elders, then send me to hunt the Tragar instead," I said. "I'll take care of the problem, and she will continue on her own."

"By yourself?" Rausery laughed. "If there's even one psion like the last one you ran into, then you'll either die or be captured. And no Red Sister is to be captured."

"Send a team, Elders," I said, unwilling to give up as I felt that frustration, already marks old and growing, now becoming hot and urgent. "We'd have the advantage, the surprise. More memories will surface, I'll discover what it is they want so close to our city. I'll bring back a sample of the element they wanted, use whatever I can, everything, like I did before. I *refuse* to die under a Tragar!"

Rausery stared as my voice rose loud, her sharp eyes piercing and deflating my tirade in a moment; I snapped my mouth shut. Elder D'Shea spoke after a pause.

"She's going out there anyway, Rausery," the Sorceress said with a lovely, small smile, her voice smoothly taking control. "That was my plan. Choose your own Sister. But it will be kept to two, as we agreed."

I stared with more surprise, waiting what seemed a very long time for my heart to slow, and for the Elder General to answer. Meanwhile, I looked at the Sorceress, wondering if she had done something unseen.

"You'll work with Panagan, Sirana," Rausery said finally. "We'll start this hunt early, and we'll send you out farther than we thought we'd have to. You have permission to 'take care' of any Grey Dwarves that threaten the recruit, but she's not to be seen or confronted by you until she's crossed over the border into the Great Cavern. She is not to be guided. Understand?"

I nodded agreement, meeting both their eyes. "I understand, Elders. I'll do it."

With my Elder seeming pleased with the outcome, Rausery called the two Leads back in and instructed Qivni to retrieve Panagan immediately.

"Tell her to bring her bow."

I looked at Jaunda, who casually folded her arms and took a comfortable stance between me and D'Shea. I waited for recognizable gestures from my Lead, but she made none.

It did not take long for Qivni and Panagan to enter.

The younger Sister indeed carried a bow and quiver of arrows, going straight to her Elder at a gesture, while Qivni, first with a small bow of her head to D'Shea, stood boldly in front of me, leaning close.

"Let me make this clear to you, novice," the Collector said with narrowed eyes. "Sisters do not kill each other, or leave each other to die on a mission, and that's what this is. The Nobles and the armies do that. We don't. Understand?"

"So long as Panagan does," I replied, impatient with a threat which hadn't been on my mind.

"I do, Lead," the archer said proudly.

"Answer her properly, Sirana," D'Shea said.

"I understand, Lead," I said, mimicking Qivni's bow as I swallowed my resentment. *They're sending me to find Jael. I'm getting what I want.*

I realized Rausery had just finished instructing Panagan about something in sign language, and I'd missed it thanks to Qivni. That was intentional, I knew. I glanced at D'Shea, who stared intently at Rausery and ignoring Qivni, but from the way she leaned, I knew she didn't have a good view of Rausery's hands. The Elder soon gave her attention over to D'Shea.

"Ready?"

"Been so," the Sorceress replied.

"Great. You two will leave now," Rausery ordered, her eyes following D'Shea, who pulled out a small, abstract object which had a cut of red-tinged, Davrin hair wrapped around it.

She nodded agreement, set the piece inside the inlaid onyx circle in the floor. "Stand next to that. It will get you to the closest jump point we've built to where she is now."

After we'd obeyed her, each of us glancing at the other, the Sorceress continued. "Make sure the recruit lives past a Tragar threat, but do not interact with her or otherwise guide her until she reaches the borders. *If* she does. Is that clear?"

"Yes, Elder," we answered.

D'Shea looked at me. "Find out what you can of what those Grey Dwarves want in our lands."

"Yes, Elder," I said.

"I look forward to the reports."

There was chant in a familiar voice, a flash of painful light, and a lurch which left me momentarily disoriented. The shock of profound quiet coupled with that sense of empty expanse took me by surprise.

When my mind and my eyes first detected the Radiants in this new space, my first thought shocked even me.

~Since when does crystal flow in the Deepearth?~

CHAPTER 15

Veins creeping through the rocks, and crystalline liquid moving inside.

I stared with a dull horror. I couldn't pinpoint the source, though this moment lasted for only the time it took for jump-circle magic to dissipate. The clear, writhing shine vanished into blackness while my other, base senses kicked in. I smelled raw rock unformed by hand or magic, with a hint of water and moss.

A soft thrum from the deep warmth beneath us sounded, familiar and seeping into my bones. The Radiants that defined the shape of the caverns in pure darkness soon became clear as a portrait to my eyes.

Just stone. Regular stone.

Panagan and I crouched down with high rock on two sides of us, silent and still and all but invisible to anything else as long as we had our cloaks on. I could make out the larger outline of Panagan's bow and quiver on her back and wondered how good her aim was in a tight place.

D'Shea had said we would be as close to Jael Aurenthietti as they could manage, but I didn't know which direction or how far. While the area felt familiar, the features were not, and we could wander around for cycles, missing our target.

I looked at my partner in this venture, who was at a disadvantage not knowing fully why we were here. Panagan only had her orders. She looked around and I knew she did not find the place familiar at all.

I signed, *What were you told about the Tragar?*

She frowned askance but at least realized we had to work alone without back-up, which meant closing a knowledge gap. She moved her hand in silence.

I was told a Ward placed near the recruit was tripped, and the Sorceress identified the threat. The General decided to send us out, far and early.

One corner of my mouth lifted. *Because she wants this one.*

Panagan jerked her chin in a nod, reading her own words signed back at her.

I was there when my Elder discovered this, I lied. *I volunteered because I already know this area. But the General still wanted you, as you told me in storage.*

Panagan's mouth twisted. *We deflect or kill Tragar. We give Aurenthin a chance to get out of this area.*

Understood, Sister, I gestured an affirmative, smiled without showing teeth. *Good to be clear.*

We start with the nearest water source. She may be there.

I had no better suggestion, not yet, and soon discovered Panagan knew signs for finding water better than I did. I took careful note. This coupled with my rising knowledge of the area as we slipped farther from the jump circle brought us to a familiar, low-based cavern in what felt like less than a mark.

We crouched again, choosing a place low-profile and defensible, and I indicated a particular hole leading to a long tunnel higher on the cavern wall.

I've been here! She will come through there, if she hasn't already. Only one way.

We must confirm which, Panagan replied with an annoyed slant to her hands.

She moved forward, and I had to admit I was impressed with her tracking skills when she found the subtle signs of a bare-footed, two-legged creature about the size of a Davrin, not nearly old enough for it to have been me.

I began to see why D'Shea and Rausery were quick to agree on their choices of Red Sisters: I had the overall map, Panagan had the experience of detail. I asked questions to glean what I could, but she was impatient; she was not here to tutor me.

She is ahead of us. We must catch up. As I track, you tell me if we're following a similar path you once took.

If she's tired or disoriented, she will, I wagered. *I took the down-hill path, least resistance.*

We shall see.

I made no corrections as Panagan led the way for the first leg of our trek. Meanwhile, memories resurfaced for me as we traveled, some clear, others murky. We headed essentially the same way I had before, with only a few divergences that still brought us back to that main tunnel that lead to where I'd first heard Kain tapping the stone.

I reminded myself to draw in a breath.

The rock in the area seemed to vibrate with a higher wavelength than my eyes might have detected before. As we continued, a low hum began to flow through my head and into my teeth; it became irritating and distracting. I didn't know whether to focus on it or try to block it out, and my hesitation must have shown.

What's wrong with you? Panagan signed, her hand flashing quickly. *Step lightly. We're closing. She's just up ahead.*

We are? She is?

I raised my hand to reply, hesitated, looking at the odd pulse in a few spots within the rock, like spiders made of light and ready to break out of their blurry egg sac.

Finally, I signed, *Psionic.*

My Sister stared at me, clearly withheld a scoff. *You can't know that.*

I shrugged. *Tragar, then.*

I see no sign.

They didn't come this way, we're not following them. My signing was insistent. *We're getting near.*

Panagan paused this time and asked me directly, *Are you a mage?*

I could easily lie, just to persuade her to take my direction. However, I didn't know how that reputation might affect things back at the Cloister, where else I'd be tested. I wanted neither gossip nor trials coming my way that I had no way to back up.

No, I'm not a mage. The Sorceress gave me something to help sense them. Temporarily, for this mission. A potion.

Why didn't you mention that earlier? Panagan signed with a scowl.

Because the General signed something to you I couldn't see at the same time! I retorted. *Can't know it all at once.*

She accepted this grudgingly enough, looking ahead. *Tragar close, and maybe psionic?*

I nodded and expected a signed or whispered curse. I read her lips instead: *Twist my web-sticky tits.*

She signed, *Inform me of any change.*

As the hum got stronger, I focused on it more, relying on Panagan to guide me forward closer to Jael while I motioned "warmer" and "colder" to her. That her physical signs for our recruit and my intangible source for the Tragar were consistently going in the same direction was not encouraging.

To my dismay, I could feel exactly when we stepped to the place where I'd killed Kain.

I stopped, my skin breaking out in bumps beneath my red leather.

They here? Panagan asked, worried and perhaps feeling the creep as well.

The pile of rocks I mounted on top of his body ...

They had been partially scattered by scavengers and there were no tools, no cloth, no bones. Everything was gone except for a few old blood stains that marred the natural patterns of the stone, as if someone had splashed opaque dye onto a bed of phosphorescent moss.

One side of my head started to hurt, then a piercing stab made me queasy. I smelled the scent of the Dwarf, felt the oil on his skin, heard our grunts in my ears as we struggled, as we coupled. I reached out to place my hand on the stone, trying to stay upright, as I felt again the wide, short prick piercing and stretching my body, ramming itself in again and again.

I want it.

I was so angry, so disgusted and horrified that I *needed* it like that, and it should have felt so *good*. I hated how far he'd fallen, how he had weakened, growing to enjoy the trap despite the magic harnessing his gift like a beast of burden. He had spurted inside me, bitten me, my back was scraped raw against the rock.

I was bleeding.

So real ...

Someone twisted my ear, and I hissed.

Silence!! Panagan signed in front of my face.

I recognized her.

What's happening? You're not acting right.

We need to ... move beyond, I replied, taking one determined step past the grave. "We need ... distance.*

I fumbled for the sign language and for another step farther down the tunnel. Panagan eyed me, untrusting. Not moving.

Silently, I snapped. *Psionic backlash! Get me away from here! Too much!*

Wary and confused by the demand, she took my upper arm in a hard grip and dragged me with her. Almost immediately I felt some relief and I gestured, *Yes, good. Away.*

Panagan kept me moving when I might have sunk to my knees as the presence in the tunnel weighed down on me. I was desperate to get those memories, those sensations which I had felt a turn ago back under control.

Easily as bad as the first time I'd worn the Feldeu in D'Shea's bed. I couldn't have described anything as it truly was in that tunnel, it was entirely inside my head. Panagan could have taken anything from my belt or pouches, she could have signed me a question, and I wouldn't have been aware, but I felt her arm touching me.

Walk. Keep moving.

Eventually my physical sight cleared, my mind calmed, and I wondered whether there had never been any Tragar up ahead and it was that particular, haunted spot. Panagan picked the place to stop so I could catch my breath, and she stared hard at me as I quickly checked my weapons and belt to make sure all was in place.

She hadn't touched anything, but I was sure she'd been trying to communicate.

You're better now? she asked.

I nodded.

What happened?

A psion died there, I answered truthfully enough, too tired to think of a better story. *The death-memory lingers.* I smiled ruefully and added, *Not sure I want to volunteer for another of these experimental potions.*

Panagan nodded. If she had doubted what I said before, she believed me now. *And up ahead? Anything?*

I pulled out my waterskin and took a swig, rinsing my dry mouth before swallowing. I took a few more breaths and tried to concentrate past a throbbing head. That hum from before was still there.

Still in front of us, even as it is also behind us. Delightful.

It scared me to think I might not be able to tell if these twin feelings were connected to the living or not. That was why I needed Panagan's solid senses to back things up.

I nodded. *It's up ahead, too. What about you? Sense anything?*

She nodded. *I can hear movement, more than one body. Sounds aggressive. Armored. Could be Grey Dwarves.*

I groaned inwardly. We knew without signing anymore that we had to catch up to our potential Sister right now. We took off.

Jael.

With each stride as my boot landed upon the barren floor of the tunnel, I imagined another stone placed atop another inside my mind, building a mental wall against any other reminders of Kain.

Tragar. Just the threat to be dealt with.

Luck was with us as we came to the next opening with the high-ground advantage, and it was easy to survey from a low crouch. We could see several squat bodies moving around the base of a surprisingly tall, bulbous boulder, and atop it was the lithe form of a familiar cait. She did not have clothes on and crouched on three points of contact, gripping a trembling short sword in her right hand.

There is our little initiate.

The Tragar had found her first. Jael had gotten herself trapped atop that stone, though given the rough shape she was in and the new blood I could make out glowing more brightly on her body, she was fortunate to still be alive.

Panagan nudged me. *Which are psionic?*

Good question. I looked back, trying to tell a difference between the energy folding around the short, hairy bodies. There were six in total with two that seemed different somehow, though it was subtle. I was making an educated guess, but a guess nonetheless.

Hatchet and Pickaxe, I answered, identifying them by their weapons. The other four held large axes or Dwarf-sized swords of impressive make. They all wore well-made armor of metal and made a lot of noise.

This wasn't going to be easy.

Some bend Radiants as camouflage, I continued. *Catch in webbing or outline them the instant they start to fade.*

She nodded once. *You engage, I'll cover.*

Why, thank you, I signed sarcastically.

I have the bow. She smirked. *You are melee. You get close, outline them for me. I shoot.*

A loud yelp caught our attention and as we looked up, I saw one of the Tragar was holding on to a rope with both hands. The other end was somehow connected to Jael's leg.

"Barbed hook," Panagan said aloud with a hiss, tensing and clearly wanting to rise and nock her bow.

She was right; I had to move now.

"Cover me," I murmured. "Light pellets only with warning."

"Right. Go."

I surged forward down into the hollow where Jael resisted being pulled off the rock. She couldn't last long and landed with a loud scream of pain; at the same time my boots hit the cavern floor.

Panagan waited until I was within distance, when my stride made enough sound to cause a Tragar to turn around, before she fired. It was a beautiful shot, lodged in the armpit as he'd raised his arm to prepare an attack. He barked in surprise, gripped the arrow with shock, and I finished him with a slim stab into the throat with my thinnest blade. Metal armor or not, there were weak points.

One down.

"*Faeriluci*," I growled, flinging three magic pellets toward the backs of three other targets.

The small spheres broke, and the spell was released, outlining their bodies in soft, magenta light for Panagan to target, just as they all turned to grasp the new threat. I appraised our advantage with delight; the Tragar did not have any ranged weapons right to hand, but Panagan and I did.

They shouted in deep throated, Dwarvish curses as I exchanged my dagger for the short-distance hand crossbow. My weapon was prepared with only one shot, but I was very close. A squeeze of my hand sent Pickaxe reeling back, a tiny poison-tipped arrow biting into his bearded cheek. He'd be paralyzed within ten ticks, fifteen if he really fought hard. Eventually his lungs would seize, and he'd suffocate.

Just don't get close again, and he'll be gone.

Two down.

Then three of them, when Panagan pierced another outlined in magenta light with a poisoned arrow of her own.

The one with the hatchet was farthest from me, him and the last two of his brethren between Jael and me. He growled as he yanked on the hook buried in the cait's calf, making her yell. His milk-white eyes gleamed with unfamiliar power, as did his teeth as he gritted them; they were all I could make out in his dark, bald head.

The other two Dwarves wore helmets. This one didn't. I really didn't like that.

They bellowed something unintelligible at me and the other two charged forward. I was faster and evaded their attacks, drawing them away from Jael and trying to give Panagan a clear shot at Hatchet. I nearly missed the large stone lifted without obvious aid off the ground, preparing to be hurtled through the air as if thrown by an invisible giant. It was aimed at the archer.

Alright, I was wrong about none having ranged weapons.

"Pani, down and cover!" I yelled so loudly my voice broke as I fished out a light pellet. I pitched anywhere in Hatchet's direction where it would break with my command word, *"Lucinitri!"*

A single, bright light lit up the entire cavern for two ticks, centered in between the two Tragar in front of me. Roars of pain and surprise exploded at the same moment I heard the harsh bang of stone colliding with stone. With no sound from Panagan, I took it that she hadn't been hit directly, but I wouldn't know for the present if she was still in the fight with me.

I couldn't see anything. I had to close my eyes and try to ignore the blotchy spots behind my eyelids and continue fighting that way.

The two Tragar tried to flank me; their confident but heavy movements told me they could blind-fight, too, but fortunately didn't have my dexterity. I took the instant I needed to strain for any sound from Jael while I dodged away from the axes held by arms with a short reach.

Where was she?

Come on, make some sound!

I heard the drag of a rope. That had to be good enough. I removed a spare steel dagger from my boot — the one that wasn't pre-poisoned, because I didn't need Jael pricking herself in the dark — and I knelt low to the ground to toss it in her direction. It skittered and bounced along the ground and stopped about where I thought she was.

I already knew she was very good fighting with two weapons, and if she had her wits at all intact, she'd scissor the thick rope that held her first.

I heard her grunt as she lunged where the dagger had landed — *Good cait.* — and I leaped away from the two blind, magenta outlines once again to get closer to the psion. I plucked a powder-filled bottle from my belt and threw it in the general direction of the bald-headed dwarf. If I hit him or the ground around him at all, I would be pleased.

"*Vahsist* — *!*" he exclaimed, not knowing at all what dusted all over his armor before he started coughing.

It would give Jael time, but after him, I heard her cough as well. Then I felt the tickle, hacking my breath once.

Fuck. Too much.

Good thing I wasn't trying to hide.

There was a whistle in the air and a grunt behind me as Panagan took down another of the fighters. Only one remained when I heard the *shink!* of two blades crossing each other and a body rolling farther away. Jael had freed herself at last.

The bald Dwarf cursed, coughed again, and turned toward the escaping Davrin. I ignored the glowing, teetering outline of the lone ax-wielder and went instead for the most dangerous. My sight was slowly recovering, which meant his would be, too, and even if Jael could stand, it wouldn't help her once he could focus with those blank, white eyes on her.

He must have heard me because something which felt like a stone golem's fist struck me directly in the chest. I staggered backward, stunned, and unable to breathe while the Tragar continued coughing on itch-dust in the dark.

An arrow clinked off the armor of the final magenta Dwarf. Panagan had missed her aim, and I had no choice but to dive awkwardly to the side as his axe struck the stone beside me, chipping it with a spark of light. Jael screamed somewhere I couldn't see her.

No!

I heard her groan the next moment and knew she still lived.

Pressure inside my head made a sudden, a too-familiar, urgent attempt to build and overtake me. I strained to stand against the mind attack while simultaneously dancing with the swinging Tragar, only half my senses working.

Damn it, they were ganging up on me. My hand crossbow wasn't reloaded, and I'd dropped it after the mind-fist had hit me anyway. My volatile poisons would affect me as well as the Tragar — range wasn't an option. Where was Panagan?

Damn it to the Abyss!

As much as I did not want to go toe-to-toe with a Dwarf's axe with my brain being addled by the thick, mental squeeze of another, I didn't have much choice. I drew a pre-poisoned dagger from my boot; all I had to get was a scratch on this one. Time would do the rest.

Three things happened at once. Another arrow struck the Axe Dwarf, embedding in something meaty this time, though it wasn't lethal; the Tragar howled, cursed, and moved to raise his axe over me again. Then Panagan cried out in alarm, stumbling like something grabbed or crushed her, as the pressure in my own mind eased by half.

Finally, I heard Jael speak.

Clear, loud, and angry.

"Your turn!"

The psion shrieked in pain, and the psychic echo which lashed out took the last-standing Dwarf, Panagan, and me all down to our knees. Pain radiated out from my crotch, and I clutched myself desperately, trying in vain to remove some invisible, sharp hook. The Axe Dwarf on the ground beside me whimpered, doing the same and grasping at his genitals. Panagan's howl was the fourth call of agony.

We felt *his* pain after what our vicious little recruit had done to him.

~*Let go of us!*~

Shocked, his mind drew back from me. ~*K-Kain?*~

"Jael, kill him!" I screamed. "Put him down!"

I heard motion, the sound of long metal slicing flesh, gurgling, and finally, the pain in my head and between my legs stopped. The last fighter did not recover as quickly as I did, and I attacked first, burying my dagger in his eye.

He flopped onto his back and died fast. Thank Braqth for *some* fucking favor! It had been a waste of a poison dose but ...

Whatever it takes to win instead of die.

At last, the only sounds were three Davrin gasping in a three point formation. My limbs shook from the lingering sensations and the exertion, and I became aware of the pain in my chest, a pinpoint bruise radiating pain as I breathed.

The physical strike that stopped me in my tracks.

He hadn't thrown a stone at me. It was a mind "push" with the power of a thrown fist. Impressive to think he could form a club from nothing and strike me with it from afar, but I was still here.

What were the limits on things like that? Had I met them already? I knew Tragar mistrusted and feared the Davrin, so had he begun with a powerful attack, but it wasn't enough?

Maybe Tragar just aren't as powerful as Ornilleth.

Maybe that was why Kain and I had fallen into endless rutting in the first place.

Shaking, I fumbled for a slow acting healing draught and quaffed it. It was stupid of me not to have taken it prior to rushing into battle, but I'd forgotten and then, once in, there hadn't been time.

Typical skirmish "plan."

The magic potion warmed my stomach and filtered its soothing power through me. It became easier to breathe as my bruised chest, ribs, and back stopped hurting, as my headache went away, and the phantom pain of hooked and shredded genitals disappeared entirely.

While I waited, I checked on Gaelan's Feldeu strapped to my lower back. It was still there as well, but it had been loosening; I reached to secure it in place. I could stand within moments and looked toward the ledge where my archer had been.

"Panagan!" I called.

"Not so loud," she answered irritably, and I could see her holding her head as if she'd drunk too much wine the previous cycle.

Alive and talking. Good enough.

I moved over to Jael next. She'd cut the psion's throat and dragged herself back from the freely bleeding body. The cait was awake but struggling to remain so, and she watched me with extreme wariness through loose, tangled hair. She could not stand, or she would have been on her feet already, I knew.

I appraised her injuries.

She'd ripped the barbed hook out of her calf somehow; I was amazed she'd had the strength. She'd then used the same hook on the psion. I started to smirk, hearing her quip just before the scream, and feeling what she'd done.

At great cost to her, however.

Her leg muscle was ruined, and she'd be permanently lame without magical healing. She breathed poorly, with too many hitches and grimaces of pain; some of her ribs were cracked, if not outright broken. I couldn't count the number of scrapes and cuts on her skin, and it looked as though one of the axes had grazed her flank as the long cut gaped wide and bled freely.

My eyes returned to her face, seeing she was at the end of her endurance, though she tried to hide it as the rush wore off. She grew paler before my eyes as she lost blood, and she had trouble holding her focus. She couldn't make it back to the Great Cavern on her own, and scavengers would come to this place soon enough, attracted by the blood.

She couldn't defend herself anymore beyond this point.

Too late.

We hadn't found her soon enough for it to matter. She was going to die out here as if we'd never come.

"You," the cait said, slurring a little even as it took great effort and pain to talk. "Re'mber ... you."

I nodded. "Wicked work."

"Th'battle or ... these?" Her eyes flicked toward the Dwarf bodies.

"Both." I crouched down and threaded my gloved fingers together. "Answer me something. You woke up next to that pond, you found your House's blade. Then what?"

Jael weaved a little, side-to-side. "Mm." She thought sluggishly. "Walked. Downhill. Thought someone was ... behind me, moved faster."

I nodded. It was probably Panagan and me.

She continued. "Heard stone chipping ... ahead. Trapped between ... too late once th- ... they sensed me. Chased me ... climbed on a stone. Hooked me, my leg, pulled me down ..."

A look of pure hatred passed over her face as she gritted her teeth and gazed at her ripped flesh, then at the body of the one who'd done it. After that one flash of fire, however, hopelessness started to seep in. She knew she had no choices left.

Damn it. If it hadn't been for …

We could have been here sooner.

I didn't even know how much time we'd wasted while Panagan had to guide me in the tunnel. It was true that we'd dealt with the threat and Jael was still alive, but not for long. I regretted that Panagan and I had inadvertently pushed her stumbling into the Tragars' path. It had turned out exactly as I had tried to prevent: an unrealistic challenge that only ensured certain death of the recruit.

I wanted you to make it. So did Rausery.

" … I saw you … attack," Jael said in a weak rasp, drawing me out of my thoughts. "One ran … before y-you."

I blinked. "What?"

"*Seven*," she whispered, drawing on some speck of will inside. "*Female.*"

I counted the bodies again — six, all male — and looked to Jael again, my gaze intense. "You're sure?"

She nodded, wavered, and finally fell over to lie on her side. She seemed to be feeling less pain and if she still breathed at all, it was shallow. She didn't have long.

Panagan had finally seen fit to climb down off the rocks and join me. She caught me taking another bottle from my belt.

"What are you doing?" she demanded.

I kneeled beside an unconscious Jael and used my teeth to uncork the bottle, gathering the injured Davrin up into my arms so she was less likely to choke.

"Stop," she said. "Don't you dare, Sirana, that's yours, you might need it!"

I ignored her and dribbled part of the most potent potion I had across Jael's cracked, swollen lips. Fluid entered her mouth, that tiny spill just enough to revive her a little. I tipped again; she swallowed reflexively and coughed. Grimaced. Eyes still closed.

"We're not to aid in her trials!" the archer barked. "Elders' orders."

I spat out the cork and hissed as Panagan moved to take the bottle from me. "I was *ordered* to take care of a threat and see the initiate get out of the threatened area. That's what I'm doing."

My Sister paused but got my meaning and made an ugly face. "Are you insane or just stupid? The Prime will just kill her! And then kill *you*, after making you sorry you helped her!"

I bore down on the fear trying to rise. *Always more than one way to follow orders ...*

"We missed one!" I said, grasping for some justification. "A female Tragar. Jael saw her before we got here. We must track her *now*, or she'll bring more Grey Dwarves to this area, and they'll follow us instead. I'm also not leaving a Davrin body behind for those mind-fuckers to take back to their stronghold. At the very least, they'd eat her!"

I fed the potion to Jael as I spoke, and she kept swallowing the bitter brew with intermittent, weak coughs. She *wanted* to live, though she probably couldn't hear our words.

"You're going to fucking drag me down with you!" Panagan said. "The Elders were extremely clear on parameters!"

"They have to be, yet even a novice can sort priorities," I retorted. "Nothing works like it's *supposed* to after you release your first arrow, Panagan, you *know* that."

She paused, taken aback, perhaps a bit scared how quickly all the consequences of this mission had changed. Hells, even I didn't know what would happen back at the Cloister, because the mission wasn't over yet.

Jael had finished the draught; I lay her back down and stood up, picking up the cork and putting it and the empty bottle in a pouch on my belt. Panagan shook her head, lips tightly pursed before she spoke.

"It won't be a true test, it's compromised. The Elders can't justify it to the Prime to save your skins."

That was true if I returned only with my current, limited knowledge and a set of empty hands. But there was more to be had, if I seized it, and my Elder Sorceress's biting words after my first solo mission echoed in my mind.

I expect more from you. Every mission has an opportunity, and you have the ability to spot it. Your trials demonstrated this without any doubt on my side.

No doubt. Every mission has opportunity.

"Quit arguing, Panagan," I said. "The Tragar is getting farther away. We have to find her."

She hissed and ground her teeth as we watched the cait heal with unnatural speed. The wounds in flank and leg stopped bleeding first, and the ragged flesh knitting together rapidly within a subtle glow. Eyes still closed, Jael whimpered in discomfort as bones grew back together and swelling lessened, as the magic made her whole again.

She blinked, bewildered at first, but a cry tore from her throat as she rolled away from us. Before either of us could respond, Jael had seized her House blade and my dagger nearby. Grabbing both, she brandished them, growled something indecipherable at us.

"You little —" Panagan began.

"Excellent, you're up," I said, boldly held out my hand. "Thank you, Thietti. I'll take my blade now."

Jael hesitated, eyes flicking between us as I stood ready, waited to see what she'd do. Ultimately, she handed my blade out to me, handle first. Like me, she was prepared to act if either Red Sister so much as twitched. I realized I was smiling as I took back my dagger; between that grin and Panagan's snarl, the recruit was very confused.

I glanced at my fine-pointed weapon and saw it was covered in blood smears from tip to handle. If she'd only used it to help cut the rope, it wouldn't have looked like that, maybe handprints on the handle. I guessed I knew now how Jael had gotten the barb out of her leg. Her own short sword would have been even less refined than this as a surgical tool.

Determined and resourceful. Fearless. She's perfect for us.

Then Panagan pointed in the general direction of Sivaraus and growled, "Say nothing and run, recruit. Go. Now!"

Like a huntress poised to escape, Jael took a step back on bare feet while glancing at me. On impulse, I winked at her, and that healed, attractive mouth twisted dryly on one side. Next moment, she turned and ran fast, still nude and holding only her House blade, white hair streaming behind. I witnessed the power of the potion I'd given her, seeing how her body was in perfect working order.

And what a body it is.

"Find sign to track the female Tragar, Panagan," I said as I picked up my hand crossbow dropped during the fight. "She's got a half-mark head start."

Chapter 16

Unlike tracking Jael, I didn't need Panagan to determine which direction the missing Tragar had gone. The recent path of seven Grey Dwarves coming into this area, all wearing metal and hard boots, using tools, was clear as candlelight even with my lesser skills.

The female Dwarf had backtracked that path, going the opposite direction in which Jael had just run. Panagan and I followed at a fast, sustainable jog, closing the gap as we knew that the Grey Dwarves, like the Ketro, Pyte, or any other short-legged, squat creatures in the Deepearth, were not endurance runners like Dark Elves.

Our target would stop soon and burrow in somewhere, and we assumed the need to be wary if we caught her too close to her own territory.

While the skinnier Ketro were just smart enough to construct pit and collapsing traps around their dens and run at first glimpse of trouble, the brawny Tragar used these basic ideas for hunting but rarely ran. In instances like these, I'd been told, the non-psionic Tragar could still be expected to choose a good spot to stop running, turn around, and fight with all the will they possessed.

Panagan and I had taken the stance that this female likely did not have any traps set up in advance. A single Ornilleth, if outnumbered, would always have planned an escape ahead of time, complete with deadly surprises. A group of Tragar, even psionic ones, were more likely to pull together a trap quickly and under duress, as they did not imagine themselves to be in retreat and pursued.

The best Tragar obstacles and traps were at their strongholds, and it had been centuries since the Valsharess' Army had seen it necessary to assault one of those. Here in the wilderness tunnels, with one survivor and the unlikelihood that this escape had been pre-planned, we only had to catch up with her before she got close to home.

We ran into one of those hasty traps just as I felt a mental itch just up ahead, as the tunnel widened into another cavern. Panagan knew to stop and study before entering such a prime ambush or trap spot, though I had already slowed down from the early warning. We attempted to check it over before going forward, but the trap triggered without our having to touch anything.

~Move!~

I shoved Panagan to one side, and we barely avoided being crushed by a sole, compromised boulder falling from a ledge over the tunnel's mouth. Our prey made the mistake of shouting something at us, a threat and a crow of confidence not unlike her male counterparts.

Certainly less bass to it.

She was outside of range for our Dark Sight but with the noise, I still pinpointed her most likely position just as Panagan stood up, withdrew an arrow and nocked it. She drew back and released right where I would have said the Dwarf was standing.

We heard a cry of alarm but not of pain.

Caught armor or clothing, I signed.

Panagan nodded with a scowl. *Hope that shuts her up. Can't stand that hack and gargle sputtering they do.*

I smirked but made no comment. It didn't sound as coarse to me anymore, but I had a good reason for that. Part of it was strapped to my lower back. I'd even understood her.

"Let me be, Davrin, or this place will make your tomb."

Not very creative, but I heard the determination in her voice and something else I couldn't define. Not fear, maybe Tragar were too stubborn to fear much, but ...

Something causing a lot of tension.

Panagan put up her bow and drew a dagger. ★Flank her,★ she signed.

I nodded as we sprinted in opposite directions, creating two targets and circling around intending to trap her. There was no obvious escape route for her unless she could climb the rock very quickly. As we closed on her, she ducked down out of sight and didn't come back up. From my angle, I saw the tunnel leading downward.

Oh, fuck Braqth's snatch with a pincer staff.

Approaching the hole in the stone, I heard no scraping of metal as I imagined the Tragar must be moving quickly on hands and feet in a narrow space. When we reached the mouth, we saw why. She'd shed the bulk of her armor and her helm and left them behind. Both a good and a bad idea, but at least she wouldn't become hung-up by it if the passage got smaller farther in.

Been there.

Panagan cursed with her hands but stayed silent, then looked at me. ★I'm not going in there. She'll collapse the tunnel on us.★

No doubt. Or there might be other traps. This tunnel was intentional — built, not natural — and that close space would be very hard to fight a psion. The same dexterity and speed that won the fight before would mean very little here.

★We don't know where she'll exit,★ Panagan continued.

★So, she's escaped?★ I replied.

She hesitated, not wanting to admit that outright, but did not have any ideas on what to do. I only had one idea that might off-set our disadvantage, but I could not do it with Panagan watching. I took a slow breath to decide.

Kain.

One of that troupe of seven had recognized his voice in my head. There was a good chance this female psion would as well.

I took off my cloak and rolled it up. ★Carry this?★

She jerked her head no, so I wedged it between two rocks. Less obvious than the discarded, Dwarf-sized armor.

My Sister signed, ★What are you doing?★

★Going in. I'll flush her out. You stay up here, watch for her to pop up.★

Her look of disbelief also held mocking laughter. ★Go on, novice, walk into the trap!★

I wasted no time, ducking down and slipping into the narrow crawl-space headfirst, just as I'd seen the Tragar do. I wouldn't know if Panagan stayed up there until it was too late to stop the Tragar from rolling a rock over the exit. She might leave to go after Jael to kill her off after I'd broken the rules, to avoid the punishment of the Prime.

My body flushed to think of these things going wrong outside this closed space, yet I could do nothing about them this moment. Not with the strong pull of the psionic Dwarf just ahead of me.

I must catch her. I must have something, or D'Shea can't defend me.

I crawled on knees and elbows to get out of sight of Panagan and reached back to loosen the Feldeu from my belt. So many risks to be squirming with a ready erection after a short, female dwarf, but part of me hoped that, if I was in a Tragar-made place, the gamble might see true knowledge rise.

Anything useful.

I loosened and tugged down my pants, squirming to get it over my hips with the bulbous end of the phallus crammed in my mouth. Pants down, I sucked off the dust and grit that had collected, spit it out, then slickened it up with as much spit as possible. Winning the fight and seeing Jael run off in perfect health gave me some delight to warm my body, but I still needed the added moisture.

I lay on my side and opened one leg until it touched the top of the passage, pressing the bulb into my sex without delay. It burned a little as I stretched, but soon I had it seated, and I whispered the command word.

The attachment and rush of pleasure was not much diminished for the lack of foreplay. Instead of lying there stroking it, however, I hurriedly pulled up my leathers and secured them, repositioned my belt, and marveled what it felt like to have this live magic straining to be released.

My new limb pressed scalding hot against my belly and formed a visible ridge beneath my clothes. It made me want to crawl faster.

Now. Go after this … this …

I breathed raggedly for a few moments, and after recognizing the scent of the stone, I tried to think past the rising lust and watch the tunnel around me. My eyes adjusted, my vision seemed to shift a little, and I saw the scrapes left by pickaxes and chisels.

~Not fresh but not old, maybe a score of turns. There are several of these in caverns between here and Rothlech Deep. For emergencies like this one.~

It would lead to an underground source of water and another chance to lose any pursuit. I gritted my teeth against the persistent distraction of a randy cock, kept moving. She didn't have to cover more than a mark of crawlspace before she'd reach the water and vanish.

I slithered along as quick and quiet as I could, my only goal to keep moving forward. Soon, I heard the Dwarf scrabbling up ahead, breathing heavily and not nearly as silent as I was. I could smell the heat coming from her ore-dusted skin.

~I will catch her, and I will grab her, hold her down. She'll give me relief.~

I wanted to snort. Oh, yes, indeed. She had large muscles in her arms and legs from working for the males in the forges every cycle of her life. Imagine a slender Elf wrestling with her in a small space and see if that turned out any better for me than it did the last time.

I wondered exactly what I planned to do once I caught up.

~Just touch her, touch her skin.~

Then what? There was no response. I didn't know.

I spotted the trap hatch above my head immediately, as if I knew it should be there. It was a simple trap, but potentially nasty. I could hear as something slapped a bare tail against the enclosure. Something poisonous was in there and ready for when I snagged that impossibly thin metal wire that she'd set up as she passed by this spot.

I reached into a pouch and pulled out a small metal wedge that I could either press into softer substances or hammer into stone using the pommel of my dagger. I didn't want noise, so I forced it in at an angle through the material that made up the hatch door itself and the filler they'd used to camouflage it.

Somehow, I hit the sweet spot, and it sealed the hatch closed. Now I could remove that wire which I could neither crawl under nor over, and I continued past unmolested.

~*Foolish Tugren. Just wait.*~

My quarry had paused up ahead to see what happened with the trap. It took her too long to determine that I'd somehow gotten past it without tripping it, and I could make out the smooth, bald line of her round head before she saw me and uttered a sound of surprise.

My muscles seemed to explode at the noise, in a surge I would not have tried without the hard prick pulsing against my abdomen, but it surprised her as well. She got one good kick — a hard one — to my side before I grabbed her leg, hauled myself up and threw my relatively slight weight on top of her.

Stupid!

Tragar impulses guided me.

In the proper body, the male's weight on its own would have prevented her from doing much. My mass was awkward for her but nowhere near dense enough to keep her from throwing me off and against the stone. She prepared to do just that when my *real* training kicked in.

I wanted to live.

I had a blood-stained dagger out and in front of her face, very close to her blank, white eye, just before she could throw me off.

"*Shh,*" I said aloud. "*One scratch. All it shall take.*"

I was telling the truth, and she knew it. Something else shocked her into stillness, but only when she spoke did I realize what it was.

"*Wh-why have you not already, Davrin?*" she hissed, as wary as she should have been with the poison dagger so close.

I'd understood her so clearly, and she had understood me. It hadn't been the trade language. I'd spoken in her tongue. Her expression changed as my weight shifted, settling on her so our joints didn't grind together, to a look of dawning horror as she felt my erection.

"*Are you … man or woman?*" she asked.

I half-smiled and didn't enlighten her, only pressed the Feldeu into her and rubbed against her. It felt good, and she didn't smell so greasy as the male Tragar. She had no hairy beard; indeed, it looked as though she did not have any hair at all: not on her head, her cheeks or chin, not on her bare arms or the backs of her hands.

She was smooth, dark-skinned but lighter than my own, with strong features — the heavy jaw, cheeks, and brow, plus the large nose and prominent lips common to the Tragar. She should be ugly to my eyes.

She wasn't.

My favorite quality was the incredible plushness of her breasts — much larger than mine and soft enough on which to lay my head down and sleep, though I would never risk that. Almost everything about her was hard from many turns of physical labor, except for those breasts. Something told me she was a young but fully-grown Tragar, and comely for her race.

In fact, Kain knew she had worked for thirty-three turns so far.

"Unnatural creature!" she exclaimed in a hoarse whisper, stiffening beneath my next dry hump. *"Get off me — !"*

"Be still, Tugren," I commanded in a tone unfamiliar to me, but she stopped her struggle immediately. I was surprised at her obedience, though I felt no discomfort or uncertainty weaponizing my cock so soon. I should have.

~*Tugren.*~

The last time I heard that word, I was fucking Gaelan. Wearing this Feldeu. I remembered why Kain had been where we'd first met; I knew Jael was in danger.

I tried again to reach for a meaning of the word.

"Kill me or release me, but be done with it," the Tragar interrupted. She seemed to recall that she wasn't required to obey me. *"I will fight to my last breath than endure your sick torture, Blood Elf!"*

That was one opinion where we differed quite strongly. Not that I felt the need to debate that with her. I was comfortable lying atop of her, my Feldeu pressing against her inner thigh and her breasts pleasantly overwhelming mine.

I hadn't yet touched her skin, I realized, though the heat of it was building between us in the small space. My gloves and uniform alone prevented contact because, out of her armor, she wore a short-sleeved leather work tunic. Her thick, muscled arms were exposed, as was her bald head.

"*Why did you run?*" I asked, still speaking fluent as I watched her eyes and face.

She trembled beneath me. I could smell her fear. Sensed her indecision.

"*You and six others chased a Sivaraus Elf,*" I prodded. "*I never saw you, so you ran before I arrived to stop them. Why?*"

The female shook her head defiantly.

"*You will answer every question I have, Tugren, or I numb you from the neck down.*"

I gestured with my tainted blade in front of her eyes. She was scared but did not focus on my question. Perhaps she required more detail to understand.

"*If this blade pricks you, you will have to watch every 'unnatural' thing I do to your body and not be able to lift one finger against me. It will only hurt after the poison wears off and you remain alive. Until then, you'll feel nothing while seeing everything.*"

The threat hit her very deep; her broad face flinched, and her blank, white eyes watched my mouth moving. I felt the flash of heat flood her body, heard her heart rate double.

"*Y-you intend this either way, Elf,*" she accused.

"*Maybe not,*" I said, believing I was telling the truth. "*If you talk with me.*"

~*I can't face you like this. No ...* ~

I tilted my head, hearing that inside, not out. "*You **are** a mind-lifter, ya?*"

Her white eyes moistened, blinked. She nodded.

"*Why did you run, Tugren?*" I asked again with force.

Her muscles were rock hard, quivering with tension. She tried. She did try.

"*I-I thought I heard ...*" She swallowed, her throat locking up; it looked painful. "*The kregburen saw a naked Elf. Insane, running toward us. They*" *expected more and were right.*"

"*That does not explain why you ran before the fun began, Tugren.*"

"*Stop calling me this!*" the Tragar cried, anger making her face bright in the blackness. "*I am not your Tugren! I will not be again! I'll fight you!*"

At last, a meaning found purchase in my mind. A Tugren was like a consort and a servant together but more strongly bound. Ritualized. Restricted. Entirely so a *kregbur*, a digging fighter, could know for certain that *he* was the sire of any children that came from her womb. Him, and no other male.

It took a lot of work and a lot of paranoia to make certain of that. Most didn't want to know how often they failed.

Tugren. I shook my head; Gaelan was not that. She could not be a bound consort or servant who bore me children; this had confused Kain as she begged me to fuck her.

Maybe it could also mean whoever submitted their body to another? The one intended to be used was the Tugren, whether for pleasure or breeding. Maybe either counted.

I was quiet thinking about this, and the female Dwarf shuddered once. I heard her breath catch on a surge of emotion.

"*Why did you run?*" I asked for the third and final time.

"*I sensed you,*" she whispered. "*It must have been you. I hear his voice in your mind.*"

"*Who is 'he'?*" I asked, dreading this to be a mistake, but I still needed … something. Information. Some connection.

I received that in plenty.

"*Kain,*" she said, white eyes unblinking. "*It is you, ya?*"

Her voice was soft. Submissive.

~*She knows. She knows me. She still wants to please me.*~

The Tragar stiffened as my dagger wavered closer to her skin, and my other hand closed on one of her large breasts. I growled low in my throat, fondled the tit absently as the heat in my groin generated sweat between us. Her scent was pleasant to me. Her presence, a comfort.

Even though she had run away from me.

"*Stop,*" she whispered. "*Tell me what else you want, Davrin, you said you would not ..."*

~Help me, Lana.~

She fell silent after that plea. Rightly so.

~Free me. Don't leave me here. Take me into yourself, find me a new body.~

Her revulsion was putrid in our eye contact. Her thoughts, surging raw and honest, were so bitter of a backlash that I sucked in a startled breath.

~Never!~ the bald female sent back. *~You deserve this, Kain! I don't know how the Black Elves did this, but I'm glad it happened!~*

~Shut your mouth!~

I had always known she had never enjoyed me, though we never said it. The Tugren submitted, bent over when I told her to, or spread her thighs while on her back. As was my right. She was passive, a warm sheath to hold my pole when it ached. Because if she didn't, she was beaten. She had never questioned, never fought back.

Now she resists? Now she hurls venom at me? What changed in so short a time?

~Talk with me.~

I felt memories swirl and mix in a dark spread of stone, metal, and smoke. Her naked, curvaceous body was Kain's to use as he saw fit, and he worked her very hard, in many ways. She expected his brutality, and this proved to the other *kregbur* that Kain's Mind-Lifter Wife was no weakling, while he was still powerful enough to control her.

Especially with *her* gift of the mind.

~No longer can you control me! You're dead, Kain! You're dead!~

Like a crossbow triggered, I relived that death yet again, and Lana saw it. She cried out in disgust and horror at the way that it had happened.

~What did they do to you?! Why?~

Psychic hooks snagged hold of my memories, my *real* memories of my Sisterhood trials which led to it: the ritual on the altar, the divine magic and fever-pitch lust that sang a song entirely alien to the psionic Dwarf.

My life was the tale of horror and dread Lana had been told to expect of my race. I *was* the very nightmare whispered about the Davrin Queen and her Magus Inquisitors. Fear and hatred were clear, true, and justified in the sequestered female's fracturing mind.

I was not sane to them, and, like all the other Blood Elves, I *relished* living that state.

~How can you?!~ Lana screamed. *~How can you not know what the next waking will bring?~*

I knew what she meant. She spoke to Sirana, the child. Sirana, the Noble. The Red Sister.

Lana saw the continuous plots and cruel, extended effects of Davrin magic, magic which no other race possessed, and how we used it against each other ... this frightened the Tragar to her core. It churned her vitals, this thought of it never stopping, the rules changing all the time.

And I hadn't even grown up in the thick of it.

~At least our beatings and deaths are direct and expected!~ the Tragar claimed.

I couldn't help but laugh, an unsettling sound which filled the crawl-space of our heads. In return, I saw her upbringing, her cyclical waking moments, filled with control and fear. Harshly physical and immediate, but no different from mine in its tenant: the stronger will overwhelms the weaker.

Those most brawny in the ways which matter make the rules. Endurance, fortitude, stubborn determination. Those with the will to work another cycle, to worship a violent, uncaring Chief who granted no mercy to the weak. The Chief's Tragar crawled over the bodies of the dead to find their place, to find the ore, the water, and the food.

Find the ore ...

I saw what it looked like, at last. Thick, hard-worked hands dug it out of hardest stone.

In true light, the ore was the deepest blue.

~Do you have any? I must find it for my Elders.~

Tears leaking out of Lana's white eyes. Again, she shook her head in defiance.

"You deserve this as well, Davrin. For killing my new Vungren."

I did not have to try to understand that word. The male counterpart to the Tugren; the dominant, the one in control. Kain had been her first Vungren, but I knew, I could *feel* how Lana had much preferred the second.

She had enjoyed him even before Kain disappeared. I saw it in her mind: her silent pleasure-peak had come for the first time in her life when this other *kregbur* had his cock patiently stretching her dirt hole, teasing her in slow, full strokes.

Unlike Kain's painful pounding as he made her wail for other males to hear outside their burrow.

~That weakling left his leavings in her shitter? They ... these two may have been doing it even while my own cock was buried between a spider-slattern's narrow buttocks!~

How I relived that pounding. Vividly.

Climaxing from a stubby, fat, Dwarven meatpole.

I had come because I *was* insane at the time.

"Cheating whore!" I hissed aloud, shaking my head. *~I cannot stay! Separate us! Free me, now!~*

Lana's eyes widened, still wary of the stained dagger held by a red glove, so close to her eye. I wouldn't accept her refusal; I moved the blade to the side and leaned down to kiss her. So much flesh to her lips, soft and full. It felt like I pleasured a swollen, highly aroused set of female netherlips.

~Just touch her, touch her skin.~

A flash in the back of my skull caused an even greater disconnect between my mind and my body. Suddenly, I was aware of Lana formless, nude in different way altogether, both familiar and foreign as Kain forced the merging of our consciousness together.

The first feelings to pierce through the veil were grief, denial, and fear. There were no actual words, no language, but I still struggled to understand them, forcing them into some type of translation so I would not fall irreparably insane in that very instant.

~Confess, Wife! Tell me every filthy thing you did with him after I left!~

~It's mine! You're only a ghost, Kain, an echo! I won't help an echo, I won't be tricked! You deserved this punishment! You earned it! Stay out!~

I became enraged; it was hot and immediate. Burning so hot, I had to strip off her clothes, make her yielding holes vulnerable.

~No! You're dead! No, please! Don't! Stop!~

~Be still and accept me! Do your duty and free me!~

In the middle of the struggle, intense pleasure flooded through our connection. I felt it, I shared it, but in her I recognized the shock and denial, because I'd felt it our last time together, too. A prick she very much didn't want had invaded her body.

My prick.

Serves the cheating wisp right!

I surfaced only enough to feel the hard stone scraping my knees as I pushed forward, her trousers stretched tight across her ankles and partly in the way as I scrabbled to settle myself between her thighs. Overbalanced, I flopped down on her breasts. I felt her body's dryness and discomfort, and the impulse was there to chastise her for not being ready for me. She'd had plenty of warning that I was ready for her, how dare she try to refuse me?

~I'm glad you're dead, Kain, I'm glad!~ Pure, hateful emotion surged balefully between us. *~It brings me rare joy that a stronger female killed you with your prick hanging out!~*

~The Sloppy-Second was no better,~ I sneered, both insulted and with an odd urge to laugh in pure satisfaction. *~He died with great dignity. Hooked in the balls by the very Davrin he hunted, with his own barb!~*

The surge of genuine grief, feared but now confirmed, infuriated me. Made me jealous, possessive. My pride was wounded, and all I wanted to do was make her sorry she'd said she felt more for him than me. I thrust harder and she strained; spikes of pain jumped between us — I wallowed in it, knowing it meant she received her punishment. So much better than coupling with a non-psion where I couldn't feel it so clearly.

She was my prize, not his. Mine.

~You're mine … ~

~No — ~

~MINE!~

~What have I done? You're not Kain!~ the Dwarf pleaded. *~Don't drown*

in the echo! I'm sorry, Davrin! He's not the pure Will! **You** *are!~*

I kept fucking her harder, hurting her. I'd strangle the very breath of the cheating, ungrateful Tugren when I was done and my male seed dribbled out of her hole—

~Sirana! R-Red Sister! Listen to me, you must remember!~ Lana took a great risk to wrench loose a memory foreign to her. *~Please, tell me. Who is this?~*

I slowed down my pace, a bit of warmth returning to my cold chest. Who?

~He is Micraen. My first bua. The first eve I wasn't alone when I awoke at the Palace.~

Lana nodded, unquestioning. *~And him?~*

Ohhh, Goddess.

The Royal Consort at the Worship Ball.

~Auslan. My hidden treasure … So beautiful.~

Then she switched my focus to another male. *~And him. This bua. Who?~*

~Callitro.~

The Wizard's Tower. I had to go back for something.

I wanted to return.

~He makes me something. A gift. I want him again.~

~Yes. These buas are all treasures, I see.~

Lana held and soothed me, cooled the fever; she stopped a rise leading to a violent murder. Our struggle eased, and her pain stopped crackling through my head. I stopped, and we were breathless, me lying atop her. Still connected in body and mind.

~So many mates,~ she murmured. *~All of your own choosing, Davrin. Tell me, why so many?~*

~Fun.~

I knew she was confused by that. *~And … ?~*

~Desire. Challenge. I want them.~

~Not for children?~

I laughed inside our head. *~A different challenge. My Elders bet I will avoid children. The Priestesses bet I won't.~*

~*Strange choice.*~

~*Games. Our Goddess commands that we play.*~

~*I have heard. I think a Tragar would be driven mad in such play, to take on the death-memory of a Davrin. You, Sirana, have taken the memory of Kain and live with it. You shall continue living.*~

A fearful surge tried to come up as I gripped her harder. My mind's voice deepened to Kain's. ~*Surely there must be something you can do, Tugren!*~

Lana painted my long line of buas across our linked minds again like a thick blanket, and Kain's maleness was smothered. It was Sirana with whom she communicated, not her old Vungren.

~*It's not Kain in your mind.*~ She seemed to be thinking to herself, no longer panicked or spouting mental vitriol. ~*It's not possession. Just a shard causing a wound not healed. I feel shame for talking back to it, for making him real again. Kain is dead, and I'm well rid of the middens he was.*~

She spoke as though to smooth out the hot spot in my head while her fingers touched my hair. Inside, it felt like different fingers were spreading and patting it down like damp clay. Her body shifted with discomfort, and I became aware enough to withdraw the Feldeu from her cunt without climaxing. She sighed in relief that I was not pressing so deep.

For the first time when under magic's influence, I did not feel the need. I was not driven, not compelled to seek completion. I could still feel its heat, its stiffness, but it was controlled. I controlled it. I had hesitated to believe this was possible.

~*You absorb the shard, Sirana. In time, you will be well.*~

I believed her, but Lana's thought felt tired, as if she'd given up and submitted once more. As she had been doing for her whole life.

~*That thing attached to you ... is helping you but, with time, you will not need it. The shard loses its cohesion and will become one with you. You understand that no Tragar would want to dissolve into chaos.*~

Cautiously, I nodded. ~*He died that way.*~

~*Yes. He knew it as he died.*~ Lana's thick, full lips turned upward in satisfaction. Her tone held no accusation whatsoever, no regret. ~*And he is dead, Sirana. You killed him.*~

Only this Mind-Lifter and me within this crawlspace. No one else. I was myself and always would be.

Lana spoke with her physical voice then. It was hoarse, wheezing, and I heard that she wanted to weep. *"Kill me now, Blood Sister. For my help, I beg you … make it quick and clean. No magic. No further torment."*

I had to work to see the details around us with my own eyes. Pants down, skin scraped, weapons askew, moisture and heat pressed between bare thighs. I still gripped my poison dagger in one gloved hand and the other held her throat.

"Why?" I asked, easing the pressure on her windpipe so she could speak more easily.

"I know too much about you."

She could not have been more accurate if she had pinned a beetle with a dart from twenty paces. Only one of us could leave this tunnel, but I was confused at her lack of spirit after our first contact and her bold words.

"You don't want to fight for the chance to live?" I asked, prepared for a bait and switch. *"You've taken it as a foregone conclusion it will be me who walks away?"*

"My second Vungren is dead, and I have no protection now," she whispered, blank eyes not seeming to see me as her face fell to passiveness. *"There is nowhere to go."*

"Wouldn't your knowledge of me be of some worth to them? A bargaining coin for your life?"

She shook her head. *"The men would not believe me. And they do not deserve to have what I know. I will miss my Vungren too much, and I am tired, Davrin. I am ready to stop working."*

Ready to stop.

To say such a thing back at her Stronghold, I knew, would mean the Chief would oblige her only after a sound whipping and wringing the last bit of work that he could from her hands and arms and back. Digging stone, moving any cart or crate that needed to be moved. She'd stop working only when her malnourished body failed her for the last time.

"For my help," she said again, *"make it quick and clean."*

I could grant her that, yes. And once I did, the entire group would be dealt with according to my mission.

"Have you any of that blue ore?" I asked.

Lana shook her head, face hardening. *"We never found all of Kain's old sign. But the Chief might bid us return. That none of us return now means there will be more Tragar next time."*

I nodded. I still pressed the Feldeu to her thigh, and I shifted on top of her clumsily. She winced and cursed at me, trying to close her legs against the false phallus, and it was apparent that her muscles were cramped. I got off her, crouched so my head and shoulders barely missed the low ceiling, and I scooted backward from her, placing my blade behind me to tug up my leathers and cinch my loosened belt. I would have to double-check all my pouches again before leaving here.

Lana sat up, pulling up her pants, and watched as I gave a cursory cleaning to my dagger before sheathing it. She glared at me, her white eyes flashing dangerously.

"You will not kill me, Red Sister? You should, or I will kill you."

"I already did," I replied. *"It won't take long."*

The Dwarf blinked and reached to the side of her neck with her bare hand; I could see in her face the moment she felt the sting of the scratch. Lana withdrew her hand and saw the blood on her fingers.

"You said this poison would ... s-stay my life ... to watch the harm you do."

I shrugged. *"I lied. It will kill you instead. Surprised?"*

Lana shook her head in the negative, even as the deep-seated fear of dying was clear on her face. I sensed a surge of mental threat in the tunnel and moved fast. I retreated as fast as I could scramble. I did not want to be anywhere near another psion at her moment of death.

I left the psion to suffocate as the poison seized her muscles and, eventually, her lungs.

CHAPTER 17

So focused was I on getting out before Lana died that I hauled myself up and out without checking the exit. It must have looked as if something was biting my toes.

"Sirana?"

I took Panagan's voice — and her genuine surprise — as a peace sign, as she had remained waiting at the mouth of the tunnel. Belatedly I realized the Feldeu was still between my legs, straining my pants, and now I couldn't remove it with Panagan watching. I grabbed my cloak where I'd stuffed it for the added cover against that hard ridge and tried not to be distracted by a magic erection rubbing against soft leather.

What in the Abyss happened down here? the archer demanded with loud hands.

Did you hear anything? I asked first.

Distant Tragar tongue, two voices. Were there more down there? She looked me over; I knew I was disheveled. *You are injured?*

Mild, and yes, another lay in wait, I responded, glad she couldn't understand the Grey Dwarf language. Even more interesting that she hadn't been able to tell it was me. *The Tragar planned to escape with one left behind to watch their mounts.*

And you killed them both? she asked earnestly. *I saw none surface, though I paced this entire cavern.★

　★Both poisoned, dead,★ I affirmed. ★No witnesses to tell tales.★

　★Grab any proof? Ears, fingers, organs?★

Fuck.

I shook my head. ★Dangerous to touch psions when they die. But you can check the edge of my dagger for Dwarf blood.★

Panagan agreed and gestured that I show her my blade. She gripped my wrist to hold it steady once it was unsheathed and sprinkled a bit of powder on it while murmuring a word. There was a reaction which I assumed she could read, as she narrowed her eyes at mine before either deciding to believe me or figuring my Elder could weigh the burden of proof herself. For certain, she wasn't going down in that crawlspace to check on what I claimed.

　★We catch the recruit if she makes it to the border,★ she signed.

　★Impossible,★ I complained. ★Her lead is too large.★

Panagan rolled her eyes. ★Back to the jump circle. We'll arrive ahead to lay in wait.★

I blinked. ★Can you use it?★

The archer nodded. ★One time. Elder gave me a home gem.★

Abrupt excitement flooded my belly as my eyes widened. ★And if we catch her?★

Panagan was still displeased with my actions; her eyes flicked to the side.

Probably thinking of the Prime.

　★Option to fuck her before the others, or skip it and turn her in.★ Now the archer smirked a little. ★Hasn't been that long since your turn. Thought you'd remember.★

For the next few ticks I imagined "initiating" Jael as had been done with me.

After the Sathoet attacked her at her House. After the Prime beat her up and took her in for more of the same. After nearly dying from blood loss and a Tragar hook and chain ...

Gaelan never knew all I'd already gone through when she'd caught up with me, but I supposed it had been enough to "go easy." I had the insight to know even more about this young recruit, and her life was still at risk for my having given her my healing potion, regardless of her own efforts.

How much must a novice take before she proves tough enough to be a Red Sister?

Though I questioned, I knew Rausery would say: *As much as she can.*

We had to retrace our steps past the scene of the bloody battle. Scavengers had already arrived and were spreading the meat, bones, and tools, but nothing larger than us or half as intelligent was among them. They growled a threat to defend their find, and when we passed on the edge without interest, they returned to eating and dragging carcasses away.

Returning down the tunnel where I'd felt Kain's ghost, I was afraid. I did my best to hide it from Panagan, breathing slow and determined not to lose my senses once again. My magical cock remained hard in my pants and my mind drifted to how Jael's body might feel wrapped around it.

My Sister. Not his Tugren.

If we caught up to her, we would have the option to fuck her first.

I'll take it.

Heart pounding louder than I would have wished, I made it through without drowning in memory. I knew where we stood. I smelled Panagan's scent, though I recognized where I was, where I'd killed him.

I glimpsed a raw, beautiful blue out of the corner of my eye and paused.

~*There it is. Just beneath the surface. I need a pickaxe or a chisel ...* ~

Come on! Panagan's fingers rapped my shoulder.

I'd ruin my blade's edge using it as a poor substitute, but I had nothing else. I drew it and signed, *My Elder wants this.*

Wants what?

Dwarf stone. We retrieve some, it's protection against the Prime's wrath.

Fucking rock?

She's a Sorceress, archer. She told me she wanted this.

Though aggravated, Panagan aided me after I'd rushed to the spot, tinkering with places soft and brittle to work some of it out of the crevice. It was clear that the stone wasn't like sapphire to Panagan's eyes as it was to mine, but the mage could at least tell it was a true element over basic bedrock. She didn't sign that I was crazy, and she pocketed a piece herself. I noted where.

Done? At last?

I nodded. *Let us catch her.*

Observing the sentries, Panagan and I knew that Jael had stopped somewhere short of the gate. Perhaps the recruit was still working out how to cross the border unseen and unseized. Meanwhile, we had used the jump circle and were on the side of Sivaraus already. Unlike the Dwarven confrontation with which the recruit had collided, we made it in time to prevent the one with the sentries.

If she makes it to the border, we grab her.

I understood now that this was enough. Jael didn't have to make it past the sentries, the wards, the obstacles and into Sivaraus proper. Neither had I, during my test. That I discovered that tunnel to swim through and come out within the Great Cavern, finding Auslan on a farm of solitude, was something which surprised the Red Sisters, Gaelan in particular.

It's gone now, Panagan had told me when I suggested using it to approach Jael from behind. *The Prime ordered it sealed after Elder Rausery told her how you got in. House D'Verin was required either to raze that outlying hovel or staff it properly with Guardsvrin. I heard some sacrificial Noble Daughter was fucked for the negligence in place of the Matron.*

I smirked. Outwitting my seekers held its own satisfaction for me but hearing that the Matron could buy her way out of a Red Sister assfuck did not surprise.

Did the Matron choose to raze it or guard it? I asked.

Guard it. You think they'll give up even that spit-sized plot of land to the bordering House?

Of course not.

Boast confidence to the border keepers, the archer signed to me. *We tell them to, and the sentries will let us through.*

My grin widened in the dark. My first solution to any problem had never been to demand others to obey me — that had been Jilrina's method — and I still wasn't used to the idea that I could order most of our people's defenses around.

But I held that power now. If I needed it.

I watched Panagan the first time, noted which sign she used to gain the mage-captain's attention, and how she phrased it. I stood bold and stern as her flanking Sister, maybe mimicking Jaunda a little. Except for the officer, the Guardsvrin were all caits not much older than me, and their eyes widened to see us here. I could smell a change in the air.

They are afraid. Worried it is one of them we've come for.

It didn't occur to me to wonder whether any of them had specific reason to believe so; I wasn't looking for it. I was looking ahead. For Jael.

There's a Davrin out there, Red Sister? the mage-captain asked with appropriate caution, not a slant of her hand toward skepticism.

Yes, Panagan commanded the mage-captain. *Suspend and open the Gate, only a sliver's width.*

This was not a simple, one-step action, from what I understood. Suspending the Wards on a giant metal door was akin to unfurling a layered work of art made entirely of many-colored spider silks in exactly the right order and holding them there until one was ready to drop them down again. I imagined a mage hoped it didn't become tangled.

The captain remained calm; she needed the aid of two other subordinates and one peer, and Panagan and I needed to be patient before they could open the Main Gate to Sivaraus even a little bit, just enough for us to slip through. The moment we were on the outside again, we bolted into the black without a foot fall's echo.

Panagan found a spot where we could hole up and wait for sign. Comfortably I crouched down with her, waiting for long enough that I felt for the raw stones in my pouch again, feeling the shapes. It helped my patience, aided my focus. No caravans passed by in the time we waited; nothing of size wandered through. The huge tunnel was largely empty.

Just us and the frogs, rodents, and pincer worms.

Finally, there was Jael.

I was sure it was her. I sensed exhaustion, a will worn down to a nub. Uncertainty bled out like a deep wound. A lost sense of direction. I knew how that felt. I had thought it was a good idea to try to steal my way back to the Palace. Jael didn't even have that as a goal.

What? the archer signed as I lifted my chin and turned my head toward the wilderness.

She's coming, I replied.

Panagan made a face in the dark, irritably turning her own senses in that direction. I waited through the pause. *How do you know?*

I hear her coming.

Sort of the truth.

My Sister blinked twice, all astonished skepticism and annoyance, but she waited long enough to finally get that physical proof she sought.

Right, she acknowledged, pulling out a familiar wave of cloth, which she draped over her knee. *We seize her. Put the black bag on her head to hide her face. Take her through the Gate as a prisoner. You help me get her to a holding spot not far away, I'll show you. I want to spear her ass first. It's my right. You can go second, if you want.*

I nodded, though now reluctant and bewildered at this response. I had enjoyed the mental image not long ago of seducing the naked scrapper, of experiencing her body pumped up with spirit, having survived the danger that she had. I imagined making the Aurenthin cum before the other Sisters got her, like I had Reishel and Gaelan, but realized that wasn't realistic with the archer here.

Panagan wanted to mount her as a status symbol only, and she would enforce rank. I also knew exactly from whom she had learned that focus. My netherhole and I'd suffered under Thena's rule of caits for three straight cycles, and I'd wanted to kill her, to kill all four of them, Panagan included. I wouldn't be waiting for Jael now if I had. If Jaunda and Gaelan hadn't come to pull me out of their room.

I pursed my lips. *Gonna make it hurt?*

The elder frowned at me. *Haven't learned, Sister? It's what we do.*

I haven't tortured a new Sister yet, archer, I returned, mouth askew. *Just been on the other side.*

So?

So Gaelan fucked me when she captured me, but didn't make it hurt.

Panagan made an ugly face. *So?*

So, it made me curious about the Red Sisters. Jael will be the same.

You were under the influence of Priestesses. Jael's not.

She's already taken the Prime and a hoard of Sathoet. What's the point trying to top that?

*Speaking of which. We've got a bigger problem: your healing potion *and* the Prime.*

I blinked, leaned back, repulsed. *Will you try to 'undo' the healing on Jael?*

I saw white teeth flash in a snarl, and the archer nearly barked with her hands. *Wouldn't work anyway, and it doesn't have to hurt, but unavoidable if she struggles too much. She should know that by now! The croot just has to learn her place.*

Somehow, I didn't think Jael would care. New threat, new fight. Simple as that.

*What if we talk — * I began, but Panagan cut me off.

She's here!

I held still. Silent. I spotted the vague shape of living Radiants stepping out of the pitch darkness. Jael's feet were sore, I could tell, but she moved normally otherwise. She hadn't run into anything else trying to take her life. She had made it close to the border, had found the way back to Sivaraus. We crouched, ready to lunge as we watched for other signs of interference, but nothing raised its head by the time we were prepared to spring our trap.

Finally, we grabbed her, and her furious roar filled the tunnel.

"Rraugh! Let me go!!"

Panagan took her wind by punching her gut. I slipped the black hood over her head, cinched it closed. It took both of us to bind her wrists behind her back as she kicked and struggled despite not being able to breathe. That tactic caught up with her and she went limp when she could no longer gain enough air through the sack.

"Come on, grab her ankles," Panagan huffed, looping arms under Jael's pits and clasping her hands beneath the recruit's naked breasts.

I did better than that, lifting Jael's butt off the ground with the archer by hooking my arms behind her knees. This close, we could both walk forward to the Main Gate, if turned slightly sideways, and I could sneak a glance down between Jael's open thighs now and then, admiring the lay of Radiants that was her white pubic fur.

Don't get too distracted now.

Jael was partly aware, emitting a mix of groans and growls as Panagan and I brought her through the Gate with the help of the mage-captain and her sentries.

"Sisters," she acknowledged with a salute, eyeing the mysterious Davrin we hauled in. There was a tentative question in her tone, but she likely knew she'd get no answer.

"Well done, Captain," Panagan said. "May the Valsharess favor your vigilance."

We left the Gate with our prize, safer within the Great Cavern itself as Panagan showed me where yet another cache lay for the Sisterhood's use. Not much different than the one to which Gaelan had taken me, perhaps a little smaller. It had the same long, low entrance, but this one required a boulder to be moved with a spell or a Red Sister item — one I might be awarded sometime after I'd earned it.

Interrogation implements and restraints had been stationed here as well, plus a source of water. First focus for me, however, was the one spot we could kneel or lie down that wasn't on bare stone: a cool, dusty chaise for a Red Sister to lounge.

Jael seemed very confused when her pert tits rested flat against the firm-stuffed platform. I straddled her back, facing her ass and bound hands, and sat down on her shoulder blades, rubbing my still-present erection against her back as I held the in-curve of her waist tight with both gloved hands. Then, I reached behind me to loosen and tug off the black bag so she could breathe better.

Meanwhile, Panagan had lit a smokeless torch, offering a small light so our capture could see the other places in the room she could be bound, instead of where the comfy place she was with me. I watched as Panagan eagerly loosened her leathers, preparing her own Feldeu.

"Goddess, just stop," Jael wheezed, despair and aggression mixing in an odd tone through her dry mouth. "*M-More* of this shit? Why didn't you j-just tackle me back with the Dwarf corpses!"

"Calm, Jael," I said. "Try to think."

Panagan raised an eyebrow at me, a warning not to guide as she stepped up with a glossy, black phallus in place. She shoved Jael's ankles apart and stepped between her legs, closer to the chaise. Jael lay on her stomach, helpless, squealed in anger and tried to twist abruptly, a vain hope to throw me off. I was prepared; Jaunda had taught me well, and the recruit was still in place when Panagan reached out to squeeze the recruit's buttocks, parting them to look at her target in the light.

I recognized the leer on the archer's face.

"Wait," I said. "We have some time, right?"

"Not much." Panagan caressed her prick with one hand, held Jael's buttock with the other as one knee hit the chaise. "We should hurry."

She gave me a look as she spoke, suggesting that I make space.

"I don't see why," I said. "We report and turn her in to the Elders when we're good and ready, right?"

She peered at me with resentment that I was eating time talking about this, but I knew Jael beneath me was listening closely.

"Let me prepare her asshole for you, Panagan," I offered.

"Why bother?"

Jael growled underneath me.

"Because it's different," I said. "I bet I can make her cum."

Panagan tilted her head up and laughed. That made me return a smile.

"If I do," I wagered, "then we talk what to do about the Prime after you're satisfied. I have an idea how to get both Rausery and D'Shea to back us. Something the Sorceress taught me."

"What? Is this something to do with — ?"

"She cums. You cum. *Then* I tell you."

"Fuck you, Sirana."

A chuckle slipped out of me as I moved my crotch along the spine of our new meat; a little farther forward and I could lay my cock in Jael's hands. "Come on, Panagan. My Lead always says it's easier to talk strategy with a clear head, and fucking clears hers. Get off on her ass while you can but let me make her pliable first."

"What about you? Are you going to spit-roast her with me?"

Heh. Jael bites, no doubt.

"I'll wait," I said. "Make sure you're not interrupted."

Panagan glanced down at the straining rod inside my leathers. "When did you get that, anyway?"

I winked, leaned forward, and spit a glob of saliva right on Jael's tight, newly healed pucker. Dead center. She moaned in angry dread, the crinkled muscle flexing, having the side benefit of spreading the lubricant around. My elder Sister watched with easy fascination and desire.

The archer nudged the recruit's bare thigh with her knee and spoke to her. "You're quiet for once, cait."

Jael wasn't *that* quiet. Her breath was ragged as she struggled for enough air under my ass, her head turned to the side and cheek pressed to the chaise. Her fingers clutched and clawed at empty space, and a startled moan slipped out of her mouth as I reached forward to rub my fingertip in a circle around her netherhole, spreading my spit a bit more. My finger poked inside, just a little, and she whimpered, not eager to be sodomized yet again.

No wonder. It's been almost a span since we grabbed her from her House.

More important, however, Jael lay still. She listened to me, as I had to Gaelan. I could tell she was biting her lip to keep from talking back to Panagan when the Red Sister prodded her twice more about fighting yet another inevitable prick up her ass.

"Well?" I asked my Sister. "Deal?"

Thank Goddess, Panagan was a little curious than others.

"Fine. Deal."

"I make her cum by myself," I clarified.

"Fine," she grunted again. "Don't draw it out too long. We don't want a Lead or Lunent sent out to find us."

"I imagine they'd be irritated."

Panagan nodded. "Probably ass-fuck us both before dragging the croot away."

"Don't worry. I'll use *all* my tricks. I've already slurped one climax out of this one's holes when they were raw, and right now, she's fresh."

"Yes, so I heard."

Panagan backed away, pulled up a stool, and got comfortable to watch, lightly stroking her length. "So. Dive in, cuntsucker. Show me what you've learned since you burst your head and needed Jaunda to put it on straight again."

Yeah. Been working on that ever since.

"Sure, Sister." I grinned. "You got it."

Leading to this point as we talked, I had been stroking Jael's naked body with my warm gloves, smoothing her flanks, her ass, and thighs, slipping fingers underneath as far as I could to caress her belly. Some of the tension had leaked out of our new catch as I did this, even more when Panagan moved away, and I hoped Jael was more receptive now. At least, her skin would be awake and sensitive.

Without speaking, I coaxed Jael into position on her knees, face down and her ass up, and turned us perpendicular to the chaise. This allowed her head to hang off the edge toward the stone floor, her spine held in a straighter line as I trapped her upper body and arms in a firm hold between my thighs.

Next, with my ankles crossed and knees tight against her sides, her head just escaped my buttocks, and she wouldn't fall off. If I passed gas, it would flit right by her nose. Jael made several irritated noises and ultimately disliked her position, I could tell.

But she isn't fighting.

Now I had the freedom to use my hands, which I would need to coax her to climax without triggering a stubborn streak that I wondered might grow to be legendary.

If she survived long enough.

I grinned with anticipation, reveling in the feeling of kinship along with the tidy shape of her netherlips. I twisted my spine slightly, whispered down toward her ear.

"I can't wait to taste your ass again. Enjoy what I've learned, scrapper, and maybe you can pay me back."

Jael balanced on her knees but stopped breathing for several moments. If I could have seen her face, her expression might have been one of bafflement.

I left her to whatever state she was in as I continued caressing her everywhere, from mashed tits to flat belly, flanks and haunches, thighs and everywhere in between. I dipped my tongue into her crack, grinding my Feldeu against her back as I nudged the smooth, sweaty pucker open to deeper exploration. Her fingers strained to brush the hard ridge in my pants a few times.

Ohhh, yes ...

My hands rubbed her inner thighs, fondled, and explored her clit, mound, and sex. It took much longer for the recruit to feel my red leather fingers slipping into her twat than it had my tongue spearing her netherhole, and Jael grunted when it finally happened. She adjusted her knees, opened her stance a little wider to let me go deep. Panagan huffed, sounding halfway impressed.

"Those *are* good tricks," she commented.

Jael's ass squeezed shut on the tip of my tongue and pushed it out.

"Shush," I suggested.

We almost had to start over, the recruit and me, but Jael relaxed into my ministrations more the second time. I knew she was trying to let it come, because climaxing could help her survive, just as I had learned before her.

I touched her, exploring. The naked cait twitched, her toes clenching as she grunted again, catching her breath.

Good. Good novice.

Jael trembled, breath shaky as my tongue slid as deep as I could go from this angle. My fingers from each hand teasing her cunt, all of it from hole to nub to crowning fur. I didn't care how slimy and stained my gloves got, because the contrast of textures made Jael squirm as she slowly lost her hold upon her fear, her anger. At least for the moment.

Worth it. I'll trade Gaelan something for a true-clean spell on my gloves later.

"*Mm-nngh!*" Jael groaned.

Her pucker flexed around my tongue and against my lips. Her deep, slick channel grasped at inquisitive digits while her hard, pink button rose up stiff and proud against the soft red leather of my fingertips. She was close. Panagan was stroking her cock harder and harder, eyes wide as the recruit writhed in my inverted hold, as I dry-humped her hot body. I was near the edge as well.

"Ah ..." Jael uttered on a gasp. "Ah! *Ohhh ...* "

Her climax started with a flutter, then accelerated to a roll with a low, animal grunting. It turned into a crashing wave and a loud, long cry. A squirt of fluid gushed out over my fingers. Messy and inelegant; not a thing faked or performed.

That did it for me.

"*Fuck!!*"

I came just after her, grinding my magic cock as it sizzled and throbbed between my legs, sweeping up into my burning head. There was a little pain, but not as much.

"Jael, fuck!"

As I came down, I didn't hear Kain's voice. Quiet. Just the shivering cait beneath me panting, groaning, and Panagan's fapping until she got to her feet and joined us, standing facing me, her jutting Feldeu aimed at Jael's sopping cunt and ass.

"Hold her still," my Sister demanded.

Jael choked on a yelp as the archer dipped her Feldeu full-length into her slit, stroking to get it good and wet. I held Jael's ass cheeks open as Panagan pulled out and pressed the head to the glistening, relaxed pucker. Jael tensed up.

"Shhh, easy," I said, not sure who I was talking to. "Take it slow. No hurry."

Both seemed to listen, which was one small, divine favor, and with her red uniform and red cloak still on, only her leather pants open and pushed to her thighs, Panagan fucked young Aurenthietti up her ass, relishing the tight grip and easy domination.

The Red Sister was not *too* rough, and Jael did not fight so hard as to be hurt, possibly because I was there the entire time, guiding them. I watched as the black cock sank into Jael's bung over and over, stroking the cait's clit some more so she enjoyed some of it.

Jael found a way to grip my own erection while she held in place to receive a Red Sister how she was supposed to when she was at the bottom. If we had been on a bed or pallet, I wondered if she might have bitten the blanket like Reishel did. By the end, as Panagan found her release with her toy inside the younger female, she was in a much better mood. She pulled out, smacked Jael's ass with a playful slant, and sighed deeply.

"Ahh. I needed that."

Jael still panted beneath me, licked her lips and swallowed to try and wet a dry mouth. I crawled off her at last, prepared if she decided to bolt — the exit was blocked, there was nowhere to go — or if she attacked us. Fortunately for her, she did neither. The young Noble from the poorest House sat back carefully on her backside, grimaced a little, and lifted her gaze to look directly at me with bright, copper eyes. I smiled and offered her a drink from my waterskin. She took it, and I nodded, satisfied.

Now you know you can do it once. You can do it again and still get back to your feet.

We just had to bend enough to get past the Prime's rock-rigid rules so that Jael could pass her trials and live to fight another battle.

CHAPTER 18

I DIDN'T EXPECT PANAGAN TO BE FULLY BEHIND MY PLAN, EVEN IF SISTERS weren't supposed to leave each other to die. She would throw me under the falling rock if she thought it might save her skin. I wanted to do one better and keep the rock from falling in the first place, but part of that plan involved guessing what Varessa D'Shea wanted.

As it seemed Jaunda was still interested in keeping my ass around, and I still owed her a "chase" for that favor earlier, the Lead sneaked us unseen to meet Elder D'Shea, who then began to inventory all our belongings. My Sister and I were stripped as naked as Jael, though not blindfolded and bound as she was.

The most awkward moment was when D'Shea found Gaelan's Feldeu on me. She raised an eyebrow.

"It proved useful," was all I said.

The Sorceress considered me, took a delicate sniff of the magic item, and set it down beside my other weapons without giving me a hint what she thought about that.

With stubborn protest from Panagan and steady coaxing from Lead Jaunda, the Sorceress agreed to bring in Elder Rausery before the full inspection of the recruit, and to share in the first debriefing from the two Red Sisters returned. My heart pounded with her arrival as I hoped I could persuade them both once again. Lead Jaunda was sent outside, and the Elder General joined us soon after. Rausery scanned Jael where she sat quietly on the floor.

"Aurenthietti is alive," she remarked, and I didn't consider it a good sign that she still called Jael by her House name, not a recruit or a novice. "And in fairly good shape, assuming she still has eyes behind that strap."

"She does," D'Shea answered, her arms folded, shoulders square. "It remains to be seen if she uses them beyond this meeting. I've already determined she drank Sirana's preserver potion, negating the trial according to tradition."

I spotted the moment when the Elders met eyes and then D'Shea's dark red eyes shifted, landing squarely on me.

She added, "I'd like to know under what circumstances."

Rausery smirked. "Kinda curious, too."

The Elder General walked around Panagan and me. Her slow circle did not show her a lot of what we'd been through. Most of the marks from the Tragar battle on each of us were gone, and I only had a few new ones on elbows and knees from my struggle with Lana. The archer was quivering with fear, however.

"I told her not to give it to her, Elder," Panagan blurted. "She didn't listen to me."

I glared at her. So much for letting me talk first. Smoothing my expression, I lowered my eyes before my Elder Sorceress. "Permission to pick up the dark brown pouch, third from the front?"

"I see not what that has to do with your empty vial, Sirana."

"I wager you're curious where the link is, Elder."

D'Shea chuckled. "Permission granted."

I stepped forward and retrieved the pouch which contained the element which Kain had died trying to extricate. I upended it into my palm, releasing three pieces for which I had ruined the edge on my dagger to lift from the rock. D'Shea gazed at them, slowly rubbed a finger across her lips, her thoughts in a calm center.

"They just look like rocks to me," Rausery said frankly.

"They appear like sapphires to a Tragar," I said. "A psionic one."

"How do you know?"

Rausery's focused gaze told me she had not forgotten the "Kain-wound" in my mind, but Panagan was here, and I had told her a different story.

"The potion the Elder D'Shea gave me to help sense mind mages nearby on this mission." I explained my bald lie, and Panagan relaxed to hear me tell it. "They look like rocks to me, too, but at the time, I could see them. They're a bright blue."

The General looked like she might laugh for a moment as her umber red eyes landed on her peer. The Sorceress, as I knew she could, picked it up gracefully.

"There *is* a subtle, blue aura around them, Elder," she acknowledged, and I couldn't tell if that was true or not. "It's interesting. Not certain if this stone is of any use, however."

"Odd of you to say. I could take one to the Wizard's Tower," Rausery offered, never blinking as she watched D'Shea. "Let someone study it. Someone pretty good at finding the best spells to imbue stones and gems with."

The Sorceress's body was extremely still. Her eyes appeared black for a moment, as if a dark emotion had rushed through. I blinked, and the dark red color was back; I wondered if my eyes had just played a trick on me.

My Elder smiled then, her voice chilly. "We shall discuss it. For now, I want to hear how this stone pertains to Aurenthietti. Sirana? Summary first."

"We used the jump port and tracked the recruit," I began with confidence, "but accidentally pushed Aurenthietti right into them as she knew she was being followed. There were six male Tragar, two of which were psions. They had trapped her, and though she still fought them when we caught up, it was only a matter of time. They were armed and armored. She wasn't."

Jael tensed on the floor, shoulders hunching as she pressed her mouth closed, making no sound. The Elders noted it but waited for me to continue.

"Panagan and I took care of them, as ordered," I said. "They are *all* dead. Aurenthietti would have bled out as well, but she mentioned a seventh Tragar. A female. To learn more, I gave her my preserver potion."

Rausery glanced at the cait on the floor. "Half a chance she was lying, Sirana. That's a known trick. A desperate one."

"I knew she wasn't, Elder, and we caught up to the Dwarf. Panagan saw her, too. Heard her. She went to ground, and I went in after her. I ran into another Tragar as well. Her ... mate. For lack of a better word. I poisoned them both, they didn't get away."

Both Elders glanced at all my equipment laid out. I knew they looked for fingers, ears, organs ...

"The female was a more powerful psion than the one I ran into last turn," I said with utter truth. "I rushed to escape as soon as I knew my blade had cut her. I *know* better, Elders. It's dangerous to touch a dying psion."

"So I've heard," Rausery said with an odd tone as one corner of her mouth lifted. "What happened next?"

"We caught up to the recruit using the same jump circle and gem you gave Panagan, and we caught her."

"And took your pleasure with her?" D'Shea asked, peering with deliberation at my cum-stained gloves.

"Yes, Elder."

She would see all the evidence eventually.

"Hm." D'Shea looked at Rausery. "No lies."

I held my face steady. *No lies that you don't already know about.*

"You broke the rules of a trial and directly disobeyed orders," Rausery said, "because she warned you about another enemy nearby, which Panagan would probably have found trace of anyway?"

I drew breath to speak; Jael beat me to it.

"I know the Grey Dwarves turn that stone blue somehow, Elders." The blindfolded cait swallowed; she was very nervous but continued. "If that's what I think it is, my House recorded blue-laced axes carried by some of them, starting about two generations ago. They won't ever trade for a weapon that color, not even on the Fringe. They're not that desperate, at least yet."

Jael stopped, and the room was quiet. I clenched my teeth to make certain my jaw didn't sag in surprise. My entire plan, which was shaky at best, was thrown off.

"You told Sirana about blue stone weapons while you were dying?" Rausery asked her with plain disbelief as she glanced at me. "And that's why she healed you?"

"Never said that, Elder," Jael muttered, keeping her chin down. Her eyes were still covered, and her wrists tied behind her back. "I told her there was a seventh Dwarf she missed. The females are rare, so I noticed her, even being chased."

"Why tell her that while bleeding out?"

Jael shrugged. "The Red Sister fought like I saw before, against the thralls. She killed the fuckers, straight-in, as they were ripping me open. She gave me a weapon and instruction, both to me and to the archer, so we could beat them. And I *saw* them beaten, three against six, before I knew I was dead. She's ... a good leader. I ... wanted her to *win*, even if I blacked out. There was one left, I knew it, and I didn't want the female Tragar to get the Red Sisters from behind because I didn't *try*."

The room was silent. Maybe it was easier to say those things with her eyes covered, because I sure as fuck knew I couldn't make my mouth work at all being able to see the expressions on my Elders' faces.

"Good leader, eh?" Rausery finally said, amused as she looked at me, then at Panagan. "Do you agree?"

The archer shook her head with a frown. "The novice is clever and persuasive, perhaps. Not the same thing as a leader. *I* wouldn't follow her."

Jael said nothing. Not one argumentative sound. I wasn't sure what she was thinking about, but it could have been the deal over how to use the recruit's asshole in the cache room. At least, that's what came to *my* mind when the archer said that.

I didn't want to be a leader, anyway.

"I want separate reports," D'Shea said then, looking at her peer. "I'll start with Sirana, you with Panagan. Then we'll trade."

Rausery didn't fight that demand; she nodded agreement. "Let me stow the recruit somewhere safe. Don't take too long, D'Shea, I still have questions for you. We don't want to be interrupted before we have a plan."

"Very well. Be swift."

A plan? What kind of plan?

Somehow, as I stood in the Cloister with most of the truth out but none of my case made to defend my decision, Jael was a "recruit" again, and Rausery and D'Shea wanted a plan.

How did this happen? What will happen now?

I closed my mouth and went with the Sorceress, hoping to learn the meaning behind even a portion of those looks the Elders had been sharing.

No doubt that comes with its own price and discomfort.

Once again, Aurenthietti was held somewhere I didn't know, and after our separate reports with each Elder, I waited alone in a small, quiet room for either of them to return. My Elder D'Shea's questioning had been familiar, weighing my actions against my motives and experience in a thorough and intellectually broad exploration.

"Extraordinary insight into the Tragar, Sirana," the Sorceress said, ultimately pleased with my telling her everything — almost to the point she might have been aroused had we been alone in her quarters. "And you sought and achieved a path I can work with in my study of Kain, and how much of his shade might remain."

She paused, her eyes drifting to a random spot on the wall as she considered something. She added, "We won't need Lelinahdara's assistance as I thought. Share none of this with her, especially the stone and the female, Lana. Let me manage any curiosity she retains on the matter. With any luck, I can persuade her it was a temporary trauma which faded, no matter what else we discover."

"Yes, Elder."

I exhaled in relief at the same moment I detected in my Elder some small regret that a Priestess of Braqth knew about this at all. I agreed with her but, for now, it was enough to believe I wouldn't have to give up my body and mind to an altar-sucker over this again. My Elder was convinced I could adapt and handle it — that I had helped myself and made more progress alone.

Unlike after my first mission executing my own sister to save my Matron and her unborn, the Sorceress seemed satisfied that I had exploited all opportunities possible under the circumstances. I understood better what she wanted from me.

In contrast, Elder Rausery's debriefing had been brusque, focused mostly on my actions and trying to understand the "wound in my head," as she phrased it. She was equally fascinated with the peek behind the fortress that I had learned in interrogating Lana; the Elder even seemed impressed that I had used the Feldeu to intimidate the Tragar and "got her talking."

The experience had been more than that. It had reached far deeper in my mind than I could describe, the link far more intimate. I *knew* her. She had known me, and I understood why she had asked me to kill her.

Without the mage's studies and experience that D'Shea had, without the decades spent watching me and gathering insights, Rausery worked only to figure out my current limits and what to expect from me short-term. Her questions went back to a comatose Reishel in the infirmary after the battle more than once.

"Did you prod her awake? Choose her over the other two?"

I shook my head vehemently. "No, Elder."

"Are you so sure? Did anything odd happen? Think back."

I didn't want to claim it, because I was terrified what she might ask of me in the future if she thought I had some actual skill against Ornilleths.

"Nothing I can describe. Nothing I did on purpose. I wasn't intending anything against my Sisters, especially nothing malicious, Elder, I swear. I don't know why Reishel woke up and the other two didn't. We had no special bond."

"You do, now," she pointed out, having yanked the details earlier on why I had stolen Gaelan's Feldeu in the first place. "If D'Shea isn't already planning to train a new team in you three, maybe the recruit, too, if she makes it, then I'm going to recommend it. It'll help in dealing with the Prime."

My heart thundered at this mention, and Rausery raised an inquiring eyebrow.

"Are you going to tell her?" I asked. At the same time, it was a plea against it. "I swear I don't understand what's happening much more than you."

The General chuffed, her hands propped on her hips, far more relaxed than me as her chin lowered in thought. "Anyone else knows about this, Sirana, and it won't be just the Prime who will want to kick you out and hand you over to the Valsharess for containment. On a good cycle, nobody here trusts a Davrin who had their mind twisted by a psion. You saw how tough it was on Reishel, trying to come back, and it will be a while before some Sisters will work with her."

She lifted her chin and looked directly in my eyes. "Now imagine their reaction to one sharing memories and abilities with a psion she killed. Talking like him, in his language, so that even Panagan didn't know it was you." She watched my face and nodded. "Yeah. I imagine the Priestesses would demand control of you, whatever the plan, because it looks like possession. Something they have experience with. They could convince the Valsharess, easily."

I was shaking. Sick to my stomach. My vision faded out briefly. "Please. No ..."

"Head down. Breathe."

I did. She watched me for a few moments before speaking again.

"Keep this in mind, Sirana, and keep your mouth shut. Don't show your hand to anyone, don't confide in any Sister, not even Jaunda or Gaelan. Like D'Shea, I don't want to hand you over to the Sanctuary before figuring this out. You have potential, and we want that for the Sisterhood, not for the Priesthood. But we could be forced to if anyone finds out about this. Your Elder and I will talk. *You* stay silent. Understand?"

"Y-yes, Elder. I will. Thank you."

Now, I waited alone in this tiny room inside the Cloister. A shiver went down my spine when it was Lead Jaunda who let herself in next, not either Elder. I felt the prickle of having been in this position before.

I saw a flash of myself, still as a Noble at House Thalluen, small and powerless as I waited to be blamed for Jilrina's death. It was the same here. Jaunda had remained with me in my own bedroom at my Matron's House, keeping watch, until her Elder had time to announce my fate. Back then, I hadn't been sure if the warrior had wanted to fuck me.

Now, there was no doubt.

My Lead twirled her finger, her face set in a happy leer. "Knees on the ground. Elbows on the chair."

Sitting at a height of fear, Jaunda's command caused a surge of arousal in my gut as I seized on the blatant opportunity to de-stress. My hands had already released my chair and I reached to undo my weaponless belt before I fully grasped my actions.

Spawn of an Abyssal slit.

When did my cunt start thinking for me?

This was my life until I gained rank in the Sisterhood.

Very soon I was gripping the back of the fiberstalk chair, my leathers bunched around my knees, and Jaunda spearing my netherhole with her familiar cock, deep enough that I could feel her fur pressing against me. She began with long, powerful strokes, both of us grunting.

She enjoyed that pace for a while then leaned over to lie atop my back, wrapping her strong arms around my middle. A hand slid down between my legs to flick at my sensitive pearl, and I flinched.

"Aw, yeah," she chuckled. "Squeeze that cock, Sirana."

She did it again, and I gripped her pole, a hum slipping out of me. I adjusted my stance, offered that steady platform as she took her time. She slapped my ass appreciatively then stroked me some more. Her mouth was close to my ear when she spoke, her fingers circling my white bush and the folds just beneath.

"Gaelan told me her Feldeu was missing. Figured you took it. You were the last to leave the room."

I squeezed her again though I knew it wouldn't distract her. "Confessed to our Elders."

"So it wasn't an order from either?"

"No, Lead."

She lunged in, her breath hitching just before a throaty growl. My cunt was wet, aching with emptiness as she filled my ass. She spoke next through a tighter throat.

"So, you can use it now. Gaelan said she taught you how. On her and Reishel."

"Yes, Lead," I gasped, the chair legs thumping and scraping against the floor with our heavy motions.

"You weren't done when I interrupted you with Reishel? That why you stole it?"

I swallowed. "I had finished, Lead. Although ... there's more I can't tell you ... without D'Shea's say."

"Got it."

Jaunda chuckled with odd satisfaction, asking nothing more. Her one hand left my crotch so that both hers could wrap around mine, trapping me as I gripped the back of the chair.

"You know, cait, you're a lot like your Grand Matron. The way you push and pull."

I jerked in surprise. *Huh?*

"My ... ?"

Jaunda let loose the reins then, fucking me hard, rutting my ass with glee, spending many lewd compliments on my well-trained, talented netherhole. Through it all, I felt my slit drooling down my thigh; arousal hit a high pitch, yet I couldn't climax. She teased me too much with the mention of a Davrin I never knew. Perhaps this was Jaunda's own style of interrogative torture for me before D'Shea got here.

An event which proved to arrive very shortly.

The Ward suspended, and the Sorceress stepped in while I was joyfully fucked. D'Shea just watched in silence at one side, standing patiently and giving Jaunda time to finish inside me. My Lead wasted no time, then; she sped up, throwing herself fearlessly off the edge.

"*Yeeaahh!*" she growled, holding herself deep, groaning through clenched teeth as she squeezed my hands with hers. I whimpered a bit, a sound I knew Jaunda enjoyed but also because I'd be sore either standing or sitting while D'Shea told me what came next.

Plus, I still needed to cum, whether my pucker was raw or not.

Abyssal slit.

"Wait for me outside, Lead," D'Shea instructed with elegant calm once we had disconnected.

Jaunda stood up, put her toy back inside her leathers, and straightened her uniform. She obeyed without a sound, signing her acknowledgment and respect. Then, it was just me and the Sorceress. D'Shea waited while I gingerly pulled up my pants and put my tender ass back in the chair. I waited for her to speak.

"Panagan believes she's absolved of your doings concerning the recruit," my Elder began. "And she believes the part about your taking a potion to sense psionic presence. Fortunately for me, such a potion exists, though not easy to make. My instruction for you is to say nothing of this to any who ask. In time, it shall be forgotten."

I exhaled, nodding. "Yes, Elder. The General said the same thing."

More or less.

D'Shea offered a cunning smile. "I know. Rausery and I have a report which will satisfy the Prime, I believe, and we'll put Aurenthietti through the Cloister, see if the Red Sisters accept her. If they do, we'll train her."

I opened my mouth.

"You are not to ask details," she interrupted before I could ask, "and speaking those you know is very dangerous for you, Sirana. If the Prime asks you directly, all you know is that *I* gave you instructions to chisel out that stone and find that group of Tragar. *I* told you to look for and interrogate the female among them, and you crossed paths with the recruit by happenstance. You made your decisions in the field to fight and aid her based on my order to capture the female for interrogation. Nothing more. Understood?"

I nodded. It was close enough to the truth for me to remember, though it was clear D'Shea was once again stepping between me and the First Sister. Taking on more risk. Both her and Rausery.

"Yes, Elder."

"Good. Now. I have a task for you, and you shall perform it immediately after we are through here. Again, ask no details. Look for opportunity."

My heart again pulsing in my ears, I nodded. "Yes, Elder. Thank you."

CHAPTER 19

WITH A SILENT SIGH, I PAUSED IN MY RATHER LONG WALK TO THE WIZARD'S Tower, removing to study again the sealed vial Elder D'Shea had given me, along with two of the three Dwarf stones I had collected in the field. I might have anticipated that D'Shea would twist something I had looked forward to into nothing more than another tease.

"This vial will get you into the Tower," she had told me, her face stern. "But you make certain you accomplish your assignment *first*, Sirana. If you have the time before I call you, then you may reward yourself with the young wizard if you want. But, if two marks have passed since you've taken this prevention draught, do *not* take *any* prick in your cunt at all."

*Yes, yes, mouth and ass only. I'm **quite** familiar.*

My shitter was still sore from Jaunda's use.

Two marks, though. It was not very generous on first study, seemed like a weak potion, as Phaelous had claimed that his lasted for over twelve marks. But, then again, he *did* say male seed remained "viable" inside a womb for some time afterward. If that was the case, then D'Shea's potion probably lasted for an equal time.

But not a mark more.

I knew these mages could make something long-term for the Sister-hood to prevent catching babies, if they tried, but I also remembered what the Headmaster had said when I asked him: *I have nothing I am allowed to give to you, Red Sister.*

Fuck.

With deliberate, inefficient methods based more on abstaining through willpower, a Red Sister *had* to get pregnant every so often. Then, she would be kept in the Sanctuary until she dropped the babe, and it was a marked failure for the Sisterhood and a boon for the sterile Priestesses. Another tick on the game board, as the Valsharess just turned it into another method of control between the two most powerful groups.

I resented how the older females could make me feel a little *afraid* of a few cocks in the Tower. *Spinneret suckers. All of them.*

Soon, I stood at the front door of the Wizard's Tower. As at my first time, Headmaster Phaelous long knew of my approach in being allowed past the various ward-points, and he met me in the main entry. This time, instead of it being empty, there were a few buas cleaning. I felt their eyes on me even as they tried to be subtle.

Phaelous tested the potion D'Shea had given me to satisfy his requirements, and I caught a few hand signs to each other.

★Blue eyes … ★

★ … she's back.★

★Shh! She'll see!★

"Very good, young Sister," the Headmaster said, handing me back the vial. "Please drink this and come with me."

I obeyed, having several witnesses to this, and kept the empty vial with me. We walked past the young wizards to the nearest jump circle, and Phaelous' calm, aged face did not change much, perhaps a little amused. I wagered he didn't rule his nest with a spiked club the way the Prime did, or there would have been some easy "examples" to be made just now.

"It seems you're easy to identify, young Sister," the ancient wizard commented after we had jumped to a quieter floor.

"When the torches are lit, yes," I agreed with a shrug. "The battlemage has been talking?"

"Word spread of your visit, though not solely from his mouth. Regardless, some of the others will hardly let him be, asking for details about you. They also noted his change in behavior afterward. He's been focusing very much on his crafting skills."

None of this surprised me; the buas at the Court were the same way even without magic. I cleared my throat. "Speaking thus, I brought something on behalf of my Elder."

"Indeed?" Phaelous' long, leisurely gait flowed unabated. "Let us find some privacy."

The Headmaster's notion of "privacy" took the form of a small, round library on the fifth level which held both protections and — if I chose to guess — a hidden entrance or exit somewhere. Maybe a jump circle behind a scroll case. Once we were alone, he motioned me toward one of three, heavy and fine-quality study tables. I moved closer but didn't take one of the wide seats with comfortable cushions; I remained standing.

"May I see your message from your Elder, Red Sister?" he asked politely.

"It isn't a note."

"Everything sent here from the Elder Sorceress has a message attached."

True.

I removed the two Dwarf stones from my belt, setting them upon the table an equal distance between us. They appeared just like ordinary, greyish-blue stones in this light, and I watched Phaelous' face for any sign of either recognition or skepticism. I saw neither.

"Instructions?" he asked.

"Do you know what it is?"

He smiled with patience, the corners of his eyes crinkling. "Is that your Elder's question?"

Damn it. I shook my head. "No, it's mine."

"Ah. Well. It would be reckless of me to answer without understanding what you already know of it, young Sister."

"Mm. Still alive through good habits, eh?"

"Accurately stated."

I fidgeted, straining against my orders. Phaelous watched me without blinking.

After a moment, he said, "I take it your Elder does not want you to share what you know with me."

Fuck.

I shook my head. "I'm the one who found it. She instructed me to bring it here to you."

"But I may not know the circumstances. Very well. Is there any goal at all? A direction?"

"Well. We heard on the Fringe that sometimes this stone turns blue."

The Headmaster could tell I had couched the truth in a lie; it was obvious in his fine-lined smile. "Does it? Very curious. Perhaps I shall have to discover when and why it turns blue, hm?"

D'Shea is going to kill me.

"That would be welcome, Headmaster," I said, breathing out my nerves. "Plus, anything more that you learn about it."

"Certainly. Is there anything else, Sister Sirana?"

"My Elder said that the Elder General is also an acceptable contact for anything you discover."

"Inform her that is understood." The elder wizard looked again at the drab stones with unhurried curiosity. "And?"

"And, um, to use all resources available to you."

Obvious, perhaps, but that part *was* explicit in my instructions. This wizard had a lot of resources that I did not.

He bowed a slow nod. "Very well, Red Sister. Allow me to call two of them right now, before you leave for the seventeenth floor to visit Callitro."

Hm? Why?

It annoyed me that I imagined feeling the potency of the prevention draught fading away. Another test from my Elder. *Finish my task first.* I got a grip on myself.

"Certainly, Headmaster. I will wait."

I remained standing rather than sit, thanks to Jaunda. I ambled, acting as if to browse the library, sneaking a look at Phaelous and whatever he was doing with his hands near a smooth plate of gloss stone next to a small basin of liquid.

I *was* curious about the scrolls within reach, about the parchment-filled codices on the shelves surrounding me, about whomever would be coming, but I was fooling myself if I imagined I understood the markings and colors which seemed to categorize the knowledge written down.

The markings were familiar enough to recognize a Davrin hand, to see our language, but changed enough to be unreadable to the average literate Noble. It was a complex system I knew nothing about, not even where to start.

Wonder if that's why D'Shea is unconcerned with sending me here.

"Headmaster?" I asked when the old Elf seemed to be finished with his summons.

Phaelous turned toward me respectfully. "Yes, Red Sister?"

"Do many of my Sisters come here as messengers for the Elders?"

"Not regularly, only when necessary. There are other methods." He paused. "A messenger is never a mage, I notice."

He gave me that last bit for free.

"What about non-messengers? One coming for her own purpose. Any mages recently?"

"Not for a little over two centuries, young Sister." The golden flecks in Phaelous' crimson eyes seemed to twinkle in the smokeless torchlight. "But ... for her own purpose? Like what, young Sister?"

I shrugged, thinking about Callitro waiting up-level. "Play that isn't political, the way it is at Court."

He chuckled softly. "Many of your Sisters have never been to Court, and most don't seem to see wizards as much fun in that regard. My buas are studious objects kept clean and safe, largely ignorant of the grit of Sivaraus. Collected Davrin which cannot be broken and must be handled with care. This limitation doesn't intrigue many Red Sisters, but the residents here remember those who are, as she seems interested in something more than his body."

I felt an odd prickle up my back and neck, warming my cheeks and my crotch both. "Hm. Any of those recently? Non-mages, I mean."

Everything about him remained poised and patient. "You could ask around the Cloister, I suppose. Forgive that I am not at liberty to name them, and my learners have been warned against loose lips."

I figured that would be as far as I got. Too direct for this ancient, clever male, but I was keenly aware of where I wanted to go and of the time it took for whoever was coming.

Then, finally, they arrived.

Two wizards in dark blue robes entered the room. They were far younger than Phaelous — though that description might fit about every wizard here — and older than me by a century if it was a cycle. Neither seemed pleased to be here or openly intrigued by my presence, not like the younger cleaners on the main level. If anything, I thought them wary of me, even if they hid their thoughts from their face. They had learned to stand at ease with a patient, placid face like their Headmaster.

I stared at the young wizard on the left. That poise and expression wasn't the only thing in common with the elder wizard. He shared the same eye shape and color, as well as general form with the Headmaster, if a bit shorter in stature. There was no fooling anyone; if Phaelous had not sired the bua, then they were close relatives.

So, maybe Phaelous is still virile at his age? Impressive.

"Who — ?" I began.

"This is Raegal and Shyntre," Phaelous interrupted me, introducing them with a wave of his hand. "They each have talent for working with stones, determining which types of magic may fix to or interact with it. I shall be using your Elder's samples to further train them, so they shall be handling the items you've provided. Recommended you inform your Elders of this, as they will ask and expect you to know."

The two wizards each bowed at the waist, stiff and less elegant than their Headmaster. "Red Sister."

Their voices soft to the point I turned an ear to hear them. A bit high. Similar. Both were tense, and the one *not* clearly related to the Headmaster, Raegal, could have been of any House. It was more likely he was from a House either around or below mine, if only because I'd grown familiar with the attitudes at Court, and he did not hold himself like a male in the Top Eight the way Shyntre did. Although, I couldn't know for sure just looking at their faces.

"Alright," I said. "Raegal and Shyntre will be handling the stones with you, Headmaster. Understood. Which Houses may then hear of this curiosity?"

"None, Red Sister," Phaelous answered with confidence. "My learners are like yourself. They hold loyalty first to the Valsharess, to Her Priesthood and Sisterhood. Their Houses are not privy to what they learn inside this tower. They rarely ever go home unless called to help quicken a womb."

"I see. Very good."

Not good. A clean block to what I really wanted to know, and the old male knew it. My knowledge reached its limit about then, and pride held me back from prodding more. Any question I asked about what they intended to do would reveal that I couldn't read any of the encrypted language in this room.

Neither of these buas, both older than me and trained with very different expertise, seemed like they would be as indulgent of my curiosity and respectful of my station as the Headmaster. It also wasn't a good idea to bring up psionics and those sensitive to them, so I had no angle where they would have to raise their knowledge base to answer me.

Damn it.

Phaelous smiled at me. "If there's nothing else, Red Sister, you may go about your duties."

I checked the candle. Still over a mark left before I hit my time limit. Enough for a little foreplay before I watched Callitro's face as he spurted up my twat.

Ohhh-kay, I'm ready.

"Nothing else, Headmaster, thank you. How would you have me get to the seventeenth level?"

Phaelous turned to the two wizards. "Would one of you volunteer to escort the Red Sister to Callitro's dormitory?"

Both their somatic reactions were notable, including a few facial tics, and I blinked in surprise. *They hate me.*

Or, at the very least, they hated my uniform. Phaelous was testing them, their poise and wit under pressure, just as my Elders did with me and my Sisters.

"You can do it," Shyntre offered to Raegal, his precious wizard's hand casually gesturing his way.

The other bua whipped his head around to glare at him. "What? Blight on you, Shyntre! *You* do it."

The wizard's dark red eyes were half-hidden by tight, scowling white brows. "I just got back from the Sanctuary. I have catch-up to do."

"You think *I'm* not busy?"

"Not as busy as I am."

"Some special toad, aren't you? You just want first look at those stones."

"No, Raegal, I don't care. You can have first crack at those, too, if you escort the Red Sister."

"I shouldn't have to." The other bared a petty expression as he snarled, "You're the one that always gets called by the Headm —"

"Shut your gap!"

"Fuck you, let me finish! I already agreed to —"

"*Right!* Alright, you puking waste of components!"

My jaw hung completely loose to witness the bickering, and Phaelous did nothing to intercede; the elder wizard acted like he watched a boring pair of jesters on a stage. For the first time, I wondered if this all-male Tower could be worse than the pettiness at Court.

If only for the fact that they have fewer outlets for their frustrations.

"It is decided?" Phaelous asked with bland interest.

Both young males turned to him, their hearts pounding and their bodies warm to my eyes. I sniffed, noting the stronger scents as well; not just the result of body heat but as if they had both been elbow-deep in potion extracts for the last cycle and hadn't bothered to bathe before leaving their work. If that's what they were doing when summoned to come here, I could be glad, at least, in that they hadn't wasted my infertility potion.

"I'll escort the Red Sister to Callitro's room, Headmaster," Shyntre said, clearly enunciated and resented.

"Very well. I shall get started with Raegal, but you return here immediately after she has reached her destination. No detours or loitering."

"Yes, Headmaster," Shyntre said, almost a growl through clenched teeth.

The elder male next looked at me. "I respectfully request his delay in returning here be kept at a minimum, Red Sister, so he may help fulfill your Elder's request. I require his skills."

Shyntre made a face before returning to scowling, and I imagined Phaelous was doing his best not to show favoritism to his likely son. Not when the entire Tower is filled with buas for whom he was responsible.

I shrugged and nodded. "I have no reason to delay him, Headmaster, I'm here to see Callitro."

I detected a tiny smile on the Headmaster's thin lips. "Very good, young Sister. I am certain he shall be glad to see you."

CHAPTER 20

SHYNTRE WALKED ME OUT OF THE LIBRARY, LEADING ME TOWARD THE NEAREST jump circle. He was burning up, heat flowing off his dark robe, and he stank like mushrooms boiled in urine. I wrinkled my nose.

"What were you working on when the Headmaster called you?" I asked.

He opened his mouth, thought better of what he was about to say, and tried again. "I am not at liberty to say, Red Sister. I direct your question back to my Headmaster."

Oh? I smiled. "Something to aid the Priesthood or the Sisterhood?"

His body flushed hot again as we stepped into the nearest circle. "Red Sister, I need to concentrate if you want to make it up-level with all your limbs attached."

Gruesome threat.

"Very well. Do I need to hold your hand to assure that?"

His body language screamed, *Don't touch me.*

"No, Red Sister. Standing in the circle is enough. You should know that from the Ornilleth battle."

"Ah? You know the particulars of that?"

"Only what the battlemages said. That the Red Sisters appeared out of nowhere to turn the favor for them. I know the Sisterhood moves around quickly using them. It makes sense."

"You were guessing?"

"Educated but, yes. Now, please be quiet a moment."

That was surprisingly difficult, and my stomach lurched even more on that account. I tilted and just caught my balance when we left a level smelling of books and arrived at another smelling of bua bodies holed up in their bedrooms for a long time. I inhaled deeply, enjoying it despite the sourness of the wizard next to me.

Shyntre stepped out of the circle and led me where I had wanted to go before deciding how fast I wanted to get there. This wizard seemed like a fun one to tease, though in a far different way than I intended to tease Callitro. I was curious that both he and Raegal showed no fear of my uniform, or perhaps covering it behind strong dislike. I wanted to know why. Could be for many good reasons; I just wanted to know which one.

Especially if they'll be handling the Dwarf stones.

"Wait, wizard," I said, but I had run out of time.

Shyntre placed his palm on the smooth stone by Callitro's door, and I heard movement behind it as the young battlemage responded.

"My Headmaster requested that I not dawdle to chat with you, Red Sister," he said coolly without looking away from the door, which opened the next moment.

Callitro seemed to recognize Shyntre, nodding his head to acknowledge his presence but did not have a specific reaction to him. That was, perhaps, because he was too quickly looking at me. The young mage smiled in a genuine pleasure I had only seen a few times at Court.

"Welcome, Red Sister," he said. "I was hoping to see you soon."

"Progress report?" I asked as an answering urge to smile dragged up one side of my mouth.

"For certain, and my pleasure to confirm." His burnt orange eyes slid over my red leathers. Callitro did *not* hate my uniform. Quite the opposite. "Will you come in?"

At last, I grinned. "Why I'm here."

"Excuse me," Shyntre said and left, his heartbeat fading with his sandaled footsteps.

Callitro and I glanced at his surly retreat. Since the younger wizard shrugged, unsurprised with the behavior, I stepped inside so my new bua could close the door. As before, I could already see evidence of his welcome beneath his robe. I knew I had about a mark, and my netherhole was still on the raw side. I could take him safely in my cunt, but like before, he probably wouldn't last long enough for me to cum, too.

Might have to suck him again and use his nut gland to hurry that second ride.

The wizard read my face accurately this time and began to undress, keeping his peace for the moment about the progress report. I probably grinned like an absent fool as he pulled soft fabric down to reveal bare shoulders, arms, and chest. I held my breath until he fully undid the tie at his waist and dropped the robe at his bare feet.

"I was told to expect you," he said, his cock good and hard. "I know your time might be short. I've already climaxed once, Red Sister. It will take some time to do so again."

Oh, you clever, precious treasure.

I swept Callitro up into my arms and kissed his mouth, thrusting my tongue inside as I held his naked body tight against my leathers. He relaxed into it so fast I imagined he must have been dreaming of it before now; he put his arms around me and kissed me back, yielding his lips to all the sucking and nibbling I desired. I gripped his ass, pulled his standing prick hard against me, squeezing it hot between our bellies; he responded eagerly, grinding his erection against me.

Moaning in approval, I tested one more thing as I held his buttocks with both gloved hands. Parting them, I fingered his hole, and a powerful rush swept through me when he gasped in surprise but then relaxed. He allowed my fingertip inside, even being a little dry.

I wished I had Gaelan's Feldeu.

"Fuck, yes, bua," I panted, pulling my mouth away, grasping for some self-control.

Callitro's heart beat strong and steady against me; he watched my face with a low-lidded gaze, surely able to feel my quivering. He waited, didn't have to say a thing. He smiled, slowly, and did anyway.

"However you want it, Red Sister."

I smirked. "I *want* to ride you into a soggy, brainless lump."

The battlemage nodded, showing his delight. "Do it. Please."

"I *want* you to fill my cunt with a bigger load than you shot in my mouth."

He groaned, gripping my armored shoulders eagerly. "I want it, too, Red Sister."

"Sirana. When we're alone."

"Sirana, yes." Even in this light, I saw the bua's cheeks flush hot. "Sirana, fuck me."

"I mean to. Get on your back. On the bed."

My eyes were fixed upon his lithe body as he obeyed, upon every bend of his back and rise of his bare shoulders as he watched me try to get out of uniform without tearing anything. I was sweating enough now that parts of it wanted to stick.

Stupid fucking thing. Come on!

My cunt was so ready by the time I was naked and ready to pounce that it ached to slip even a finger in there. Callitro couldn't blink as he watched me do it, and he saw the string of stretchy slit juice as I finally pulled my hand away to show him my swollen netherlips, ready to swallow him whole.

He nodded, licking his lips, holding his cock by the base so it stuck straight up. His sex was leaking, too.

He had a candle lit with markers on his workbench; I grabbed it and set it on the cluttered bed stand before I joined him. The young battlemage welcomed me, settling back and lightly holding my hips with his hands as I got into position over him to grab his pole and nestle it between my legs.

I took him with a mutual groan, felt my ready body accommodate him with overt greed, fluttering and settling around every bit of him from tip to base.

"S-Sirana," he breathed in awe, his hips jerking with involuntary urgency. "Ohhh, hot ..."

I glanced at the candle marks, noted where we were, how much time I had to enjoy my ride. I found myself snickering as I breathed out, preparing to torture us both in the best of ways, right up to the very limit.

"Probably should've jerked it twice before I came up here," I whispered, holding his eyes and grinning with pure wickedness. "Suggestion ... for next time."

NEITHER THE HEADMASTER NOR A MESSENGER HAD COME TO CALLITRO'S DOOR by the time I had exhausted the both of us.

My legs and arms rapidly approaching a liquid state, I flopped over to one side with a bounce, forcing Callitro to shift closer to the wall to make room for me on the narrow bed. Our limbs overlapped; hips and shoulders pressed together, we gasped for breath, our chests coated in sweat.

My coveted, creamy spunk had been sprayed up inside and now oozed out from between ruffled lips, and my vision had come back while my blood still rushed in my ears.

Callitro, the little fucker, fell right to sleep.

Unusual.

As our breathing had begun to settle, I checked the candle mark again. I'd made it, I saw, cutting it close as I could, and I smirked as I fondled my semen-coated lips, lying in the young wizard's bed. The risk only added spice, which was not a good thing, really, but easily the most Abyssal, insane set of climaxes I'd had in turns. Maybe a decade, if I didn't count the most recent Priestess ritual.

Two if I don't count either of them.

Not in any hurry to report back to the Cloister, I lounged in a bed far more comfortable than the pallets in the barracks. I stared at the ceiling, at the odd strings of shriveled plants or mushrooms hanging to dry; I wondered what the wizard used them for. His workbench seemed full of partial projects awaiting his attention, and his bookshelf was not nearly as organized as the fifth level library.

That reminds me ...

I nudged the battlemage awake. "Hey. You owe me a progress report."

"Hmn?" Callitro was caught in a yawn that nearly locked his jaw as he hurried to close it. "Oh …"

His eyes flew open as he remembered where he was. Who he was with.

"Oh!"

He scrambled up, crawling over me with legs wide open to get his foot on the floor. I snickered, reaching for a playful swat to his swinging bits as he stumbled trying to avoid it.

"*Whoa!*"

I laughed hard enough to hold my stomach as he knocked over a basket of stained cloths. He launched back to standing, spinning around as if to get his bearings in his dwelling.

"Surely my presence doesn't make this place unrecognizable!" I hooted.

At first the wizard didn't know what to say. He opted for grinning with a familiar shyness, his eyes flitting over me. In his rumpled bed.

"Almost, Red Sister."

He'd stopped calling me by name as soon as his prick wasn't inside me. Good call.

I winked as I rose up on one elbow, turning my hip. "So. Your report?"

"Uhh, yes. Uhm." He looked around his room to locate something and spotted it on the left side of his workbench. "Aha!"

I sat up with interest, putting my feet on the thin throw rug beside the bed as he retrieved it and came and sat down next to me. Callitro opened his palm to show me a plain, golden ring.

"If you please, Red Sister, choose a finger where you might wear this so I can size it right."

"Hmm. Does it matter which hand?"

"Ideally, the one you use to strike with."

I smirked at him. "I use both."

"With a weapon?"

Oh.

I shook my head, lifting my right hand for that. "Mostly this one, unless it's broken."

Callitro nodded. "And a preferred finger? It can be whichever you like."

I grinned, shifting my hand into a lewd gesture. "Either of these two would be fine."

The wizard bit his lip as his shoulders jumped a time or two with amusement, and he chose my middle finger, slipping the gold band on and seeing where it got stuck. I adjusted the angle of my hand so he could work on it more easily, watching his lips as his bright eyes focused only on what he was doing.

I heard him mutter words I didn't know, though they sounded like Davrin, and they were sort of musical.

My hand tingled as he held it in his, and the ring loosened by itself to fit over my knuckle and slide into place like the jeweler had known it was for me from the start. I was pretty sure it had been sized for Callitro's hand just a moment before.

Rubbed my thumb against the smooth metal, I waited expectantly then uttered a sound of surprise when it warmed abruptly in response.

"What's that?" I demanded, though it was already cooling.

"That's good, Red Sister," he reassured me. "It just harmonized with your aura. It'll recognize you now and will fit well no matter if your fingers are swollen or not."

"Alright," I said. "Now share why I'm wearing this."

Callitro rubbed his mouth, paying less attention to my naked body and his sated prick as he considered his own magical theory. "Well, it's not quite finished, it still needs more testing. The Headmaster has been helping me with it, since it's my first serious craft and, uhm, intended for one of the Sisterhood."

I adjusted my question. "What do you *want* it to do, once it's finished?"

"Give you a true aim when you really need it," he said.

"Huh? When I really — ?" I thought about it. "So, not *all* the time."

My battlemage shook his head, looking shy. "No, I'm not yet skilled enough to create items which offer continuous enhancement when worn, and those that do get made are only commissioned and awarded by the Valsharess, the Prime, or the High Priestess, anyway. But once this is working right, it'll be useful to you, Red Sister, just as you asked. I only need my Headmaster and your Elder's permission for you to keep it, if it passes inspection."

I had forgotten my own nudity by this point, unabashedly curious about a lot of things. "Continuous enhancement?"

I need permission?

"Wait," I interrupted myself, "how many wizards here can make magic items?"

"Well … all of us. Mostly potions and spell-gems for the Nobles and army."

I rolled my eyes. "No, I mean things like you're describing. Something we wear that lasts a long time, for many uses."

Like the fucking Feldeu.

Callitro grimaced. "Um. I don't know exactly. I only just got started. I was interested before and now have a reason."

I squinted my eyes skeptically.

"We aren't all taught in the same room, Red Sister," he tried to explain. "A lot of it is private study and coaching, and the older ones keep their mouths shut about things they make. If it's powerful enough, there's a gag rule attached, I know that much. I'd never know if a Noble or a Priestess or a Red Sister was wearing something one of the wizards here made for her, because he never brags about it."

Frowning, I gave that some thought. Sadly, it didn't take long for me to think of a reason for this type of training. "Blur the line for abduction," I guessed, "any time a particular wizard is out of the Tower? Especially a battlemage?"

"That's one reason," Callitro agreed. "And keep the Houses from trying to use details like that to twist their status. If an item is made for the Valsharess, the Priesthood, or the Sisterhood, it doesn't matter which House the wizard originally came from."

I grinned. "And which one is — ?"

I saw his change of expression, the instant hesitation and anxiety, and stopped without finishing a question which he'd be required to answer. It wasn't supposed to matter anymore to me, either, yet I recalled thinking the same thing looking at Raegal and Shyntre without a second thought.

Always the way it had been before, the first question: Which House are you? Hmm. Bad habit I need to break.

I studied the ring on my finger. It was a simple but well-made piece. Only when I looked closely did I see tiny runes etched on its perfectly straight edges, running parallel to each other and framed by the darkness of my skin. For when I needed "true aim."

I smiled, reaching to tug on the ring, asking a silent question. The young wizard nodded, and I easily slipped it off, handing it out to him.

"It sounds very useful, Callitro. I look forward to its completion."

He breathed out, accepting it back with a warm smile. "Thank you, Red Sister. It's an honor."

"Mm-hmm," I acknowledged, my smile growing to show teeth. "Would it be an honor to have a Red Sister teach you how to suck a cunt?"

He blinked in surprise at the hard shift in conversation. "I have ssuu …"

I leaned back on my elbows and parted my thighs, feet flat on the floor. Callitro stopped and gulped, his cheeks warming.

"I mean, yes, Red Sister. It would."

"Wonderful." I bore down, squeezing some of his cum out to freshen the glaze on my netherlips. "*Mnh.* Want me to wipe down first or do you like it sopping nasty?"

He started at the white globule. "Uhm. I would relish bathing your mind-blowing cunt for you, Red Sister."

I threw back my head in a laugh of delight. "Now you're learning."

Although, he was lucky; my Sisters didn't give me the choice.

I opened my legs wider, scooting my butt closer to the edge. "Have at it, wizard. Prep it to your liking because you'll be there for a while."

THE SUMMONS FINALLY ARRIVED. MY MOUTH WAS FULL OF COCK AT THE TIME.

"Red Sister, your Elder has called you back to the Cloister."

Damn.

Callitro was very close, quivering on the tipping point as he kneeled above me with his prick halfway down my throat as he clutched my thighs and sucked devotedly on my crotch. I had already peaked twice from his mouth and had been working toward a third. Alas, I was too far to ignore the summons until I made it.

Callitro might as well, though.

I pushed a saliva-slick finger into his netherhole, surprising him, although I had milked his nut-gland once before. The battlemage cried out with his face still buried between my legs, and his hot seed spurted thick, gliding straight down my throat with me hardly tasting it. I rubbed that familiar spot inside his asshole a few more times, just to get those last shudders of ecstasy out of him. He pulled away voluntarily when he became too sensitive for me to continue.

"Red Sister?"

It was Shyntre.

"The Headmaster is unavailable to see you out, but you need to leave now."

He sounded impatient in his endless, reluctant duties. *What a sack.*

I sighed audibly, lying askew on the bed, staring up at the decent height of the ceiling. "Coming!"

Callitro cleaned up and dressed as I did and beat me only because he didn't have so many pieces to put on. He came with me to the door.

"I could see her out, Shyntre," the battlemage offered, breathing deep and still a bit unkempt. He looked adorable; my chest puffed up with pride.

The older bua made a face. "I would take you up on it, given the option. Sorry, you stay here and stay quiet. Like before."

Callitro pursed his lips, breathing a sigh out his nose, and looked at me. He grasped for some type of farewell but was careful to say anything about our visit with the door open to the hall. Small wonder, as I heard a few others open around the circular level.

Subtle.

I grinned and tugged on Callitro's forelock of hair that had escaped his tie. "I'll be back."

The bua smiled at me, and that had to be good enough for both of us.

I left with Shyntre to go to the jump circle. After we stepped inside and before he could concentrate, I said, "You need a bath."

He blinked in surprise, tossed a scowl at me, and replied, "So do you, Red Sister."

Goddess, he's got spine. Not a glimpse of worry for the risk of insulting me.

I smirked and kept my mouth closed while he worked his magic, getting the both of us down to the main floor in two heartbeats which always seemed to last a bit longer. I gulped my stomach back into place and took a deep breath, waiting to see if I would puke.

"Rough trip," I commented. "Still practicing?"

"Says the Sister who distracts the mage at a crucial moment."

As Shyntre stepped out, his voice sounded odd. A little different from before; it wavered, like it wanted to be lower than Raegal.

I shrugged. "Like I said. Still practicing."

I saw his fist close with irritation as the barb hit. He made as if to speak, coughed and touched his throat, then said nothing as he led me to the front door. I kept an eye on his bare hand until we reached it, when he lifted his hand to place his palm upon some runes.

Peering at his frowning, focused face, I witnessed him cast a silent spell to open the door as easily as Phaelous.

Huh. So, this wizard could let me in, too.

He just wouldn't want to.

"Sire teach you that?" I poked, trying to get him to speak again.

Shyntre stopped moving for a moment, drew in a slow breath and let it out as he chose not to reply. It took effort, I could tell. He stood at the door and bowed respectfully to me; it wasn't bad, a solid effort, even though I knew he didn't mean it. He signed with his hand.

⋆Your Elder summons you, Sister.⋆

Stubborn wizard.

There was plenty of space for me to leave; for how wide Shyntre had opened the door, two Sisters abreast could walk out comfortably, three, if a bit snug. But I noticed how the wizard hugged the frame, keeping back as if I had a disease, ready with his hand upon the panel. It was clear he was going to close it as soon as my bootheels cleared the line; he wanted me out, so he could go back to whatever it was he had been doing before I had arrived with the Dwarf stones.

I took a detour to the far right and came very close to him.

I said again. "I'll be back to ask after those stones."

He nodded but didn't look at me, just the panel, and though I tried, I couldn't hear his heartbeat this time.

"Hmph," I grunted, finally stepping out.

Then I caught a whiff of his *real* scent, not the spell he'd been using to mask it, and I froze in place until the door closed behind me, nearly catching my cloak as I whirled around.

I heard nothing, then. The Cavern was silent as the wilderness after the spell locked into place.

My heart pounded in my chest as I stood with my mouth open.

His voice returned to me, too. Recognized too late but hinted at when the spell used to change it had broken down after that "distracted" trip through the jump circle.

The invisible wizard from my trial.

Shyntre. The Headmaster's son.

Fuck!

Chapter 21

★What's wrong?★ Gaelan signed.

I jerked my hand. ★Nothing. Can you show me again?★

She and Reishel exchanged a glance, and Gaelan demonstrated the proper motion to flick coughing powder with more precision and control than I had against the Tragar. I practiced with an inert equivalent, taking it from my belt and trying to tag a moving target without also enveloping myself.

Reishel smiled as she protected her eyes from the floating dust, coughing from simple irritation. ★You're getting it.★

★Again,★ Gaelan instructed. ★This time, we come from behind.★

I pursed my lips and nodded, somewhat satisfied.

But still distracted.

Gaelan ended up knocking the entire pouch from my hand.

"Fuck!" I hissed as she counted coup with a hard jab of her sheathed dagger.

I was dead. Sourly, I retrieved my pouch.

★Again?★ Reishel asked, but Gaelan motioned against it.

★Not where her head is at,★ the mage said. ★We're wasting our time.★

Neither of us argued, and Reishel asked me, ★Where *is* your head?★

Gaelan guessed, ★Either the novice in the Cloister or someone in the

Wizard's Tower.★

★Or both,★ I grudgingly confirmed.

★Not the best place to be,★ she signed wryly.

★Our Elder still hasn't asked me about the latter!★ I vented.

★It's only been three cycles,★ Reishel said.

★Yes, and Sivaraus goes on even with a new Sister to initiate,★ Gaelan said. ★The Sorceress is always busy anyway. What's wrong? Ready to burst in the telling?★

I narrowed my eyes at her. Not an invitation, but fuck it. I checked around us. We weren't far from the quiet cave where my Elder had debriefed me after my first mission of execution at my former House. I knew this place was difficult to find and had wards to warn us of approach, but I still didn't want to talk out in the sparring area.

I exhaled and signed, ★Crouch with me?★

My Sister nodded and motioned to Reishel, leading us into a protective gap where we couldn't be seen if someone stumbled in, but we would see them. Gaelan didn't even have to prompt me once we were there.

"Remember my trials in the candle chamber?" I whispered, and both nodded. "I found the wizard who force-fucked me. I remember his scent. His voice."

All of it had come back in vivid detail while I had stood slack-jawed outside the door Shyntre had closed in my face. My head and heart had been furious, but my stupid cunt had been hot and aching to play rough again. I figured that response wouldn't be a one-time thing, and it annoyed me to no end as I awaited D'Shea's attention.

Reishel showed an innocent surprise while Gaelan's eyes flicked to one side.

The former asked, "So? You can't do permanent harm to the wizards."

"Nothing *permanent*," I repeated with a devious smirk.

"He was ordered by the Prime to participate, Sirana," Gaelan said. "He couldn't refuse."

I sneered. "The bua enjoyed it too much."

Gaelan's mouth twisted. "Yeah. As much as a caged *canurso* enjoys being thrown scraps and then whipped until he eats them."

I narrowed my eyes at her. "Him, a hunter?"

Gaelan shrugged then shook her head. "Could've been one, maybe, if he'd been born a cait."

"You know who he is?"

My elder Sister bit her lip, glancing at Reishel as if passing the question to her.

"That was Phaelous' son, right?" she said, crossing her arms with a casualness that looked genuine. "I heard he has a temper but rarely gets put in his place because he's a Priestess favorite."

"Which Priestess?" I asked with interest. That matched what he'd said about "catching up" after coming back from the Sanctuary.

Reishel shifted. "Erm. I don't know. Maybe more than one."

Bit of a slut, then.

Gaelan looked at her, shrugged noncommittally, then her eyes were back on me. "I've never spoken with him, just watched your trial. It was the only time I've heard his voice. I still don't know his face."

"Either of you know which House he came from?" I asked. "Which Matron or Noble bore him?"

They shook their heads. Disappointingly, I had to believe them as neither of them had been Nobles before the Sisterhood. They wouldn't have been to Court or been in position to hear much gossip about bloodlines.

"What do you want from D'Shea once you tell her?" Reishel asked curiously.

That was the frustrating part.

At first, I thought the satisfaction of discovering him and receiving praise from my Elder in tracking him down would be enough. I already knew it wasn't, but I didn't know what to ask next. I had promised to play with him, to pay him back in my time, but the difficulty and distraction of that was significant and less desirable now than it had been at the time.

I have much more to which I should pay attention. I'm walking a fine line with both Elders, and they protect me from the Prime. The Dwarf stones, Callitro's ring ... I have reasons and excuses to visit, but what to do, now knowing both much more and still not enough about him? No wonder D'Shea was smiling like that.

"I don't know," I admitted.

"Maybe forget it, then," she suggested.

I ground my teeth. "Maybe."

Not likely.

"Can we practice holds instead?" I asked.

We were back to the Cloister in time for more tasks, more chores, more shoveling down "dung-spread fiberstalk" in the Mess Hall. The food was warm, at least, if not inspired.

Gaelan, Reishel, and I received our first interrogation mission together from Elder Rausery, who hooked us coming out of mess, asking us to step into her quarters. I took a deep whiff when we arrived but didn't smell Jael here recently.

"Servant's been softened up," the General said, seeming to think about three other things as she briefed us. "Paranoid, catching a glimpse of red here and there. Fairly sure she saw whoever grabbed their healer. Get what you can out of her. A name or symbol would be great."

"Yes, Elder."

On our way out, as we collected our gear in a stock room, I commented, "Didn't know Matron Shenpra *had* a healer."

The House was Fourteenth, only two below mine.

Gaelan nodded, focused on her hands. "A bua. Her nephew. You don't hear about the ones that can heal by touch instead of brewing. Otherwise *this* happens."

Reishel nodded. "Almost guaranteed that another House abducted him. He'll be buried deep by now. Whoever's got him will try to warp him to serve only her. It's a short window before he's broken and useless to everyone."

And the Sisterhood is looking for him. I pursed my lips. We were only one small team, available for some less urgent branch of the investigation, but we might get lucky.

"If his House can't hold him," I asked, "why are we being sent to get him back for them? He'll just get grabbed again, now that *someone* knows."

"We're not bringing him back," Gaelan said, keeping her eyes on the floor. "The Elders will take him to the Valsharess if he still has a mind, and then She will probably give him to the Priestesses. There's a reason they call them 'divine healers.' "

"He'll never go home," Reishel added. "I can count the number of touch-menders who've been born in my lifetime on one hand."

"That you know about," I added.

Her smile was grim. "All of them are in the Sanctuary now, and of Noble blood."

"Huh. Nobody *really* important, I take it?"

"They're all male," Gaelan cut in.

I blinked. "No female 'divine' healers?"

She smirked at me. "None who aren't made to be Priestesses. Lelinahdara healed you by touch."

Oh, right.

I already knew we didn't have any bua Priestesses, but regardless, it was obvious as a strike in the forehead that the Sanctuary would want control of this kind of healer.

Maybe they have something to do with the Consorts as 'sons' of the Priestesses?

The search for the young Noble appealed to me. Even if I would never get very close to the discovery of his location, moving about over the next two cycles without Reverie, I learned a lot from watching Reishel and Gaelan during the interrogation of the servant of House Shenpra, and from the other opportunities we were able to exploit.

Gaelan was familiar with many areas around the Market where we followed up on whispers, and Reishel understood more about the outlying farmland than I'd realized.

Meanwhile, though each had a basic knowledge of the Noble pedigree, they always looked to me to give them a short-cut or confirmation with the current names at Court. Jaunda had warned me, D'Shea would not allow me to fall behind.

As a result, we covered a lot of ground quickly, and what we brought back helped. I knew it the moment I saw Rausery's face during our last report.

"Excellent," she said. "This is the lead I needed."

The three of us didn't know how it was, exactly, but something had linked together in the Elder's eyes. She was grinning like a hungry thief about to nab a pie cooling on the table.

"Take a break, Sisters, you've earned it," she said, and her tone made me feel warm and proud. "Oh. And Jael's still here after five cycles, hasn't gotten herself killed yet."

Unconsciously, I smiled. *Calling her by her name. Good sign.*

"Take your turn, if you get the chance. I might ask your opinion later. Dismissed."

"Thank you, Elder," we said.

Hmm. Sleep or sex? Always a tough call. Then again, was I up for holding down a biting, nut-hooking bruiser? *She must be in worse shape than I am by now.*

Given the choice, Gaelan had already made hers by the time we reached the first ramp around the curve. She shook her head in the dim light. "Just want some Reverie. Maybe later."

Reishel seemed to want to follow her but hesitated, looking to me. "You want her, Sirana?"

Well, when she says it like that … I nodded an affirmative. "Yeah, I do."

"Can't loan you my Feldeu," Gaelan said before I could ask, giving me an irritated look, as though it wasn't her idea but she'd still paid for what happened last time.

I nodded again. "So be it."

I didn't want to court a resurgence of Kain's shard while initiating a new Sister, anyway. I hadn't heard his voice since making peace with Lana and hoped he might be gone for good, but I couldn't tell if my mind was truly healed or just numbed.

Given how much I'd enjoyed Reishel and Callitro recently, my way and *without* a cock, I had more confidence leading again now than in a long time. Better for Jael that she sees this side; few things had led me to accept my role and place in the Sisterhood more than Lead Jaunda when she welcomed my ass into the Cloister with both hands.

There was no doubt that she thought I belonged.

I wagered that, as I found out more about each Red Sister, I'd find the Sisterhood was all misfits in Davrin society, anyway. And Jael Aurenthietti was, for certain, another misfit.

"I'll help you find her," Reishel offered, stifling a yawn, and I grinned in thanks.

I wouldn't say it aloud, but I felt relief when we found the Sisters who currently had the novice. It wasn't Corpora Thena and her team, but a pair, Red Sisters Mela and Graer, who had no particular grudge against me or Reishel.

They both owned Feldeus, and Mela sat in a worn chair holding Jael's ears, the recruit's face held firm in her lap and phallus lodged full between her lips and down her throat, while the other kneeled behind her, enjoying the ride in one hole or the other. Jael was tense but tolerating it, neither fighting nor particularly engaged.

Mela looked up and grinned at me and Reishel. Graer noticed and glanced over her shoulder, still holding tight to Jael's hips. She smiled as well, and their focus and teamwork in double-ending the new Sister seemed revived.

They like being watched.

I winked at Mela and reached to squeeze Reishel's firm backside cupped tight in her leathers. Reishel squeaked, offering a fun expression of surprise and a chuckle. Jael couldn't fail to notice the heightened energy of the pair, and she grunted, making more noise as the two Red Sisters demonstrated that enthusiasm in rutting her.

"Oh, that's good," I murmured, rubbing my crotch through my leathers watching the pair.

Mela took one, abrupt moment to shift her chair with a scraping thud. It hauled Jael into an erotic profile so that Graer could get a better look at Reishel and me as she lunged with her phallus deep inside the recruit. Their eyes traced my body, my hand, and they enjoyed Jael so much more on that account. Better for her, if Rausery really did ask for opinions.

Inspired, I stepped behind my Sister, arms coming around to molest Reishel from behind, my hand heavy and rough, mauling her mound through the red leather. My Sister submitted, leaning back against me with a soft moan.

Mela and Graer murmured approval, grinned and panted as they spit-roasted Jael, and I showed teeth in a wide, hungry grin, tugging at the hip ties of Reishel's uniform to expose her dark skin and white puff adorning her sex. My red gloves fondled her, and Reishel made more noise.

This helped my other Sisters climax faster, and they reached it almost at the same time.

"Shit!" Mela gasped, thrusting a couple more times, slowing down. "Shit ... ah, yeah ..."

With a deep, rumbling sigh, Graer pulled her cock out of Jael's slit, and I could be glad that the novice's netherhole had received a break. I slapped Reishel's cunt just as she was starting to get aroused, and she yelped in protest; Mela and Graer laughed.

"Our turn?" I asked.

They nodded, taking hold of Jael at each end and shoving her away from them, toward me and Reishel near the doorway. Jael barely caught herself so her chin didn't strike the stone, but then she fell, trembling and too spent to stand up.

"Have at," Mela invited, leaning back to relax in her chair, a spit-soaked, black prick sticking up and hovering above her belly. She didn't move to pull up her leathers around her ankles.

"Pucker's probably had a chance to tighten up again," Graer suggested, putting her leathers back into place as Reishel tightened her own and set her skewed belt back into place.

"Excellent."

We stepped forward to claim the newest Sister, each taking an arm and pulling Jael to unsteady feet, and she shivered. I saw tiny bumps spreading across her skin and glanced at her dark purple nipples. Enjoying the turgid, tight form, my gaze drifted farther down her flat belly to her mons. I blinked in surprise.

Her pubic fur was gone. Her crotch was only smooth skin, like a juvenile Davrin.

What the fuck?

Furtively, the Aurenthin glanced up at me, wary and uncertain, as I looked toward the other two Red Sisters. Graer read the question on my face and shrugged.

"Not us. Someone who had her before took the fluff. She hasn't said who."

"We didn't ask," Mela corrected, and Graer smirked.

"Got it," I said, nodding toward Reishel, who might have looked more sympathetic in private. "Doesn't matter, I guess, just weird."

"Eh, her slit feels the same if you don't look at it," Graer confirmed.

I nodded again, and Jael's flushed, swollen mouth pursed tight as we led her away to another section of the Cloister. Reishel took a sniff and looked at me.

"Let's stop by the sluicers," I murmured.

The scents and saliva of probably seven to ten Red Sisters remained to clean off the novice before I would put her on my pallet. I had gone through the same, passed around from one place to another. A good portion of it, I was in a magical high that blurred a lot of detail, for better or worse, but those cold showers in between gangbangs had always brought me aware for a while.

I could wonder how much of this Jael would remember clearly later, but for certain she'd recall the sluicers. The shock of cold was enough that she yelled and started fighting us.

I grabbed her mouth to muffle her, bent her backward as she stood in discomfort on her toes, water spraying her sweaty belly, running down her thighs to her feet. Gloves off, Reishel kneeled and began rinsing Jael's well-used crotch as the novice writhed like her bald cunt was too sensitive.

"Quiet," I whispered. "We're lucky we have the place to ourselves right now, but that won't last if you keep making noise."

The young fighter quivered, nodded agreement, breathing hard through her nose. The tight tips of her small breasts wrinkled still more as I watched, and I grinned in delight. When I removed my hand from her mouth, she didn't make a peep.

I can wash, she signed, acknowledging this was a short opportunity to get clean.

Prepared for rebellion, Reishel and I released her, and Jael scrubbed herself without our help, willing and urgent. She was thorough.

I grabbed a towel from the cabinet, wrapped it around her, and Reishel and I hustled Jael out before she'd barely begun to dry herself, leaving wet footprints upon the stone as she clung tight to the only covering she had possessed for the last several spans.

We stopped by one of the storerooms so I could grab some dry rations then we moved to my small room in the barracks, located not far from Lead Jaunda's. The three of us relaxed when we got the door closed behind us without being confronted by other Red Sisters. Reishel exhaled, smiled at me, and I smiled back, chuckling when she fought another yawn.

"Reverie?" I asked.

Reishel rubbed an eye. "Hmm. Truth, yes. Been a long two cycles."

I nodded. "Go ahead. Join Gaelan, if she'll let you. Thanks for the help."

Reishel smiled at that, looking at Jael, whose bright copper eyes flicked back and forth between us as she kept her mouth closed. My Sister brushed Jael's cheek with her fingertips, and the novice jerked her head up in surprise and annoyance.

"Don't be stupid." Reishel nodded with visible affection to me. "And secure the door."

"Will do," I said as she stepped by us to let herself out.

I waited until she was gone then followed through. The ward itself had worn out — I needed Gaelan to refresh it — and I would receive neither magical warning nor barrier against a Sister determined to enter, but a chain attachment I'd installed would at least slow her down.

Jael looked around the sparse room before I pulled her damp towel off her shoulders and pushed my hand against her bare back to guide her toward the pallet. She went, although reluctance still radiated in each barefooted step as I hung the towel on a wall hook. She kneeled to crawl onto the mat and rolled to sit on her backside with her knees drawn up.

The Aurenthin looked up at me as I began to undress and secure my weapons out of easy reach. A tightening of her mouth was the only show of dismay once I was fully nude, but I noted it.

She was tired. I was far from a loathed or frightful figure to her, but in this state, it didn't matter who had her next. At the same time, I knew I wasn't up to the task of impressing her, so maybe that made my decision for me.

I picked up one of the small bags of rations and sat on the pallet with the recruit. I ate first, dipping into the mixture of rich pods, seeds, dried meats, and toasted pastes. Chewing methodically and swallowing, I offered some to Jael from the same bag. She didn't take long to accept; she had been watching my hands, which I kept in full view. The risk in eating was as low as she could expect.

We consumed the first, and she watched me open and sample the second before accepting more. She was as hungry as I was. When we had finished the two bags, I kept the third for later and twirled my finger.

"Roll over, Jael. On your side, facing the wall."

This would put her back to me, and the muscles in her arms flexed as she stared at me. She glanced around the room again then back. I watched her without moving. Once given long enough to consider her alternatives, Jael did the smart thing and obeyed.

I lay down and moved up close, cradling her back and buttocks with my body. With one arm folded beneath my head, my free hand drifted over soft skin and the occasional bruise, over her flank and hips and right buttock. She flinched when I caressed her ass, and I kept my hand away from her orifices since it was not my intent anyway.

She was toned and strong, and I enjoyed her lean scent up close; fragrant and earthy without being tart, neither too musky nor of heavy perfume. I stroked her arm up and down and then reached beneath it to cup one breast, first rubbing my thumb back and forth over her nipple, then in slow circles.

She drew in breath and tensed as I nuzzled through her damp hair and nipped the back of her neck. My nibbling turned into lazy draws with my lips, and the slow circles around her nipple grew even slower.

"What are you doing?" she asked through clenched teeth.

"Whatever I want," I responded, my breath hot in her hair.

"So … Do it already."

"I am. Be quiet. I'm very tired."

She huffed a laugh tinged with bitterness. "Tired? Oh, poor Red Sister! So sorry to have burdened you with my eager and awaiting cunt!"

I couldn't restrain the chuckle against her shoulder.

"What's so funny?" she sneered, a tremor passing through her naked body. "I didn't *ask* to be made bald!"

Is that what she worried about? I gave her nipple a little squeeze and a twist. I was just playing with it, but she tensed and squeaked. "Who did that, anyway?"

Jael growled, then swallowed her answer, her shoulders hunched up. The loaded silence stretched long enough that I wondered.

"The Prime?" I asked.

She hesitated, murmured, "You said to be quiet so you could rest, Sister."

Huh.

I removed my hand from her breast and spread it flat over her abdomen if it might help her take a deeper breath. I drew air myself, deep in then back out, nice and slow. Enjoying her scent and managing to relax despite the situation. I closed my eyes and listened to life signs faster than mine and felt her charged energy as we were pressed skin-to-skin.

She still waited for something to happen. Nothing would, unless she acted first. The quiet stretched as Jael's muscles softened a little at a time, if only because she couldn't maintain readiness to fight when exhaustion dragged at her as it did me. Jael struggled to stay awake until I drifted into Reverie.

She probably only lasted a score of heartbeats before falling into the same.

CHAPTER 22

"Talk to me," the Matron whispered. *"With your hands, with your lips, however you can. What happened?"*

"Demons," the youth confessed upon drawing enough courage. *"Yellow eyes watching me sleep. In my room, in the deep shadows. They have white manes. Claws."*

This Matron was young for having had four Daughters and two sons already. She had probably been barely more than a cait herself the first time she'd caught a bua's seed. There was more concern on her beautiful face than there was on any female of power at Court. Her bright eyes, the same color as her young Daughter, sparkled with intelligence.

"Damn them," the Matron whispered, straightening up. She put her hand to her lips, thinking deeply. She seemed to come up with nothing new for she shook her head and said it again. *"Damn them ..."*

"What, Mother? Please?"

The older Davrin frowned at the worn desk still holding together past the time it should have broken a leg and needed to be replaced. There were old, brittle notes taken by previous Matrons, and resilient leather wraps trying to keep them contained.

"The Priesthood may come for you when you're grown," she said with frank sobriety, her thoughts unfiltered. *"It has been so through the time of many Matrons. Sometimes, they just come and take one of us. The one they choose vanishes, we*

never know what becomes of them. Those Sathoet are always the first sign."

The cait blinked her wide eyes, hand clenching into a fist as she shook her head with fear. "No! I'll run away! Like Franek."

The Matron shook her head. "They track the Daughters, my baby. Sometimes the sons can get away to the Fringe, but …"

"What should I do, Mother?" the youth implored.

The Matron swallowed. "Learn to fight. Perhaps a Red Sister will notice you and challenge the Sanctuary."

JAEL JERKED WHEN I DID, EACH OF US STARTLED BY THE SUDDEN MOVEMENT AS something jarred me awake. My heart pounded in my ears, but I still held the novice against me; by the scent and the warmth surrounding us, neither of us had moved for quite a while.

The voices and images from my Reverie faded from my mind's eye, and I heard Jael lick her lips and swallow as she came fully awake. She shifted her head slightly, trying to look around. I wondered if she didn't recognize where she was. It was possible.

"Rest well?" I asked.

She tensed against me but didn't pull away or twist around. I was sure now that she had rested; the comparative tension which returned was stark.

"Sirana."

I smiled even though she couldn't see it. "I am."

Jael paused. She hadn't yet looked my way; my breasts were warm pressed to her back. "How did I get here?"

I frowned. "What do you mean?"

She swallowed. "I … I only know I've been fighting for spans to stay alive. Th-the Sathoet came for me, probably because I insulted the Fifth House healer."

"True," I said.

"Then you and Elder Rausery were there. Grabbed me away from them."

"Yes."

"Put me through all this ... lying, so the Prime could accept me."

"Mm, as my Elders decide. I mostly watched, but it seems that way to me."

"But you *didn't* just watch. You fought for me! You wanted me here, among you."

"We need new Sisters," I confessed. "Two of us didn't make it through that Ornilleth battle where we met."

Jael was surprised. "I ... never heard a whisper that Red Sisters died in that."

"They were taken away before anyone could see."

It only took a moment's thought, and the youth nodded her head in understanding. "I've heard ... things. The others were talking as they fucked me. I know you are the youngest, besides me. Did you just want a new cunt to take your place at the bottom? Figured I'd be used to it?"

I smirked. "Not just any 'new cunt,' Jael. You are right for us, and you made it back to Sivaraus alive. Being on the bottom is a necessary test. Every Red Sister who gained her leathers has gone through something like this."

"So you watched me. You are the reason they came for me?"

"No." I wagered that she knew this already; she was testing. "You are the reason they came for you. My assignment was to observe."

"Which you didn't do when I was trapped by Tragar."

"D'Shea hates wasted opportunity. More so than Rausery, I think."

Jael huffed a skeptic's laugh. "So, the Elder Sorceress follows strict orders only when it's convenient."

I chuckled. "Sounds about right. Working within to make them work for her."

★"Pfft!★ Gonna blow up in her face one turn."

"Well, she's six hundred, at least, and still alive. You could do with less rebellion and more bending. Your trial with the Prime should have told you that."

She was dead silent for a long while. "Still watching me?"

"When possible. Not then. What happened at the Sanctuary when the Prime dragged you there?"

Too late, I knew the mistake. I had pushed her past a breaking point with that one.

She jerked away, and I only just caught her back to me. She cursed at me and tried again to escape, whether to strike me or scramble to the other side of the room, I didn't know, but I had Jaunda and Gaelan's tutoring to thank for managing to hold onto the initiate now.

Jael wouldn't give up, and I was forced to turn my new Sister onto her belly and climb on top. It wasn't a hardship for me; the wriggling and flexing of her buttocks against my groin made me purr as I held on to both her wrists above her head and pressed down with my weight. The side of her face pressed to the pallet, she looked up at me with one eye through her hair. Her teeth were clenched.

"You're going to do it now?" she hissed. "Fuck hard as you want to, you won't impress me. Neither did the Prime, no matter what she tortured me to say!"

Her heart seemed ready to burst in memory of that torment, the sheer helplessness beneath both Prime and Sathoet. Her breath was ragged, getting worse.

She must calm down or she was going to pass out.

I lay on top, held her immobile, kissed her ear. "Maybe soon. You *do* smell good. But first, tell me what Elder Rausery said when we captured you running away from those first Sathoet in the barn. Who she was talking to? Do you remember? I can tell you if you don't remember. I was there, soothing your netherhole for you with my tongue."

Jael blinked, clear in her memory of me doing that. Satisfied, I watched as her eyes narrowed as she reached farther back. It was not swift, but I waited. Soon she had focused enough, determinedly expanding her lungs to talk.

"She complimented Lead Qivni on 'snaring' them in her first word."

"Yes. I've seen the Lead do it before, sending away a Sathoet attacking me. And she did it for you. Qivni is the only one who knows how, I think, but I know the Priestesses can't randomly send the demonbloods here because we have her."

"The Lead blocks them." Jael began to relax, perhaps seeing the Cloister in a new light.

"Yes. She's only impressed with self-discipline, however, so you may have to work harder to impress her than you have with me."

Jael was quiet but I could almost hear her thoughts racing; some of the frustration on her face melted away, along with the tension in her body. It was abrupt enough to make me wonder whether I could be wrong about something I'd just said.

"Or has she already seen you?" I asked.

She nodded an affirmative.

"And approved?"

"Yeah. Lead Qivni was the first."

As Lead Jaunda had been mine. *Huh.*

"Does she like you?" I asked.

Her hips moved under me again as if she was trying to wriggle out or tease me. It had been brief.

"Jael?"

"Shut up," she mumbled, white eyelashes down. "She warned me not to talk to you about her."

I stared in disbelief but felt an honest glee that Qivni cared enough to mention me to the recruit. The connections and balances were still growing, still changing. The very thought energized me.

Jael wiggled again, and I pulled her arms down to cross her wrists at her lower back so that I could keep her in submission but have one hand free. She made an enticing sound, wordless but protesting as I slid my fingers down her side and in between us, along the crease of her butt and thigh, touching her sex. She squealed softly as I felt her netherlips and probed at her hole with a finger.

She was a little moist, but only enough to suggest recent arousal — as we struggled but not before. I thought she wasn't fighting me as hard as she might.

"As you wish," I said, sounding pleased.

I released her, lifting my weight and moving to one side, and kept her between the wall and me. She rolled and scooted to gain a little space between us then she looked at me with high suspicion and incredulity.

"What the fuck are you playing, Sirana?" she demanded. "Or are you frigid with caits and only suck cunt around here?"

I burst out laughing and took her hand, leading it between my thighs, onto my naked, hot netherlips. "If that feels frigid to you, let me know!"

I was far wetter than she was, and her fingers played around with my sex. Lingering. She snatched her hand back as soon as I moaned aloud.

"Little tease," I chuckled.

"So, you're just playing. Qivni told me you only make light of things."

Neither of them had seen me ranting about Shyntre not long ago. I propped my head on my palm and smiled, studying her face. "I think I know what this is. You both have that serious streak with a low threshold for prank. Am I not dour enough to arouse you?"

Jael scowled at me, not taking the jest well. "Fuck you, Twelfth, *you* don't expect to stay on the bottom for long. I've never stood anywhere else!"

"This is about our former Houses now?" I shrugged. "I can say I have no idea where anyone else came from, they won't tell me. Not even D'Shea or Qivni, both of whom seem to have stronger ties with the Sanctuary. Yet everyone seems to forget, or not talk about it. You survive long enough, Jael, I bet you'll have a lot of younger Red Sisters under you who have no idea you were from the Lowest House. And you're not, anymore, you're in the Sisterhood."

Copper eyes narrowed like sharp daggers, but she said nothing on this. She changed the subject. "So why did Qivni warn me about you? What did you do to flick her off?"

Had a bad dream in her room while stinking of divine magic.

I opted not to share that. I shrugged. "I couldn't get her off. She didn't want me, Jaunda did. What about you? Did you make Qivni climax?"

Jael seemed a little disoriented despite my letting her lead our topic. "Um. Yes."

I smiled. "I'm impressed. Jaunda laughs while she fucks me. I think I prefer that, after trying everyone here, but Qivni might find it fucking annoying."

I spotted a tiny smile on the novice's face. Just a little on the right side. "Yeah. She does."

My smile became a grin. "Goddess, you *have* had some good conversation with the Lead, haven't you? Doubly impressed. She barely said anything to me. But I did figure it out eventually."

"Figure out what?"

"Juicy lips down low loosen lips up high."

Jael huffed again, a soft laugh. "Lead Jaunda talks to you, huh?"

"Center web." I winked. "She's my best shield. If you move your tongue to get Qivni to move hers, then she's your best shield. Listen to her, and never refuse her when she's horny."

Jael gave me a look; perhaps she realized we were talking too much about our Leads. I was satisfied it had taken her this long to notice.

I reprised. "A Lead likes you. That counts for a lot, Jael. Don't do anything stupid, like try to kill another Sister, and you'll stay with us. Give it time, forge some successes, and we start to forget how we came to be here."

"But you're still new," she said. "How do you *know* they'll forget?"

I thought about that. Mostly, I got that impression from how fluid Reishel's status had proven after she returned to us from a coma. Jael was right about one thing: I was already off the bottom rung, but it wasn't because we just nabbed her.

"Most Sisters seem to live in this moment of time," I said. "Only a few are required to live in perpetual forethought. I mean, you lived in your moment at your former House, Jael. Whose task or burden was it to live in the future?"

She didn't even hesitate. "My Matron's."

"And in this Cloister, who has that burden?"

"The Prime ..." She noticed my smirk and the slight shake of my head. "Hm. The Elders. Rausery and D'Shea."

I nodded. "Do what you do best and, as their show of appreciation, the others forget where you came from."

Jael thought this over in silence, staring at a spot on the wall before she looked at me again. "You'll be one of those forethinkers, won't you?"

Now I looked to the side. "Maybe."

"You are. I can tell." She shrugged. "And you can have it. Things get tight, just tell me where to stab, I got it, and my mouth stays tight, too."

I blinked in genuine surprise, a laugh of disbelief slipping out of me. "You're jesting."

"You're not stupid or petty, Sirana."

I snorted. "So sure, novice?"

"Yeah." Jael straightened her shoulders, offering a nice display of her breasts. "Panagan was one of Thena's, and *they* mentioned you, too, while they fucked me. How you almost fucked up when they made you snap." She swallowed. "But you worked with Panagan to find me, pushed a grudge aside. You have your reasons to do things, better thought out than most. Especially if D'Shea favors you. So, I mean it. If things get tight, just tell me what you want me to do."

I stared at her. She could hear my heart; she made that plain as she tilted an ear.

No cait had ever handed me that kind of power, and no bua had ever sounded so sure of doing it. Especially this soon after any sort of bond.

My eyes wandered as I considered what to say; my gaze trailed down her body, coming to rest again on that odd, bald patch at the junction of her legs. I missed the white, curling fur crowning her thighs. The white hair had still been there in the wilderness, and I had made it through my own trials still adorned.

Which Sister opted for this? And how? Why?

Ultimately, I could think of nothing to say to her promise, having no plan at all to use it. I released a long, thoughtful exhale as I stared at her, reaching out now to nudge her shoulder.

"On your back, Jael."

She blinked, but obeyed readily enough, rolling herself in place to recline. I moved closer on my side and smoothed my hand along her inner thigh. I could smell her fragrance, though much subtler without the hair.

If the scent were weaker for the lack, then maybe the texture would make up for it.

Jael's gasp was incomplete as I pulled her leg open and crawled between her thighs on my elbows and knees. I kissed the bare mound. It was incredibly smooth, as if the shave with a superiorly sharp blade had just happened. I didn't see how, though.

I ran both hands along her inner thighs and ended by rubbing both thumbs slowly along her pouting netherlips. Her hands gripped the blanket and I had to wonder what she expected, or dreaded, from me after what she'd just said?

I admired the novice's naked slit, noticed the raw, dark pink look between her purple-tinged lips, and on closer inspection I saw tiny, swollen bumps where the individual hairs should have been. I touched and peered closely, realizing only then that no blade — no matter how thin and sharp — could have removed not only the hairs but the roots as well.

"Did a Sister pluck every hair out of your sex?" I asked, letting her hear the surprise in my voice.

She shook her head but didn't elaborate.

"No? This wasn't done with a blade. How was it done?"

"Melted candle wax," she said shortly, staring up at the ceiling.

"Who?"

"Thena and Suna. Used strips of cloth dipped in wax to rip it all out. They had to tie me down."

I imagined that and grimaced. "Did they say why?"

She tried to shrug it off but was too anxious. "Not really. Not beyond just wanting to see what it looked like."

I frowned at that, gently rubbing my thumbs along her lips again. I didn't see any torn skin. Just hairless. Slightly pebbled.

Trimming and sculpting our crotch fur was quite common among Davrin of both sexes but, at Court, a denuded Elf was either being demeaned or disgraced by shaving the head, too, or had been ordered to satisfy a Noble with suspicious tastes in lovers.

Given the Sisterhood's strict line barring the rape of children with our Feldeus, I supposed Thena and Suna had simply been demeaning Jael.

Except they hadn't cut her hair, too. No one would have questioned if they had, but now I did.

The thought turned me off, so I set it aside. I could still admire the full, mature lips and the lovely symmetry, and the grown scent, even without fur. I leaned forward to enjoy a whiff of her slit. Closing my eyes, I lowered my mouth onto that naked sex, offering sucking kisses and flicking my tongue gently over the smooth flesh. She drew in her breath.

I tasted her body deeper, felt the heat of her slit — greater than my tongue — as I tested the spongy, swollen flesh. She was indeed sore. Forceful penetration might make her draw away from me. Her body language told me she was waiting for it, expecting it. Ready.

So am I.

My mouth settled into a quiet contemplation exploring her smooth skin, and I did not think about much except for the scent below my nose, the pure taste of her cunt, the warm give of tender flesh against my tongue and lips, and the moist heat on my cheeks which reminded me of an underground hot spring.

Sometimes I'd withdraw and let her feel the chill of the air as I blew soft breath onto her wet skin, then I'd lick lightly, suck with pure enjoyment, and always keep her wondering when I'd turn from lavishing to punishing as my hands explored her thighs and buttocks. I heard her arms move, and I looked up.

Her own eyes had closed, and her left hand was gently twisting one of her nipples. Her eyes opened almost instantly, and she stopped, either sensing my gaze ...

Or she had just felt my lips smile against her.

"Mmm," I hummed, encouraging. I saw her mouth open at the sensation.

Her hand fell back to her side just before I closed my eyes again, continuing to service her. Her lingering soreness and wariness made for a very slow climb, but at least the climb was there. Her tension through it changed at last from the anticipation of pain to the acknowledgment of pleasure.

When Jael involuntarily started closing her legs, a little bit at a time, and when those smooth, strong thighs finally squeezed my ears, I wrapped my arms more tightly around them, forcing them open, choosing my preference over hers. She gasped at my first show of force, and I dove in, mouthing her with more enthusiasm, finally pushing her toward that steeper part of her climb.

It's time that she be pushed.

"Ah! Goddess ..." she moaned, and for a moment she sounded afraid as she gripped the blanket in both hands. "S-stop —"

She was losing control of her responses, and maybe it hurt just a little. *Good.*

No cait in her right mind should stop at this point.

I pierced her with a spear-shaped, stiff tongue, over and over, alternating with harder strokes against her clitoris. She yelped and shifted her legs, then I felt her heels digging into my back. She gave me an aborted scream when I released one thigh to push a single finger inside her, rubbing hard a few times at the firm ridge at the roof of her cunt.

That's it, little scrapper. Let it go. Submit again, it's just you and me.

Jael moved her hips of her own accord and made frequent sounds — chirps and calls and groans — such a contrast from her earlier silence that her voice drove my excitement higher. I worked to push her farther, to see how far she could go.

I was so aroused now, aching, I wished I had Gaelan's Feldeu ready to penetrate her, to feel her slick body clutching around me as our breasts pressed together, her legs wrapped around my hips.

I used two fingers now, thrust them into her, drinking in those delicious, sloppy noises warning me the novice might stain the blanket below us very soon—

At that worst possible moment, the door broke inward, the chain sheered with a magic burst.

"Ha! Found you!"

Jael jerked away from me, her gasp of utter horror, her climb crashing in an abrupt halt. I was up and moving before I had a thought beyond something venomous, and the intruding Sister was ready for a response as I charged her in the tiny room.

But she still fell for a feint.

Her eyes focused on my arm and my fist as I wound up for a strike, at the last moment, I side-kicked her knee instead, following that with a thrust to her face with the heel of my hand. She stumbled and fell to all fours, reaching for something on her belt. I snatched my metal washbowl and smashed it down on her hand just as it came back up.

Thena cried out, dropped her pouch, and I barely had time to fall on her, rolling her into one of Jaunda's holds. I wrapped my legs around from the back and hooked my heels at her knees, slipping my arms beneath hers and clasping my hands together at the base of her neck.

"Gotcha," I said, and the Corpora screamed in shocked rage.

"Let me GO!!"

We rocked and thrashed for good long time, the jutting points of her armor and weapons bruising and scraping my nude body. Jael remained on the bed at first, watching but frozen with indecision.

"Been a while since we last fought, hasn't it?" I panted.

"Get off, Sirana! I'm going to split your ass for this!"

"Whatever. So, where's Suna? Surprised she wasn't attached to your belt, too."

"Don't need her to get the croot from *you*."

"So, she's on a task and you're looking for someone to alleviate boredom? Came to the right place. Hey, Jael? Start stripping her, would you?"

I saw Jael think about it, and she started moving toward us.

"No! Jael," Thena warned, her voice rough in her intensity. "I'll make it so much worse for you later!"

The novice slowed up, I saw her expression; she thought twice, and I even agreed. Neither of us had a working Feldeu or any other sexual equipment, so breaking Thena would be difficult. Jael *would* pay a high price later, and I wouldn't have discouraged Thena one whit from trying to push her around. I hadn't even managed to get Thena to stop forcing *me* to spread for her over this last turn.

I changed my instruction. "Jael, take off her belt and weapons, then step back out of reach."

"*Cunts!*"

I accepted quite a lot of pain to hold Thena as her struggles intensified. If she could have gotten to any of my nerve points, it would have been over already, but my recent practice paid off. *Thanks, Gaelan.*

I managed to hold Thena long enough so that Jael completed what I told her, and I enjoyed the sight of her smiling, standing over us with Thena's entire belt in hand, her naked thighs still glazed with her own lubricant which I'd drawn so patiently out of her.

Sexy.

"Now pull off that third pouch on the right side, the one with two knots side by side."

"*Sirana!*" Thena yelled, her voice reverberating in the small room.

The Corpora gasped constantly from her efforts to break free, and I gained another deep bruise and a ringing head as she slammed us against the floor and snapped her head back, striking me in the ear. I'd turned my head just enough that she didn't break my nose. The novice was holding up a familiar pouch.

"*Agh, ow* ... Yes, that one," I groaned. "Open it and sprinkle a pinch over her face."

"I'm going to fucking kill you!" Thena seethed.

I laughed, impulsively kissing my captive's ear while my left one throbbed. "Oh, come on, Corpora, sometimes we're just in the wrong place at the wrong time. This is one of your times. Jael, make sure she breathes it in."

I held my breath and closed my eyes as Jael followed through; Thena tried to do the same, but the youngest Sister took her opportunity. Jael punched Thena straight in the stomach, forcing her breath to explode and draw in air again immediately; the powder was already on her nose and lips. The elder Sister coughed and moaned and cursed us both.

Given enough time, Thena fell unconscious, going lax in my grip. I kept hold of her, breathing out, very slow, my mouth and nose pressed as low on her spine as I could reach, then inhaled with caution. My lungs burned for more air, but I waited to see if Thena was acting.

Jael saved me some time by slapping the older Sister's bloodied face, nice and hard. When there was no response at all and the Corpora was truly dead weight, I let go and pushed her off me to get to my feet.

Jael's eyes were bright; she laughed softly, looking from Thena to me. "Now what?"

"Now we dump her and her equipment outside where other Sisters will find her, then we move over to Gaelan's room." My eyes flicked to her visible slit. "And pick up where we left off."

"Naked?"

"Absolutely. Although keep the sleep powder and a dagger, just in case. Be ready to pass it to me."

Jael nodded, thinking. "Why Gaelan?"

"She's got stronger Wards on her door."

"Ah."

With Jael's help, I managed to drape the unconscious Sister facedown over my shoulder, and the novice opened the door, followed me as I carried Thena out deep into the Cloister. This tested my endurance, but we managed to find Mela and Graer again; they sparred in a practice room near Qivni's room.

I kneeled in front of them to lay Thena on the stone, managing not to crack her head, though she would have deserved it.

They blinked and stared at me, seeing the clear marks on me from the struggle, noting Thena's bloody lip and nose, and the fact that the elder Red Sister was still fully clothed. Jael tossed her belt and weapons on top of the bested Corpora and stepped back behind me, holding on to one sheathed dagger and the pouch.

I said, "Please tell Lead Qivni I may be a little longer with the novice but will bring her to her quarters when I'm finished."

After a silent moment while I waited, ready for any response, Mela covered her smile behind a glove. The two each looked at the other, and Graer said, "Sure, Sirana. We'll let her know."

I bowed, a bit Court-like, with a clear smile. "This interrupted cunt thanks you."

They chuckled, watching as I hooked Jael's waist with one arm, taking the dagger from her, which she surrendered willingly, and I pulled her away with me. I listened for movement at our backs, but no Sisters approached. My witnesses had decided to let me keep what I'd earned, and it was up to them what to do with Thena.

I felt as if I was floating, able to punch straight through a stone wall. There were no words as we made our way quickly to Gaelan's room.

I've never done anything like this before.

Gaelan grudgingly answered the door, probably with Reishel's prodding, and they let us inside where the defenses against another walk-in were stronger. Jael watched and listened to us share remarks with quips and familiarity, and I could sense genuine excitement in her. I slid my hand down to cup her rump once and squeezed; again, I heard that soft laugh.

Jael enjoyed laughing. She just didn't know it until now.

"Can't fucking believe it," Gaelan said as I set both of Thena's tools on a nearby flat surface.

"This one's going to burn," Reishel agreed.

"Hope it causes blisters in her cunt," I said, folding my well-toned arms with a smirk.

Jael couldn't wait any longer. She approached me and lunged into a kiss, pressing herself close. I reacted on instinct, clutching her hard and keeping our mouths locked, stroking inside hers with my tongue.

"Whoa! Okay," Gaelan said. "Get on the pallet, you two. If I'm not going to sleep, at least let me watch."

More chuckling in the room as I pushed Jael to step backward toward the bed. She explored my back and my backside as we went, squeezing and scratching with her fingernails. As we settled onto the pad on our knees, facing each other, she leaned down to suckle my breasts, and one hand reached to stroke me between my braced thighs.

Jael sure knew what to do with a cunt.

"*Fuuuck,*" I moaned.

Her intense enthusiasm left me spinning, it was so different from her behavior before. My skin was bruised in many places and my bedmate pressed many of those sore spots without thinking, yet I couldn't help chortling, kiss after kiss.

Something buoyant and powerful remained in my chest; it surged now and then as Jael whispered that she wanted me, wanted to please me, and did I like it *this* way — ?

I groaned, threading my fingers into her loose hair, her fingers inside me, and soon I felt not a lick of pain that didn't blend with pleasure. Then Gaelan took my wrist, gently tugged it out so she could lay something cool, smooth, and firm in my palm. My fingers closed around it before I recognized what it was.

"Initiate her, Red Sister," murmured she who had initiated me, a tone both lurid and wry.

"Yes!" Reishel agreed, breathless with her own fingers between her legs. "Then fuck Gaelan again!"

"What," I said, getting the cock in place, "to pay her back for the safe room and the prong?"

"If you insist," the mage snickered, "I accept."

Gaelan touched her breasts as I laid Jael upon her back, as our newest Sister clutched at me in tense anticipation, glancing at the two other Sisters. Her eyes were wide, almost orange as she stared up at me, spreading her legs while I leaned between them, the head of my phallus parting her hairless lips. Her mouth opened as I slid in, but I was the one who groaned loud.

I paused, trembling, waiting. No pain in my head yet. No voices in the room except for my Sisters. No Dwarven words in my head.

"*Fuck me,*" Jael pleaded, rolling her hips to entice.

Growling low, I did, and I wouldn't stop until all four of us had peaked at least once. Until we would fall to a pile, a Reverie inspired by afterglow. By then, we all knew the Sisterhood was one more Davrin strong, and I had attained some new heights to defend.

I looked forward to the next test.

No demons but us.

Chapter 23

"House Itlaun."

"Pardon, Elder?"

D'Shea frowned a little. "Curgia, the Second Daughter. Have you visited her and her family lately?"

Braqth's Bobbling Tits.

"The last time was while you were at the Sanctuary with the Prime and Elder Rausery," I said. My body flushed with a sick feeling; my Elder noted it. "I have a report waiting on that, still."

She lifted her brows. "Oh? Did you forget?"

I cleared my throat. "Within my Elder's limited availability and other recent urgencies, Elder. Yes."

"Fine qualifier." The Sorceress was smirking.

"I am ready to report now, if you are ready to listen."

"Something noteworthy, then?"

"Yes, Elder. While I watched, Curgia proved distraught enough to use a weapon on herself."

"To kill herself?"

"No, Elder. To end the pregnancy Priestess Wilsira forced on her, but it was not well thought through and resources were limited. She may have died by accident digging up inside herself."

D'Shea expression showed comprehension. "If?"

I tried a smile. "If I hadn't shown myself to her. We talked a bit."

Her eyes burned through me; she was still for three, long breaths. Then she rubbed her face with one hand. "And this interaction is how old?"

I wetted my lips. "Three spans."

"How time flies," she sighed, tapping her stylus against her desk. "Tell me what you said. What she said."

I confessed the speculation I'd been doing about the Priestess's intentions toward the demonblood in Curgia's belly. I described how Curgia had listened to me and agreed to wait until Wilsira made another move toward her, and that the young Noble expected me to call on her again.

"You said the Valsharess doesn't allow the Sathoet to breed, Elder," I said. "How could the Priestess intend anything other than scare tactics against an ignorant youth without being caught in treason?"

My Elder nodded once in acknowledgment of the logic, but then shrugged. "Never underestimate an old Davrin in lust with her own son, Sirana. But it would be time to check on the Second Daughter again. See if she still lives and carries, at minimum."

"At once, Elder."

"Then, go. Now. I will see no delays in your report this time."

"Yes, Elder." I paused. "I also identified the invisible wizard from my trials, the last time I was at the Tower. The Headmaster's son, Shyntre."

She nodded curtly. "I am aware, Sirana. Gaelan told me."

Of course. My own fault for not being able to hold it, and the Sorceress was ahead of me, as usual. Any possible response she didn't want me to see was blocked.

"She also said the Prime ordered his involvement," I said. "Is that true?"

Her frown became a smirk. "True. It wouldn't be his first time working with the Sisterhood."

"Pleasant duty," I remarked. "Explains why he hates our uniform."

D'Shea's shrug was nonchalant. "The Wizards have many old connections with the Sisterhood, even if we can trust them about as much as we can trust the Priesthood. Kerse was 'on loan' from Priestess Wilsira as well, you already know."

I considered that. Jael and I had faced the half-bloods of the Sanctuary. I wondered about Gaelan, as a mage, how her test might be different?

"Is every recruit tested by Priestesses as well as Red Sisters?"

"Frequently enough. The Sanctuary likes to know a new Sister's face, if she makes it."

"But you're not required to share trials."

"No, but it's noted, and cooperation elsewhere becomes difficult. It's also not unheard of for the Sisterhood to assist with novice discipline for the Priestesses."

Ah, politics.

"House Itlaun, Sirana," D'Shea said then, cutting off the tangent and returning to her script. "Come right back afterward and tell me what's changed, if anything, since you last spoke with Curgia. I'll make time."

"Yes, Elder."

I resolved to bring up Shyntre again once I came back, weave it into the follow-up as I had here. The Sorceress had acknowledged my find but offered absolutely nothing else, as I'd expected. I still wasn't sure what I wanted regarding him, anyway.

When I arrived at the Noble lands of the Tenth House, I confirmed easily that both the Second and Third Daughters were still pregnant. It had been just over a turn, and they were just past the midway point. Bellies were showing now, and the Noble sisters would both be eating a lot, but their twin swells wouldn't get *really* big until the very last quad-spans.

Unborn Davrin took their time to get up to size, I'd been told, but when they were ready to put on weight to prepare for birth, the Mother's body worked to pack it on in a matter of spans. My Mother back at House Thalluen would soon be entering this stage, beating the Itlaun sisters by almost half a turn.

Kerse's offspring can't possibly make it that far, can it?

The quickest way to gain insight on current events was to ask the Royal Consort, but I had to rely on chance for when he might be alone.

Unfortunately for me, he was not allowed to return to his quarters for the eve following a hefty dining experience with the cluster of females, which included the First Daughter, now present for a visit from Court, or wherever she had been — a detail I would need for my final report to D'Shea.

I watched the plantation from a couple different angles through the first two marks of our most common Reverie period. Activity was usually slow, although there always seemed to be someone awake and moving around at any point in the cycle.

When it became clear Auslan was wherever he was within the mansion for longer than this, I infiltrated the garden and the hidden passages again, eventually letting myself into the Consort's empty bedroom. I enjoyed a deep sniff of the air, exhaling with a smile.

I would wait here for a while. My exotic bua would be tired when he returned, and that might be the best time to question him as his endurance might be low, along with resistance.

Plus, if there are any marks of abuse on him from the Matron or Daughters, he won't have time to hide them.

While I waited, I poked around. The basics I expected were here: fine bedding and clothes, a variety of self-grooming and cleaning options, decorations and gifts aplenty, some intended to be worn as jewelry and others just to clutter the room with added importance.

In drawers by both the bed and his vanity were little locked boxes which might contain potions, perhaps healing or ones related to fertility, but I wouldn't know without breaking the ward and the lock and peering inside.

I didn't have time to do that, as Auslan was soon escorted back by the House Guardsvrin. I flushed with excitement and hid myself inside the walls, my ear pressed to listen. A Davrin checked around, swept the place for female ambushers, like me. If I had moved anything too much, it wasn't to the point this bodyguard would recognize it.

"Thank you, Jaezred." Auslan's voice was a quiet murmur. "Have a good eve."

The Guardsvrin sounded amused. He was male. "Most are waking now. But yeah, you look like you should lie down."

"I mean to. I appreciate the escort."

"As I am bid. Good Reverie."

I peeked out a crack as Auslan closed, locked, and warded his door. Smart to keep the female Guardsvrin from coming into his room alone, or I might have to put her to sleep if she loitered too long.

Now was my chance. I stepped out of hiding. He saw me in his periphery and spun to face me. The beauty's gasp of surprise was as delicious as his mouth.

I grinned and signed, *Just me.*

I wagered his shoulders would have fallen into a slump had the weary groan I saw in his eyes slipped out from between his lips. This was excellent timing as far as I was concerned. I stepped closer to him.

Strip, I commanded. *Show me your skin.*

He closed his eyes and turned his head slightly away, taking a slow breath. His long hair was braided but a little sloppy, as if it had been redone without a comb.

I am unhurt, Red Sister.

Show me.

Auslan swallowed. *We agreed ... * he began, then hesitated to finish.

I smiled. *I recall. It is still in effect. Show me. The sooner you obey, the sooner I leave.*

He pursed his mouth and reached to loosen the sash at his waist, soon shedding the silky, pale garment from his shoulders and arms and down over his hips and legs to step out of it. He kept his sandals on, his clothes tight in one hand, and let my eyes drink in the sight of him.

He wore his white bush trimmed and groomed tidy atop his hanging member. I could smell the musk of other females on him, not a detail I enjoyed but it was to be expected.

Turn around.

He did, making it full circle, letting my eyes linger on his back and buttocks for several long ticks before continuing around again, likely to be certain he could see my hands. Confirmed, he had no marks, and I had a stupid grin on my face.

★I shall report the Nobles here aren't abusing the Gift of the Valsha-ress,★ I said, a thinly-veiled official note. ★Unless there is anything you want to add?★

This was when Auslan reminded me again that he was twice my age. He shrugged with graceful indifference and walked nude over to a simple washstand, pouring cool water into a basin. I checked that my mouth wasn't hanging open.

"As it ever is, Red Sister," he said aloud. He used a pleasant, liquid soap in the water and a soft, blue cloth to wipe himself down after the sex. "Report what you see, I have nothing to add."

Nodding, I moved on. "When did the First Daughter come back? And from where?"

"Two cycles ago," he answered, "and from the Palace and surrounding areas. She made attempts to get her foot in the door of higher Houses closer to the Palace."

"Overall success versus anything specific?"

"Mostly unsuccessful, no particular deals she brayed about," the Con-sort said. "She returned because of fallout with the Seventh House at Court, she didn't want to be anywhere near. Her Matron and Aunt said she would return as soon as the 'heat cooled.' "

"Oh?" I asked. "What happened with House Lospure?"

"What I heard, they stole Matron Shenpra's nephew for their own."

Huh. "Did she say why?"

Auslan paused and quirked a brow at me like I was being coy. "No, she did not. But there are few reasons the Valsharess would care to send the Elder General of the Sisterhood to retrieve one bua over whom two Houses begin fighting."

He waited. Apparently, it was my turn. I smirked.

"You have a theory, Priestess son? How interesting. Do tell."

The Royal Consort seemed confused at my response at first, then said, "The Noble must be a healer by touch. That is the one mage's gift in a male which does not go to the Wizard's Tower, but the Sanctuary. His Matron could only hide him so long, and Lospure has made a notable mistake."

I nodded agreement. "So Itlaunadara came home during the chaos at Court. Washing her hands of it, grabbing distance."

"Yes, Sister. I think something scared her. She may have heard whispers of the Shenpradalik and been tempted just before the discovery broke, but that is speculation."

"Noted. Any action she confessed to you?"

"No, Red Sister. Itlaunadara was unnerved by Elder Rausery's unexpected appearance at Court. She described it in great detail at her family dining this eve." He paused. "She requested me to 'soothe' her after, and the Matron granted it."

I was grinning despite everything. " 'Unexpected appearance.' The General doesn't come to the Palace often?"

"You should know that, Red Sister."

"I do, but so what? You're older. You've probably seen her more than I have."

Auslan's eyes squinted briefly but he shook his head. "No. I have never seen the General in person. Reputation, only."

Hmm. "What about the Elder Sorceress?"

The Consort nodded in clear recognition. "Yes, Red Sister. I have seen the Sorceress a few times when I'm not assigned out to a House."

"Has she ever spoken to you?"

"Not directly, no."

I watched his lovely face a few moments, deciding where to go next. "Tell me what the First Daughter described about the General. What caused her to panic."

Auslan nodded. "A short tale. The General didn't bother calling Nobles together or making a show. She walked in during a party with two Red Sisters, said nothing until she approached and grabbed Baedit Lospursareci by her neck and slammed her down against one of the decorative tables. The First Daughter said whatever Elder Rausery whispered in her ear caused the Noble to wet down her leg."

I was grinning again, wishing I could have seen that. I'd never liked Baedit.

"Shortly, the Red Sisters left again with the Third Daughter bound and soon the Matron herself was being called to Court over the abduction of a Noble son. That was when several lower Houses left, including Itlaun, though all Eighth House and above were commanded to stay."

A pause.

"Is that all?"

"All spoken at the table, Red Sister. I was not to speak as I helped her relax afterward."

"A pity. And boring."

"Oh?" He smiled a little. "You commanded the same, if I recall."

I blinked. "A bit of spice on that mild prick, eh? I didn't want to gag you, but excess noise was unwise then."

His eyes brightened with humor. He bowed. "Of course, Red Sister."

Saucy slut.

My wits required gathering. "Curgia." The reason my Elder had sent me. "Tell me about her belly."

"She has not aborted, though now the House knows, and she still refuses to name the sire," Auslan said. "The Matron is not pressuring her in public. I must imagine she has been told and they are ... hmm."

"Planning?" I suggested.

"Yes."

"Have there been any messages or contact from the Palace, Sanctuary, or Sisterhood that you know of?"

The Consort shook his head. "No, Red Sister."

Neither good nor bad, I supposed. Still in a waiting period, if this was the reality, and I hadn't missed anything during Jael's initiation.

"Has she bedded you?" I asked. Pure curiosity.

"At the start of my residence, yes," Auslan said, sounding a bit wary. "She was ... on the edge of violent, but without true injury. But I knew why, she doesn't want the baby she carries." He paused. "She has not visited my rooms in the last half-turn when I would have seen the bump."

"Tulia?" I asked.

A nod. "Regularly. The Matron, too. And the Aunt. But never all at once, they prefer privacy."

Not unlike my former House.

I waited, watching as he dried himself and chose a different silk tunic to wear. "Anything else unusual occur since last you saw me?"

"It had been quiet until the First Daughter returned from Court, Red Sister."

I thought over anything else my Elder might want to know. At least I could think a little clearer without him standing naked.

"What about your Priestess, Wilsira, and you? Have there been any messages exchanged? Observations you've provided her?"

The Consort nodded, seeming resigned. "Required once per span, if nothing is noteworthy."

"And if it is?"

"Two."

"*Pfft*," I scoffed. "Not every cycle?"

"That is ... too immediate, she has said. If it is urgent, she sends another to watch and report. I am not her favored spy, she doesn't trust me."

"You specifically," I asked, "or all Royal Consorts?"

Auslan hesitated, glancing toward his vanity, of all things. "I believe it is me. Although I do not truly know how she treats the other Royal Consorts stationed at their Houses. We are dissuaded from comparing notes the few times we are gathered at the Sanctuary."

Which was only once every five to ten turns, I knew. Not much opportunity to build strong bonds after a Consort reached breeding age.

"Hm," I grunted, and Auslan watched my face for a few moments.

He dared to say, "Your questions seem less focused on the Noble sisters now, Red Sister."

I could show my annoyance, discomfiture, or anger. Instead, I shrugged casually and winked. "I'm just learning more about how you live. Always consider the source of any information gathered."

"Thus says the Sisterhood?"

His smile paid for his forgiveness; I saw admiration and respect in the testing.

"For millennia," I agreed then paused. "Do you know if Wilsira has already sent another spy here following the First Daughter's sudden return?"

Auslan shook his head. "I am sorry, I do not."

"How likely is she to do so when you make your next report?"

"I already made it," he told me. "When the First Daughter arrived."

"How?"

He grimaced and spoke frankly. "I will die if she learns I leaked this."

"Nix it, then," I granted. D'Shea might already know and I only showed my own ignorance. "Answer the other. How likely is she to send a spy, now?"

"Likely," he said, "as she has designs on the pregnant Daughters, and the First Daughter is not yet pregnant."

"Is that likely to change, and involve you?"

"If Itlaunadara stays, then yes, and yes, Red Sister."

"So, you'd be watched more carefully and not necessarily know who else was reporting to the Sanctuary."

"Correct, Red Sister. Though all Davrin talk if a new Guardsvrin or servant unconnected to another shows up from somewhere else. The Matron would know, for certain. I would not, as I am an outsider."

"Always good to recognize your limitations," I said.

"Indeed." Now he smiled. "It prevents me from overpromising and upsetting a powerful female."

I chuckled. "I'd be looking for a new Davrin, either related to or vouched for by one already established, or a long-term Davrin on 'retainer' who changes his or her behavior."

The Consort nodded his agreement with a face so calm I couldn't help but smile. "Or a Davrin who has already arrived from Court with the First Daughter."

"Or that."

Then something returned to me. I frowned at the thought which struck.

"You said Wilsira has designs on the pregnant Daughters. Tulia, certainly, but where did you think the Priestess has designs on Curgia and her unwanted one?"

I sensed his face warm. Had I caught him off guard?

He lowered his eyes. "The … unborn is touched by the Abyss, Red Sister. I wager you already knew that."

"You can tell?" I asked, confirming without saying.

"Now, yes. Not earlier. But she conceived at the same time as Tulia, at the Palace, and I have heard that Curgia beseeched Wilsira herself for a Consort before the Worship Ball. I can guess who the sire is."

I was fascinated by his deduction. "Tell me your guess, Auslan."

He swallowed to hear my name aloud but obeyed. "Kerse, Wilsira's Sathoet."

My clever Consort. I grinned. "Mm. Good guess."

He could read that he was correct; the lovely bua nodded modestly and didn't ask how long the Sisterhood had known. Thus, he would understand more why I turned up here now and then, and it wasn't only to torment him. I had long decided I would keep the details — that I'd fucked the same Sathoet and that he had seemed a little too interested in me at the Worship Ball — out of my conversations with the Royal Consort.

Conversation, hm? Yes, it feels like that.

A bad sign. A weakness should I grow lax, too comfortable with him.

"Does any cait or mata talk with you this long before they fuck you?" I asked, intentionally crass.

Auslan shook his head in the negative. "No, Red Sister." He paused. "There was one once, but she is dead now." He looked at my face, anticipated my next question. "My first Priestess in the Sanctuary. The one who trained me, before I was given to Wilsira."

Such an intimate, voluntary confession. Hearing it sped my heart for a reason I didn't grasp right then. "Her name?"

He paused, though grasped the pointlessness to keep that back. "Priestess Juliran."

"When did she die? And why?"

He swallowed. "Five decades ago. For similar reason Red Sisters die, and Nobles are assassinated or meet with accidents."

Oh, yes. I know about accidents.

"It's possible no one of the Sanctuary remembers her anymore," he said, "except me."

I shifted in discomfort and cleared my throat, reining in my own eager curiosity. One other female had talked with him, had cared to know more of his thoughts, if he was being truthful. At first, I didn't think it was possible, then reflected on my own upbringing.

It's possible.

Why did I feel so strange now to know this?

Auslan sighed with care. "If you are finished with me, Red Sister, I am … very tired."

Yes. I was dawdling, staring at him, enjoying his voice for the sake of it. Prodding. It was time to report to D'Shea, though I'd do one more sweep on the chance that some Davrin seemed new to the grounds. I had time; I only should not spend it all in this room.

As much as I want to.

"How about a kiss and I'll be off?" I asked.

I saw the alarm on his face, caught in an unwary moment. I swallowed the impulse for insult though my voice still came off as a gripe. "Nothing *more* than that."

"Red Sister, please," he murmured. "Command me if you've changed your mind."

If I had altered our agreement already, is what he meant.

"I cannot refuse you," he continued, "but I remind you that my Priestess has ways of discovering if I am being promiscuous outside the Noble family in any regular way. It is part of the agreement between House and Sanctuary."

Great. Now he was afraid of me, and I soured in jealous constriction.

He waited for me to speak. I sighed.

"No commands this time, Consort. Until next time."

CHAPTER 24

I RETURNED TO THE CLOISTER WITH A FEW NAMES AND DESCRIPTIONS I WANTED to transcribe from my shoddy field notes before reporting to my Elder, to make sure I had it straight. Gaelan's room was the only one I knew to have writing tools, so I stopped there first.

Luck was with me as I found her there. She released the ward, letting me in. She was brewing potions for the Sisterhood at her tiny workbench. Recent memories of my last foursome here rushed in, nearly flooding my nose although my Sister was bubbling something with less erotic scent in a vial under a small, open flame.

"Well met, Sister," I said.

I knew my voice sounded light, and Gaelan smiled as she glanced over her shoulder.

"Hey, Sirana."

"May I use your table and supplies to rewrite some notes?"

"As long as you don't take my Feldeu again," she looked back at the bench, "sure."

I gathered a small square of parchment, the ink vial and quill, and sat at her one-cait study desk. It reminded me of where my tutors had me sit while I learned to write.

"Don't tell me you've hidden your cock back in the same spot I took it?" I nudged with a smirk.

"Nope." She shook her head, carefully measuring a powder. "It's better secured now, must be, or D'Shea will whip my ass and have me brew standing up for a span."

I snickered, admiring that ass a moment, sitting on its stool, then got to work. We didn't speak again until we'd each made progress and found a breakpoint, then Gaelan spun on her seat, wiping down a metal stirrer.

"Hey, Sirana, I want to ask you something."

I blew on my wet ink. "About?"

"About Reishel."

I pursed my lips. "I don't know why she woke up."

Gaelan shrugged. "I believe you. But D'Shea might have called me to help heal her after she made it through the Prime's courses. She didn't, our Elder called you."

"Says who?"

"Reishel."

I frowned. "Who else knows about that?"

Gaelan shook her head. "Nobody. It was just me and her."

"You want to hear about whipping asses if she knows you two gossiped within spans about that?"

My Sister smirked. "Reishel didn't describe a thing. I didn't ask. I could fill in the blanks when she talked about you being there when she woke up, twice. And you had been deliberately trained to wear the cock at the same time *and* instructed not to tell me. Or so you said at the time."

"So, you just guessed?"

"Yep. And you confirmed."

I scowled. "Stop looking so smug."

Another shrug. "Why did D'Shea call you to be the conduit instead of me?"

"D'Shea said you were too used up after the Ornilleth battle," I grumbled, feeling foolish.

"You're not a mage, Sirana. What's the Sorceress training you for?"

"I can't tell you that," I said, "or I would have by now. I didn't ask why you were so fucked up from being a 'conduit.'"

"You mean unaware and unable to fight as you played with me?"

I dropped my forehead in my hand. "I apologized, I'll never do it again. I'm still curious but figure you can't say more than you have. Just like I can't speak about some of the things I'm doing."

Gaelan watched me for a few moments, and it was clear she had something else to say. Then, or perhaps instead, she asked, "Will you check on your Matron after she gives birth?"

I blurted a laugh, shook my head. "No. I have no reason to go back, and I wouldn't ask. D'Shea would have to assign me, and I doubt she will. I don't see how it benefits her."

The young mage said dryly, "And it's all about that, isn't it?"

She sighed, turned back around on her stool. Worked on something, not a new potion. Taking notes. I glowered at her back, resting my head on my fist.

"What?" I growled.

Gaelan shrugged. "If you think everything the Elders ask of us pertains to something which happened in just the last few turns ... "

"I don't think that," I said, insulted, "but I don't know enough about my new *present* yet to nudge the past and avoid the poisonous pincers."

"Fair," she granted, slowly turning around again to face me. "Often we can only start with ourselves and trace the silk threads from there."

"Qivni would think I do too much self-serving stuff already."

"So does she." Gaelan looked like she didn't care. She also didn't say anything more.

I huffed, annoyed. "Why are you being oblique? What do you want?"

Her mouth tightened. Her shoulders hunched.

"What is it?" I pressed. "You *want* me to go back to see the new heir when she's born?"

After a swallow, she spoke, voice starting uncertain but gaining momentum.

"It would be worthwhile keeping touch on the places and the Davrin you just left, Sirana. I know there's no danger of you becoming too attached to your past, you've made it clear. You've achieved this much already, you clearly belong here. But everyone keeps secrets, and while we can watch and look in on each family, sometimes only those who once lived with them can see important changes later."

Makes sense. Then I shook my head.

"Wouldn't D'Shea tell me to do this if she agreed?" I challenged. "Do the others? What about you, do you go back to the Markets where you were born?"

"Yes," she said flatly. "That's how we got those leads on the missing bua so fast."

That shut me up. I tapped the quill. Then Jaunda came to mind, again.

"Lead mentioned that I was like my Grand Matron once, while fucking me," I volunteered, watching Gaelan's face.

She seemed interested but neither surprised nor amused by the circumstances. "Your Grand Matron? What was her name?"

My mouth twisted. "Matron Siranet Thalluen."

"Oh! You were named for her?"

My Sister's surprise was genuine; she hadn't known.

I shrugged that off. "A *Third* Daughter. Not First, not Second. Clearly Matron Rohenvi and her Mother didn't respect each other."

"Well, seems our Lead invited you to ask about that, given the opportunity."

We sat in silence as Gaelan let that sink into my stubborn head.

"D'Shea and Jaunda have been watching House Thalluen for a long time," I said. "And when Jilrina died, it's possible my Matron called them specifically. Maybe knew them from before."

A nod. "Sounds probable to me."

Gaelan was smiling now, pleased. She had gotten something she wanted. I wasn't quite sure that I had anything more than new questions and curiosities.

Isn't that why the Davrin continue to exist? We always seemed to need something beyond whatever next meal we could pull out of a cavern pool.

I sighed, thinking back at the start of the talk. Gaelan tilted her head expectantly.

"Whenever you can tell me what happened to you after the battle, with D'Shea and the Priestess, why you were the way you were, I'll try to answer something about Reishel's healing."

My Sister nodded slowly, considering. She was wary. "I'll think about it."

That was my cue. I stood up with new, dry notes in hand. "I have to report to our Elder now. Thanks for the parchment."

"Sure. Until later."

Gaelan secured her door behind and, I presumed, returned to making potions.

The Sorceress consumed my report, quick and thorough. At least she seemed satisfied where we stood with House Itlaun and the Bred Consort of Wilsira Tachnathon.

"You are making interesting progress with that bua, Sirana," she said. "I see the value in natural grown curiosities but be wary. Remain vigilant how at ease you feel with him. You cannot trust a Priestess's son, ever. You harm the Sisterhood if you do."

My nod of agreement was earnest. "Yes, Elder. I feel that same danger."

"That shall have to do for now. I will be watching." The Sorceress looked down again at my notes. "Very good. Logical thoughts. Useful descriptions. I can use this for research. It will refine my directions in your future missions."

I bowed my head to acknowledge her. I said nothing, but I felt good.

D'Shea tapped two graceful fingers as she contemplated something more, and I waited. It crossed my mind it might have been a sign of nerves, yet it was common enough of a gesture for me to discount myself.

Until she spoke.

"There's been some progress on the Dwarf stone you found," she said.

I blinked. "Already, Elder? It hasn't been a span."

"Phaelous and his son are very intelligent males. It's a good thing the Valsharess keeps them locked up and away from the Nobles, or those female idiots would ask for objects that would rupture their own Houses." Her dark red eyes looked up at me. "It *was* a bit too fast, though, even for them. Unless they were given a direction?"

My stomach tightened and my face heated; she could tell. I confessed. "I might have mentioned the Fringe, what Jael said when we brought her in. No names or mention of Dwarves. Just a color."

The Sorceress was visibly annoyed. "Well. That answers that. I am glad you didn't speak of the Tragar in association with this stone, Sirana, but there is still one problem. Phaelous reports direct to the Valsharess, and with the color and the Fringe being mentioned to him, it's only a matter of time until some Priestesses becomes aware, and Lelinahdara hears it trickle down then follows up with me about you."

My jaw tightened, although I wasn't sure of all the connections D'Shea saw between what I'd said to Phaelous and Priestess Lelinahdara coming around. "What about the Prime hearing?"

At least my Elder shook her head with certainty. "That, at least, Tarra would never do."

"You're certain?"

"She finds the Prime's impatience and blunt choice of weapons a waste like I do. And this new gem might help our direction. Don't forget, Rausery is backing us as well."

"What's the … direction?" I hesitated at her sharpened gaze. "I think I've fallen behind."

My Elder smiled a little like I had amused her. "You never caught up. But you should, given you are at the core of it. The direction, ideally, is Red Sisters resistant to psionics, independent of the Sanctuary or the Wizard's Tower. New methods to block or return their power back at them. Tools we can train other Sisters to use."

She paused, studying me without blinking. "The changes you've experienced are more than a curiosity to Rausery and me, Sirana, but we must be careful how we approach this goal until we understand more.

First, so that the Prime doesn't cull you and Reishel immediately with her narrow and fearful mind, and second, the Priesthood doesn't try to claim rights to study you as well."

"The latter was your first direction, Elder," I pointed out.

"A regretful one," she admitted readily. "I believed it had much more to do with Tarra's magic, but you've since proven to me it does *not*. All I can do is delay her involvement and slow her own study until Rausery and I have something set in stone," she smirked at her own pun, "which the Sanctuary cannot usurp or claim. And I believe I am safe to assume you will cooperate in this, Sirana?"

I nodded. "Absolutely. I don't like Priestesses, Elder."

She chuckled. "Yes, I know." She spread her hands in an open gesture. "In truth, neither do I, and I have worked with them for almost six centuries now. They are as necessary for maintaining Sivaraus as the Sisterhood, and demonstrably powerful. If there was a similar group of Sorceresses kept in one place, we might attain similar influence with the Valsharess."

"Instead, you're spread out over the city," I guessed, "and the only mirroring group of mages are male, and thus, less in Her Eyes."

D'Shea nodded. "The Sisterhood benefits most from those tools both the Tower and the Sanctuary grant us, thanks to the Prime's early visions for us. Now we are in a rut. But, if we develop our own defense against psionics, Sirana, well … That may change the balance of things with the Valsharess, and the Sisterhood may gain back some of the autonomy we lost to the Sanctuary over the last four centuries."

I listened eagerly, my eyes unblinking as I tried, with limited success, to imagine how the Sisterhood might be independent of the Daughters of Braqth. "This loss was something both you and Rausery have witnessed."

"Yes."

"And the Prime is satisfied with new tools in the same structure as it's been."

"Maintaining a deep mistrust of all psionics, yes." My Elder was pleased with me. She hummed. "I enjoy that you keep up, Sirana. Now, we shall visit the Tower, you and me, and see their progress. Obey me in all things and do not question me while we're inside, understand?"

I exhaled, abruptly excited and oddly nervous. "Yes, Elder."

"Likewise, if you spot opportunity somewhere," she added, winking with surprising charm, "do try to let me know."

ELDER D'SHEA AND I DIDN'T WALK IN THROUGH THE FRONT DOOR OF THE Wizard's Tower, and I didn't have to walk yet again past those huge, unnerving Drider constructs.

From the strategy room in the Cloister, we appeared in the center of a jump circle placed within a small, round chamber. The interior mimicked the dormitory levels I'd already seen, but this one was tiny. There was only one door upon which to call, but we didn't need to.

We hadn't even stepped out of the circle before Phaelous exited that door, a dark satchel over one shoulder. The tall, elder male faced us full and bowed formally to my Elder and me, bringing with him a pleasant mix of scents clinging to his dark blue and gold mage's robes.

"Elder D'Shea. Red Sister Sirana. Welcome to the Wizard's Tower."

I nodded my chin, although my Elder barely acknowledged the greeting. I waited to see if the Headmaster would demand to see some fertility suppressant vials from D'Shea, as he had from me.

It did not even seem to cross his mind.

The Headmaster invited my Elder, "Shall we go to the library, Elder Sister?"

Which one?

The Elder Sorceress held out her hand for his satchel. With a pause of careful consideration but without protest, Phaelous slipped it off his long arm and gave it to her. D'Shea transferred it to her other side for me to take, which I did, biting my inner cheek to hide my surprise as she next briskly frisked the Headmaster, checking his pockets and seams, inspecting the rings on his fingers, and feeling his scalp through his long, golden hair.

He tolerated it but even his composure was wavering, showing me a discomfort fascinating to witness.

Was my Elder overstepping her authority? I wasn't sure but she'd touched him all over without seeming to enjoy any of it, while he stood like she had just stripped him naked in front of me.

The Sorceress stepped back and scrutinized him in a way I probably couldn't see. "Remove the ruby ring and hand it to me. You'll get it back before I leave."

Phaelous seemed baffled with this demand. He weighed his options first — he was *not* responding because of fear of her — then did as she said, slipping the ring over his knuckle and placing it in her palm. He was holding her eyes as she closed her fist around it.

Impertinent.

If I could see auras the way I'd heard Gaelan describe, I wondered if these two would be crackling with friction. I hadn't thought anything could ruffle the Headmaster, but in hindsight, a powerful Sorceress pushing him around inside his own place of power would do the trick. I didn't understand the nuances but found it entertaining, nonetheless. Not that I dared to laugh in this atmosphere thickened like stew.

"*Now* we shall go," D'Shea agreed with a confident smile, gesturing to me to hand her the satchel. Like the ring, she received the bag without protest. "My transport spell, not yours, Headmaster, understood?"

"Yes, Elder," he said, stepping into the circle with us, standing on D'Shea's right as I was on the left.

By the web, there was a long history here. When my Elder said she didn't trust the wizards in the Tower, she meant it!

I also noted that she knew exactly which library Phaelous had suggested, and how to get there. We arrived in the blink of an eye and only a tiny lurch to my balance.

"Ninth floor," my Elder told me, and I motioned my understanding.

The space design and architecture were like the fifth level, though this one was fuller. An older smell linked to more objects and art of the arcane upon the shelves, on pedestals, and hanging, either taking up precious wall space or in free swing from the ceiling. The library was well-lit with no exposure to real flame, seeming more colorful as a result, with only two study tables instead of three.

D'Shea motioned for us to step out of the jump circle and carried the Headmaster's satchel over to one of the tables. She set it down, turning to him expectantly. "Show us. We don't have long."

Phaelous nodded without speaking and came close to unpack the bag as the Sorceress took a step back to give him room. I saw a bound book of handwritten notes, a couple small jars and vials, some jewelers' tools, and a soft cloth he unfolded, inside of which was one of the two Dwarf stones I'd brought. It was smooth and polished, no longer raw, and shaped like a small lizard's egg. Now it appeared to our color vision as a dark, muddy blue.

Not as bright as seeing it beneath the stone, but ...

"Where's the other?" D'Shea asked, pulling out the third stone from her own pouch, setting it next to the polished stone. It was still drab grey, a raw, ugly pebble.

"Shyntre and Raegal are working it still, Elder," he said. "Do you wish me to summon them to offer their progress?"

She jerked her chin once to the side, her eyes boring into him. "No, I do not. That's why I brought her."

She indicated me, starting to smile at him, almost like she intended insult. My eyebrows lifted a moment before I caught myself; had Phaelous not been staring unblinking at D'Shea, he might have seen my genuine surprise. I had not the first instruction or goal regarding the Headmaster's son after having found him, but it seemed my Elder wished to place us in the same room on this very trip.

"Tell us about this one, Headmaster," D'Shea commanded.

Phaelous lowered his gaze and bowed his chin, plucking up the smooth stone and rubbing the pad of his thumb in a circle over it. "This is a very hard, precious gem. A pure element compacted to impressive density in crystalline arrangement. Currently, the Davrin have no name for it, but the closest likeness would be a sapphire."

D'Shea jerked her chin in a nod, waiting for him to continue.

"It responds strangely to magic cast nearby, seeming to mute it or perhaps absorb it. There is a tonal shift when this occurs, subtle, very difficult for a mage to hear without enhanced senses."

"What made you search for a tonal shift, of all things?" my Elder asked.

"Logic," he said with humble calm. He set the stone back down. "Most of our magic incorporates sound. Language is vital. A gem muting a mage's words would have one of these shifts, Elder. It's also the farthest I've ever witnessed, in the opposite direction of the bloodstone. In truth, I hadn't realized a precious element this extreme could exist."

The Sorceress rubbed her mouth with her red-gloved fingers, thinking deeply on advanced knowledge in which I had no training, yet what Phaelous was saying made sense even to me.

The Davrin had magic-detection methods aplenty, yet none of those worked for psionics as well, as far as I had heard. There existed means for sensing mind mages, my Elder only recently informed me, or my lie to Panagan about why I knew the Tragar were nearby wouldn't have worked.

The Headmaster's thoughts gave me the insight only in this moment to wonder if psionics occurred in absolute silence, despite the voices I heard in my head, and if such detection by a Dark Elf mage had more to do with revealing a void where sound *should* be, rather than a presence of it?

"These gems cannot be imbued with our spells," the Sorceress stated.

"We have not yet confirmed that, Elder," Phaelous said, "but it is likely that even if they can be, it would not be worth our resources. It could take more of every aspect just to have the same result, or a reduced effect, compared to a gem which readily focuses and transfers our magic."

D'Shea nodded. Her interest and fascination in what the Headmaster said was clear on her face, making her seem warmer toward him than when she had first stepped in here. She seemed pleased with the discoveries thus far.

"How did you turn this one blue?" she asked, indicating the polished one.

"It occurred on its own during testing," he said without a hint of deceit in his voice or his entire frame; I believed he was telling the truth. "Exposure to spells seemed to have done it. It started dark grey and lightened with each casting."

Somehow, I found that disturbing. Jael had described Tragar weapons which were a stark, bright blue, and that they didn't have a long history of her family noting them. They were recent. If magic might be required to make them that color in true light, then where was the exposure coming from?

My Elder seemed to be thinking along the same lines, although I saw why we must keep the link to the Tragar and psionics out of the Headmaster's study. His observations were worth more when his studies weren't directed, when he wasn't biased to look for or explain something specific.

I had been surprised that D'Shea, of all of us, had the willpower to let Phaelous meander about with something new without the expedience of sharing what we already knew, but now I mentally rolled my eyes at my own ignorance.

If D'Shea is the only one with all the pieces, she can take them from each source and put them together ahead of the Sanctuary, the Tower, the Prime, even the Valsharess. And Rausery wants her to succeed.

This was how a Sorceress gained more power, no doubt, and probably how all the Priestesses worked, especially Wilsira and Lelinahdara in their own contact with the Sisterhood. My loose, novice's mouth was a weak point and a risk my Elder *must* accept, only because I was the one with my head turned upside down by Grey Dwarves. Otherwise, I'd be blind like Reishel.

I resolved to keep my mouth shut and not make it harder for her, even if Shyntre walked in the door.

"What are your plans for further testing?" D'Shea asked.

The Headmaster gently shrugged his shoulders. "I am not certain. The obvious qualities revealed themselves immediately, and they do not suggest much potential for us. Some insight on where Sirana found this and why she thought to bring it to you might help."

The Sorceress chuckled. "Not right now. Perhaps later, if I deem it necessary to advance the work assigned."

Phaelous nodded like he had expected that answer. "Then I am finished for now, until another idea surfaces."

"Very well. I will take my leave for now but shall return in a few marks. Sister Sirana will remain here and receive the report from your students on their findings. I hope they are ready soon."

His back stiffened. "If the Red Sister stays without you, I require she take your fertility suppressant."

My Elder laughed softly. "I find it amusing you are so concerned about that, Phaelous."

The wizard called her bluff with a fold of his arms. "You might tease, Elder, but I know you will protect this new Sister from the clutches of the Priestesses as I will defend my own learners. Surely you brought the draught. If you did not, there are two on the table."

D'Shea made a face. "Presumptuous wilter, aren't you?"

Phaelous said nothing, only waited. My Elder rolled her eyes, removing a vial from her own supplies and holding it up in front of his face. He flicked his fingers at it, focusing a moment, then nodded his acceptance. D'Shea handed it to me.

"Drink, Sirana, and stay here until I come for you. Do not speak on the context of their study. I want pure conclusions, not what they think I want to hear."

"Yes, Elder," I said, stepping forward to take the bitter potion and toss it back with a swallow. This was, what, the third time? "If time allows, may I check on Callitro and his progress with my ring?"

Both powerful mages looked at me in surprise; I didn't know why, unless they were distracted by each other's politic positioning.

"What?" I asked and smiled, handing the empty vial back to my Elder. "He's a fast learner."

The Headmaster nodded, looking at D'Shea. "No sooner than a mark from now, but beyond this, it is well with me."

"Very well," the Sorceress agreed. "If time allows. You'll respond immediately to a summons once I return, Sirana, I don't care if you're fist-deep in his ass at the time."

Whoa! He's not trained that well, yet.

"Yes, Elder," I chuckled.

The Sorceress nodded, reclaimed her raw stone and took her leave from the library. I felt when she used the jump circle, a subtle *whomp* of sucking air and a weird tremor in my teeth.

Then we were alone, Phaelous and me, waiting for Shyntre and Raegal to arrive with the third stone.

Chapter 25

The library on the ninth floor remained quiet in a way the Cloister rarely was. I stood at attention because I saw no opportunity to prod Phaelous in a way that didn't make me look like a childish Noble clumsily pleading for gossip at Court.

Still, after seeing Elder D'Shea fence wits with the polite, placid Headmaster, after witnessing his responses, I had begun to understand how Shyntre could be his son, and perhaps why a bua with a brain was both maddening in its delight and dangerous as a conniving Priestess.

It's a good thing the Valsharess keeps them locked up, my Elder said.

And I am to be locked in here with both? That was a sticky web.

Phaelous lifted the polished stone and held it out to me. "Would you like to hold it, Red Sister? Take a closer look."

The answer was yes, but I hesitated at such a direct suggestion. If this element was unknown to the Headmaster and was almost opposite of a magic stone, what would happen if I touched it again? What might he see about me that I didn't want him to?

I replied with a casual smile. "No, Headmaster. My Elder said I should just observe and receive the report on her behalf."

True enough.

The old male didn't push it. With a nod slow and deep, he returned the gem to a pocket within his dark, gold-and-purple threaded robes. Something occurred to me.

"Did you receive back your ruby ring?" I asked.

"No, young Sister, your Elder took that with her." Phaelous smiled with amusement; no insult I could detect. "I assume she meant it would be returned when she retrieves you and leaves for the second time."

"Is there a chance she'll simply keep it?"

"What is your guess, Sister Sirana? You know more of your Elder's current mind than I do."

Thinking on it only turned me in circles, and I soon stopped. "I don't know, Headmaster. She does as she wills, I never know why."

Phaelous chuckled softly. "An accurate and succinct description, young Sister."

I almost asked why she had left at all rather than staying for the other report but stopped when I decided not to reveal how little instruction the Sorceress had given me in bringing me here.

Drider pits everywhere I look.

"What does the ruby do?" I asked instead.

The fine creases around his eyes showed in a cheeky, closed-lip smile. "Headmasters are not encouraged to define their tools to anyone who asks, Sister. Forgive me."

I rolled my eyes. "You don't require my forgiveness, Headmaster. And there's only one of you."

"Living, yes. Correct on both counts. I'd not annoy you or any intelligent cait needlessly, however. The Sisterhood has made another fine choice for collection. I look forward to you gaining status within your clique. Perhaps we will work in cooperation more often, as we do now."

The warm pride in my chest appeared before I could consciously challenge it. I wrinkled my nose. "You flatter me to distract me, Headmaster."

He bowed his head. "Flattery or insult work equally well in each other's presence."

"But the latter only causes trouble."

"So does flattery. At least insult is consistently honest."

I squinted. "So, you're lying to me, Headmaster?"

Another calm, bemused smile. "Not consistently, Red Sister. Rarely, when necessary."

Now I felt annoyed, needless or not. "No wonder D'Shea compared you to a Priestess."

"A fair comparison." His eyes drifted toward one of the bookshelves. "We are where we are because we made our choices and avoided death for a little longer. How we continue breathing isn't always up to us."

A moody, useless statement. Maybe more a reflection on his centuries? Did any male who survived to be his age prattle on like this? I wouldn't know. There hadn't been many buas at my House older than three hundred, and they were Guardsvrin or servants.

I didn't reply, for I had none. The silence stretched for a bit as Phaelous opened a book to read and I just stood there. Then, finally, someone tapped the door.

"Enter," Phaelous said, closing and shelving his book.

Shyntre let himself in. Alone.

"Where is Raegal?" his Headmaster asked.

His son pursed his mouth, looking at the floor, speaking in his natural voice. "Raegal is being spineless. Wouldn't leave his dorm. Says he'll accept your punishment, Headmaster, whatever it is."

"Noted." Phaelous wasn't pleased; I could tell this much.

I also wondered how close we'd come to Shyntre blighting off and saying the same thing; I wagered he had better cause. Or at least, a specific one standing in the room.

"If my Elder had been here," I said, "I imagine she would send me out to drag him here."

"Perhaps. He is under my authority however, so I shall see to his punishment, Red Sister." Phaelous gestured to Shyntre to come closer. "For now, let us see the third stone."

The wizard from my trials did not speak as he obeyed, pulling it out of his robe pocket and placing it on the table in front of his sire. He hadn't looked directly at me, yet, though I watched for the moment, until the polished stone itself distracted me.

I blinked several times, trying to clear the vivid, blue corona which must be my color vision going awry. It wasn't. The color was just as I'd glimpsed it underneath the rock before I dug it out.

Goddess, that's beautiful.

"What do you see, Sister Sirana?" Phaelous asked me.

"It is much brighter blue than yours, Headmaster," I said with every effort to sound level and calm, even though I wanted to pick up that stone right now. "That's what you see, too, isn't it?"

"Hm. Correct, I do." Phaelous looked at Shyntre. "Inform the Red Sister how you and Raegal achieved this change, Shyntre."

The younger wizard's fingers twiddled nervously. He inhaled then exhaled, still not looking at me. "I believe it's … reactive to the emotions of the caster, Headmaster. The stronger intensity, the greater the change. It doesn't seem to matter which emotion it is."

"You're bucking me, wizard," I scoffed.

He heard my tone. He recognized it, I knew he did; I could listen to his heart beating in the library. He said nothing and I cursed my tongue. I should have just shut up and let him talk. Now I might not get details of the testing for D'Shea.

"Hm," the Headmaster said again. Politely, he motioned to me. "Please come closer, Red Sister."

Gladly.

Grinning, I joined the two males at the study table. Shyntre wasn't covering his scent this time; I leaned in, taking a whiff. His body pitched me a familiar, annoyed air.

"I *knew* it was you," I said, triumphant. "Nice to know your face as well as your prick, Shyntre."

He flicked a sharp glance at me. I saw hatred beyond just me, though I was securely balled up in it. "I wager you preferred my mouth, Sister."

Delightful. I couldn't have stopped smiling if I tried.

"True. Lips-on-lips *was* the only time you weren't complaining." I paused, listening to the speed of his heart; it was faster than mine. "I don't know what you're afraid of, I can't hurt you here."

"Or anywhere, Red Sister."

I took another deep sniff. "You smell afraid."

Another ugly look. "Only of my own actions. What I might do if you touch me uninvited."

I snickered. "Would you *invite* a touch from me?"

"Never with a Red Sister."

" 'Never' is a long time, wizard."

"You have no idea."

"Neither do you, unless you claim *intimate* knowledge from your mentor."

He ground his teeth. "Piss your cunt, Sister."

Satisfied that my barb had hit with that nasty comeback, I finally glanced at Phaelous, who'd been silent, listening to us bicker. I saw no amusement at the free entertainment this would have been at Court. The elder male wasn't even watching Shyntre and me. He was watching the stone.

"Headmaster?" I asked.

"Would you pick up Shyntre's sapphire, Sirana?" he returned, thoughtful, as his son followed his gaze.

"Why?"

"It's shifting tone to your proximity."

Damn. Maybe the wizard was *too* smart.

"I am here to observe."

"You've already failed," Shyntre gibed.

"You found the element in the wilderness," Phaelous said. "And although observable change occurs around mages, you are not one, as far as we know."

"It changes around strong emotions," I countered, sneering at the younger bua as I spoke to the elder. "Your 'learner' said, and I have *many* intense thoughts about him."

"Indeed. Will you pick it up?" he asked again.

"No," I said for pure spite. "And you're wasting my Elder's potion, Headmaster. Finish the report, and I will go somewhere else to assure Shyntre isn't *afraid* of his own actions around me. I have another, far more pleasant bua to check on while I'm here."

The Headmaster may have been disappointed but didn't show it, turning his gold-flecked eyes toward the bua with the same trait. He nodded. "Finish your report, then escort her to Callitro's room."

Shyntre sullenly obeyed. "There's a difference in the color change whether the magic cast evokes something tangible or not."

"Examples?" Phaelous asked.

"Light, fire, and shield strikes cause a brighter blue than passive effects —"

"Like invisibility?" I asked.

Shyntre glanced at me, losing his chain of thought in a glower. Phaelous snapped his fingers to gain it back.

"Passive effects. Focus."

"Yes, Headmaster." Shyntre wetted his lips. "I tried glamour, communication, and persuasion spells. These hardly changed the color at all. The evocation of offensive force spells shifted the blue to be this bright."

"So those evocations require a strong emotion to cast?" I asked.

"A good question, Sister," Phaelous said with a smile. "No, they do not. It can enhance the strength of the manifestation, but I've also seen such strength evolved by using other foci than emotion. Each mage is different."

For certain, that counted in the two mages before me. I nodded and waited for anything else.

"That's basically all," Shyntre finished brusquely. "I'm assuming we're still not being told where or how it was found?"

"We are not," Phaelous agreed.

"Then what else are we supposed to do with it, Headmaster?"

"We will leave that to the Elder Sorceress, although I may have a recommendation, if she will listen. I'd not keep in a treasury for very long." A casual shrug from the ancient Elf. "Are you ready to head up-level, Red Sister?"

I *was* ready, but I hesitated. I was shoving an opportunity away with both hands, the same as at my Mother's House on D'Shea's first mission for me? I felt slight panic at the thought after my Elder's obvious disappointment, but I brought it under control when I decided D'Shea would rather explore that proximity thing on her own with me.

"You'll give her the stones?" I asked.

"If she asks for them, right away."

"You said you haven't confirmed if they'll even take a spell. What was it, imbue?"

Phaelous nodded patiently; I caught a tightening of Shyntre's mouth like he was biting back a remark. Smart.

"Will you test that next?"

Another patient bow. "We could right here, if you wish. You still have half a mark before you should call upon your bua."

Shyntre wrinkled his nose and kept his eyes on the far end of the room. I couldn't tell if he was reacting to the further testing or Callitro, but I suspected it might be the latter.

"Yes," I said with mustered confidence. "I want to see if you can. Which spell you think might be easiest?"

"Light," Shyntre answered, probably without thinking as he cleared his throat and looked up at his Headmaster apologetically.

"He is correct, Red Sister," Phaelous said. "Almost any gem can be imbued with light, from a subtle glow to a blinding flash. It also needs very few components and could be done here."

Eagerly, I nodded. "Show me."

Phaelous pulled out his drab blue stone as well, motioning a reminder on the magical spell to be used, and it was what was discussed though I didn't get the nuance. The two males moved to opposite ends of the study table to give each other room.

I stepped back and stood in the middle, enjoying that they coordinated, demonstrating just for me, though I didn't drop my guard. Each wizard removed what looked like the same powder from a tiny bag within a larger pouch on their sash; I was wary until it was clear they were not about to pitch it at me.

First Phaelous then Shyntre, both cast a spell upon their respective blue stone through familiar verbal and somatic ritual, adding that small bit of material to will their desired effect into being. Their voices were distinct, the tones different, and I saw a bit of what Phaelous meant about mages having different foci, not all of them emotion. Phaelous' expression was still as the stone he worked, his presence as intangible as a tingle up my spine.

In contrast, although Shyntre's face wasn't grotesque or exaggerated, I could still read a progression there. I could guess with some accuracy, I wager, when the spell had begun and each stage where he felt something different until it was completed. I also felt a stronger pressure coming from a void. I could believe something had changed, but I didn't know what.

The wizards exhaled, shared a look and nodded confirmation to each other. Phaelous motioned an invitation to his son, who grudgingly obeyed, picking up his stone and coming closer to me.

My arms were crossed, though I looked curiously at the glinting sapphire in his palm. I leaned over a little more as he held it out; he seemed ready to snatch back his hand as if I was a caged beast that would bite it off.

The blue color seemed just the tiniest bit on the purple side, now.

"You should already know the command word," he said. "Same as the outliner pellets."

Faeriluci.

"Nice attempt," I said, keeping my hands trapped beneath each arm. "I told your Headmaster, no."

When Shyntre glanced that way for a prompt, I grinned, adding, "Unless Shyntre strips down and places both hands on the table while I milk his nut gland."

The younger mage whipped his head back around to me as I finished, "*Then* I might reconsider touching his sapphire."

With genuine shock his temper rose up, right on cue. Seeing his face, I snapped first.

"You dare to look *indignant* after last time, Shyntre? It's only a matter of *when*, not if. Get used to the idea now!"

His fist clenched tight around the blue stone, Shyntre stared at my eyes without blinking. He spoke an insolent growl through clenched teeth. "I don't cower for Red Sisters. Nothing *you* could do would surprise me, novice."

I couldn't help but pick that apart, and I was blunt. "Intimately familiar with the Feldeu already?"

"You all look ridiculous wearing it," he replied by way of an answer.

In that case …

I punched the wizard in the stomach, dropping him to the carpet. He choked, struggled to draw a breath. Then, finally, he gasped.

"How it *should* have ended in the candle chamber," I said, holding my fist tight. "I don't *enjoy* hitting buas, Shyntre, but you *deserve* it this one time."

I heard him growl his predictable opposition, gradually regaining his wind. "Had to."

"Then don't act so shocked I want a piece back."

Shyntre had dropped the sapphire on his way down but grasped it again before pushing back to his feet, hunched over but stubbornly refusing to cover his aching middle. I smirked, my eyes drifting back to Phaelous, who observed without comment.

As it always was when he wished it, the Headmaster's face was an unreadable mask. Meanwhile, I was quivering, and he could tell. I hoped he couldn't also tell that my slit had grown hungry beneath my leathers.

Goddess, is it time to see Callitro, yet?

"Nothing permanent," I said to them both. "Yet the Prime comes close to killing one of *us* all the time. I don't have your protection."

The young wizard snorted, his body now shaking more than mine. He tried to speak but was incapable, and not because I'd knocked the air out of him. Shaking his head, Shyntre walked away, putting the sapphire into his pocket.

Displaying his back to the room, the young wizard said hoarsely, "I'd like to leave, Headmaster."

"A moment, Shyntre," Phaelous said, finally showing me an expression. "Red Sister, did you mean it?"

My face was stuck in a frown, my focus on the quivering mage. "Did I mean what, Headmaster?"

"That you don't enjoy striking buas. Just 'this one time.' Was a fist in the gut truly enough to settle the score from your trials?"

Now the old one had put me on the spot. *Had* I meant it, or would the humiliating burn come back again? Would it lessen over time? I breathed in, then out, noticing the knot inside was gone; I did feel better. The punch was cathartic, and I knew all my words had hit when he couldn't speak at all. It was obvious this would eat at Shyntre regardless, locked up here.

While I could let it go, if I wanted, make that call. I had that freedom.

Plus, now I was horny. *Stupid cunt.*

"Yes, Headmaster," I said with an easy smile. "The score is now settled. I've wanted to locate and punch the invisible wizard from my trials for the last turn. Now I've done that."

"Red Sisters always do a lot more than the original insult," the young mage snarled, turning his head toward me without turning his back. "Wait until they call you weak for letting me off that easy. You'll be back."

"Oh? Do you *want* more, Shyntre? 'A lot' more?"

"What I want doesn't matter, does it?"

"Poor bua!" I snorted, crossing my arms and rolling my eyes. "It was the petty ass-fuck at the end which flicked me off, Shyntre. It wasn't necessary, you're just a poor loser. I know you didn't have a choice about the rest, and I've faced the Prime, too."

When he didn't reply, I shrugged, looking to the elder male in the room. "Truth, Headmaster? The rest was fun. I like power games like that. If he wanted to play again, I'd consider it. I don't see feisty ones like him wandering about."

Now Phaelous' son turned halfway around and shot me a withering look. My face split into a white, challenging grin. Meanwhile, the Headmaster was smiling with apparent genuine pleasure.

"Hm. We appreciate your generosity on this complicated subject, young Sister —"

"No, we don't," the younger male mouthed, and I chuckled.

"If the grudge is indeed satisfied on your end, Sirana," the old wizard continued, throwing a warning glance at his son to be still, "my compliments to you. We don't see many such as yourself in Sisterhood, Sanctuary, or the Palace."

"Yes, I'm aware."

I exhaled, liking this lifted feeling somehow. Unlike female Davrin, whom I could insult and draw lasting back-and-forth, there was only so much Shyntre could do for a punch to the gut, especially as payback for a specific action. My holding on to this would mean I was as petty as him.

I nodded with confidence in my decision. "The grudge is settled, Headmaster, Shyntre. *Unless* he'd like to start it back up. In which case, I'll gladly top him." I winked. "Every time."

Phaelous bowed his head with grace and gratitude on behalf of his son, seeming to have let go tricking me into accepting one of the blue stones. "Shyntre?"

"I'll believe it when I see it," he said stubbornly, at last rubbing his sore middle, a sight I enjoyed. "But I'll not touch her again."

I smothered a laugh. *Infamous last words.*

Satisfied in one way, now I ached for satisfaction in the other. "Will Shyntre escort me to the seventeenth level now, Headmaster? Before my Elder returns."

If I had strangled my glee just now, Shyntre had a chokehold on his groan.

"If he is willing," his sire said in a surprising show of leniency, offering the young wizard an exit on a silver platter.

"I'll do it," Shyntre said, just short of a grouse.

Ha. Stubborn bua.

I had a guess why he'd refused the easy way out. It wasn't too different from some of the things I tried in my determination to show Jilrina I wasn't afraid of her. So I told myself.

Bidding the Headmaster a good eve, I happily followed Shyntre out of the library and towards the jump circle. I bit my lower lip to make sure I didn't "distract" him at a bad time; he was having enough trouble with that on his own. Knowing this, I recognized the feeling similar when I'd thrown Thena back from Jael and me when she was unwanted.

I could fight back and cause real change in those around me. At last.

An *urp* escaped from my mouth as we jolted our way onto a familiar-smelling floor, and I nearly reached out to take his shoulder to keep my balance. That would have been a mistake, given how he almost vibrated with tension.

"Relax a bit, your muscles will snap," I whispered, righting myself as the vertigo passed.

The sour wizard might have mouthed something obscene, looking toward the bend in the hall away from me.

"Are you always going to act like this?" I asked.

"Shh."

I ignored that; my slit was thinking for me at this point, anyway. "I mean it, Shyntre. We can play. You have a beautiful tongue when you aren't using it to talk. And I've learned a few things since then. I can show you."

He spun on me; we hadn't even left the circle yet. He cast something, and the air around us seemed to deaden. A voice-muting spell.

"Will you stop?" he demanded. "Let me fucking breathe!"

I glanced down at the front of his robe. No erection poking through to betray him. *Damn.* I sighed. "I spoke truth to your sire, wizard. You and I are even for the game we were forced to play. Might be better by choice next time. Don't you think?"

"Next time?" he repeated incredulously.

When I just grinned at him and said nothing, Shyntre scoffed and shook his head, dispelling the mute shield, and stomping the first few steps toward Callitro's door. I followed, not making another peep. He had a nice ass, what I could see of it.

As before, Callitro answered quickly, greeting me with his bright smile. "Come in, Red Sister."

Shyntre bowed his head, barely enough to be respectful in front of the other and turned to leave without a word.

My blood singing in my veins, my netherlips already drooling, I slipped inside, and we closed the door. The young mage's eyes widened, his heart surged, though he held his place, waiting for me. I seized the willing bua into my arms, pushing him backward as I kissed him, ready to fuck him deep into the mattress.

"Goddess," the battlemage gasped, trying to breathe, though he responded to every kiss, returning them if quick enough. "Sirana."

His heel kicked a fiberstalk box on the floor by accident, sending it beneath his bed. He didn't notice as I plunged my hand down the front of his wizard's robe, caressing his smooth skin. He finally got to stripping naked.

What Callitro lacked in Sister-like aggression, he always made up for in enthusiasm.

CHAPTER 26

D'SHEA HADN'T SUMMONED ME BY THE TIME I HAD WORN THE WIZARD AND myself out. Once again, Callitro felt safe enough to drift into a light doze, and I was tempted to do the same. I struggled to stay awake, however, playing with my sloppy, buzzing crotch and allowing my mind to wander.

I had always enjoyed any bua's cock at Court, especially their proof of pleasure; the bitter, slippery eruption when they lost control that I would never get from a Feldeu. However, Callitro's body and responses quickly grew familiar. I could drink deeply of him, be assured I'd get what I wanted, even though it had been Shyntre to whet my appetite this time.

Despite either intent or effort.

How was this? That such disrespect, such resentment and resistance in the spoiled, insolent son of the Headmaster had made me so hot.

It's a challenge, a defiant prick swinging in front of my eyes. Of course, I want to reach out and grasp it.

I'd never truly forced a bua into sex until Auslan, and sometimes I felt confused how his consistent dissuasion afterward, even though I *knew* he wanted me since our first meeting continued to feed my appetite. And Shyntre resisted, too, but he had forced *me* first; despite motive or circumstance, that didn't change the fact he'd jammed his cock down my throat, spitting insults, or had the gall to mount my backside like he held some soiled high ground.

Games.

I'd just called it that in the Headmaster's library. A new kind of game I hadn't played much with males at Court, but I said to Phaelous quite plainly that I knew I liked them. It was like the games with Jaunda, but I was on the dominant side.

Or at least, it felt that way, and I had suggested to Shyntre we do it again sometime, when the Prime and the Elders weren't arranging it like a gladiator fight. Goddess, his expression when I said that. It had caused a burst of pure delight down between my legs.

Games and those who would play them. A less acidic version of what my older sister had forced me to play, perhaps.

Perhaps. Careful you don't become like her.

I'd promised myself that decades ago.

I watched Callitro sleeping, looking disheveled in his somewhat disorderly room. The cooperative bua was play for me as well, genuinely enjoyable but of a more familiar kind. He did not receive a lot of sex in general, sequestered from the nosing females of Sivaraus because of his inborn talent. He was as hungry as me and quite a bit of fun, although …

I made a face to myself. *He isn't all that I want.*

I couldn't let myself be exclusive with any wizard at the Tower, anyway. There was nothing wrong with having a couple favorites here, and just like my Sisters, I enjoyed some buas more than others at Court. Feeling a desire as I had for those who had become my favorites, I *knew* I wanted to win Shyntre's reluctant cock.

My way, next time. I'll have him spurt in my cunt, where it belongs.

It was the only hole of mine that he hadn't yet creamed, after all.

My fingers diddled faster with my thoughts, my mouth stretched into a distracted smile as I contemplated waking Callitro by sucking my own, drying juices from his flaccid prick. I glanced at the candle. We might have time for one more.

Callitro inhaled, deep and sudden, and opened his eyes. Caught me staring at him. He blinked. Waiting and willing to submit, an unconscious response.

I smiled hungrily. "Anything new on my ring? I know it hasn't been long since I tried it on."

"Um —"

"If not, I want to go again."

His penis throbbed, just starting to swell under my gaze. *Yum*.

"The ring is almost finished, Red Sister," he said.

"Do you need anything from me?" I asked, and he shook his head. I rose up on my knees to lean over his hips, reaching for his sex. "In that case —"

I slurped him down, and he gasped, his erection plumping up between my lips, spongy and hot, gradually growing turgid. Another experience I never got from the Feldeu.

I pushed his thighs apart with one hand, and he obeyed, spreading for me and bending his knees as I slickened two fingers in my own twat before removing them and prodding between his cheeks. Callitro lifted his legs, knowing what to expect, and groaned as I penetrated his ass with both fingers at once.

I savored how he yielded, how metal-hard his cock in my mouth became as I found and stroked his nut gland. Though nowhere near ready for a fist, as my Elder had jested, Callitro responded well now to a cait exploring his pucker. It hadn't taken long.

Neither did I, this time, as I soon removed my fingers, wiped them on his bedding, and climbed up to get that properly-prepped length up inside. I didn't know how much time we had. I fisted his hair just above his nape, gripped one shoulder, focusing on his face, and began to ride. Hard.

Callitro clutched my hips, moved with me without restraining me, closing his eyes to breathe slower when my gaze grew too intense for him. He worked hard to avoid climaxing before I did, and he must, for I didn't make it easy on him. Perhaps he thought of something less arousing to hold out, while I thought of something even more.

A mottled, fanged Dread Spider with enormous tits, leaking yellowed milk, versus a struggling bua with gold flecks in his eyes, bound to a table and still spitting insults despite the root stuffed in his mouth.

Just as example.

I blinked, shook my head as my pacing stumbled, and Callitro groaned. The trickle of fear coming into me made me hold him down; instinctively he resisted, writhing in a gasp of shock.

"Yes!" I whispered, my jaw slack as I trembled, clasping his shoulder, now slightly sticky with sweat. "Fight back. Resist me. I'm gonna cum …"

Callitro obeyed, his burnt orange eyes unfocused, the flicking about recalling a flame, and his whole body tried once to throw me off him. He moaned like he had something in his mouth; I wasn't sure how he did that without practice, but it made my arousal surge, accelerating the climb.

"Yes, bua!"

I held him down. Fucked him harder, his body tensing as I reached and gripped one wrist, pressed it down. Held his hair, his head in place as I anointed his cock with my slimy markings, thrust after thrust, cramming him in. Hurtling toward that intangible, black edge.

"G-God … Goddess!" I gasped, my cunt rippling, clenching.

"Mmmrrghh!!" Callitro cried, teeth clenched, lower lip quivering, his cock throbbing inside me. Spurting!

"Yes!!"

~Fuuuck! Fuck me! Oh, OH!~

Sweat. Heat. Pounding, pulsing, pleasure.

I collapsed, rasping, forehead to the mattress. Cock softening amidst goo between my legs. He was shaking. A hand on back. He whimpered softly.

"H-hurt?" I asked, my head still spinning.

The mage took much longer to answer — to decide how to answer — than I would have believed genuine if it had been any other words to come from his lips.

"I-I don't know. My head. Aches."

As did mine. Fuck.

"You need water," I said, and Callitro nodded agreement.

I pushed myself off him and went to get it from his stand. I noticed when the wizard sniffed his own source.

"Let me, um, purify this," he said. "Just in case."

"Alright."

Afterward, we both drank thirstily; we consumed all there was, saying nothing else. I wiped down and started to dress as Callitro pulled a blanket to himself. I hadn't yet received a summons, but there wasn't time for another round before the potion I'd drunk would wear off anyway. It might be a first, not being interrupted or hurrying to gear up with someone waiting outside the door.

"Are you better?" I asked, my headache having faded by the time I finished.

The mage nodded, his brows still drawn, a mystified look on his face. "I apologize, Sister, it felt like … someone tampered with my water. I hallucinated just before I … climaxed."

I held myself still. "What did you see?"

Callitro tried to shrug it off. "It wasn't real. Like a dream in Reverie."

I shrugged, my stomach tightening as I sat down on the bed's edge. "Tell me. I'm just curious, not angry. You're a good fuck, mage, like always. I'm satisfied."

He glanced at me, wariness and reassurance clashing in his eyes. "Mm. I saw the Drider Keeper. She's been in bad dreams before, the warning tales I've heard. What she does to young buas tied up and left in her Pit." Callitro glanced at me. "You've probably seen her. I hope I never will."

I kept my mouth closed, listening. I knew similar stories, geared more for Nobles who might think they could avoid being sacrificed on an altar if they overstepped their bounds. But, no, I had never seen the Keeper, either. It only now occurred to me that, as a Red Sister, I just might. A grotesque delight waiting.

"She … the Keeper was fucking me," he murmured. "Milking me before sucking me dry with her spider fangs. Just for a moment, I forgot it was you, Red Sister." He swallowed. "No insult to you, I swear upon the Grace of the Valsharess. As I said, one of my 'brothers' must have slipped something into my water as a prank. I wouldn't have fought you if I recognized you."

I nodded. "I believe you. You're well now?"

Callitro exhaled, considered, and nodded. "Yes, Red Sister. I am. Thank you for asking."

Self-suspicion and guilt had wormed its way in by now, and I leaned to kiss his lips, lightly. I tried a smile. "I should return. Wish to escort me down?"

The battlemage looked about his own cluttered, well-worn space and nodded. "Yes, Red Sister, I wish."

It seemed a change of scenery would help. I stood up so he could get to his feet, wipe down, and get dressed, waiting as I tried to think about something other than being fucked by Driders. I spied the small, grey box under the bed.

"You kicked something underneath," I said, nudging the corner with my boot as Callitro glanced my way while rubbing down.

"Hm? Oh, there it is." He nodded. "That's your ring."

I smirked. "You put it on the floor?"

His face warmed. "It fell off when I got up to answer the door."

"And you were too excited to pause on the way?" I chuckled.

"One should *never* keep Red Sisters waiting," he said with a charming smile. "It's safe advice."

I laughed. We had both relaxed a bit in the banter, and I followed Callitro's lead as he opened the door for me and then closed it again, securing it with a ward significantly more complicated than the ones I was training to break or withstand. He didn't trust his Towermates, especially not after believing one of them had drugged him for fun.

That could work against us the next time we need battlemages to fight, but I can't tell him. I should tell Elder Rausery about it.

I sighed softly at the thought, took two steps just behind Callitro as he moved toward the jump circle, and then the door in front of us popped open.

"Callitro!"

Two grinning wizards around his own age. Not battlemages, no brown sash.

"You emerge at last!"

"Introduce us?"

My escort glanced at me — I put on my bored expression — and shook his head. "No, we answer a summons. I must take her to the main floor without delay."

"We'll come with you."

They stuck like burrs.

"No!" Callitro said, annoyed. "Cluttered circles give everyone headaches, you know that!"

The first one shrugged while the other studied my armor intensely.

"So we'll follow after."

More doors around both bends were opening at the same time, at the very least curious about the raised voices. My mouth twisted in response. *Fucking Abyss …*

One bua was fine. A troop of buas, each wanting something? At the very least, a look or some attention? I'd never get out of here, and I knew I was finished playing in the Tower for the cycle.

"Go back to your rooms," Callitro insisted, gesturing the first two away without effect.

"You can't tell us what to do," the first burr said.

I wondered about this not happening when Shyntre was my escort. Happenstance or significance? Maybe I'd find out later. For now, I waited until a few more buas could see what would happen next.

"You'll stay on this level," I said, and the two wizards froze in place when I looked each in the eye. "Where you belong."

Their gazes dropped.

"Um, b-but we'll assist you, Red Sister."

A last, desperate shot when, clearly, I didn't need any. I knew what Jaunda would do if I pulled this shit.

With an annoyed exhale, I lunged, my cloak billowing as I took four, quick moves to stun and hook each bua off his feet. They landed upon their backs on the hard stone; both grunted, and one lost his breath. Four other wizards saw me do it. They stopped, two others coming up behind, and only one was smart enough to retreat right then.

"Back to your rooms!" I barked, my voice hurting their pointed ears, if nothing else.

They scrambled, running the way they had arrived. I gave a few extra flicks to the two on the ground, but the one lingering while his brother still gasped for air, I kicked him in the ass with the hard tip of my boot. He yelped.

"Go! Don't tempt me in what I'll do next!"

More scuffing sandals, another door closed, and finally, it was just me and Callitro on the seventeenth floor. I grabbed his arm to drag him to the circle.

"Now don't fuck us up," I teased, my voice still rough with aggression.

"Never, Sister!" he gushed assurance.

"Do it."

Despite the last-moment excitement, Callitro gave me a smoother trip down to the main floor than Shyntre ever had. Could be the battlemage was simply better at this spell. The place wasn't empty, and we received a lot more looks, but I walked out front this time as I headed straight for the door. Callitro barely kept up with me.

"Wait!" he whispered, and I turned to where his hands would be blocked by my body, reading, *I can't open the main door. Only those the Headmaster chooses.*

"*Now* you say?" I whispered.

He could have mentioned that when I asked to be brought down here. What did I think I was going to do, lounge in the waiting area listening to the bua mages natter at me?

I smoothed my expression and signed sternly, *Call your Headmaster.*

Callitro nodded and went for a smooth panel while the three interrupted in their tasks watched, and I stood in the middle of an all-male residence, unable to leave when I chose. I felt awkward but wouldn't show it.

Still, it was odd that Elder D'Shea hadn't summoned me yet. I wagered she would have come to take me through that same, small level back to the Cloister instead of having me walk. Unless something had happened unexpectedly, and she was dealing with it.

Abruptly, the main door opened without anyone touching it.

I stared at the tall line of yawning blackness beyond before I snapped myself out of it and moved toward it. Callitro met me at the double doorway while the gawkers moved closer with care, as if they wanted to peek outside without getting too close to me.

I shook my head. What did they think they were going to see? Then I paused as I saw the tense expression on Callitro's face and detected movement at the second gate closest to the Tower.

Oh, yes, them.

The Drider constructs. Not real ones, but real enough that a bua who had sleep terrors about them wouldn't want to go wandering about the grounds. Callitro wasn't the only wizard with that opinion, from what I saw. We couldn't hurt the magical buas, but if one betrayed us, perhaps the Keeper's Pit was a consistent sentence, and they knew it? I'd have to ask D'Shea.

I did something mindless to straighten my uniform, squaring my shoulders, trying to look and sound official. "Thank you for your aid, wizard. You have your orders. Continue forward as we've discussed."

Callitro nodded, seemed like he had something else to say but was both distracted by the constructs outside and trying to work out my cryptic message. All at the same time. Alright, so his focus outside of battle could use a little work.

Bowing my head, I left the Wizard's Tower, intending to run all the way back to the Cloister and break a message pellet to my Elder as soon as I got within range. I hadn't quite made it to the eight-legged monstrosities when I heard someone running up behind me. Turning around, not quite putting my back to the Driders, I identified Shyntre, of all Davrin.

Well, well.

I smiled, but at least remembered not to show my teeth out in the dark. Still and silent, I waited for him to catch up. If he held any fear for the Guardsvrin at the gate, he didn't show it, nor did he give away anxiety for being outside the safety of the Wizard's Tower. Indeed, by the time he slowed and stopped before me, this could have been the most relaxed I'd seen him yet, despite the heavy breathing.

Somehow, the older bua still scowled at me. Possibly his "resting" face.

I signed a greeting. *Need something?*

Shyntre held out a dark pouch with one hand, signed with the other. *Take this and give it to the Elder Sorceress.*

With whose regards?

The Headmaster's.

Eyeing the size and apparent weight of the object inside, I might guess what it was. Phaelous was one stubborn spider-fucker. *Like sire, like son.*

Carefully, I lifted the pouch by its ties at the top, tucked it into a larger spot on my belt where I had room. I scanned upward at the massive, empty space above us but for the Tower itself, then behind me, then back at Shyntre with a smirk.

You seem courageous out here. The rest of them are still huddling at the doorway.

Clearly, Shyntre could think of nothing he would opt to say. He only shrugged.

Untouchable or indifferent? I asked.

He snorted, making the insolent noise. The wizard didn't answer me but turned and walked away, having delivered the object for his sire. Goddess, if my pride were as parchment-thin as some of the Nobles I'd known, I'd be furious, planning already a spiteful way to get him in trouble with a higher female.

As it was, I took this as a sign he'd continue the Game with me.

This was a challenge and a tease, opening the way for that future, victorious moment when I got his cock up between my legs again. He had all but confessed to know the Feldeu as I did; maybe he couldn't help but resist until he was forced to submit.

Perhaps the Prime and the Priestesses had trained him that way, and that was the only way he could get his own prick up to violate caits recruited for the Sisterhood, to force her to contemplate something that never happened to us in Sivaraus.

Being forced by a real bua who wasn't afraid of females.

I watched until Shyntre was back inside, and the door had closed, then continued past the guarded gate. I barely felt the creep up my spine from four pair of eyes peering through shaggy, grey hair, while thinking over this revealing visit among the sequestered wizards.

I pitched my body into a fast jog. Not only because I had to get back, but because I had renewed energy to burn off before I got there.

CHAPTER 27

D'SHEA RETURNED THE MESSAGE AS SOON AS SHE RECEIVED MINE.

My quarters. Immediately.

Uh-oh.

I paced myself and loped over stone and through crevices, using the well-worn methods for breaking up my trail as I approached my hidden Cloister. Kneeling beside a camouflaged entrance closest to the wing where I needed to go, I disabled the trap, slipped inside, and reset it behind me.

Before emerging from the trap lock, I listened for approaching Sisters, certainly for any I didn't want to explain my way past if they felt like delaying me.

Three Red Sisters walked by without speaking, so I didn't know who they were but at least now the way was clear. I entered the Cloister and moved fast to D'Shea's quarters, where she was waiting to let me in.

I smelled the wine on her breath, saw the heavy lids of her eyes, and hadn't worked through my surprise before she planted both hands just behind my ears and pulled my lips to hers. I froze like a virgin bua, letting her explore my mouth because ...

What else can I do?

"Disarm and strip," she commanded after pulling back. She was

346

pointing to a cleared space on her workbench.

Alright, there's that.

"On my bed, Sirana. Don't dawdle."

At least she knew my name.

As I obeyed, I saw a small pile of shattered glass at the base of the wall across from her desk. On the desk was Phaelous' ruby ring and a mostly-empty bottle of wine. The glass was missing. Or rather, it was no longer in one piece, a spray of dark spots drying upon the stone.

I sat naked on my Elder's bed. *What has happened since I was in the Tower?*

My Elder approached me, pushed my shoulder with one hand to get me to lie back as she climbed onto the mattress. She wore the silky, deep purple robe with silver and red threads which I'd only seen on her inside this space. Kneeling between my thighs, her larger-than-average Feldeu in hand, I watched the Sorceress draw her tongue around the bulb intended to go inside me, then leaned down to do the same on my slit.

I sucked in my breath, my head whirling as tremors arose in my limbs. I wasn't sure if it was fear or anticipation.

Oh Goddess, she's drunk … I can't lose control again —

Another moment, the bulb was locked in place. She spoke the magic word and, an instant after that, I felt every stroke of her hand along my phallus. She was eager. Impatient.

"E-Elder," I stammered.

She climbed over me, her robes askew, teasing my view with only part of one breast. The silk draped over my thighs as her warm, smooth buttocks slid down, her hips settling into place. The tip of the Feldeu ready to receive the plunge down.

"Augh, Godd —" I groaned as my Elder took me.

She rode me as desperate as I had Callitro. I watched her breasts jiggle and bounce, and I clasped helplessly to her thighs, wrinkled the fabric in my grip. My view of her hungry cunt swallowing me was partially obscured by the robe.

"Look at me," she growled.

Mouth slack, I ripped my gaze away from our pumping, fragrant joining. The Sorceress stared into my eyes.

"Kain?" she demanded.

I shook my head, recalling I had to breathe on my own. I sucked in, filled my chest full to answer. "No. Sirana. Elder, I-I know you."

D'Shea nodded, satisfied, stoking the fire in her loins higher. Her robe slipped off one shoulder, exposing it and a full breast. Her nipple was tight. I thrust up once, and she fought me over the rhythm. Immediately, I submitted and built a focus instead. Self-control.

Because one of us needs to.

"*Nngh*, yes, Elder," I encouraged, touching her only over silk and not her skin. "Feels good. More."

She moaned, nodding, her balance not quite so sure and her grace suffering from the wine. Her eyes were closed, her focus completely on bringing her orgasm forward without concern for mine. This was fine with me; between the two of us, I would have said she needed it more.

Much more.

She also didn't need me to speak. To distract.

I laid back and let her use me as she would.

Before much longer, the Elder Sorceress yelped just before she came, her cunt clutching hard then rippling its way along the rod buried deep in her twat. She grunted and ground her hips, fingernails digging painfully into my ribs. She came down, her desperation now shifting up from her lower gut to her exposed chest and getting enough air. Her eyes had been closed the entire time.

I watched her shoulders relax as she remained on her knees astraddle my hips, her body snug around the Feldeu. She licked her lips. Weaving slightly, as if dizzy from her indulgences. I reached out and held her upright by her arms, my eyes still lingering on her breasts framed by wrinkled, elite robes.

I either heard something or felt it. I wasn't sure, but then D'Shea looked toward her workbench with a bewildered expression as well. She tilted her ear toward it, swinging one leg over to get off me.

"What *is* that?" she muttered.

I breathed out slowly at the chill of a wet, unsatisfied Feldeu so swiftly abandoned, shaking my head at the annoying buzzing just beyond my hearing. I watched as my Elder searched my belt, found the spot where I had tucked the pouch Shyntre had given me.

Oh, yeah.

"Mm, sent with … best regards," I mumbled, propped on my elbows, "from Headmaster Phaelous."

My Elder tugged open the pouch, looked inside, then upended it into her palm. It sparkled in the candlelight, the color captivating yet so familiar. She brought it very close to her face, too close to be wise with an unknown, perhaps, but I had time to notice the metallic silver shining next to the sapphire blue.

"The Dwarf stone didn't look like this," she said, seeming less inebriated. "It was mere marks ago."

"That's not the stone the Headmaster showed you," I said, sitting up and scooting to the edge of the bed to sit up, my cock still jutting up from between tight thighs. "Shyntre worked on that one. He brought it in after you left, but it didn't have the metal. That's new."

"Yes, it looks very new," she murmured, turning the jewelry over to inspect it carefully. "Just mounted. It's a pendant." Her eyes swept over and pinned me. "Did either male say anything, give you instruction?"

I swallowed. "Phaelous wanted me to hold it. I … refused."

"Why?"

"Gut feeling."

"Hm. And then?"

"I visited Callitro. And when I was leaving, Shyntre caught up to me and told me to give my Elder that pouch with Phaelous' regards."

D'Shea's face seemed on the edge of some expression I couldn't define. "Did you look inside?"

I shook my head. "I guessed that's what it was. Just the stone, though, I didn't expect the pendant."

"No instruction. No context."

"No, Elder. Both sire and son made a similar comment about us in that regard."

The Sorceress rolled her eyes and sighed, seeming calmer, more like her usual self as she chewed on the curiosities of the blue stone closed in her hand. "What warning did you feel in touching it?"

I looked down. "The Headmaster could tell it responded to me in a mage-like way, but I'm not a mage. He wanted me to hold it so he could study ... something. I figured you'd want to see what happened when I held it, first."

D'Shea nodded approval. "Good instinct." She held it out. "Will you? Now?"

I glanced down at my "little head" still peering up at me. "Can you please remove the Feldeu, first? Just in case."

The Sorceress blinked, then surprised me with a smile as she chuckled. "Ah. Of course, Sirana. Yes, we should control the factors in any test. Open your legs and hold still. Relax."

Soon enough, the wide bulb stretched out from between my nether-lips, and D'Shea and I had made the exchange, magic cock for non-magic stone. I didn't feel any sort of jolt, no surge or vibration while I held the pendant. I felt calm, and the buzzing in my ears was gone.

I could appreciate the work done on it as a magnificent decoration for any female to wear; it only lacked a small chain or length of cord from which to suspend it around one's neck. I sensed nothing like the Davrin magic within it or the runes or wards, those complexities I was gradually being trained to recognize.

With me sitting nude on my Elder's bed, Shyntre's sapphire was only a quiet, beautiful stone resting in my hand.

"Astonishing," D'Shea whispered, seeming to take in me and all around me. Maybe she studied my aura, if I had one.

"Elder, wh — ?"

"I have a theory," she said, rushing to her desk as she lifted a finger for me to await her.

I watched as she picked up Phaelous' ring from next to the standing, green bottle and put it on her middle finger. She spoke a word I didn't recognize then commanded me.

"Choose a face, Sirana, and do not tell me who it is."

I chose and nodded. D'Shea came closer to me, her gaze drilling into me.

"Imagine this face as a wide tapestry at the fore of your mind," she instructed. "Make it as clear as you can. Do not resist, and do not change the image."

I was tempted to do exactly that, because the face I chose wasn't clear, anyway. I had only seen her once, hiding at the top of a set of stairs I'd once known well. But, no. I kept it consistent, thinking about Natia, the unknown cait my Mother seemed to have adopted sometime after I left. She was too old to have been born before, so where had that child come from?

My Elder shook her head, her mouth beginning another lovely smile. "Nothing. I see nothing."

She was excited at this. I drew breath to ask.

"Now," she said, "set down the pendant on the other far side of my workbench, if you please, then come back here and picture the face again."

Alright.

I obeyed, returned to the bed without the stone, and focused on Natia. I felt a subtle pressure pushing at me now, coming from D'Shea's gaze. I tensed.

"Do not resist," she commanded, frowning in disapproval.

Reluctantly, I submitted. The spell felt like a writhing worm working into my ear, and I grimaced in disgust, fisting the blankets as I waited for it to end. D'Shea blinked in surprise then, taking a few extra heartbeats to be sure.

"Natia Thalluen'rith?" she asked. "The Matron's handmaiden?"

I nodded. My jaw locked in my tension.

"Hm. I did not expect that. Are you jealous, Sirana?"

I unstuck my teeth. "N-No, Elder. Just curious."

"Interesting. What are you curious about?"

"Sudden appearances at any House are always suspect," I said. "Even more when they are close to the Nobility. I reported on *exactly* this detail at House Itlaun with the First Daughter's return."

"Ah. Reasonable." D'Shea thumbed the Headmaster's ring. "I could tell you that Rohenvi Thalluen obtained the child in an orphan bid. Those happen from time to time, when a head of family is executed and she has multiple children and grandchildren, as this one did. The Sisterhood is always aware of where those children go."

"Yes, Elder," I acknowledged, somehow feeling impatient with the explanation.

"Retrieve the sapphire again, Sirana, and choose another face. I will try harder."

Joy.

I was tempted to go with a familiar, pleasant face since I expected more unpleasantness but chose Raegal, the wizard too cowardly to be in the same room with me.

The Sorceress stared, drawing upon her significant power while the very edges of my ears tingled in the closed space. I clutched the Dwarf stone, now transformed and unrecognizable as such. It would blend in with the pieces in any Noble's treasure box, and I enjoyed the cool, calm center of it.

I was aware of the Sorceress trying to break into my mind, and I wanted to retreat as she kept trying, especially when she moved beyond subtlety. Once she clasped me by the ears, bringing me close to peer into my head through my eyes, I ached to lash out. To pull away.

"Stay," she whispered intensely.

I didn't blink. I expected something to explode, some backlash to what vibrations I sensed in my jaw. But, deep inside, it was quiet.

Finally, with a gasp, D'Shea deflated, and whatever spell for which she had used the Headmaster's ring fizzled. She released me and stepped back, looking at the ruby on her finger. Again, she was excited at the failure. Elated. Tilting her chin up toward the low ceiling, she laughed in a way I'd never heard.

"Elder?" I asked.

"Sirana!" she cried, still laughing. "Oh, Goddess, that motherless mongrel!"

I was only further confused so I stayed quiet. I waited as D'Shea hurried to a standing chest, opening a lid and then a small drawer inside it, searching about. She returned with a strongly woven black cord, her empty hand outstretched.

"The sapphire," she demanded.

I handed it over, watched her thread the cord through the pendant's metal loop with nimble fingers, and tie the ends before casting a quick cantrip to seal them. My Elder handed it back to me sooner than I expected; in fact, I wouldn't have been surprised if the blue stone might have gone straight into her own specialty chest.

"Wear that *every* moment in your next audience, Sirana," my Elder said. "Do not allow it to be removed under any circumstances. In fact, keep it hidden when possible. Whether he knew it or not, Phaelous just gave us the means to keep you alive and free for a little longer."

I opened my mouth. Closed it. I stared at her, then put the pendant over my head, flipping up my frazzled braid to let it settle around my neck to hang in front of my pounding heart.

"Your audience is at the Sanctuary," my Elder elaborated, folding her arms beneath her silk-covered breasts. I could tell she was pleased with my choice to shut up and listen. "Priestess Wilsira has asked you to stand before her without me. Without any of us. Alone. The Prime has overridden both Rausery and me and granted the Priestess what is owed."

"Owed?"

"From your trials. The one using Wilsira's Sathoet son, specifically."

I risked a glance toward the pieces of shattered wine glass near the wall, and D'Shea followed my gaze. She harrumphed.

"It seems your instincts about Kerse's intents toward you at the last Worship Ball may be correct, unfortunately. If Kerse has spoken your name to his Mother even once, then I fear Wilsira is jealous and wants to inspect you. She has the right to ask, and now she has. After you've been with us barely more than a turn."

I slipped my hands underneath my ass so they wouldn't quiver, getting to know the new weight of the pendant as it swung gently between my naked breasts. "What is the significance of the timing, Elder?"

D'Shea nodded smartly; it was a good question. "Short enough that the Prime believes you won't compromise the Sisterhood spilling anything

Wilsira doesn't already know, thus is likely to agree. Long enough that the Priestess has likely confirmed I have investment in you, making her doubly curious."

My bare shoulders prickled with unease. "A rivalry between you?"

D'Shea's smile was humorless. "Immense. She dislikes Lelinahdara, as well, who rises in stature within the Priesthood and may threaten her some cycle to come."

"Do you think she knows about Auslan as well?"

My Elder made a face. "No, I do not. I'd expect you to keep your ears open for any such hints." She glanced down at the sapphire. "With this Dwarven sapphire shielding your thoughts, Sirana, that Consort may stay hidden as our informant if Wilsira does not yet realize it. Although if she learns what I *do not* want her to know about *you*, then 'Auslan' is far from your primary concern."

A scenario had come together in my mind. Again, I looked at the wall, the spatter marks, the glass. Imagining the mixture of fear and anger it might have taken to cause my Elder Sorceress to pitch her final glass of wine at the wall rather than guzzle it.

"The Cloister received the request from the Sanctuary," I said, "and despite your opposition, the Prime will still send me, as is 'owed.' You believed I would walk into the Sanctuary with no defense, and … ?"

"Be broken by the Priestess, first," she answered harshly, "to give up all you've even begun to understand about yourself. Then either be imprisoned or sacrificed while Wilsira tells the Prime, and both of them come after me for hiding something like this."

I felt the cold down to my marrow as I stared up at my Elder. "And … Rausery?"

The Sorceress smirked, her mouth twisting bitterly. "With any luck, depending what was wrung out of you, she might pretend ignorance and evade the same fate. Or she might not. And the Sisterhood is culled according to the Prime's preferences."

Tears came to my eyes, surprising in their abruptness. I swallowed a hard knot in my throat. "I-I am … this dangerous to you, Elder? Because of what happened with Kain?"

Why does she dare keep me?

Reading my expression, she leaned down and took my shoulders. My eyes flicked down the front of her robe then back up to her face with a silent chiding.

"Listen, novice," she said.

I did.

"Each of us still living began where you are. *None* of us lived through our first five turns in the Sisterhood on our merit alone. There had to be something worth protecting in the eyes of another Sister. Someone had to fight for you. That's why we're the Sisterhood, not the Priesthood."

My mouth was dry. "The Prime doesn't teach that."

"We know," D'Shea said. "Our Cloister was different at the beginning, and the gap between her and the younger Red Sisters only grows. Rausery and I will protect you, Sirana, because you are a path to further change for us. But *you* in turn must protect *all* of us by never revealing your mind's wounds to anyone."

"But h-how can I?" I stammered. "Lelinahdara ... a-and Phaelous just made —"

"Let *me* deal with them," she said, her face pure determination as she lifted the sapphire pendant off my chest, displaying it in her palm. "You protect yourself, your mind, from the Daughters of Braqth. You do this at all costs, understand?"

I could hear my blood rushing, throbbing in my ears as I nodded. "Yes, Elder."

"Good. Now get into your full uniform with all equipment. I'm going to teach you such that a novice Red Sister might visit a Priestess alone within the Sanctuary and come back out on her own two feet."

I nodded then gave her an odd look. She saw it.

"What?" she asked.

My mouth rose at one end. "Is that why you fucked me in such a drunken heat, Elder? You thought it would be the last time?"

Some of the familiar, haughty confidence returned as my Elder lifted her chin. "If you knew all I do about that venomous place, Sirana, you'd take *all* private moments as if they were your last."

Private, huh?

And she wanted to keep me that way.

I bowed my head. "I'll bear it in mind, Elder."

Although, ever since the moment I had almost died on Jilrina's altar, I was certain that I already did.

CHAPTER 28

"Queen's Grace, Sirana. You are looking well since last I saw you."

I smiled, stepping inside the boundary. "And you shine with Braqth's faith, Priestess, as always."

Tarra paused from where she had just closed and sealed the small, camouflaged door in the dim, long hallway. She turned and planted hands on her hips as if she didn't like my tone.

"No Court-inspired lip service here, if you please, Red Sister."

I bowed without hesitation. "I've forgotten the Court, Priestess. You healed me with that faith. Could I not be sincere?"

The Liaison glanced down at my crotch and back up with a smirk. "As long as you're not wearing that *thing*, I suppose it may be possible."

I smiled. "I am not wearing it, Priestess."

"I can tell."

"I did not even bring one," I added. "I am repentant about what happened last time."

"Yes, so your Elder informed me before your arrival."

Tarra's green eyes trailed over me again, narrowed in the heatless torchlight. She also scanned the space around us and seemed satisfied with her own privacy.

"You still insulted me greatly, novice," she said.

I nodded acknowledgment. "Yes, Priestess, I recall it. I dug at a reopened wound. It was a stumble back, but it'll not happen again."

"Yes, so your Elder claims." The four-century-old Priestess paused, studying my face. "Given why you're here, *do* you realize, at last, that you need me, that your Elder needs me? Don't forget, she *knows* me better than she knows you, and I know her better than you ever will. I am not her enemy, I am her Liaison, and for good reason if the Sanctuary and the Sisterhood are to continue working together for the Glory of Braqth. I am the only one who sees this clearly."

"Yes, Priestess." I bowed again. "She has corrected my behavior. I beg your tolerance."

Tarra weighed this with the expected suspicion but protested no more. "Enough for now. Still your tongue and follow me."

I maintained a smile and a bounce to my gait despite being required to admit all fault. It was easy, given the mental image of the Liaison's tongue most certainly *not* being still at my Elder's netherhole while I had fucked her.

With a longer stride than the Priestess, I kept up with her down the long path, my cloak flowing out behind me. The Sanctuary was enormous, central to Sivaraus compared to the hidden Cloister of the Red Sisters. I held genuine interest in the various internal spaces I would see which I had no access as either Noble or a novice Sister.

Anyone on a Palace balcony outside could see the Sanctuary looming next to the Palace. The two were attached both in architecture and policy even though one would never mistake one for the other. The Palace had used a darker stone, and although both were curvaceous more than square, the Valsharess' space overall contained more straight edges and stately vertices than the softer molding and swirls in the view of its bigger sister.

Each was covered with ornate, carved decoration with many spider and web motifs, of course, but also entwined with our most common objects of beauty: crowns and religious headpieces, long flowing hair, perfect bodies wrapped in silk and armored in balance, jewels and gilding enhanced some of the more abstract designs.

Upon my arrival at Court, I had seen more sets of piercing eyes than any other interpretive pattern.

Now, I entered the Priestess' home through a backdoor to which I'd been directed, stepping into a near-empty, oddly straight passageway which conflicted with all the public areas. Something told me I was on a floor below the surface, in the deep foundation. From this one place, I could not gauge or sense the same vast space that one could see from the outside.

The farther in I walked with Tarra, however, the more the halls and stairs curved like our Cloister; there were no straight-shots which lasted longer than two-eights of running strides. The ceiling was less high than the Cloister, however, the walls not as wide. I might use a weapon the length of my forearm, but nothing which was most effective in a spin or full swing.

"Why the good mood, Sirana?" Tarra asked, her hips swaying slowly in her silky, purple gown. I noted the same ornate black belt and ceremonial dagger she'd been wearing at the altar of my final trial.

"A rough ride upon waking," I said, keeping it simple.

The Liaison snorted delicately, her mouth widening in some humor. "But your Sisters seek any and all holes nearby, with high frequency. Is it still such a lift for you, then, after a turn of being the youngest?"

I grinned. "It is, Priestess. Another notch in my bedframe. It's become so thin it may crumble and send me to the floor one of these cycles."

Of course, I had no such bedpost, but I also knew Tarra didn't come to the Cloister except to visit D'Shea, who did. The Priestess seemed surprised, perhaps tempted to be amused as I hoped she would be. She gave up the topic with a shake of her head.

"Well. Wilsira wished to meet you at once upon arrival. Do you need anything first?"

"No, Priestess. I came prepared. Even my bladder is empty." Her eyebrows crawled up at that, and I winked. "You know, in case she's as frightening as they say. I won't soil my uniform."

Tarra relaxed. Just a little. Again, she seemed tempted to smile. "Very well. Come."

Thanks, again, Jaunda.

Starting just one floor up, the walls and open rooms of the Sanctuary now looked like the Sanctuary. They were colorful and decorative, lined with a tasteful number of tapestries, banners, metal sculpture, and murals. Small tables existed for no other purpose than to display a figure or fine design, and there were quite a few more sources of water with regular, small fountains for washing and probably blessing, though I wouldn't drink from them.

The sconces held either smokeless torches or delicate candles with real flame, depending on burning hazard or some other significance I didn't know. As we went up three additional flights of stairs, each floor had a dominant color I would be blind to miss. Purple, gold, blue. Red was either missing or I hadn't found the level yet.

I was accustomed to dealing with less light given the sparseness of the Cloister's torches or no light at all as we crawled around outside. The Sanctuary was very well-lit by comparison, all the better to show off the beauty of its aesthetics. This brought back more memories of the Court and of my House, how accustomed I'd once been to candles and decorations just *being* there without my really thinking about them.

Now, my mind cataloged them all as possible impromptu weapons or tools; as disadvantages or advantages depending on where I stood in any given room.

How quickly some things change.

I anticipated the blue-themed floor, the third above the ground, and heard the subdued voices of children and a few low wails of hungry infants as we passed through.

D'Shea had warned me children were being raised within the Sanctuary itself, adopted Davrin who did not leave in their lifetime until a Priestess bid it, always for a particular purpose.

These Davrin were unknown to almost all of society. They belonged to no House and, like the Consorts, found it impossible to have any identity or status outside that which the Priesthood gave them.

D'Shea would not tell me the how and why, but I'd correctly guessed at least one purpose: the breeding and raising of the Consorts.

"Yes," my Elder had granted. "Not the only purpose, however."

"To raise and train more Priestesses?"

"Perhaps."

"Perhaps, Elder? But, to get Consorts, do they not need a place and function for the caits as well?"

D'Shea had shaken her head. "Their rituals are powerful, Sirana, you know this. They prefer males for better control. They *select* for buas." A pause. "I cannot do that with my arcane magic. No one can."

I had blinked in disbelief. "They *never* get a cait when they want a bua for a Consort?"

"It seems so," she'd said. "Or they abort as soon as they know it's female, but that would be a lot of breeding and birthing happening completely out of sight within their fortress."

I had shuddered. "What about us?"

"Us?"

"Are there any pregnant Red Sisters on that floor now whom I might see, Elder?"

She had shaken her head. "No, fortunately, there are not. It's been some centuries since we've lost one of ours to the Sanctuary. Don't ask whether there are any children of ours there now. They wouldn't ever be certain if their Mother had been a Red Sister."

I focused down the third-floor hall, decorated in tones both rich and somber, toward noise which I hadn't heard much of in my lifetime. Clusters of Davrin children together. Perhaps a score, and possibly the single largest group of them that I'd ever been aware of in one place for any length of time.

What would such an upbringing be like?

No single Matron to look to for decisions; many Priestesses of all ranks; far too many siblings, whether of blood or not, they were of similar age; and little knowledge of the city and plantations outside. All this would alienate them.

That Auslan had called himself an outsider to any House made more sense to me. I grasped why he'd opt to refrain from interacting much with House Itlaun except as he was expected to perform. The rest of the time, he just watched and listened.

And reported to Wilsira.

Lelinahdara paused in her smooth stride. "Is there a problem, Sister?"

I heard layer of chill in her voice and shook my head, replying honestly. "I've never heard so many children in one place, Priestess."

She nodded. "A necessity. We are very protective of them, Sirana, don't become too curious. We are only passing through."

I bowed my head, and yet, with all the secret passages I knew were here somewhere, had Tarra truly *needed* to take me to this floor at all? I wondered.

"Not to worry, Priestess. My function doesn't involve children."

Ironic, that. Given how often that function involved fucking.

"Good of you to say, Sister. Come."

We went up another well-decorated, spiral stairwell. As Tarra gently touched a smooth, polished stone on the wall five steps from the top, I felt an odd feeling in the pit of my stomach, as if I'd just taken a trip through a jump circle and all color vanished ahead of me as the door slid open.

What in the Eights?

Wary, I stepped out of the exit, surprised to see this floor was dominated by whites, grays, and dark shades not quite black. I stood out in stark contrast in my red uniform.

Most tapestries contained scenes of which I was not sure what my eyes were supposed to see. The feeling was mystifying to me. Patterns somehow nonexistent in a form of art which came into being *only* through rigid order and progression.

Tarra allowed me to pause so I could look closely at one of them. I saw abstract, interpreted magic and energy flow, as if I was seeing with my Dark Sight, but also smears of red and orange.

Somehow, I understood that they were violent images, though the menace in them was often blurred with blackness and forced boundaries which seemed unnatural and temporary. Casting voice or magic into a void, perhaps. Not unlike Qivni calling darkness to force utter blindness around me as I sensed her threat nearby.

Then I understood.

The Abyss.

"We're on the floor holding the Sathoet?" I asked.

Tarra folded her bejeweled hands before her. "Indeed."

"Only a floor apart from full-blood children? I thought Sathoet were hostile toward them."

"They *are* hostile."

"And the Abyssal floor is near the top of the Sanctuary, isn't it?"

"Twelfth level, yes. We skipped a few just now." Tarra's smile was small and smug. "I'm glad to see Varessa gave you *something* with which to work. I grew worried."

A soft chuckle, then she turned around to lead me farther down the chaotic slings of white and black.

There was not as much object art on this floor; mostly banners and tapestries, plenty to look at but less to shatter or destroy. I smelled a strong scent up here of larger bodies with greater heat putting off a greater volume of musk. Not overwhelming, but it did not have the undertones of soap and perfume, or the general fastidious cleanliness by other floors.

The halls twisted for a while until I was sure we'd walked to the far side of the Sanctuary. Next, I was led to a thick, double-wide iron door inscribed with runes and magical carvings.

"Was our last recruit tested here recently?" I asked.

Lelinahdara was silent, her hand pausing before it touched the next panel. She glanced at me. "This exact place? No. Kennitha's Fourth Daughter faced the Sathoet in an arena on another floor. She would have had an unfair advantage here."

"Unfair?" I repeated skeptically.

"Yes. Sathoet magic is restricted inside this room."

That didn't sound well for Jael. She had refused to talk about it.

"Is this where the Priestess Sons have their Reverie?" I asked.

"They don't experience Reverie, Sirana, but they do rest. This is where they are kept if one's Mother does not want him with her at any given time."

I frowned. "Why are we here? I thought you were taking me to see

Wilsira."

"I am." Tarra shrugged. "She likes this place."

Shit.

My Elder had guessed this one to be the least-likely meeting place. What had changed that she'd be wrong?

My guide rested her palm on the inscribed panel and murmured a chant which did not sound arcane. Something heavy clunked deep inside the doorway and it ground the floor far more than any of our typical sliding doors did. Only one side opened, just wide enough for us to walk through single file.

The Priestess went in first with me following. The door closed automatically after my boot heel just passed the threshold. I coughed, making the first noise in this quiet, ominous place.

A lot of scents in here. They clogged my throat all at once.

The dim light available was of odd quality. No candles, and the wall lanterns had been soldered and bolted to the stone, glowing with a heatless, unsettlingly pale glow casting many shadows.

I would have preferred either brighter light or none. This half-way illumination was a similar trick upon the eyes as in the Cloister's hallways, yet due to the smells and wide-open space, it felt far more dangerous to leave the wall and walk forward.

Shifting bodies and quiet hisses. At least one happy giggle. I saw none of them as shadows bulged and flowed unpredictably around creatures capable of masking their presence.

I shut my eyes against the useless light and stood listening to those menacing sounds, letting the subtle air move across my face, feeling their living energy. In a few moments, I could confidently place five of them in the room.

One was right over my head, on the high ceiling.

I would not have been prepared without D'Shea's counsel, but she had pressed on me the importance of setting boundaries early on. Had reminded me that I'd already done it once, I could do it again.

Tarra barely had time to raise her hand, a protest on her lips, as I withdrew my crossbow pistol and shot straight up over my head. I moved to the side, pushing the Priestess ahead of me deeper into the room, as the blunt head of the specialized bolt struck the ceiling near the skulking Sathoet.

The packet of sneeze powder burst on impact and the dust sprinkled down slowly to where I'd been standing. Even though my nose and lungs itched, Tarra and I were out of the direct effect. I had to confess in a smile how amusing it was to listen to a Sathoet go into a sneezing fit for a solid half a tick.

"Braqth take you," I said to him toward the end of it, a broad grin on my face. "You might want to get off the ceiling, Stripe. I have more, and I revel in target practice."

Lelinahdara saw that I had done nothing to injure the creature and relaxed. Her eyes watched some movement I couldn't see, though I could hear the scratching of claws along the stone. The Sathoet headed toward one of the outer walls, away from me. Sure enough, soon he was climbing down, grumbling low in his chest.

"Well," my escort spoke softly, as if she was still deciding whether to be impressed or not. "Interesting."

Whatever proud, revealing entrance Wilsira may have been planning, the mood had been spoiled for it. The elder Priestess simply walked out of the shadows at this point, elegant and poised in her shimmering gown — like amethyst blended with emerald this time, instead of with garnet.

Wilsira's impassive face was framed by the same headpiece of a stylized, black spider, her white hair with gold streaks loose and flowing down her back. Her silver belt of many tiny chains looped and draped around each other to perfection at the curve of her waist, cradling her left hip in ornate, shining metal against a dark sash.

Lelinahdara bowed, as did I.

"Tarra," she said to acknowledge, though in the name was a quiet rebuke, possibly for not bowing fast enough. For the moment, Wilsira ignored me.

The younger Priestess straightened. Her smile held, and she did not look afraid. "Priestess Wilsira, I've brought to you Red Sister Sirana, courtesy of the Red Sister Prime. She sends her regards and requests a confirmation message in return."

Wilsira nodded. "Grant it to her. You are dismissed."

Tarra did not bow again but nodded, turning to leave. She met my eyes, and I thought I saw an eye twitch — not a wink at all, but the intensity of her gaze suggested an interest in following up later.

The Sathoet in the room were quiet and tense as the Priestess opened the door and let herself out. When it thumped back into place, the sound echoed loudly. Some of the hisses translated as the rushed exhalations of a greedy, delighted sycophant.

"Hherrr, too ... ?" I heard one whisper.

"We get hherrr nnow?" rumbled another.

Wilsira waved a slow, patient gesture, and the excited whispers quieted. She was waiting on me.

I bowed again without taking my eyes off her. "Queen's Grace, Priestess."

The Priestess nodded once, her voice mature and low. "Bless the Davrin, Red Sister. I am Wilsira Tachnathon, Priestess Daughter of Braqth, but you shall call me the Conceiver."

"Indeed, I shall," I said. "The Conceiver is a unique station, created specifically for you by our Queen over three centuries ago."

Because 'High Priestess' was already taken.

Her mouth twitched at my lack of subtlety in being coached. "The title has many layers. I bear it proudly. What is your House name, Sirana?"

No possibility she didn't know, yet this was not why I shook my head. "I am of no House, Conceiver."

"No longer," she corrected. "But once, you were."

"I was, yes. Apologies. You asked of the present, Conceiver. I answered you."

"So I did, and so did you." The Priestess smiled, pretending to be playful in the tilt of her ear. "It seems I shall have to be precise how I word my questions to you, won't I?"

She lied, as I saw it a greater chance that any political mage worded *all* her questions precisely.

"You will have many questions for me, then, Conceiver?" I asked.

She chuckled. "Of course, or I'd not have asked for you to come here."

"Now that I am, Conceiver, would you grace me to know why?"

Her yellowed brows lifted together. "You have the gall to claim ignorance?"

"I am aware of a connection to my trials, Conceiver. That is all. It would be pure arrogance to claim anything except ignorance where the knowledge of a Priestess lies."

This pleased her ego, at least, as she hummed softly with pleasure. Her gaze traveled slowly about the chamber, seeming to summon another round of eager shuffling and sniffing in her wake. I did not make the mistake of looking away, since I couldn't make out the shadows anyway.

Eventually, her attention returned to me.

"Would you rather be elsewhere, young one?" she asked me. "I believe I heard you are not fond of those who are Called to clerical ambitions at the Sanctuary. Something about a ... *familial* strain?"

The Sathoet around me cackled in the dark.

I frowned with mild confusion. "Jilrina is dead, Conceiver, her memory is irrelevant. I serve as the Sisterhood bids me now, to guard Sivaraus."

Wilsira grunted skeptically, lifting her chin as she peered at me with maroon eyes which had taken on an odd, purplish mist in the pale blue light. "I have never been impressed by the Sisterhood *insisting* they no longer have families but for each other, child. It is a false shield they hide behind; a gap between them and Braqth, intended to suppress or mute the Davrin passions which would better serve the Spider Queen and our Valsharess. It is almost impossible to erase the first century of upbringing, and, for certain, one can *never* erase shared blood."

I bowed. "Thank you for your divine view, Conceiver."

She stared at me as I straightened or perhaps at my expression. "If you would dare to laugh at a Priestess, Sirana, do so."

I swallowed. "You first, Conceiver."

"I find nothing amusing about you."

I smiled at her, as there was nothing left to do when she didn't get the jest. "A pity, Conceiver, and genuinely dismaying. Would you have been

Lead Qivni's tutor once?"

I'd done it; I had surprised the Priestess, and she had given me a tell in her face. The moment after, I regretted the probable mistake. Wilsira had stepped back from our debate, but not in retreat. She was reevaluating.

Then she *did* smile. Like the Drider Keeper might in discovering a new bua in her Pit.

I cleared my throat. "Yes, that's it. I'm delighted to have entertained, Conceiver."

"I was thinking of something else, Sister, but I believe I shall be. Soon."

Wilsira had been standing three paces away but now took one step closer to me. The maroon of her eyes became darker in the odd light.

"I was not present when my son tested you," she said, choosing to speak plainly. "But I now believe the story I've been told has some weight. What did you think of him, Sirana?"

"I do not know him, Conceiver. Just the one engagement during my trials, many cycles ago."

"Just one. But memorable."

I nodded an affirmative, contemplating if she may have answered a lingering question for me: Had she set up my run-in with Kerse at the Worship Ball?

Perhaps not. Or perhaps I couldn't read her in all things.

"Well, then, Red Sister? What was your impression?"

She's 'in lust' with her own son, D'Shea had said.

"He is a smart bua, Priestess. And well-endowed."

Wilsira's smile was less strained this time, but it was wry. "Yes, he is. And it was consensual, as I've been told? You willingly accepted him. You climaxed on him."

"Yes, Priestess. Or, rather, with him on me. He pressed me on my back."

Kerse's Mother enjoyed that image better.

"Given the circumstances," I added, "it was better to play with him than endure him."

Her finely wrinkled mouth tightened. "Any animal can 'play,' Sirana.

How did that suggest he is 'smart' to you?"

I shrugged. "Given how little I knew about Sathoet before, I was impressed that he could talk, and bargain."

Wilsira's mouth tightened further. "Yes. He certainly knows *your* name."

Damn it to Abyss.

"I never told him, Conceiver," I said. "I assume he overheard it from my superiors. Did you hear my name from your son, then?"

Wilsira nodded, narrowing her eyes slightly. "Shortly after he was returned to me."

Odd.

D'Shea had said they liked to "know the faces" of our recruits. Did they regularly fail to ask the names? Especially considering Wilsira's stance on denying any family at all.

"I trust you were not mystified by my name for long, Conceiver?"

"I found it in the archives quickly enough." She smiled slowly, eyes never leaving mine. "I paid a visit to House Thalluen. A cait's Mother can provide many insights into a child who sets herself apart."

Swallowing a slight panic, I maintained eye contact, keeping my smile light. "Indeed? I set myself apart chatting with a Sathoet while Jilrina languished in mournful obscurity, Conceiver? Had she but known. Although, she didn't like buas at all, no matter how divine, so it would have been pretending. Like everything else she did in her pointless life."

One of Wilsira's bejeweled hands closed into a loose fist, and the Priestess took the remaining two steps necessary to close the distance between us. I could smell her clearly now, separate from the clinging morass of the whole. Not as many floral or soapy scents as I might've expected.

She smelled of incense, powdered fungus and herbs, and sweat, like Jilrina when she was high and horny.

My heart sped up behind the sapphire pendant beneath my armor.

Don't panic, Sirana.

I didn't move from my spot and let the heat of our bodies blend in the space between us. Wilsira and I were of similar height, I realized; neither one of us needed to look up to the other. The Priestess only seemed larger in her presence and full gown.

"You flip between being direct and indirect," she commented. Her breath smelled of a recent, potent tea. "Your method is not focused. I would rethink it."

My brows lifted. "I have followed your guide, Conceiver. Which do you want? I am still bewildered why I have been called to stand here."

"Hmph," she smirked. "You shall see."

She walked past me, her purple silk barely brushing both my leathers and the floor, distracting me. When I looked up, one of the Sathoet had dissolved silently from the shadows and leaped straight at me.

No weapons. No injuries.

It took more skill by far to track and hold his demonic yellow eyes, to stand still, than it would have to draw from my belt again. Claws dug hard into the stone floor as the half-breed stopped on a coin in front of me, breathing in my face. I would have preferred the scent of hallucinogenic tea.

"He's got a rotting tooth, Conceiver," I commented, challenging the Sathoet to blink first. "That, or he needs to chew on some sweet moss, or something."

This one wasn't her blood-son, and Wilsira stood silent somewhere behind me. I couldn't hear her, and I hated not being able to see her yet could not turn my back to this beast. I'd already learned what happened when I turned from Kerse, and the others could hardly help but chase when Jael had escaped their clutches.

And if Qivni or a Priestess didn't care to direct them otherwise … ?

Yes, I knew what happened.

The Sathoet champed teeth at me and growled, a lecherous grin growing on his maw. His hand movement down below suggested he didn't wear a loincloth, but I didn't look down to confirm. I didn't need to. His male scent wafted up briefly as he rearranged and started caressing himself.

I stood in this staring contest while two more Sathoet appeared in my peripheral vision, flanking me on both sides as they crouched down, ratcheting up the tension as it became much more difficult for me to stand still.

Wilsira behind me, her pet beasts on the other three sides, and no escape. In any other circumstance, I'd have done several things quite differently by now. But, like the wizards in the Tower, I'd been warned not to injure one before a Priestess.

It will give her any excuse she wants.

But if I did not fight, if they piled on me instead, maybe this was how Wilsira wanted to soothe her pride. Watching me be debased by other Sathoet, not her precious son.

Would it soil me in a demonblood's wandering gaze, I wondered? Would that even suffice for the Mother?

The one in front of me still sniffed at me. Still clutched and rubbed himself. The tip of his prick leaked, making that distinct, male sound.

"Rather cruel to tease them, isn't it, Conceiver?" I asked boldly.

The Priestess chuckled. "How do you know I am, Sirana?"

"This one in front seems rather close."

"Perhaps that is his preference, Red Sister. To watch, to release all over the object of his desire."

I smiled, watching the Sathoet in front of me, coughing delicately at his next smelly breath as he huffed and stroked. "I just cleaned my uniform for this visit, Conceiver. My Elder will likely send the costs of magical components needed to repair and refresh it again to you personally, as this wasn't in your request to the Prime."

She didn't appreciate my answer; she forced a bit of a laugh. "Repair? Assuming of violence and victory, Sirana?"

"More a basic assumption of contact with anything that has claws, Priestess, supported by the claw marks on my back from last time."

Wilsira was silent again. Then, "Would you kill them if they *all* fucked you, Red Sister?"

"No, Conceiver. I'd probably cum again."

She made a doubtful noise.

Then Sathoet to my left reached out and caressed three claws very lightly down my thigh. Truthfully, I didn't know if that was his initiative or the Priestess's unseen direction. I hadn't been told if she could instruct multiple demonbloods motion-by-motion, like so many puppets, but—

Maybe they know hand sign, too?

I did not flinch, and his first caress avoided even snagging my leather. The Sathoet shifted his path to curve long fingers around my hamstring toward my inner thigh. I was already tense, my legs spread in a stable stance I could hold for a long time, but it was agony being so vulnerable — less for his exploration and more that I feared deep gouges at Wilsira's petty command.

D'Shea had guaranteed the Priestess would test my nerves, and there had been too many possibilities to guess. Plus, the Prime hadn't been very clear to her on how far "inquiry" could go, and I only had two healing draughts.

If it was only a matter of giving into a group fuck, I didn't fear that, but Kerse might not even be here with his "brothers," and Wilsira hadn't yet exposed what she truly wanted.

The Sathoet's control was too thin, his desire too greedy to resist pressing the pads of his fingers into the crotch of my leathers. A surge of energy entered my bloodstream, as did an influx of arousal that gave me some relief from the tension. The touch was blunt and firm but less clumsy than I would have expected.

He purred low in his chest, the Conceiver hummed in thought, and the rustles in the room increased so I could count three others surrounding me. The boundary I had to defend grew much closer.

The Sathoet to my right now grew bold enough to copy his brother, reaching to stroke my other leg and gingerly play with my buttocks. The Sathoet in front of me finally broke our lasting gaze, looking down to watch the other two grope me, his nostrils flaring, his hand fapping. With his gaze went more of the tension, and I sighed quietly.

The left-side creature withdrew his hand to sniff it, and his brother in front immediately replaced him, clutching and rubbing my mound through my pants before also pulling back to inhale my scent. He rumbled and nodded, licking his lips and pounding himself harder as the right-side Sathoet traded my ass crack to take his own time, sliding a long swipe along my cunt.

I quivered as he finished with a flourish, noticed my breath was in sync with theirs. All three touches were different and fanned the rising heat between my legs as they alternated, long and slow. My face grew hot.

It occurred to me that Wilsira might not be able to see the details standing behind me, as my cloak obstructed her view. She certainly knew where they were touching me, though, and must know the one in front was determinedly on his way to a loaded spurt.

"Very nice," I breathed, and all three Sathoet paused to listen to my voice. "Good buas. Are … are they often this docile, Conceiver?"

"Not often," she murmured. She sounded almost fascinated. "They would not remain so if I were not here. They may not even now."

"Mm-hmm," I hummed, a sound too languid as I became aware how warm Shyntre's sapphire had become against my chest. Pleasantly so, like a living, turgid cock settling between my tits for a stroke.

The pulse in my head slowed down, matching the claw-tipped strokes between my thighs. Without conscious choice, I reached to touch the mane of the Sathoet on the left. He ducked as if expecting a strike but, after a glance up at me, he returned his attention to sharing my nether region with his flanking partner.

In fact, after that, his focus on pleasuring me became *better* as my gloves shushed through the coarse hair along his spine. The Sathoet in front churred at the sight and leaned down to nuzzle my crotch directly with his nose, snuffling urgently as I jumped.

Ohhh, my … uh!

Hot breath seeped through the material as he insisted on sniffing more. Meanwhile, the one on the right clicked in his throat as he started tugging at the leather ties on my right hip, clearly wishing the garment gone.

Fuck.

The lack of fear on my part was odd. I felt a floating, passive sensation with a sense that being the center meant I had control. I knew that I could let them take down my pants; I wouldn't resist. They could smell me, and no denying they would find me wet. I could climax from what I knew they wanted to do.

Because, apparently, I'd fuck anything.

My belt remained in place, sheaths and pouches nudged out of the way as claws carefully hooked the edge of my leathers, dragging down. A few more tugs and pulls before the three had bared my puff of white fur to the eager, yellow eyes of the one in front, and the swell of my ass to either side. The unadulterated scent of my arousal smeared my swollen netherlips.

~Touch me.~

With a savage squeal of glee, the front Sathoet dove right in. My pants were not even halfway down my thighs as he crammed his muzzle between them and ate voraciously like I was his final meal.

I gripped his mane with both hands and barked aloud, "Oh, fuck!"

The left-side brother lunged behind my cloak, turning his head so that his long, slimy tongue plunged between my ass cheeks. He managed to find the center of my pucker in a couple of swirls, and, fucking Eights, a full breath later he was inside, prying me open.

Two rasping, demonic tongues squirmed and churned within my creases, one in each hole and lapping my clit.

Fuck me … more!

In no time at all, an abrupt orgasm jumped on my back and tried to pound me to the ground. Hunched over with my legs apart, I gripped the rough mane in front of me to keep from dropping to my knees.

"Yes!" I wailed. "Goddess, *yesss!"*

All three males erupted on me somewhere, their eager tongues whipped back to yowl and bawl in delight. Thighs, cloak, boots, they splattered all over me. I supposed I may end up sending the requisition for the cleaning spell to the Sanctuary after all.

Then, once the blood in my ears had finished its roar, I noticed the noise inside the room, outside my head.

"Enough," Wilsira commanded. "Stop."

I blinked.

At first, I wasn't sure who she commanded, but the three Sathoet who had just finished flinched at the voice of the Priestess. They obeyed, slinking backward, soon disappearing.

Even as I caught my breath, I sensed just how many more there were in the darkness, trying to come forward.

Uh-oh.

The sense of urgency increased as I pulled up my pants.

They snarled and brayed, ready to attack as one.

"Creuhn-shaleh'thra!" the Conceiver bellowed, casting a deep report in the chamber which added an intense undercurrent of power to her voice.

The roil of Abyssal creatures trembled like a wall of water about to burst, hesitating with clear intent to come forward. With the Davrin Priestess there at the gate, however, her power twisting and changing the boundary even as they sought to discover it.

My mental count had passed twenty before I lost it.

"Obey," Wilsira growled, low and barbarous. "Or I shall make you *suffer!"*

Finally, they backed up. The Sathoet melted back into the ever-changing shadows, hisses of deep resentment trailing after them.

The light in the room grew brighter.

The Conceiver stood next to me, and I couldn't think of a single word which might make it through my open mouth.

"We shall go elsewhere," Wilsira said, her voice belying any concerns she might have of what might happen if we didn't.

I made not one smart remark as the Priestess of Braqth let me out of the Sathoet chamber unharmed if not clean.

Once she had the iron doors sealed to her satisfaction, Kerse's Mother turned to study me in the black, white, and grey hallway. Her dark red eyes were intense, hardly blinking as she noted the cum stains of three pent-up males dripping down my red leather and boots.

I could only expect to see her displeasure and, indeed, that irritation and disapproval crawled on the mature mata's face and through her body's language.

What I hadn't expected to see was a tremble in her hand of which she did not seem aware, or the slight confusion creasing her brow as she peered back at the closed double doors.

Wilsira smoothed a palm slowly down her belly as if she were drying it off, and she took a slow breath in, held it, and let it pass back out. She touched her lips once as if to keep herself from saying anything, though clearly, she had questions.

So did I. I had a lot of questions.

First among them, *What the fuck did I do?*

"Were you not disgusted, Red Sister?" she asked.

Disgusted?

"By what? Pleasure?" I licked dry lips and shrugged, not even faking the afterglow. "Someone taught them how to touch a cunt. It felt good, Conceiver."

Another pause as Wilsira contemplated the novice before her. I could only wait.

"It has been significant turns," she commented, "since I've witnessed a youth appreciate my gift so frankly."

Her hand had stopped trembling, and her tone sounded warmer, less chilly. I didn't believe that any "gift" had been her original intent leading me into that room, but I offered a nod that I hoped appeared respectful.

Fortunately, she wasn't peering for insults right then. The Priestess stroked her belly again over her gown, her dark cleavage swelling in its royal purple casing with another deep breath. I caught her hand dropping a bit lower before she stopped herself, jeweled fingers twining tightly into silk as I counted to three.

"We shall meet our Confessor again so she can lead you out," said the Priestess. "Return to your Prime, Red Sister. Tell her my curiosity is satisfied."

One of them, maybe.

"Yes, Conceiver. I shall."

After she handed me off to the Liaison, I found it disturbingly easy to imagine Wilsira rushing off like that because there had been one Sathoet demonstrably missing in that chamber.

Kerse would be awaiting her in her private quarters.

CHAPTER 29

JAUNDA RELEASED AN ENORMOUS SIGH, ONE ARM BENEATH HER HEAD ON THE chaise inside the cache. Her eyes drowsy as all stress from our hunt evaporated.

"Mmm, so. Blue Eyes."

"Hm?"

"Your ass good and sore like I promised?"

I snickered, turned on my side and facing her. I rubbed one glowing buttock. "Oh, yes, Lead. None better than you when I want to stay on my feet for a span."

"Heh. You want to suck on mine some more, I'll let ya." She chortled, relaxing more. Eyes all the way closed now.

She was still awake, though.

"How many ya got now?" she asked, her voice like the slow grind of her hips.

I blinked. "How many, Lead?"

She didn't open her eyes. "Sisters watchin' your back. Besides me and Gaelan. Seems you've been finding enough tease an' trouble to test it out, right?"

I counted without using my fingers. "Reishel, Jael, Elder D'Shea, Elder Rausery."

"Not bad." Now she opened her eyes, her irises the color of crumbling rust. "Very top and very bottom, though." She shrugged. "Doesn't surprise me. Something told me, if you made it, you weren't gonna go 'middling' Sister."

I smiled dryly. "*Have* I made it, then?"

She closed her eyes again, one arm muscle flexing. "Since the first time I fucked you. Only question now is how long you're going to last. Making it this far only means it gets trickier from there on. The easy span was the last one."

That certainly seemed to follow the course.

I took a risk. "How did you start, Lead?"

"Loud and irritating," she replied, her mouth breaking into a grin.

I quirked a brow. "So, nothing's changed."

She knuckled my upper arm before I could even flinch.

"Ow!"

"Quit whining. Trying to sleep."

"You are not, Lead, you haven't kicked me out yet."

Jaunda chuckled, opening her eyes for good this time as she rolled to face me, snatching me closer to start biting my throat, sucking my tits. I gasped, and she growled happily, slapping my ass before releasing me. I rubbed my bottom again when I could; it still stung. My heart was pounding in my ears for her next words.

"Fine," she said, resettling herself for comfort rather than ordering me out of the cave right then. "What's on your mind?"

"Well. I still enjoy buas," I told her.

"Yeah, figured you would. But you earned some Sisters. Discovered hot slits are still good, right?"

"Yeah." I grinned. "Does that mean you'll offer yours?"

"Fuck, no." She jabbed a knuckle at me again and I yelped. "Offer? Are you fucking jesting? If you can't beat me in a fight, sweetmeat, you don't get to pound my holes."

"That what it takes?" I smiled cheekily. "Some century soon, then."

"Some century *later*, maybe."

Jaunda turned on me again, and I submitted to another rough mauling in her arms, chortling and enjoying my Lead's musky scent as she started to sweat again. She was still streaked with the grime and dust from the chase, having insisted I be the only one to dunk myself after she'd caught me and dragged me here to "pay with my ass."

I risked another question as she nursed one nipple. "Jael made it, too?"

Jaunda's lips came off with a suck and a nod. "First time you fucked her after fighting off Thena, far as I'm concerned."

"Any guesses about her?"

"Will never let go of a bone once her jaw is locked on it. Might only know the bones by smell, though."

The strong Davrin got to her knees and settled between my legs, Feldeu ready to go.

I watched her. "Odd thing to say."

"She's an odd cait. Comes from much weirder stock than you."

"Yes, that reminds *mmEE!*"

Jaunda had bottomed out with a grunt, and I gasped as she thrust a fast tempo. She definitely had a second wind.

"Y-you mentioned my G-Grand Matron?"

"You *really* wanna bring that up now?"

"*You* did! You kn-knew-w her-r?"

The Lead grimaced in concentration. "Gawdess, cait, lemme cum first!"

Jaunda lifted my legs to her shoulders, folded me almost in half so my cunt was tight around her cock. She pounded away and didn't take long.

"*Unngh!* Fuck! Ahh ... okay. Whew ... Better."

She flopped down onto her back so hard, the chaise threatened to break. Panting, she watched the ceiling, rubbing her short white hair into random spikes. I expected another deflection of the topic, but she didn't need a nudge.

"A lot of connections between us all in Sivaraus, Sirana," she said. "Goes without saying, because where *else* are we gonna go?"

She shrugged in answer to her own question. "Except for the Nobles trading sires, no one talks about how deep the links go, or tell their caits because it muddies the water. The way we live, the ones at your back are the only ones you should find out more about, if you can."

"Because?"

"Because they're either helping you watch it, or they've got a dagger pointed at it."

Jaunda watched my face as that sank in. She smiled. "Matron Siranet once watched my back when I needed it. Not gonna tell you how, not yet, you're not ready. But remembering the dead isn't easy for Davrin. If we do, there's a reason, and it's always personal. Remember that."

Later in private, after Jaunda had released me, I retrieved the sapphire pendant from my hiding place in my tiny, solitary room and sat down. Holding it in both hands, I turned it with care and stroked it with my thumbs. I had studied the details frequently so I might recognize it quickly if it was ever swapped out for a fake.

It probably wasn't necessary; I'd recognize it just from the quiet spot which formed from touching it.

I wondered which wizard had done the silverwork, Phaelous or Shyntre?

The mount covered the whole back of the gem, but there was a thick, metal cradle on the left side that stretched around to come to points on the right side, just failing to meet. The fattest part of the silver had knotted designs and markings I couldn't read, if they even said anything. The detail was very fine, the curves almost perfect.

Was this done by magic or fire? Or both? How would he have had time to finish it and give it to me *without* magic?

I still wasn't sure which "he" I meant when I asked myself about it.

Elder D'Shea had been holding the pendant for safekeeping when I wasn't on an active mission where she had deemed that I might need a strong mental shield, but her annoyance had shown when she gave it back for me to keep for the long term.

"You're the only one with any use for it," she complained. "Plus, it drains the potency of volatile magic if you keep them in the same box! I need to dispel and recast far too many weakened vials, thanks to that!"

I opted not to tell her Phaelous had guessed that already; he said he'd never keep it in a "treasury." I had also noticed that my Elder still had his ruby ring, though she didn't wear it regularly, and I assumed she had not gone back to the Tower to hear further thoughts from the ancient wizard.

Maybe later when she remembered he still had the semi polished Dwarf stone.

For now, her instructions were to keep it out of sight and hide it when I had bedmates. It was only a matter of time before a Sister jumped me successfully and stripped me for a fuck but even if they saw it, I knew I wasn't the only one who wore a necklace beneath her armor.

The Prime didn't like them to be "too pretty," of course, and this one probably was for her tastes, but it absolutely *had* saved my ass against Wilsira and I'd discovered that from the Prime, herself, when she had deliberately walked in on a map-making and map-reading lesson Elder Rausery was giving me.

"Good work on the recruit, Elder."

The General tilted her head, glancing at me. "Haven't tested her map skills yet, Prime."

"Not that. The Conceiver."

"Wilsira?"

A nod. "Said the lowbie faced off with a Sathoet and still held concentration to shrug off a fear probe. You know her old tricks. First-turners usually fail. She's impressed." The Prime's cold eyes slid to me. "Priestess said she might be interested in requesting Sirana as a bodyguard sometime. Next time we need a favor from her."

Rausery watched her with complete calm, while I wondered if D'Shea might throw another glass when she heard this.

"I see," the Elder said. "Very good, Prime, thank you."

"Keep it up."

The Prime left then, sniggering at her own joke.

As it turned out, the Elder Sorceress did not waste any wine when I told her, but she sighed. Deeply.

"I expected it," she said. "She's still curious about you. From your report, I'm not certain which of you affected those three demonbloods more at the time. That's concerning."

I pursed my lips. "I do regret any difficulty, Elder."

"Surviving is never a fault, Sirana." D'Shea stared at the top of her stylus, seeming deep in memory. "You bend under pressure and speak your mind when you can now that you have a choice. You will never fade into a wall with those eyes of yours, either, so you might as well take point more often. Jaunda and I will teach you how."

Later still, I would lie down in Reverie with two other caits near enough to my own age, connected by the same thought-flayer battle. Like me, Jael would never "fade into a wall," either, so I knew we'd make a good team when we needed to be loud like Kiren and Lawret. We just needed more practice together.

In contrast, Reishel seemed to blend in with my presence, like how I'd noticed Gaelan's did to D'Shea. Even though Reishel had begun that Ornilleth battle as a Corpora, after she had fallen, she didn't seem to remember or yearn for the lost rank. She was a novice, like us, and she was my Sister. She was one who watched my back.

"Fuzzy," she commented now, petting Jael's tiny, short hairs at her crotch growing in once again. She smirked mischievously before rubbing them the wrong way.

"Stop that!"

My scrapper swatted at her, copper eyes firing up, and Reishel chuckled, reaching over me to tickle Jael, who yowled. My Sister taunted that bristle patch some more with reverse fingers, and next thing I knew, I had an accidental hip in the gut as they piled on top of me, wrestling.

"Hey!" I cried. "I'm not the arena, here!"

"Sounds like denial, dear Sister."

Reishel's breast brushed my face.

"Ha, I like how the arena lies," Jael agreed, hooking her strong thigh around mine and pulling them open. Her hand darted between to fondle me. "Don't you?"

"Oh, yes." Reishel winked at me. "There is a warm spring to drink from, too. Sometimes she gushes."

"That's Jael."

I was sure to point at the *real* youngest of the Red Sisters, and Reishel tried for a ferocious scowl. She failed miserably.

"Shut up and be fought over, Sirana."

"Yeah!" Jael agreed and attacked.

I laughed, diving into the gratifying rough-and-tumble with them. Coveted by caits I wanted in return was a peace I'd earned, and I could enjoy it this time.

Even knowing the experience wouldn't always be as pleasant as this.

**The Conceiver wants to ruin me for the Sisterhood.
I can't let this happen.**

Read The Daedal Pit: Sister Seekers Book 3 now!

Thank you for reading about Sirana and the Davrin Elves of the deep! Help others to find the dark fantasy they want and leave a review for Book 2 on Goodreads, Bookbub, or your favorite retail site!

Sister Seekers is an adult epic fantasy with an ever-broadening scope. Found family is a core theme throughout. Perfect for fans of entwined plots, challenging themes, immersive worldbuilding, and elements of erotic horror. Sexuality and inner conflict play into character growth with nuance, intrigue, action, and magic.

[Follow Etaski and Subscribe to her newsletter at her website]

Do you enjoy fantasy maps, timelines, and glossaries? Do you love to read extra tidbits about the characters and places in the story?

[Be sure to visit Etaski's series lore at World Anvil!]

Read the next book in the Sister Seekers: The Daedal Pit

I stumbled into a place I wasn't supposed to be. Priestess Wilsira isn't angry. She demands penance at her side, only too delighted to wreck my Elder's plans for me.

Serving her and her demon-blooded son, I'm caught in a cascade of revelations and begin to understand the real powers which govern out city, consuming most of us eventually.

Will I fall prey to city's worst monstrosities like so many fighters before me? Or can my private battle gain an edge for the Sisterhood when the sweeping chain of events finally reaches its end?

In *The Daedal Pit*, intrigue and horror, action, and drama weave Etaski's third act of the Spider Queen's web into a consummation of promise. Fulfilling that promise catapults one determined survivor to a place she once could see only in her dreams.

ACKNOWLEDGMENTS

Always a joy to work with my long-time beta team & ideamongers:

NecrosisBob, Eris Adderly, Axelotl,

Gerrit, Ile Depak, Leonard,

Gazukull, and, always, Dear Hubby!

A very special thanks to these supporting patrons:

Baelus, Richard Laney, Cittran, Dreya K.

Dark Pulse, Mehrphy, John K., Katie Lily

Stacy & Roy Meyer, Sir Cumference, Does , Dora B.

Brianna R., Simon H., Jager, Jonathan H.

Josanna, Rachel C., Lexanii, John S.

Nymerias Howl, Larry F., Paul M., Devodebo

Phillip G., Nigel, Kia, NotSoWeird

Jack K., Charles H., David, Matthew S.

Jonathan M., Julie S., Michel C., & Alienated

ABOUT THE AUTHOR

Etaski has entertained herself with fantasy stories since the first day she sat on a school bus looking out the window. When hand-written letters were disappearing, she wrote no less than five pages to be worth the postage. Her early stories were written by hand, and she had a writer's callus and three embarrassing (but complete!) novels before graduating high school.

She chose to study a broad range of topics; science, archaeology and history, as well as theater. Frank discussion of sexuality was rare growing up, so she wrote theories and observations within stories, inviting the reader either to contemplate deeper or just be entertained.

History rarely speaks on sexuality, yet biology demonstrates how it sways basic choices. Drama reveals our strongest bonds but may still fade to black. In the Sister Seekers, the sex and the story are inseparable, and connections made within will forever change the story of Miurag without cutting away.

Etaski's Website: etaski.com
Etaski's Book Page: etaski.com/sister-seekers
Etaski's Series Lore: miurag.etaski.com
Etaski on Patreon: www.patreon.com/etaski
Etaski on GoodReads: www.goodreads.com/etaski
Etaski on BookBub: www.bookbub.com/authors/a-s-etaski
Etaski on Facebook: www.facebook.com/asetaski
Etaski on Mastodon: mastodon.online/@etaski